E B B.

Pregnancy
Surprise

BARBARA McMAHON
SUSAN MEIER
JACKIE BRAUN

Published in Great Britain 2014
by Mills & Boon, an imprint of Harlequin (UK) Limited,
Eton House, 18-24 Paradise Road, Richmond, Surrey, TW9 1SR

PREGNANCY SURPRISE © 2014 Harlequin Books S.A.

Parents in Training, Her Pregnancy Surprise and *Expecting a Miracle* were first published in Great Britain by Harlequin (UK) Limited.

Parents in Training © 2008 Barbara McMahon
Her Pregnancy Surprise © 2007 Linda Susan Meier
Expecting a Miracle © 2008 Jackie Braun Fridline

ISBN: 978 0 263 91174 9
eBook ISBN: 978 1 472 04469 3

05-0214

Harlequin (UK) Limited's policy is to use papers that are natural, renewable and recyclable products and made from wood grown in sustainable forests. The logging and manufacturing processes conform to the legal environmental regulations of the country of origin.

Printed and bound in Spain
by Blackprint CPI, Barcelona

PARENTS IN TRAINING

BY
BARBARA McMAHON

Barbara McMahon was born and raised in the South, but settled in California after spending a year flying around the world for an international airline. After settling down to raise a family and work for a computer firm, she began writing when her children started school. Now, feeling fortunate in being able to realize a long-held dream of quitting her day job and writing full-time, Barbara has moved with her husband to the Sierra Nevada mountains of California, where she finds her desire to write is stronger than ever. With the beauty of the mountains visible from her windows and the pace of life slower than that of the hectic San Francisco Bay Area, where they previously resided, she finds more time than ever to think up stories and characters and share them with others through writing. Barbara loves to hear from readers. You can reach her at PO Box 977, Pioneer, CA 95666-0977, USA.

Readers can also contact Barbara at her website, www. barbaramcmahon.com.

Jessie McMahon, spread your wings and fly!
Love from Mom-Mom

CHAPTER ONE

ANNALISE stared at the plastic stick, stunned to see the positive indicator. It took a moment or two to register. The plus meant she was pregnant. Impossible.

She carefully wrapped the kit in the brown paper bag she'd brought it home in and stuffed into the small bathroom trash container. Then she pulled it out. Too obvious. She carried it to the kitchen and stuffed it into that trash. Picking up the container, she went to the hallway incinerator chute and emptied the telltale evidence.

Fifteen minutes later, she stood in McClellan's Drugstore buying another brand of pregnancy-test kit. Without a second thought she bought two. No sense taking chances on a faulty reading.

When both of those kits confirmed what she secretly wouldn't admit she'd known, she went to flop down on the edge of the bed. This couldn't be the worst thing that had happened to her since marrying Dominic, but it seemed like it. His sentiments played in her mind. They'd had a discussion about having children just recently, when her twin sister announced she was pregnant.

Lianne had been trying. Annalise had not.

She *so* did not need this.

Dominic was going to hit the roof. Things had been a bit testy between them for the last few weeks. Thinking back, she wondered if it coincided with her confiding in him Lianne's quest to have a baby before it was too late. He had said unequivocally that he was satisfied with their marriage. They'd discussed having children years ago and decided not to. He had not changed his view.

Annalise wasn't sure how she felt, but she knew when he learned she was pregnant he was going to explode.

Annalise felt a bit overwhelmed herself. She'd never pictured herself a mother. She had better readjust her thinking. How far along was she? There was no way she could pinpoint the date of conception, but she tried to remember her last period. Maybe two months ago? Could she expect the baby to arrive in seven months? Ohmygod—how was she going to tell Dominic?

She had to tell him soon. Try to minimize the fall-out. Convince him this would be a good thing. Only how she would accomplish that was a mystery right now— she herself wasn't so sure she wanted a child.

So when to tell Dominic? Tonight they were hosting a cocktail party for twenty-four. Should she get hold of him before? Or wait? Should she lead up to it or just blurt it out? She hoped the right words came. Rising, she went to the phone in the living room and called his cell number. It rolled to the message center. *Damn.* He must be in a high-level meeting to have turned his phone off. The seconds ticked by. She replaced the receiver without leaving him a message. Maybe he'd get home early and she'd tell him then.

Or maybe wait until everyone had left, so there'd be no tension at the party. That was what she'd do. Taking a deep breath, Annalise tried to quell the flutters in her stomach. He had to be reasonable about this. After all, it took two to make a baby. It wasn't as if she'd deliberately tried to become pregnant. She was not following in Lianne's footsteps. But something told her Dominic was not going to be reasonable.

They'd had several heated discussions about having a family in the last few weeks. Every time, Dominic had been stubbornly adamant—against the idea. She hadn't pushed. She knew what living in a large family was like. And she'd agreed years ago when he'd brought up marriage, that a childless one suited her just fine. Fresh from the chaos of a large family, the idea of only the two of them doing what they wanted had sounded to her like perfection.

Still, a small smiled played around her mouth. *They were going to have a baby.*

How amazing—she and her twin were pregnant at the same time.

Now she just had to make her husband see what a wonderful thing this would be.

The one time Annalise really wanted to speak to her husband, he was late. The party had already begun when he dashed in, making excuses, greeting their guests with the confidence of a well-respected man. She knew the instant he entered. Whenever he was near it was as if she had a special sixth sense that instantly recognized his presence.

She went to greet him, happy to see he wasn't going to be so late as to be awkward. Greeting their first guests without him had been bad enough.

"Hello, darling," she said, with a wide smile.

"Sweetheart," he said, giving her a quick kiss and turning almost simultaneously to greet Ben Waters.

Once Dominic had put down his briefcase, he began to walk through the large living room, greeting guests, apologizing for being late, stopping with one group or another to chat for a while.

Annalise knew she couldn't tell him her important news until the last guest had left, so she resigned herself to a long evening of anticipation and dread. Normally she loved to entertain. They had a wide, eclectic group of friends. She watched Dominic as he shook hands with Congressman Peters. The congressman's wife was very shy. Annalise had invited her sister Bridget to the party to meet Judy Peters. They both were avid gardeners, and Annalise knew they'd hit it off.

"Lovely to see you again, my dear," Sheila Simpson said, coming up to Annalise. "So nice to have an event to attend where I know everyone and like them. Honestly, some of the receptions and parties we have to attend are too dull and boring for words." She laughed and chatted. Her husband was with the world bank, and Annalise knew Sheila loved parties of all types. She couldn't imagine her friend finding anything boring.

"Here's Karen. I was just saying how lovely this party is," Sheila said, when the wife of one of the British attachés joined them. "You look radiant."

Annalise smiled at Karen, who was very obviously pregnant. Annalise relished her secret—soon she'd be showing the world *she* carried a baby. She hugged her friend. "How are you feeling?"

"Fabulous, now that the morning sickness has passed. I thought I'd have to move into the bath for a few months. Yuck. But now everything is terrific."

Sheila laughed and complimented her on her dress.

"I feel huge, and I'm still three months away. Imagine how large I'll be by the end. Oh, the baby just kicked," Karen said, with a startled smile.

"Really?" Annalise stared at her friend's protruding stomach. "Can I feel?"

"Of course—that's one of the best parts. Here." Karen took her hand and placed it to the side of her stomach. A moment later, Annalise felt a definite kick.

"Ah! Amazing." Involuntarily, she looked for Dominic. Would he soon be placing his hands on her stomach to feel their baby move?

Dominic glanced across the room and met Annalise's eyes. She smiled at him, then turned back to Karen Reynolds. A pregnant Karen. Annalise had her palm against the pregnant woman's belly. There was a soft smile on her face. For a moment, the world seemed to stand still. The topic of a baby had risen more in the last two months than in the previous five years of their marriage. His mouth went dry. He did not wish to discuss having a family again. He'd made his view known over and over. When they had first discussed marriage, as seniors at university, both had agreed—no children.

The topic had not risen again until Annalise's twin became pregnant. Now it seemed every time he turned around he was seeing pregnant women, hearing about someone else having another child. He couldn't do that. Not again.

Deliberately turning, so he didn't have to see Annalise, he caught the thread of a conversation between two guests and tried to concentrate.

Annalise worked in real estate, specializing in homes in the northwest section of Washington, catering to embassy personnel and members of Congress. It was a rewarding job that enabled her to take a week off here and there whenever Dominic got a choice overseas assignment. It also enabled her to meet a wide variety of people. Many of whom became friends.

Dominic worked for a computer firm which specialized in troubleshooting high-end computer mainframes. His most recent trip, to England, had been to work on one with the Bank of England. The challenges were dramatic, but he thrived on solving complex problems. He was often given the most difficult ones, and usually turned things around within a few days of arriving on site. Which then gave he and Annalise time to sightsee and shop.

With his contacts through the "computer-repair business," as he called it, and her contacts from houses sold or listed, they had a wide variety of friends and acquaintances. Annalise loved giving parties with an assortment of guests. It made the evenings so interesting and fun. She could move from an argument between opposites about the world bank situation, to discussions about tourism in Florida, to hearing how an artist had fared at the latest showing of her work, all while circling her own living room. Tonight was no exception.

Some time later, Dominic poured himself another glass of wine. Glancing up, he heard Annalise's laugh. For a moment, he just gazed at her. She was lovely. He'd been attracted to her from the first moment they met. It wasn't only her looks that had appealed, but her manner, as well. She was confident and assured in any situation he'd seen her in. Friendly and genuinely interested in people, she loved to entertain and kept up with a wide circle of friends. She was so unlike his mother had been. Involuntarily a memory rose. His mother had looked far older than her years, and had worked nonstop as a clerk in a convenience store to keep their home, constantly arguing with his father about new furniture. He couldn't remember his parents ever entertaining friends. Annalise made it look so easy. His mother would have been horrified, and probably terrified at the assortment of people present. He frowned at the thought. He didn't need the past intruding.

Maybe he should have expected it to with all the talk about pregnancy. He was not cut out to be a father. He knew it, and if the subject arose again, Annalise would have to accept the fact. Even Phyllis—

He turned away from the thought. He was married to a lovely, successful woman. Their future together was bright. He'd fought his way out of the life he'd once lived and was never going back.

The evening was winding down when Dominic finally got time to catch up with Annalise. She seemed quieter than usual. When she thought no one was watching, her smile faded. They'd returned from London four days ago—maybe she was still suffering jet lag.

The trip had been a success, both from a business point of view and as a few days' down time. He shared Annalise's love for London. Though he was partial to Rome, as well. Part of the excitement of his job was never knowing where the next assignment would be. He relished the travel, and the opportunity to pit his wits and brain against the problems that arose with various software and computer usage. Most of the time it was silly mistakes. Occasionally industrial espionage or sabotage lay behind the difficulties.

The best part, however, was seeing the world and getting paid for it. Quite a change from his rather bleak childhood in a small Pennsylvania mill town.

He moved toward his wife and smiled. She was beautiful. Her glossy brown hair was pulled back from her face. Her complexion was like peaches and cream. No wonder writers waxed poetic about such skin. It made him yearn to reach out across the room and rub his fingertip across it, feeling its silky softness.

Suddenly he was glad the first of the guests were leaving. He moved to Annalise's side to bid them good-night.

"Enjoyed seeing you again," he said as he shook Ted's hand, kissed Karen on the cheek. It figured the pregnant couple would be the first to leave. He remembered how tired Phyllis had been for months. He could feel himself tense at the memory.

"Come see us before the baby is born. It'll be hectic after that," Ted said.

"We'd love to," Annalise said. She gave Karen a hug, and then Ted. "Keep safe."

Soon the exodus began. Within a half-hour, the last guest had left.

"Wonderful party," he said casually, throwing his arm around her shoulder as they turned to survey the catering staff beginning the clean-up.

"I like this caterer. I think I'll try them again when we give a dinner party. They have an interesting menu selection. Maybe next time I'll mix European with Asian." She looked at him. "Are you listening to me?"

"Of course."

Her voice was soft and feminine. He liked listening to her—especially late at night, when they were in bed with the lights out. He could close his eyes and listen to her for hours. Not that they talked all that much in bed after dark. He smiled. They'd be in bed soon.

"Bridget made an instant rapport with the new congressman's wife."

Dominic nodded. He remembered her telling him she'd invited them after she'd sold them a home. And the Campbells had brought a house guest—a sheikh— who had graced them with his presence and had turned out to be wildly funny. Who would have thought? Everyone had stayed far longer than predicted—a sure sign all had enjoyed the evening as much as he and Annalise had.

She relaxed against him. "I'm so tired. It was fun, though, wasn't it? Did you get to hear Sheikh Ramaise's commentary on American cowboys?"

"I did. He's an excellent storyteller."

"I stand in amazement at his command of English. I could never learn Arabic."

"You don't need to. But he needs English to represent his country to ours."

"Umm." She walked to the sofa and sank down.

"Tired?"

"A bit."

But she looked keyed up, on edge.

Members of the catering staff moved efficiently through the apartment, clearing away the debris from the event. Soon the living room was back to its normal state. Dominic heard them working in the kitchen. As soon as they left, he was going to take his wife to bed.

Dominic shed his jacket and tie, then loosened his shirt collar. "Did you hear Jack Simpson talking about the problems with that country in South America?"

She shook her head, waiting.

Dominic poured them each a brandy, handed her a glass and sat beside her on the sofa while he gave a brief recap. He noticed she put her glass on the coffee table and didn't pick it up.

"We're leaving now," the representative from the catering firm said, coming to the kitchen doorway. "All cleaned up."

With a quick glance at Annalise, Dominic rose. "I'll check them out and pay them," he said.

She nodded, closing her eyes.

"Good group tonight. Everyone seemed to mesh," Dominic said when he returned.

She opened her eyes and smiled. "We'll have to do it again soon."

"Next weekend, if we're home, do you want to catch the National Symphony Orchestra at the Kennedy Center?" he asked, taking his tie and jacket from the chair.

Annalise nodded. Stifling a yawn, she said, "That sounds good. I have to call Lianne tomorrow," she said.

Dominic didn't reply. He crossed the room to switch off one lamp. The one thing he'd never completely understood about Annalise was her close tie with her sister Lianne. It was a twin thing, he was sure. They communicated almost daily, had done all their lives—even when they'd lived in different cities and gone to different universities.

He liked Lianne, but he wondered what the two of them had to talk about all the time.

"How's she doing?" he asked. He didn't want to know, but his wife would expect him to ask.

"Still thrilled to be pregnant."

He hoped that was one twin trait they didn't share. When he and Annalise had first met, at Georgetown

University, they'd hit it off immediately. He'd loved being with her, enjoyed her enthusiasm about everything. She'd been so different from his high-school girlfriend, who had been needy and demanding. Annalise had been a breath of fresh air, and he'd moved in on her like a hunter on prey.

Before long, they'd become a couple, then engaged, and had married right after graduation. Having children did not play in his plans. His own father was a shining example of the opposite of Father-of-the-Year. The apple didn't fall far from the tree. He knew from the past he was not cut out to be a father.

He didn't voice his concern that Annalise was only toying with the idea of a child because her sister was pregnant. They lived separate lives, for all they were close. Lianne had recently married, for one thing; he and Annalise had been married for five years. Lianne worked as an analyst in a security firm; Annalise was more independent as a real-estate agent.

The twins were from a family of eleven children. They were next to oldest, with two older boys also twins. Even after knowing the members of her family for half a dozen years, he was amazed at the sheer chaotic nature of holiday gatherings, and the amazing patience of their father, Patrick O'Mallory. Dominic had been an only child, and happy to leave home when he'd had the chance. He was used to the O'Mallory celebrations now, but was always glad to leave for the quieter, more tranquil apartment they owned.

He couldn't understand Lianne's burning desire for a child. It was totally foreign to him.

He reached out and caught Annalise's hand, bringing it to his mouth for a quick kiss. "I'm telling the schedulers to try for a New York assignment next time. There are some new plays we haven't seen. Might as well have the company pick up some of the tab."

"You do that. And I'll see if I can sell a home or two so we can afford the best seats."

He wasn't worried about Annalise selling property. She was a natural at it. Her sunny disposition and genuine liking for people shone through when she acquired clients. They knew instinctively that she would find the best property available for them.

And they could afford the best seats in any theater without another sale. After a childhood of deprivation, the one thing Dominic made sure of was that there was plenty of money for unexpected expenditure. They had a very healthy savings and investment plan. Never again would he experience the hardship of his early years.

"Ready for bed?"

"Not yet. Sit down. I have something to tell with you," she said.

He sat on the sofa beside her.

Annalise took a deep breath.

"What's up?" he asked.

"I'm pregnant." She looked at him, as if gauging his reaction.

Dominic didn't believe he'd heard the words at first.

His worst nightmare.

For a moment, he was eighteen again, and hearing the dreaded words from Phyllis Evans. Life as he had planned it had changed with those two words. He had never wanted to hear them again. And now Annalise was staring at him, having uttered the words that struck dread into his heart.

"How did that happen?" he asked evenly, holding on to control by a thread. Anger began to build. They were always very careful, so had Annalise had a change of heart about having a child?

It was Lianne's influence. He knew it. He had always been distrustful of the tie between the twins. He had felt excluded on more than one occasion when the two of them had been together. Twins shared a special bond, one a husband couldn't ever penetrate. But for Annalise to change their lives so completely without even talking about it with him was beyond anything.

"The usual way," she said, trying for flippancy but sounding tentative.

He gazed at her in disbelief. He took a breath, trying to get the anger under control. She looked wary, watching him carefully. Well, she should. He wanted to smash something. To tip the table over and storm out of the room. He had been through this once before—with disastrous results. He could not go through it again.

Clamping down on his emotions, he tried to think. But the only thought that ricocheted around his mind was the fact they were bringing a child into the world and life as he knew it—as he liked it—would end forever.

He stood, paced to the window, clenching his hands into fists. He felt the room close in on him. "Dammit, Annalise, we talked about this. More than once. I. Do. Not. Want. Children. What part of that do you not understand?"

"I understand it all. But I didn't do anything to become pregnant. If you'll remember, we agreed before we were married that a childless marriage would be a wonderful thing. But you and I both know the only perfect birth control is abstinence, and that's not something we practice. You and me together made a baby. It'll take some adjusting, but I'm sure we'll be happy when the baby's born. We can make it work. I know we can."

He turned and faced her. It was like looking at a total stranger. "Is this a twin thing? Lianne is pregnant, so you had to be, too?"

"No." She was quiet for a moment. "I'm as stunned as you. I didn't plan on this. You can't think that. It'll change everything."

"You've got that right. We like to travel. A kid will mean no more jumping up at the last moment and taking off somewhere. There would be so much to tie us down. What kind of life do you envision for us with a baby in the mix? Or when he's six, and in school for most of the year? Or as a teenager, giving untold grief? This is the last thing we need!"

"We'll adapt. I only found out this afternoon. I haven't had a chance to do anything but try to get used to the idea myself," she said. "And if my folks can get through eleven kids, I'm sure we can manage one."

"How did you find out? Did you see a doctor?"

"No, I took a home pregnancy test."

For a moment, a glimmer of hope rose. "Take another one. They aren't one hundred percent."

"I tried three. Every one showed positive."

He hit the wall with his fist. "Dammit, Annalise, we weren't going to have children. We agreed to that." He glared at her. "I like the life we have. If I had wanted it changed, I would have said something."

She stood and put her hands on her hips, glaring at him. "I wasn't planning anything except to go on as we've been. Do you think I want to be tied down, unable to go off on a moment's notice? I love traveling. I never was able to go anywhere but the shore when we were children. Don't blame me for this. It takes two."

"So how did it happen?"

"How should I know? Something didn't work, obviously. Now we have a situation we have to deal with. We'll have to adjust our thinking."

"I don't want to adjust." God, he knew he sounded petulant and stubborn. But if she knew the full story— He blanked the thought. The last thing he wanted was for anyone to know the full story.

"Well, tough. There it is. What else do you suggest?" Her wariness had faded. She glared at him.

He couldn't think. He was furious with the news. And afraid of the past repeating itself.

"Hell, I don't know. Why not consult your precious sister?" he said, and strode from the room. Snatching a jacket, he headed for the door. "I don't want the baby."

The moment he said the words, he cringed. How cold it sounded—especially when it echoed what he'd said years ago. And look at that result. Guilt and grief played out. He knew intellectually he had not caused the outcome, but secretly he'd always believed he had. He'd never planned to bring a child into the world, disrupting the life he'd carefully built. He still had challenges he wanted to meet, places to visit. This would change everything—if he let it.

Annalise stared at him for a long moment. "How could anyone not want a baby?" she asked. "Granted, we didn't plan on one. But now that it's on the way, we will love this child."

"There are millions of people on the planet who do not want children," he said. It wasn't only the thought of a baby but the betrayal he felt at his wife's becoming pregnant. That was exactly what he felt—betrayed.

"Well, there's not much to be done about it now," she said, turning and heading down the hall.

A moment later, Dominic heard the slam of the bedroom door.

What a mess. He let himself out of the apartment. He reached the sidewalk and turned south. Blocks away lay the Mall, with the Lincoln Monument at one end and the Capitol at the other. On the other side of the Mall was the Tidal Basin. The open space would allow him some breathing room. He felt claustrophobic in the apartment. Like the walls were closing in on him. Like the past was returning. He needed freedom.

He could hear his father's voice echoing—how having a kid had kept him from doing all he wanted. He'd blamed Dominic's mother for getting pregnant and forcing him to marry her. For having a child that needed care, which had kept his father from traveling the world and living life to the fullest. The arguments had been endless, and Dominic remembered every one.

He'd felt the same way when Phyllis had told him she was pregnant. Eighteen, just graduated from high school, and all his plans for the future down the drain. They'd been sweethearts in high school, but once graduation had come, he'd had his ticket to freedom. Only, Phyllis's news had changed that. He'd done the right thing by marrying her. Then he'd gone to work at the mill. Same as his father. History repeating itself.

Only, when there'd been a reprieve, he'd grabbed it.

He'd sworn he would never get in that position again. He liked his job, combining computer work with travel. He liked Annalise, beautiful, sophisticated. Not tired all the time and scared like Phyllis had been. This pregnancy had the power to change everything—just like before.

* * *

Annalise sat on the edge of the bed, frustrated and angry. She had *not* made a decision for them. She'd never had daydreams about having babies. How could he think that? Okay, maybe she had brought up the subject when Lianne began talking about having a baby. But when Dominic had said unequivocally no, she'd accepted they'd stay childless.

Granted, she'd enjoyed holding her sister Mary Margaret's babies when they'd been small, but she'd always been relieved to give them back to Mama when they cried.

Now she was going to have a baby of her own. One she couldn't hand back when it cried. She hoped Dominic got used to the idea fast. Sure, there'd be some adjustments. She rubbed her tummy, hoping the baby didn't feel the turmoil. Why couldn't Dominic be like Tray, her sister's husband, and overjoyed at the thought of a child?

Why should he? She wasn't as ecstatic as Lianne. This would mean major compromises when before they'd lived life on their own terms. She had to get used to the idea herself.

Still, having a baby was a good thing. She'd better hold on to that thought. There was no going back now. They both had solid careers, made enough money to live comfortably and provide for a child. It wasn't what they'd planned, but it wasn't the end of the world like Dominic made it seem. He had to come around. He *had* to.

The next morning when Annalise awoke, she realized Dominic had never come to bed. Had he even returned home? She put on her robe and went down the hall. The apartment was quiet. He was not in the living room, nor the kitchen. She went to the den and peered in. He was stretched out on the recliner, asleep, still wearing the clothes he'd had on last night. The computer screen scrolled its screensaver. Had he been working and fallen asleep? Or had he deliberately stayed away?

"Dominic?" she called softly.

He didn't move.

Annalise went to shower and dress. Then she went to the kitchen to prepare breakfast. She wanted to discuss the situation with Dominic as soon as he was awake. They had fights from time to time, but soon made up. This altercation would be the same, she hoped.

By the time she had biscuits coming out of the oven, Dominic stood in the kitchen doorway. He looked incredibly sexy, with a day's growth of dark beard and a sleepy look around his eyes. He had changed, and the T-shirt he'd pulled on delineated every rock-hard muscle in his chest and shoulders. The jeans molded his lean physique. She turned away, wishing for the easy camaraderie they normally enjoyed. If it were another morning, she'd give him a kiss, and maybe suggest postponing breakfast while they detoured into the bedroom.

After their fight last night, she knew he'd refuse, and she was not into getting rebuffed.

"Breakfast is almost ready," she said, pointing to the coffeemaker.

"The smell of coffee woke me," he said. Crossing the small kitchen, he poured himself a cup.

As always, her heart gave a small skip when she saw him. He didn't say anything, just sipped the hot beverage and gazed out the window.

"How long are you going to be mad at me?" she asked finally, annoyed he was ignoring her.

There was silence for a moment. "This isn't like the other fights we've had, Annalise," he said, turning slowly to look at her. "You've rocked my world. I'm not sure if I will get over it."

That floored her. She leaned against the counter, unable to believe what he'd said, feeling a touch of panic.

"It changes my world, too, you know. We need to talk about this."

"There's nothing to discuss."

"There's lots to discuss," she said, clutching the edge of the counter tightly. "I know this wasn't the way we planned our life going, but it's not the end of the world."

"It may be the end of us," he said slowly.

Annalise felt as if he'd slapped her. She couldn't believe she'd heard him correctly.

"You do not mean that," she said hotly.

"I don't know what I mean. Talking isn't going to change anything, is it? I made my views known before we married. Nothing's changed for me. Seems as if we've reached a fork in the road."

"Once you get used to the idea, you'll feel better about it. You can talk to my father, or Tray or Mary Margaret's husband. You must know lots of men who are fathers. They'll all tell you it's a great thing. Not something bad."

"For them, not for me." He crossed to the table and pulled out a chair. Sitting, he studied the coffee in his mug.

She dished up the eggs, placed sausages on the side of each plate and carried them to the table. A moment later, she added the hot biscuits. Jam was already out. She poured some orange juice for each of them and then sat in her chair.

"So explain to me why having a baby is such a horrible thing," she said. If he'd only talk about it, maybe they could move beyond his anger.

"After breakfast," he said. He began to eat.

Annalise didn't have much appetite. She hated confrontation and disharmony. She'd rather clear the air and then eat, but maybe it was better this way. At least the food was hot.

They ate in silence. She studied him through the meal. He never once looked up, but kept his gaze focused on his plate of food. She thought about all the breakfasts they had shared over the years. When he was away, she missed their routine. In the early days of their marriage, she'd accompanied him on most of his assignments. As her own list of clients had grown she'd not been able to take off every time at a moment's notice. But she went often enough that they had seen a lot of the world together.

They would not forever be young, and on the fast track at work. She had reached a level that gave her a good income and still allowed her time for other pursuits. To her, stability and roots were important. She was grounded by her parents and grandparents, who had lived in the Washington metropolitan area all their lives. She wanted that grounding for her child. Travel was broadening, but staying home provided roots.

When he'd finished eating, Dominic rose and went for another cup of coffee. "Want any more?"

"No." She should cut out caffeine altogether, but couldn't yet forgo that first cup in the morning. The best she could do was limit her intake.

Clearing the dishes quickly, she ran water in the sink to let them soak. "Ready?"

He shrugged and leaned against the counter.

"Shouldn't we go and sit down or something?" she said.

"This won't take long. Before we were married we discussed having children. You came from a large family and said you were content with nieces and nephews. I was an only child with parents who had to get married and didn't really want a family."

Annalise nodded.

"They were young, and I don't know if they thought they loved each other or not. But my mother got pregnant and my dad did right by her—so he told her, over and over. And he didn't care in whose hearing he complained."

"It takes two," she murmured, wondering how a man could be so insensitive to a woman's feelings.

"Getting married and having a kid wasn't in my dad's plans—at least not at that point. He'd been raised in a mill town and had plans to escape. He wanted to move to New York, see about working in the theater—not as an actor, but behind the scenes. Instead, he was stuck in a small Pennsylvania town, with a wife and a kid and an old house that needed constant work. He ended up working in the mill."

"You told me that before."

"All his life he had to settle, because of one night that changed his world."

"You don't have to settle for anything," she protested. "For heaven's sake, Dominic, you can't compare that with us. You have a great career, and so do I. We don't have some shabby house. You don't have a dead-end job."

"I've seen what that kind of life is like. Men get bitter and turn old before their time. All focus is on the children—what they need, what their schedule is. Sacrifices have to be made so they'll have what they need. Soon it seems like the parents' lives revolve around the children. Look at your sister Mary Margaret—piano lessons, soccer practice, tutoring to get into the best schools. When do she and Sam have a life of their own?"

"My parents weren't like that."

"They still *are*, Annalise. When was the last time they went on a vacation that wasn't to the cottage? Have they ever been to Paris or Rome? Gone white-water rafting down the Colorado or skiing in Aspen?"

"They don't want to do that."

"Or there is no money and time to do that. Maybe they're just better at hiding their frustrations than my old man. He let it all hang out."

"We would not be like that, Dominic. You are nothing like your father. Circumstances are totally different. You make a great income. I have my own career, which has done well the last few years. We can afford to do what we want. We don't need to sacrifice things for the sake of tight financial circumstances."

He took a healthy drink of his coffee, tossing the remainder into the sink and putting his mug on the counter.

"What you don't know, and what I didn't tell you, is that I've been in this situation before," he said slowly. He hated talking about the past. But maybe it would help her understand.

She looked at him in confusion.

"What situation?"

"Expecting a baby."

Annalise stared. She couldn't believe what she'd heard. "You have a child somewhere?" There was a pause, then she jumped up. "We've known each other for more than six years. Been married five. And this is the first I'm hearing about it?" She looked stunned.

"No. I don't have a child. The baby was stillborn."

"Oh, how awful." That explained a lot, Annalise thought. He was afraid their child would be born dead.

"Our baby won't be born like that," she said gently, still reeling from the information. How could he have fathered another child and never told her? What of the baby's mother?

"You don't *know* how our baby will be born. Phyllis had a normal pregnancy. We thought everything was going along fine. But she went into labor two weeks early and the baby never drew a breath."

"Phyllis?" she repeated. The other woman had a name—of course. Annalise could hardly think.

"My wife. Ex-wife. First wife."

CHAPTER TWO

ANNALISE felt the blood pounding through her veins. Dominic was saying he'd had a wife before her. And she had never known a thing about it. He'd loved someone else. Fathered a child. And never mentioned a word. Would she have gone to her grave not knowing about that part of her husband's past if she hadn't become pregnant?

"You never told me you were married before," she said. She sat back down, wanting to weep. Then anger took hold. "How could you never tell me about such an important part of your past? I'm your *wife*. I haven't kept anything important from you. Where's the honesty needed in marriage? Don't you think that's something that should have been talked about at the onset? What happened?"

He paced across the room and back, frowning. "I never said anything because I've put it all behind me. I married Phyllis because it was the right thing to do—to give the baby a name and a father. I did it for her, too. We were high-school sweethearts. But I had plans to leave town and move on. For eight interminable months, I thought I was stuck, with no future except a life like my father's. When we didn't have the baby, we had nothing to hold us together. We divorced before I was twenty. I saved up and headed for college. My original plan, delayed a couple of years. You know I'm older than you, but that we graduated the same time. Now you know why."

"Married and divorced before you were twenty? Why not say something? You told me back then the reason you were late starting college was that you needed to work to save enough to attend," she said slowly, thinking back to those early days. Should she have picked up on some clue? How could he not have told her something this big in his past?

"That was true. All I had saved by my high-school graduation went to get Phyllis and me an apartment. For months, I thought I was doomed to repeat the life my father had—growing to resent the baby and Phyllis as I was stuck in some dead-end job in the mill town that was the one place I'd wanted to leave."

"Would you have?" she asked, caught up by the story, trying to picture a younger Dominic with some nebulous woman. She knew what the town looked like, but he didn't seem the type to be content there for his entire life.

"Probably."

"Probably not. You aren't your father. You set a goal and go for it. Look how fast you've gone up in the company. How much you know about all the various aspects of computer problems."

"It never came to the test," he said.

"Because the baby died?"

He nodded and turned to gaze out the window. He couldn't face her when he said, "And I've had to live with that guilt ever since."

Annalise frowned. "Why? You didn't cause its death. You said it was stillborn."

He ran his hand through his hair and shook his head.

"Intellectually, I know that. But it was a shock. My first reaction was relief—I could be free. Then I felt guilty for feeling that way. But Phyllis and I found we had little in common once we lived together. It was different when we were dating. The reality was unexpected. She was as glad as I was to get out of the marriage. I know you can't *think* a baby dead, but that's how I felt. That somehow my anger and resentment at not wanting the child caused its death. I should not have felt that way. What father doesn't want his child? My father excepted, of course. And then—me."

"So that's why you feel that way about our baby," she said, crossing her hands over her stomach in a protective manner. She had hardly gotten used to the idea, but already she felt she wanted to protect the growing life inside her.

"No! I do not wish this baby dead. I did not wish the other baby dead. I just wished for freedom. All I wanted then and now was to live life the way I planned. We have a great life. We entertain a wide group of friends. We take off on short notice to travel all over the world. Vacation wherever we wish, whenever we wish. We've built our life together. I don't want to lose it. To lose us."

"And that's what you fear if a baby's born?"

He closed his eyes. "I don't know," he said at last.

Annalise was reeling from the discovery that her husband had hidden a first marriage from her for as long as she'd known him. She'd thought they were a team. That it was the two of them against the world. Now she wasn't sure about anything anymore. What kind of marriage was based on secrets? She had been open about her past—not that she had anything of this proportion to reveal. Still, she expected honesty from her husband. Now his first marriage had come to light.

She'd known having a baby would change things, but she'd never considered this. "What other secrets do you have?" she asked.

He looked at her, anguish in his expression. "I should have told you. But it never seemed the right time. And then it just wasn't important. We moved here, got our careers going, and I moved on."

"So fear of not being able to do whatever you wish keeps you from wanting children?"

"That makes it sound cold and selfish. Maybe it is. But I've seen what having a child does to people. I know how my father was. That's the kind of parenting I know. I don't want to be like that."

"Lots of families have children. The parents are happy. The children enrich their lives. You do not have to be like your father."

"And children keep other people in dead-end jobs, living from paycheck to paycheck with nothing to look forward to. Kids get them caught up in the treadmill of dreary routine, substandard housing, losing hope for any kind of a different future."

"But that's not you or me. We're young, we have good jobs, and so far, we have done all we wanted to do." She tried to reason with Dominic again, to get him to understand that their future would be different.

She rubbed her stomach slowly. She felt sad for a baby whose parents weren't deliriously happy at its coming. She hoped this baby knew nothing of what was going on.

He frowned, following the movement of her hand for a moment. "Maybe thought waves are more powerful than people think. I wished a hundred times or more that Phyllis had not gotten pregnant. Then the baby was born dead."

"It's sad. But you can't think an outcome like that. Even if Phyllis had thought that, it wouldn't have resulted in a stillborn baby."

"I'll never get over the guilt," he said softly.

He looked out the window again. "I've been called about another assignment—this time to Hong Kong. It'll give us a chance to think things over."

"Think what over? Whether you want it or not, we're going to be parents. No matter what you think or say now, you are going to be a father. I guess it's up to you to decide exactly what kind of father you'll be!"

She turned and walked to the bedroom. She didn't know whether to cry or smash something. She grabbed her tote and packed a couple of outfits and sleepwear. She was going to Lianne's. Her twin would give her some advice and comfort. How could Dominic have kept his first marriage secret? She felt a pang at the thought of him being another woman's husband. Living a life she'd never even known about. They'd had an apartment together. Made a baby together. Tears threatened. Damn, he should have told her before they married about his past.

What had the other woman been like? Had the loss of their baby been so great neither could get over it? *He'd made a baby with someone else.* The thought caused a new twist of pain.

She was not going to lose *her* baby. Maybe she hadn't wanted one to begin with, but the idea was growing. She'd have another grandchild for her parents. She and her twin would have babies the same age. Maybe they wouldn't be as close as she and Lianne were, but they'd be first cousins, sharing a lot.

How could Dominic be so pigheaded as not to even consider changing his attitude when she was expecting a child? She would love this baby if only because it was part of Dominic. He could wish it away as much as he wanted. Fear of being a father was no excuse. *She'd* never been a mother before. She'd do the best she could and hope it was enough. That was all any parent could do.

She went to the front door. Dominic was leaning against the doorjamb to the kitchen, watching her without saying a word.

"I'm going to Lianne's."

"I'll be leaving soon. I'll call you from Hong Kong."

She wanted to make a grand exit and say something scathing like, *Don't bother.* But she was afraid if she opened her mouth she'd burst into tears. Staring at him, she saw a phantom woman hovering beside him. Someone else who had kissed him, slept with him. Had a baby with him. The hurt was overwhelming.

She shook her head and left.

Blinking back tears, she made the drive to Lianne and Tray's condo in record time. She sat in the car for a moment, trying to gain control. She left the tote in the car. If Dominic was leaving, she could return home later. But first she wanted to see her sister.

When Lianne opened the door, Annalise tried to smile, but she burst into tears instead.

"What's wrong?" Lianne asked, hugging her sister. "Whatever has happened?"

"Dominic doesn't want the baby," Annalise wailed.

"My baby?" Lianne asked.

"No—ours."

Dominic finished packing and headed for the living room. He'd pack his laptop and then be ready to leave. The routine was established; he could do it without thinking.

He had seen the stunned hurt in Annalise's eyes when he'd told her of his first marriage. The image haunted him. All these years, he'd thought he'd put that so far behind him it would never rise up again. Now it was out for all to see, and his guilt had not diminished one iota. How could any man wish away a baby? Wasn't that telling enough? Who could want to be around a person like that? He was just like his old man. Worse. And he hated the idea.

No matter how hard anyone worked, they never escaped the past. Now events were repeating themselves. His wife was expecting a baby, and it was the last thing he'd ever thought they'd have.

His father had been a bitter old man long before his time. Dominic remembered his mother had tried hard to please him, but nothing she'd done had succeeded. Dominic had loved his mother, but he felt sad thinking of all she'd missed out of life by having a baby so young, and then living with a resentful man who complained about their circumstances.

Dominic had worked hard to make a different life for himself. At the cost of his lost baby. He rubbed his hands across his face. When they had returned from the baby's brief funeral service, Phyllis had told him she didn't want to stay married. It had saved him asking her for a divorce. Once again he'd felt the taste of freedom—and the guilt at having things turn out that way. Even now, more than ten years later, he could feel the gnawing guilt.

Time to shove those memories away. He had a plane to catch. He wished he could have changed things for Annalise. But he was only human, and the thought of a baby scared him to death. Maybe he'd think differently once the idea seeped in. But for now, he wanted out.

Even out of his marriage? He'd almost implied that. Did he mean it?

Marriage to Annalise had proved to be a wondrous thing. They liked the same foods and restaurants. She enjoyed the theater, symphony and traveling—all new to him when he'd come to Washington for college. They had so much in common—from books and movies to their tastes in furnishings. He looked around the living room, remembering the purchase of every item. Nothing like the floral prints her mother had throughout the O'Mallory family home. Their place was sleek and modern—like Annalise herself.

Having a baby—even being pregnant—would change her. Phyllis had been fun enough when they'd been dating. But, once pregnant, her entire existence had revolved around that state. He couldn't go through that again. Couldn't bear to see Annalise change before his eyes.

He couldn't believe the past was repeating itself.

Lianne pulled Annalise over to the sofa.

Tray came out from the back of the flat. "Annalise— I didn't know you were coming over," he said. Taking a closer look, he raised his eyebrows in silent question to his wife.

"We're having a bit of a crisis. Be a love and find something to do," Lianne said.

"Right. Think I have something to do at the office." Tray bade them goodbye and left.

"Astute man," Annalise said, blotting her eyes with the tissue her twin had provided, wishing her husband had been as astute. She was mixed up about this pregnancy, and she needed his support, not to be stunned by news of his past.

"He's wonderful. But you've always thought Dominic was, as well," Lianne said, rubbing her back.

"Before today," Annalise said. "Or last night. He was horrid when I said I was pregnant."

"And you're just now telling *me!*" Lianne exclaimed. "That's great news. I'm thrilled for you both!"

"Don't be." Annalise explained everything. "He's still in shock over the news. But he will come back," she ended. "Don't you think?"

"Of course he will. You two make a great team. And the news takes a while to process. But I can't believe he was married before and never told you. I'm more than a bit surprised by that," Lianne said.

"*You* are? Imagine how *I* feel. All this time, I thought I knew the man, and now he springs this on me. Why not before we were married? Why not the first time he met me? He could have said something like *I'm just back in the dating game from a divorce.*"

"What did he say? What reasons did he give for not telling you before?"

"I didn't ask. I was too surprised by it all. Darn it, it makes me so angry to think he kept something this important a secret. What does that say about our relationship?"

Lianne thought for a moment. "I think once he realizes what he sounds like, he'll be back so fast your head will spin. Nothing is like it was all those years ago. He's crazy about you. The two of you always seemed as if you were in a world of your own—outsiders beware."

Annalise shook her head. "Not anymore. I don't know how to get over this. I feel as if he's a complete stranger. We've lived together for five years, and never once did it come up. He deliberately kept it from me."

"It's early yet. Give yourself some time. And you've got to try and think of it from Dominic's point of view."

"Which I already know."

"Not necessarily. He was unhappy in that marriage, that's for sure. Maybe he wanted to be a carefree college kid like everyone else. There probably weren't too many twenty-year-old college students who already had a divorce behind them. I could see him not spreading *that* around," Lianne said thoughtfully.

"He wouldn't have been spreading it around to tell *me*—especially when we began to discuss marriage."

"I don't know. What you had together sounds so fresh and free—unlike his first marriage. I could see him wanting to pretend life was as it *was,* not as it had been."

"Maybe." Could Lianne be right?

"Ask him. I bet he says he wanted to forget the past and forge a new life."

"Which he did. But now circumstances are similar, and he's freaked. I didn't expect to get pregnant. I sure didn't plan on it. He's blaming me."

Lianne shrugged. "Do you realize we are pregnant together? Good grief, sis—everyone will think it's because we're twins."

"Maybe it is. Maybe I felt your longing. The birth control failed. Who knows why now, after five years of marriage, the method failed? Dominic asked if it were a twin thing."

"So now it's *my* fault?" Lianne asked with a twinkle.

"No fault. I'm going to have a baby!" Annalise said. Slowly she began to smile. "A part of me and Dominic. How could anyone not be happy about that?"

"Dominic needs to talk to Tray. That man is so delighted you'd think we invented the concept of children."

"I'm happy for you. What should I do?" Annalise said slowly.

Lianne looked at her sister closely. "What do you want to do?"

"Make Dominic as happy about this as I'm becoming. Pretend I never heard of his first wife. Make everything come out happy."

"And if you can't?"

"What can I do? I'm pregnant. That's not going to change—at least for nine months. It was a shock to me when I first realized it, but now I'm growing to love this baby. I'll have to go on, I guess." She said the words, but she couldn't really believe them. Dominic wouldn't end their marriage over this. Even if he did, he'd still be a father to their child. Had he thought of that?

"Go on?" Lianne asked.

"I make a good living. I could support myself and the baby."

"I don't mean that. I mean, what plans are you making—contingency plans in case he doesn't come around—to change his mind?"

Annalise lay back against the cushions, resting her head and looking up at the ceiling.

"I don't have any. I'm relying on his good sense."

Lianne sighed. "Sometimes people don't have good sense. Especially if they have some phobia from the past."

"So how do I combat something like that?" Annalise asked. "He needs to come to the realization that this is not the same." She didn't tell her sister the rest—how he'd felt relieved, then guilty, when his first baby had not lived. There were some things too sacred to be shared outside of their marriage.

"So you and the baby would just live with him and hope he comes around?" Lianne asked.

"Not exactly. Perhaps I need to put myself first. I can't afford to wait for Dominic to come around. Maybe I could look into buying a home to live in with the baby. One was listed a while ago with our office which has loads of potential. It reminds me of Grandma Carrie and Grandpa Paul's home. It would require a load of work to bring it up to the kind of place I envision." She looked at her sister. "I don't see the apartment as a baby's home. I'll need different furnishings, a place for a stroller and later a bike. And a yard for a kid to run around in."

"We're planning to raise our child in *this* flat," Lianne said.

"I know, but somehow I want a more traditional home for my baby. I haven't had a lot of time to think it through, but I'd love to have a place like we had growing up—complete with yard and friendly neighbors. Anyway, I'll have to think about it some more."

"If you find a home, buy it. It'll give you something to think about besides Dominic. He has to make his decision for himself. You have to make yours. I hope they coincide, but if not, you have a life to live," Lianne said.

"I want to live it with Dominic. Perhaps if he sees how serious I am about our future—all of our futures— together, he'll want to be a part of it."

"You have your baby to think about now. Whatever happens, I'm in your corner."

When Annalise left her sister's after lunch, she drove by the home she'd mentioned to Lianne. She'd seen it on a home tour months ago. Now, stopping in front, she could see it definitely needed a lot of work. The yard was a mess; the house needed paint. But it had good bones and the lot was spacious. She could imagine children running on the lawn, playing tag or catch. Maybe they'd even get a small dog.

Whoa—she hadn't even convinced her husband to be happy about the baby, and now she was envisioning them all living happily ever after in this run-down house?

Dominic would probably freak when he saw it. She'd never seen his childhood home in Pennsylvania. His father had lived in an apartment by the time she'd met him. But she'd have to make this a showplace to convince him it was a wise move. *If* she decided to do it.

Feeling marginally better with the idea, when Annalise reached home, she went to the den to pull out the listing for the house. She spent some moments calculating the figures. With luck, she could swing the purchase of the house herself—without Dominic's support. It wouldn't leave much money to renovate with, but she'd do what she could as the money came. She'd just have to sell a few more higher-end homes.

Dominic had been right. The baby would bring changes. But change wasn't necessarily bad. The apartment suited their current lifestyle. A cozy family home would suit their future lifestyle.

Later that evening, she pampered herself with a long soak in a hot tub, then went to bed early with a good book. But she couldn't read. It was the first time since she'd left Lianne's that she'd let herself think about Dominic's past, and she couldn't let it go. She tried to imagine him as a husband to another woman—with a totally different life. But their life kept imposing itself. The parties they'd given, which they'd both enjoyed so much. The boating trips they shared in summer came to mind. What about skiing in Aspen? An annual event she took for granted. And the week they'd spent in Switzerland one winter had special memories. She couldn't imagine life being different.

Her mother and grandmothers had stayed home with their children. Was that the right way to raise kids? How could she give up the work she loved? Maybe she would cut back, but she couldn't imagine staying home with a baby all the time. Beside, once the child grew and was in school, she'd be bored staying home with nothing to do.

Had Phyllis planned to stay home with their baby? What had she wanted for her life before she got pregnant? Maybe Dominic hadn't been the only one whose dreams shattered. Had he considered Phyllis at all?

She admitted to herself that she was incredibly hurt that Dominic had not confided in her before. Did that show a fundamental lack of trust and commitment in their marriage? Was she good enough to be part of a fun-loving couple, but not for the intimate details of life?

That made her angry. She fed that anger when she thought of Dominic's reaction to the news about their baby. It had been just as much a shock to her as to him, darn it. Where was his concern for her? Didn't he consider she was going through some major readjustments herself?

The next five days passed slowly. Dominic called when he reached Hong Kong. With the twelve-hour time difference, it was hard to coordinate calling times convenient to both after that. She called him on Wednesday, but reached his voice mail. He had not returned that call.

She tried to keep busy, but more and more she ended up thinking about the revelation he'd made, and how that might impact their lives. Her anger simmered each day. She was unable to have it all out with Dominic, and yet unable to let it go.

Annalise plunged into working, determined to find each client the perfect home for them. And she toyed with the idea of buying that house. Lianne urged her onward. Annalise had driven by the house each day, and by Friday, had made up her mind. She'd buy the place and hoped things worked out the way she planned.

Annalise was able to get very good financing, due to her connections in the real-estate community. Offering a much lower price than the asking price, due to the work needing to be done and the length of time the place had already been on the market, she was delighted when the owners accepted. The house was tied up in probate, and her purchase would enable it to move along the process that much faster.

The attorneys agreed to a rent-purchase agreement that allowed Annalise access to the house immediately. She couldn't wait to get started on renovations. Better to do them as soon as possible, before she became too limited by pregnancy.

With any luck, she would have all the renovations finished by the time the baby was born.

Everything would go more quickly if Dominic helped. He'd worked his way through college in construction, and he was much more knowledgeable about such things than Annalise, even though she'd been helping her father and brothers all her life.

Of course she'd ask for volunteers from her family. With that crew aboard, she'd probably have everything completed easily in no time. But she wanted the project to be hers and Dominic's. Maybe having a joint goal would get them back on track as a couple.

The days seemed endless without him. She vacillated between anger and regret that so much had changed. Uncertainty plagued her. He hadn't really suggested they consider separating. She'd interjected that idea herself, and it was one she hated.

The following Friday, she picked up the keys to her new place and stopped off after work. It was a sunny fall day, but colder than normal, and she could feel the chill in the old house. She'd called the local power company and arranged to have the power turned on. Tomorrow, when she came to begin work, she'd turn on the heat. But for today, she just wanted to wander through, decide what she wanted to do in each room and make a short list of priority tasks.

It was after eight when she arrived back at the flat. There was a message on the answering machine from Dominic. Had he deliberately called when she was not home to avoid talking with her? She checked the time. On other Fridays she *would* have been home at that time. She hated that she'd missed him. Dialing the number he'd left, she reached the hotel in Hong Kong. But he had already gone out for the day.

Taking one of the pregnancy books she'd borrowed from Lianne, she curled up on the sofa and began to read. Before ten, she fell asleep.

Waking in the morning, she had a crick in her neck and did not feel fully rested. But excitement about the new house had her rising quickly to get ready for the day.

She'd just come from the shower when the phone rang. Dashing out to get it, wrapped in her warm robe, she recognized Dominic's voice immediately.

"Hi," she said breathlessly. "Your timing's good. I just got out of the shower. It's almost dinner time there, right?"

"Yeah. I called to say I'm leaving Hong Kong tomorrow and heading straight for San Francisco."

"Coming home through San Francisco?"

"Not yet. There's a project there that needs some work. I might also swing up through Seattle and check on a couple of clients there, since I'll be on the West Coast."

Annalise sat on the arm of the sofa. "So when will you be home?" she asked, anger flaring that she was still to be denied their discussion. It was not one she wanted to have over the phone.

"You know how it goes. My job takes me everywhere. Sometimes for a day or two, sometimes for longer."

"But generally you have a break between assignments," she said evenly. She would not allow her frustration to show. He was deliberately staying away. But he couldn't live out of his suitcase forever.

"I'll call you from San Francisco."

"Maybe I should fly out to join you."

"No."

Nothing more. She swallowed hard and bit her lower lip. The rejection hurt. Any other time *he* would have suggested she join him. She didn't like this rift between them.

"Okay. I won't. Take care." She put the receiver back in place and congratulated herself for not slamming it down. *Do your own thing and I'll do mine,* she thought in defiance as she went to get dressed. She had not mentioned the house. Of course he'd be surprised—but not as surprised as she'd been to learn of his marriage.

The thought still made her angry! She wasn't sure exactly which was worse—to learn he had been married before, or not to have been told earlier in their relationship.

What would she do if he truly didn't get over her pregnancy and left her?

She refused to even think about that. She had work to do today, and was glad for the distraction.

Arriving at the house some time later, Annalise turned on the heat and carried her broom, mop, bucket and cleaning supplies into the kitchen. That would be the first room she tackled. She had the vacuum cleaner in the car, and would bring more items with every trip. She had enough cleaning to last for days. Once the previous owner had died, her out-of-town heirs had not kept the place up.

There was a definite satisfaction in washing down the cupboards and counters and knowing the home would be hers for many years. She wondered if she was getting the nesting instinct from being pregnant—or was it just the next logical step in the maturing process? The apartment had been a great first home. But this was a house that would welcome a family through all its stages, from new babies through grandparenting.

Had Dominic and Phyllis rented a house or an apartment? Had they made plans for naming the baby, for raising a child? Had they ever thought about being grandparents?

Stop that, she admonished herself. She had gotten into the habit of questioning everything—trying to envision how that earlier pregnancy had been. She needed answers to her curiosity so she could stop dwelling on the past. It was like touching an aching tooth—it hurt, but she couldn't stop. She needed to know all the details and hope she could then put it behind her and move on.

She took a quick break for lunch, and then swung by a hardware store to gather some paint samples to take back with her. Dominic's favorite color was yellow, and that would be a perfect sunny color for the kitchen.

She'd have one of her brothers help her paint the room. She didn't relish climbing on ladders or stools to reach the high part of the walls. She was taking no chances with this precious baby she carried.

The weekend flew by. Annalise was tired Monday morning, but headed off to work, already counting the hours until she could be back at the house.

Dominic exited the jetway and merged with the other travelers heading for Customs at San Francisco International Airport on Monday morning. He was tired. Changing time zones had an effect, but his fatigue was due more to lack of sleep than to his flight back to the States. How long would he wrestle with what to do? He needed to make a decision and stick with it.

Was he less noble this time around? He'd thought marriage the best thing to do when Phyllis had gotten pregnant. The baby had been his; he'd lived up to his responsibilities. And he'd done his best to be a good husband. The affection he'd felt for her had faded with the day-to-day hardships of life, but he'd always done what he thought right. Just like his father. Only he hadn't voiced his frustrations and disappointments to Phyllis. She'd had it hard enough without listening to his complaints.

This time he was already married, and his wife was expecting his baby. He should accept his duty and be there for Annalise.

Only, the circumstances were different. Phyllis had not had a high-paying job, nor a large family to offer moral support. She'd been in her teens. He'd been young, too. They'd learned a lot during the months they'd lived together. He'd never forget that year. The ups and downs and the ending.

He had never held the baby, only seen it at a distance. Since they had not decided on a name prior to her birth, she'd quickly been given his mother's— Susan—to have something to put on the tombstone. They should have taken more time to decide on a name. Once he'd left the cemetery, that bleak winter's day, he'd never been back.

What if Annalise had problems during pregnancy? He clenched his teeth. He couldn't deal with the pain and guilt a second time.

Dominic moved up in the queue, and was soon through Customs and on his way to the downtown area of San Francisco. He was tired of thinking about duty and regrets and lost opportunities. He had just left one of the world's most exciting cities and was entering another. Next week, who knew? This was the life he had craved as a teenager. The goal he'd set for himself all those years of working his way through college and honing his skills. Learning all he could, applying that knowledge and finding a job that would combine each aspect.

If he gave it up, would he turn out like his old man? Bitter, grumpy, and stuck in one place the rest of his life?

Not according to Annalise. But she'd slant things to go *her* way. He needed to get a clear view of the situation. Not be swayed by pretty blue eyes.

Two weeks of thinking still had not given him a clear-cut direction.

In the meantime, he missed Annalise.

After checking into his hotel and calling the office, he took off. San Francisco was a great city for walking. Compacted into a small space, the various neighborhoods could be reached in a short time.

Every time he thought about the coming baby, he felt

hemmed in, and he needed to get out where he felt no walls were closing in.

The air was cool blowing off the Bay. He remembered the last time he and Annalise had visited San Francisco. They had taken a few days to explore the city, from Chinatown to Golden Gate Park to the financial district. Though summer, the weather had been cool, with a sea fog that blanketed the city each morning. Today's temperatures were also cool, but he was alone. No Annalise to find enchantment in everything she saw.

Today, nothing held his interest.

Dominic walked along the wharf, looking at the sidewalk cafés, remembering how much Annalise had enjoyed eating fresh crab from the sidewalk vendors as they walked along. He continued toward Pier 39, the huge converted pier that housed stores, shops, restaurants and loads of tourist attractions. Schlocky, he'd thought. She had loved every inch. Consequently, he'd gone in almost every shop and caught some of her enthusiasm.

Stopping at a bench on the grassy area before the pier, he sat and idly watched the other people—families for the most part. For a moment, he wondered why these children weren't in school on an October Monday, but he figured they were all tourists, taking advantage of a quiet season. Children ran around laughing with glee; mothers chased after them. One man was trying to help his little boy fly a kite. The wind was strong enough, but the boy kept trying to run after the kite, rather then let it soar.

Dominic wondered what was going through the father's mind. He seemed to be having a good time, if his laughter was an indicator. For a long moment, Dominic watched. That little boy was going to have some wonderful memories. Having fun, sharing their day together.

He remembered picnics his mother had taken him on when he'd been little. Those were happy memories. He didn't remember his father being part of them.

Intellectually, he knew many families were happy together. He'd witnessed Annalise's own family enough over the years. Patrick and Helen O'Mallory never seemed to resent having so many children. Would he and Phyllis have worked things out, found some contentment in their lives, if their baby had lived?

In retrospect, he doubted it. They had not drawn closer with the impending birth of their baby. And once they'd no longer had that tie, they'd had nothing to say to each other.

Some people were obviously wired differently. He wasn't father material.

He stood and began walking again. Watching families only made him feel more lonely. If he decided not to be part of Annalise's life, he could do exactly as he wished—but alone. Would that be better than resenting the ties a child presented?

CHAPTER THREE

ANNALISE packed a small suitcase with an assortment of clothing. She included several outfits for work. The majority of the other items she placed in were clothes like jeans and shirts, that could be tossed in the washer after a hard day's cleaning. She collected a few more items and headed out. She'd had enough of going to work, then home and the house. There was no one to be home for. She might as well save travel time and live at the house.

Her brother Sean had moved the bed from her second bedroom to the house for her last night. He'd been the first in the family to see the place, and had thought she was crazy to try to fix it up.

Maybe she *had* taken on more than originally estimated, but the house was growing on her. Each room she cleaned, and planned to renovate, seemed to reaffirm her decision. She wanted to bring it to life again. Hear children laughing and running down the steps. Savor the memories they'd make at holidays and birthdays. Make her mark on every inch of the place.

She'd suggested Sean might wish to help, as well, but he'd quickly given her several reasons why he couldn't.

Not that her brother was the handiest man around. He preferred to hire help if he needed anything done.

Once she'd put her things away in the small closet in the bedroom she'd chosen, Annalise sat on the bed and glanced around. She had wanted to paint the kitchen first, but maybe she needed a happy place to stay the night, as well. The faded wallpaper on these walls needed quick removal. For a moment, the tasks facing her were daunting. She hardly knew where to begin.

Dominic would know exactly what to do to bring the house to life. The best *she* could do was to learn as she went. And daydream about what it could be instead of what it was.

By Friday, Annalise had moved more items into the house—two chairs and a small table to eat at. The television from the apartment guestroom was set up in her bedroom. Bathroom items, extra towels and sheets were essential. Enough pots and pans and dishes to keep her going. She hated to return to the apartment. It echoed with emptiness, and she couldn't forget for a moment Dominic's reaction to her news, or the surprising revelation that had rocked her.

"Don't worry, baby," she said, rubbing her still-flat tummy. "We'll be fine."

One way or another, including the time before they married, when they'd already been a couple, they'd been more than six years together. Now Annalise felt cut loose, on her own. She'd stay awake nights worrying over the future—could Dominic have really meant what he said about the end of their marriage?

She vacillated between determination to make this marriage work and writing off the man she felt she had never fully known. How dare he carelessly throw away five years of marriage? Even suggest it! What about the bond between them? What about love?

It was not a word they used frequently. She loved Dominic. She'd thought he loved her. Her family easily hugged and kissed when seeing each other. Dominic came from a background where that was unknown. She'd recognized that early on, and had gradually, over their years together, come to accept the affections he bestowed as the best he could do.

It had nothing to do with their time making love. He was an ardent lover. She missed the passion in their marriage more and more as the days went by. He had rarely been gone as long as this trip—unless he'd taken her with him.

This time apart gave her an idea of what life without him would be like. And she didn't like it.

Was Dominic returning?

She had not telephoned him since he'd arrived in San Francisco. When he got back, he'd figure out where to find her. He had her cell phone number. That was all he'd need.

Saturday, Lianne and Tray stopped by before leaving for Richmond. Tray's uncle had left him a house and they were fixing it up to sell. It was the first time they had seen Annalise's purchase. Lianne walked through the rooms of the house and said at the end of the tour that she was glad they had far less to do to get their home ready than Annalise did.

"I can put my own design ideas on it," Annalise said defensively. She was still feeling a tiny bit over-whelmed. She wanted her sister to approve. She wanted backing for the coming confrontation with her husband.

If they were to continue, she'd definitely need his help with renovations.

"There are easier ways to make your mark," Lianne said with twinly candor. "In addition to getting the house habitable, the yard looks as if it'll take forever to make it useable. Maybe you could rent it out as some horror-movie set."

"Very funny. I can learn about gardening." She didn't have to have everything fixed up in the first six months. But Lianne had a point. The yard was a disaster—nothing like the groomed lawn she could envision her baby playing on.

"Dominic will be a help with the major renovation," Tray said as he stood on the back porch, surveying the overgrown tangle of plants and shrubs. "He'll probably need a chainsaw out here, though."

Annalise kept quiet. Until she knew exactly what Dominic's plans were, she was keeping silent around her family. Only Lianne knew of any problem. Annalise wanted to keep it that way.

"Is Dominic still in Hong Kong?" Lianne asked. She shivered slightly in the cold and they returned to the old kitchen.

"He's on the west coast now, checking in with clients in San Francisco and then Seattle."

"I thought they'd bring him right home," Tray said. "He's been gone a lot lately, hasn't he?"

"I think they are on an economy kick, and want to have him stop by as many clients as possible on the way back from Asia," Annalise said, making it up as she went. She didn't want to discuss Dominic until she knew more.

Lianne studied her sister for a moment. For a second Annalise thought she was going to ask an embarrassing question about what she knew about Dominic's plans. But her sister merely raised her eyebrows and then looked away. Tray apparently knew nothing about what she'd told Lianne, and she was grateful her sister hadn't shared.

They left soon thereafter, to drive to Richmond. Annalise felt lonely after their visit. They had been full of plans for updating Tray's house, decorating it to help sell it quickly. Annalise wanted that kind of planning with Dominic. Discussing ideas, selecting colors and furnishings—as they had when decorating their flat.

Instead, he didn't even know about the house. And, after his reaction to her pregnancy announcement, she was worried how he'd react.

But a child needed a house. She had had several comfortable places growing up—the large home her parents owned, those of her grandparents and the huge house by the sea, misnamed the cottage. She wanted the same for her child.

By midafternoon Annalise was exhausted. She had not been plagued with morning sickness, but she certainly didn't have the stamina she normally had. A nap every afternoon was coming to be the norm for her to be able to keep going. She lay down on her bed, and in no time was sound asleep.

Her cell phone woke her a short time later.

"Did we get robbed?" Dominic's voice asked.

"Where are you? Home?" She was groggy from her nap. She sat up on the edge of the mattress, trying to wake up.

"Yes. The bed is gone from the second room, and the television. What else is missing?"

"Cleaning supplies, some clothes. The card table and chairs. It saves travel time if I stay here while you're gone."

"And where exactly *is* 'here'?"

Annalise took a deep breath. "At the house I bought."

Dominic uttered an epithet. "What house?"

"I was going to talk to you about it, but you've been gone a while."

"Less than three weeks. And in that time you bought a house without mentioning it to me?"

"It's perfect for children. It has a large yard, it's in a quiet neighborhood and a good school district. We had the listing, so I took advantage of a great price and bought it."

"Seems you've decided how you want your life to go. Have a good one." He hung up.

"Dominic—" She was talking to dead air.

She couldn't have handled it any worse, she thought, lying back down. She closed her eyes and thought of a dozen things she should have said. It seemed as if the only way she knew how make major announcements was to blurt them out. She needed to go to the flat and explain.

Only, she was so tired. She'd had to set her alarm so she wouldn't sleep through the appointment she had at six. A couple was flying in from New York, and Annalise had lined up two homes for them to view.

She opened one eye to check the time. Not enough to dash home and see Dominic. Not and have the discussion they needed. She'd take the time to rest up, then have a quick shower before meeting her appointment at the office. She'd get home late, but at least she knew he'd be there, and they could talk as long as they wanted.

It was after ten when Annalise returned to the flat. She had another sale to her credit. Her clients had loved the first house, seen the second, and then returned to the first for another walk-through. Annalise had been amazed at how fast the sale had gone. It was a real estate agent's dream—full list price and financing already approved.

All she thought about on the way back to the flat was that she would be able to use her commission for some of the needed repairs around her house.

"Hello?" she called as she shut the front door behind her. The apartment was dark. Only a light from the den shed any illumination. She couldn't help comparing Dominic's arrival this time with his last one. Then he hadn't been able to wait to sweep her into bed. This trip had produced an unsatisfactory phone call that he had ended abruptly.

"I'm in the office," he replied.

He sat at the computer and hardly looked up when she entered.

"Hi—glad you're home," she said, leaning over to kiss him. He turned his face so the kiss landed on his cheek.

Apparently things had not improved with time to think things through, she thought wryly. He wasn't the only one to have to think. She'd come up with some ideas herself.

"Home for long?" she asked, slipping out of her jacket and tossing it across a chair.

"Until the next assignment," he said. "I didn't expect to see you. I thought you were ensconced at your house. The one I didn't even know about."

"If you were home more, maybe you'd know. Or perhaps if you called once in a while."

"I did call. You were out. At the house?"

"It needs work before we can move in. I was just

staying there while you were gone to save travel time and squeeze some work in during the evenings, rather than run back and forth all the time. At least it gave me something to do while you were away. I'll come home, of course, now that you're back."

He looked at her, then glanced around the den. "I have no plans to move in. This is my home."

Annalise shook her head. "You haven't seen it yet. It needs renovation, but it would suit a family much better than a high-rise apartment."

His expression tightened. "I haven't even gotten used to the idea of there being a baby and now you're talking about changing everything—like our very home."

"You weren't here to discuss this with."

"You knew I was coming back. What's the rush?"

"Someone else might have bought the house." It was unlikely, but Dominic wasn't to know that. "Besides, I needed something else to think about than the fact my husband had a whole other family he never told me about," she said.

Dominic didn't say a word, but leaned back in the desk chair. His gaze roved over her figure, stopping momentarily at her waist. She was not showing. It was too soon for that. What would he think when she was fat and waddling?

He turned back to the computer.

She wanted to smack him. They were having the most important crisis of their marriage and he was ignoring it for work.

She walked over to the desk and pulled a notepad closer, writing down the address.

"That's where I'll be," she said, tossing it into the center of the desk.

He swung around and looked at her. "You're living there for good?"

"I was just staying there until you came back, but if you are going to ignore me, I might as well stay for good. I thought we could talk when you got home."

"What do you want to talk about?"

"Gee—nothing like that comment to kill conversation. I don't know. How was San Francisco? Was it raining in Seattle? Want to come see the house?"

He rubbed his hands over his face, then stood. "I've thought about the situation nonstop all the time I was gone. I can't help how I feel, Annalise."

"Feelings and actions are two different things," she shot back.

"I understand that. I have not acted on my feelings."

"Which are?"

"Frustration, anger. Dammit, I thought I had my life on track. You've derailed it."

She put her fists on her hips. "Not me, *we!* I did not get pregnant alone."

"Neither did Phyllis."

Feeling instantly deflated, she leaned against the edge of the desk. She hated being categorized with his first wife.

"Did she deliberately become pregnant to keep you there?" she asked. She wanted to know every detail.

"I accused her of that. She denied it. I've always had my doubts."

"You said *she* asked for the divorce."

"The reality of the months we were married was far different than any fantasy of marriage. She was no more interested in continuing the relationship than I was."

"What if the baby had lived, grown up?"

Dominic thought about it for a moment. "She would have been nine now. What grade is that?"

"Third, I think," Annalise said.

"Hard to imagine."

"But if she had lived, would you still be married to Phyllis?"

He looked at her and shrugged. "Who knows? I wanted out. She was reasonably content to live there."

"But we never would have met. Would that be a good thing or bad?" she mused.

"Can you imagine the last six years not knowing each other?" he asked.

She stared at him as she thought through the question. Her life would have been totally different. Would she have been as happy?

"Do you love me, Dominic?"

He stuffed his hands into his pockets, returning her gaze. "Would we be married if I did not?"

"Probably. We're good together—in bed and out. We have similar likes and dislikes. We have a lot in common, yet enough differences to keep things interesting. Do you love me?" she asked again.

"Is this a trick question? If I loved you, I'd love your baby?" he asked.

"No, but that's not a bad thought. This baby is part of you, and I'm thrilled we are having a child to be part of *us*. I thought we had a strong marriage. Now I'm not so sure. What are you going to do about this child? Whether you live with us or apart, you are the baby's father, and you will have to deal with that."

"I don't know if I can," he said.

She wanted to shake him. If she could be a mother, he could be a father.

"You do have a few months to get used to the idea," she said dryly. Turning, she went to the door. "Call me when you want to talk," she said.

"Wait."

She turned, hope blossoming instantly.

He sighed slightly and inclined his head. "Tell me about this house you bought."

As an olive branch, it wasn't much. But she'd take it.

"The sale is still pending. I qualified for the loan on my own earnings and then obtained a rent-to-purchase deal so I could take it on immediately. All the inspections are complete, and the appraisal went through. But I wanted to get started on renovations since I have a time limit."

He nodded. But Annalise wasn't sure he was listening. He looked at her, but she wondered if he really saw her.

Or was it Phyllis he saw? Was it Phyllis he was fighting against? She wished she knew for certain.

"I've started cleaning every room. And making a list of all I can do and what I need to have others help with. I think I'd like to hire a construction worker part-time. If I can manage the expense. My commission on today's sale will help. I'm trying to get enough business four days a week to enable me to take an extra day at the weekend for more concentrated time to tackle the various projects." She'd hoped he'd offer to help.

"I thought you'd enlist the aid of your family."

"I asked Sean. He sounded horrified. Lianne and Tray are working on getting the house Tray inherited from his uncle ready for sale. And they've already asked some of my other brothers, so I'll have to wait in line. There are only so many weekends. Once their place is done, maybe the boys'll help me out."

"I'm sure they will."

Annalise hated the way the conversation was going. She had more enthusiastic responses from her co-workers. Dominic was not offering any help.

"You've been gone for days, and this is the best you can do?" she asked.

He stared at her for a moment, then shrugged.

"Fine." She turned and headed for the front door. He crossed after her to stop her.

"I need some more time," Dominic said.

"It's not going to change anything. The baby will still be born when it's due. The doctor said early June. I'm trying to get a family home ready. Come see the house. It's a bit of a mess right now, but with some renovations it'll be wonderful." She outlined some of her ideas.

"What you describe is a boat-load of work to make it habitable. The house is eighty years old. You'll have to check wiring and plumbing to make sure it's safe. Even if there are no termites, how sound is the structure? Building codes weren't as stringent that long ago."

"I know. I also know the real-estate business. I've had it checked out by an engineer. The house is sound, it just needs lots of work. But the beauty of it is how wonderful it will be when all renovated. Really our place—from our own hands."

"Not ours," he said, dashing her enthusiasm. "This is *your* project, from start to finish."

"You're not even going to look at it?" she asked, dismayed. She'd thought that once he saw it, he'd offer to help.

"I'll go see it," he said.

"Tomorrow?"

He nodded.

"In that case I'll stay here tonight and we'll go together," she said.

It was a small step, but she'd do anything to get back as a couple. It was not going to be an easy sell to him—he would deliberately put up barriers. But, given time, surely he'd come around?

The next morning, it was after nine when Annalise awoke. She never slept that late—or not until recently. She was constantly tired these days, and even yesterday's nap hadn't made much of a difference. She dressed quickly. Walking through the flat a short time later, she found she was alone. The coffeemaker was keeping the coffee hot. She took a cup and walked back to the living room to check outside. It was a beautiful autumn day. The sky was deep blue. She could see the trees below blowing in the wind. Crisp and clear, she expected. A perfect day for Dominic to see the house for the first time.

She hoped it would mend some of the breach between them. Last night had been downright awkward. She sipped her coffee and gazed out at the view of Washington that she loved. She would miss this when they moved.

Nothing had been settled. She still felt the distance between them. He was so unreasonable. Why wouldn't he at least consider the positive aspects of being a parent?

She called Dominic on his cell.

"Where are you?" she asked.

"I came into work. I'll be finished in an hour."

"We can pick up lunch somewhere and eat it at the house. It's too cold to eat outside, but I have that table and chairs, and the heat's turned on."

"I can hardly wait," he said dryly.

She ignored the trace of sarcasm in his voice. Maybe she'd go over early and get it looking the best it could for his first sight.

"I'll meet you there," she said, giving him quick directions. "I'll pick up sandwiches."

"Fine."

Annalise looked at the house more critically than normal when she turned into the driveway, trying to see it as if for the first time. It looked pretty bad. The yard was overgrown and unkempt. Compared to the neighbors' yards it looked appalling. The peeling paint detracted from any beauty in the structure itself. And that was just the outside.

Nothing she could do about that today. She hurried inside.

She heard his car when he arrived forty-five minutes later. Rushing to the front door, she could hardly wait to show him around. He *had* to like it!

Dominic got out slowly and did a scan of the yard.

"It needs work, of course," she said from the porch, feeling defensive. "But I figure Bridget can help us here. You know what a green thumb she has."

"This place needs a major overhaul. And, once done, how much upkeep will it require?" he asked, walking up the crumbling cement path.

"We'll put in low-maintenance plants. Hire a gardener to cut the grass. Sprinkler systems on timers. No work at all," she said quickly. She would not let Dominic's negative opinion dampen her enthusiasm.

She watched him study the house for a moment. The paint didn't look its best in the bright sunshine. Maybe she should have chosen an overcast day—or even rain. Dashing inside to keep dry might have been a better plan.

Annalise stepped aside for Dominic to enter. He halted inside, not saying a word.

She closed the door and walked into the living room. "This will be the lounge area. I picture it with comfy overstuffed furniture—all kid-proof, of course. I'd love curtains at the windows rather than blinds. And in blues and creams—sort of a country feel. Once the floors are redone, I'd get a big area rug, so it's warm underfoot in winter."

He looked at her. "We have modern furniture. Where does that go?"

"That goes with the flat. This would be decorated differently." She bit her lip as she stared at him. "We'd have to get new furniture."

He didn't say anything, but he looked at the floor that needed refinishing, the walls that needed painting, the windows that needed calking.

"Through here is the dining room—complete with table," she said as she led the way to the next room. The small table she had brought looked silly in the large room. "It needs a larger set, of course," she said, continuing through to the kitchen.

"This will be a showplace when we're finished," she said. "See the window over the sink? It looks out over the backyard. I can do the dishes and watch the kids. And once we get the yard fixed up we can have barbecues for family and friends."

She looked at him, waiting for his comments.

He looked around, walked to peer out the window. Turning slowly, he looked at her.

"This place is a dump, Annalise. It'll take tens of

thousands of dollars to get it habitable, much less decorated. The kitchen looks like it's from the 1940s. You have modern, state-of-the-art kitchen appliances in our flat. Why would you want this place?"

"It can be fixed up. It just needs new cabinets, new countertops, new appliances."

"Flooring, wall-covering, window-coverings and a new back door," he finished, looking at the old one. "So you spend a fortune to get what you already have now?"

"But the kitchen I have now is not in this house." She was trying to be reasonable, but Dominic was making her frustrated. Why couldn't he at least be the slightest bit open to the idea of a house? She wanted one for their baby.

"If the rest of the place is in as bad shape as the rooms I've seen, you've taken on an impossible task," he said.

"Look beyond what it is—see what it will be," she pleaded.

"It reminds me of the house I grew up in. You never saw it, since my dad moved to that apartment when I moved out. No one took care of the yard. My dad was too busy complaining about being stuck in that one-horse town to care about how the yard looked. The wallpaper was faded, having been put up two or three tenants before we moved in. My mother tried to keep the house clean, but it was old, damp, and it always needed repairs—most of which we were too poor to afford. Or my old man didn't care enough. This is an old house. Best torn down and a new house built on the lot."

"Our flat isn't all that new. The building is thirty years old."

"And it was completely renovated before we moved in. We didn't have to do anything but bring in furniture."

"You're not your father, and we don't live in some

one-horse town. And we have plenty of money to make the renovations." She could counter every argument he made. Why couldn't he at least give it a chance?

"I'm not interested in this house," he said.

She stared at him. "It can be a dream place."

"Maybe, with enough work. But it's not *my* dream place."

CHAPTER FOUR

ANNALISE blinked at that. She'd never truly considered that Dominic would not eventually come around to her way of thinking. Now she wasn't sure. That was happening a lot lately. Where was the man she'd thought she'd married, the man she could read and understand?

"What is your dream place?" she asked, fearing she already knew the answer.

"The flat we bought. Decorated the way we have it," he said.

"And that's all—for the rest of your life? That's *all* you want?"

She should not be so incredulous. If anyone had asked her a month ago she'd have said their flat was the perfect home. But that had been before she knew she was going to have a baby. Everything had changed. Just as Dominic had predicted.

"I'm hoping there's a long rest of my life, so I can't say that's all I'll want. But it's what I want now. I don't want reminders of the depressing place I grew up. I don't want to feel tied to a house when I could be flying to London. I don't want to paint and repair if we could be skiing in Aspen. The thought of mowing a lawn every weekend for the next fifty years is more than depressing."

Annalise looked out the window at the mess of a yard. She saw through the tangled bushes to a manicured lawn, toddlers running on the grass, she and Dominic sitting side by side as they watched with pride. Of course, that dream took some effort, with his reaction to her pregnancy.

"I'm sorry you see this like the home you grew up in. I see it as it can be—light and airy, and full of the aroma of chocolate-chip cookies baking. Kids running home from school to share their day. Laughter and love, family gatherings—just like my grandparents' homes."

"Are you sure you aren't romanticizing this? I know your parents' home was old-fashioned and made for children. Good thing, with all they had. But it's not for me."

He walked past her to enter the dining room, and stopped at the small table to start to unpack the lunch she'd bought.

When she followed, Annalise decided not to continue to talk about the house. Maybe Dominic would never come around. Maybe she was working on the house to fix it up for another family. Or, once it took shape, would he see it differently? She could consider different furnishings. Have one room like their flat—modern and minimal. She liked the sleek lines of their furnishings. The serene feeling of rooms without a lot of clutter. She could have a family room that housed the deep-cushioned furnishing, one that didn't need to be picked up every day but had children's toys strewn everywhere. Keep the two rooms separate.

"I don't want to fight. I don't want to be apart," she

said as she sat at the table. "I just want us to be like we've always been. If you don't like the house, let's consider it my personal project."

He sat and handed her a paper plate and a sandwich. "One that will take up an enormous amount of time and money. When do you propose we do things together?"

She admitted he had a point. She'd been spending all her available time while he was gone working on the house. And she had not accomplished as much as she thought she would. Everything took longer than she'd estimated.

"When you are home," she answered. She would have to schedule her renovations for the times he was gone. It would take longer to complete the project, but if he truly wasn't going to come around before the baby was born, her rush for completion vanished. Did she still even wish to proceed?

He didn't respond. After finishing half the sandwich, he wrapped the remainder in the paper and stuffed it back in the bag. "I'm done." Rising, he went to the stairs and climbed to the second story.

Annalise could follow his progress through the rooms from his footfalls. She'd have to think about carpeting on the second floor to help with the noise. They never heard their neighbors at the apartment building.

Her cell rang. It was her brother Sean.

"Hi, what's up?" she answered.

"I've been thinking about your request for help fixing up that monstrosity you bought."

"Changed your mind?" Things would go so much faster if she had help.

"Not me. Bunny's brother."

"A bunny's brother? Is this a crank call?"

"Bunny is the woman I'm seeing. It's her brother."

"The woman veterinarian you are seeing is named *Bunny?*"

"Yeah, I think it's kind of cute."

Annalise didn't want to tell her brother what *she* thought. "Her brother can help how?"

"He works in construction. There's not a lot of building going on now, so he has some free time—a couple of days a week anyway. I met him and thought he was okay. If you want, I can give you his number. I told him you might be calling."

"What's his name?" she asked suspiciously.

"Randall Hawthorne."

At least it was a normal-sounding name, she thought.

"Okay, give me his number. How much money does he charge? I don't have a lot after buying this place." She wasn't going to tell Sean that Dominic was against the project and would not be contributing. She wondered if she could manage it on her own. Did she still want to without his moral support?

Sean quoted her a figure and then rattled off the phone number. "It won't tally up to much if he only works one or two days a week," he added.

It sounded like a huge amount to her. But the sale she'd made last evening was bringing in a large commission. Maybe she could jump start the renovations with Randall's help. Dominic wouldn't see his old home in this place when it was renovated.

"I'll give him a call. Thanks. I still wish you'd help me out. You'd come a lot cheaper."

Sean laughed. "When you have the entire crew there, I'll come. But I'm not slave labor for you, baby sis."

Annalise and Lianne were the next in the line of children after firstborns Sean and Declan. Hardly the babies of the family.

She heard Dominic descending. "Got to go," she said to her brother, and rang off.

Dominic came to the doorway. "I've seen it all, and it's a mess. That bathroom's horrid. What were you thinking? Forget that—you weren't thinking. You couldn't possibly have considered all the expense and effort needed."

"That was Sean. He's found a contractor to help me out."

Dominic stared at her, wanting to understand what had happened to his wife. They'd been married for years—he would have sworn he understood her, that they were on the same wavelength. But this was mind-blowing. How she could rush out to buy this dump and then think it would end up as elegant as her grandparents' homes was beyond him. There was more work than an entire crew of O'Mallorys could handle in a year. And the up-keep once renovated would be tremendous.

Didn't she like the way they'd structured their lives? He enjoyed it, and he'd thought she did, as well.

He tried not to resent the baby. He'd been down that road once before. But if not for this pregnancy, things would have continued as they had over the last five years. Fate had a funny way of throwing a monkey wrench into the works. He knew he was in a different place this time. But the past reared its ugly memories and he had a hard time separating the two.

It also annoyed him that she had already lined up help with the project. Maybe she'd come to her senses sooner if she had to do it all on her own. His hope was that the longer she worked on it, the more money she poured into it, the sooner she'd realize what a drain it was and stop romanticizing home ownership. They already enjoyed all the benefits of owning a place, without all the maintenance and yardwork a family home would require.

Some people could see that for themselves. As *he* had, year after year with his parents. He knew some of his resistance to this house was an echo of his old man's complaints. Maybe he had cause. Dominic had never seen himself as a landscape gardener/general handyman—which a man needed to be to maintain a home in top shape. He knew from his construction work during college that he was competent enough as a carpenter, but he didn't enjoy it nearly as much as he liked using his mind to solve computer glitches.

The house wasn't the only problem. What were they going to do about the baby? The thought sent a shaft of panic blasting through him. That situation wasn't as easy to ignore as a house. He could feel the claustrophobia closing in. He needed to get away to be able to breathe.

"I don't know you anymore, Annalise. We've been together over six years, married five. And lately you are a total stranger to me."

She stared at him, her eyes large as she listened to the words. Was she really hearing what he was saying?

"I'm the same," she protested.

"No, nothing's the same. So where do we go from here?"

"You keep asking that."

"Because I never get a satisfactory answer," he said. He turned and walked out through the front door. Leaning against the railing of the porch, he took in a deep breath of the cool autumn air. She followed him.

"I think we should just take things as they come for now," she said, standing near him.

Dominic longed to pull her into his arms, to bury his face in the softness of her hair and hold her until his world settled itself. But *she* was the reason his world was cockeyed. Every time he thought about a baby it made him almost ill. He hated what that said about him, but he couldn't stop the feelings of claustrophobia that rose whenever he envisioned being tied down again. Having his future ransomed to an infant when he'd worked so hard to get where he was. He didn't want to grow to resent Annalise or a helpless baby. But if he couldn't find it in himself to become more excited about the new arrival, things would only get worse.

He had not changed. Maybe that was the key. Her pregnancy had altered the playing field. He had to decide to accept the situation, or cut and run.

"Maybe we should have a trial separation," he said at last.

The words tore at his heart. Yet it made sense. They had grown apart, were going in different directions. They might stay together for companionship, or from habit, but the spark of passion that bound them tightly, that made them a couple, had faded. Was that what had happened with them? Did he love her? She'd asked that question last night. He had been unable to shout out a definite yes. That scared him, as well. What *were* his feelings for her?

He looked at his wife. She had the same blue eyes and brown hair she'd always had. Her figure was trim and shapely. But the bright smile he liked so much was missing as she stared at him from sad eyes. What did he want from her? Instant denial of any separation? Some argument to convince him they belonged together? She wasn't giving him that. Maybe he wanted some acknowledgment that what he was asking for wasn't so off base. He'd made it clear from the beginning that he didn't see children in the picture.

"I don't want to. It'll change everything."

"The pregnancy has already changed everything," he said.

Tears spilled from her eyes, but he could tell she was trying to hold them back. One thing he could always say about Annalise: she never tried tricks to get her own way. He felt like the worst kind of heel. Yet he couldn't reconcile himself to the idea of becoming a father.

"Think about it. I'll see you if you decide to come home," he said, and turned to hurry to his car. He backed out of the driveway, noting the large trees that lined the street. "Leaves everywhere," he muttered, as he looked at the piles lining the sidewalks where diligent neighbors had raked them. "More work. Doesn't she see that? Owning a house ties a person down. I need to be free."

He drove home on autopilot. He could only think how Annalise had changed and he hadn't. Was that the problem? Was there something wrong with him that he couldn't see the wonder of having a baby? That he couldn't enthusiastically embrace owning a home? Was there something lacking in him? The something that made her so eager to expand their family and change their living arrangements, alter their entire lives?

Though in honesty he had to admit that initially she'd seemed as shocked as he to learn she was pregnant. She had reconciled herself to the fact faster. Now she seemed to welcome a baby into their lives, was willing to make monumental changes with enthusiasm. He wished he knew her secret.

Phyllis had not wanted to stay married to him once their reason for joining up in the first place had gone. Maybe there was a lack in him that women saw and he didn't. Things were spinning out of control. He had to hold on to his own dreams. If he was no longer enough for his wife as he was, what could he offer her?

Dominic let himself into the flat a short time later. He walked slowly into the living room. Stopping in the archway, he looked at the furniture they'd selected together. He remembered each shopping trip. They'd started with the console table and built from there. The sofa had been next. Then the coffee table. It had taken them months to find one they both agreed upon. He remembered the celebratory dinner they'd shared when they brought it home.

Piece by piece, he studied it, remembering. Even the flat itself held memories of their excitement the day they'd signed the papers. They'd come back after getting the key and made love in the bedroom, right on the floor.

Now she not only wanted to move, she wanted to change every stick of furniture. Virtually erase the past and start fresh with an entirely different style. Maybe it *was* time to end their marriage. For each to go their chosen way. The thought almost brought him to his knees.

Annalise watched in disbelief as the car drove off. She felt hollow inside. How dared Dominic just walk off and not fight for their marriage? Dozens of arguments sprang into her mind. She was not going peaceably away. If he thought they were over, he had another think coming.

Returning to the dining room, she cleaned up their

meal by rote, tossing the trash out and putting the remnants of their sandwiches in the fridge. Dominic drove her crazy. It wasn't *she* who wanted to separate. She was trying to adapt to the new circumstances. Was that so wrong? In a normal progression couples married, lived together for a while, then had children. Then the children would grow up and move out, and they'd be back to being a couple again.

It wasn't the horror story Dominic seemed to think it was. But without knowing more details about his first marriage she was hard-pressed to know how to counter his arguments. What two teenagers had faced was vastly different from a mature, successful married couple. Only, she suspected he was viewing the circumstances from those teenage eyes. And reacting to *those* circumstances—not the actual ones they faced.

If she'd thought she was angry before, she'd been fooling herself. She was so mad now she could spit nails. How *dare* he?

She flipped open her phone and called Lianne.

"Where are you?" she asked when her twin answered.

"Somewhere on I-95 between Richmond and Washington. Do you want me to ask Tray exactly where? He's driving."

"No. You'll be home in a couple of hours, right?"

"Probably about that."

"Come see me, will you? I'm at the house."

"What's up?"

"Dominic suggested a trial separation."

Annalise heard the hiss of surprise. "You're kidding," Lianne said.

"No. He hated the house—thinks I've gone off the deep end. And instead of trying to work with me, he just walked away." She took a breath. "I'm so angry I don't know what to do. Any suggestions? I'm afraid to call him up right now to let off steam. I might say something I'd later regret—but at the moment, I can't think of anything that I could say that I *would* regret. Damn him! It's not like I planned this baby—or had one with another man!"

"Whoa—I'll be there as soon as I can. Do you have your car?" Lianne asked.

"Yes."

"I'll have Tray drop me, and you can bring me home later," Lianne suggested.

"Okay, thanks. Tell him I owe him one."

"Give me the directions again. He says we'll be there in less than two hours."

Annalise paced around the room as she told her sister how to get to the house. Then she tossed the phone on the kitchen counter and went to work. She had to do something to expend her energy or explode.

She was too churned up over Dominic's comments to do more than hear his words echo again and again. Nothing had gone right between them for weeks. Was she a fool to think he'd come around? How could he not want a son or daughter? Their life was nothing like he described life in his hometown. She had thought *she* didn't want children, but now she was growing more and more excited about the prospect of having a baby. Of being a mother. What was wrong with Dominic?

"Annalise?" Lianne called.

"In the kitchen," Annalise called back, wiping her hands and heading for the front of the house.

Lianne waved to her husband, and Annalise heard the car drive away before her twin shut the front door.

"You should lock the door if you're here alone," Lianne said, slipping out of her jacket.

"It's a safe neighborhood. Thanks for coming."

Lianne glanced around and wrinkled her nose. "Cleaning didn't improve it much."

"Don't you start. Dominic thinks it a dump."

"He's got a point."

Annalise glared at Lianne, who simply shrugged and passed her sister on her way to the kitchen to put the tea kettle on.

"I assume you have an assortment of tea?" her sister said.

"Yes." Both twins loved tea—different kinds for different moods.

Once the water had boiled, Lianne prepared tea and poured them each a large mug full of chamomile.

"Any place to sit around here?"

"In the dining room, or on the bed upstairs."

"Dining room it is." Lianne led the way, and once they were both seated, she studied her sister for a moment. "For someone whose husband just left her, you seem remarkably cool about it."

"You should have been here two hours ago. I think smoke was coming out of my ears. He didn't leave, exactly. Just suggested a trial separation. Then said if I decided to come home, he'd be there. Like it's my decision."

"And are you okay with that?"

"Of course not! Nothing is going right. Becoming pregnant was just as much a surprise to me as to him. But I'm getting used to the idea. I can't imagine not having this baby now. But he doesn't seem to make any effort to see anything positive. And instead of talking things through, or making an effort, it's as if he's washing his hands of me and the baby."

"And he didn't like the house, I take it?"

"Says it reminds him of his childhood home—which I've recently found out he hated. Now that the truth is coming out, I realize how much he glossed over his past and how I let him. Now I want every detail. Only, he's thinking of ending our marriage. The jerk."

"And what do you want, sis?"

"I want this baby and my husband."

"So the giving him time part doesn't seem to be working—at least not in the short haul. He's still adamant?" Lianne asked, sipping her tea.

"He's horrified I bought the house. But this is the perfect family home. I want it fixed up so it's warm and welcoming and full of love and laughter. A place we'll live in for decades, like Grandma Carrie's home. I want family parties here. You know our flat is hardly big enough for the entire family. We never can sit down to dinner together there. It's always buffet-style."

"Face it, the only place anywhere near big enough for all of us at once is at the sea cottage. Once the rest of the family marries and maybe has a few kids there's not going to be a house large enough to seat us all at one time. I picture big barbecues at the beach on the sand."

"Or in our backyard. It's huge."

"Umm…" Lianne said.

"I have these pictures in my mind. Of me and Dominic sitting on the grass as a little kid learns to walk. Doesn't that sound as if everything is going to come out right? The backyard will be a perfect place for children to run around once it's tamed."

"And what does Dominic want?" Lianne asked.

"He wants nothing to change. I feel as if he's seeing his first wife when he looks at me. That he feels trapped by the mere thought of my pregnancy. But nothing is like it was when he was eighteen. Why can't he see that?"

Lianne shrugged.

"I probably would never have learned of his first marriage if I hadn't become pregnant. But history is not repeating itself like he thinks it is. Between that and his father, no wonder he doesn't want kids. But he sees other families—how can he think his experiences are the only way to be a family?"

"Because he can't truly relate?" Lianne offered.

Annalise tilted her head slightly while she brought up the memories she had of her father-in-law. They rarely visited him. "I never saw the house Dominic lived in when his mother was alive. I know Dominic doesn't like spending time with his father. Steve is a grumpy old man who is never satisfied with anything. I never really thought about growing up with someone like that before. I guess it could warp a person."

"But once that person is an adult, he no longer needs to play those childhood tapes over and over. People move beyond hardship in youth," Lianne said.

"So what do I do now? There is a baby on the way. I can't change that even if I wanted to, and I don't. I love this baby already."

"And you want this house," Lianne added, glancing around. "Though how you can see the potential is beyond me."

"Come back in a few months. You'll sing a different tune. Sean even has someone lined up to help me. If I can manage it financially." Annalise explained, and

Lianne burst out laughing when she told her about Sean's new woman-friend.

"It can't be serious," she said, her eyes dancing in amusement.

"Probably not—when is Sean ever serious? But if the guy can help me, that's all I care about."

"Forget the house. Concentrate on your husband."

"But what about me and what *I* want? It can't be all about what Dominic wants. What kind of marriage is that?" Though she missed him already. Or was it his support she longed for? Something to validate the choices she was making now? Where was the feeling she'd had of being one of a strongly bonded couple? She felt adrift. How often did trial separations end in reconciliation?

"Then you need to think about what kind of marriage you have. And where you want it to go."

"Not much of one if the first hiccup in the road of life has him suggesting a separation." She thought a moment. "We've had a wonderful five years—full and fulfilling. Lots of friends. We travel more than anyone I know."

"But how close are you two? I know you have a great life together, but where's the intimacy if he keeps major things in his past a secret?"

Annalise nodded, feeling hurt again at Dominic's revelation.

"You know, Lianne, the more I think about it, the more I think we had a fair-weather marriage. We both love entertaining. I like nice clothes, and I think he likes me looking nice when we go out. He's gorgeous, and I love being seen with him. But you're the one I go to with problems. What does that tell you about our relationship?"

"I know how he looks at you—as if he can't wait to get the two of you alone."

"There's never been a problem there," Annalise said pensively. "But is that enough for a strong marriage?"

"Who knows? But you have a history together, a basis to build upon. You have similar interests, similar passions. Find a way to reconnect. He's an only child from an unhappy marriage. Then he himself had an unhappy experience with marriage. Granted, he's been thrown in the midst of our family since day one, but at the end of the commotion and chaos you and he return to that ultra-serene flat and the tranquility that's there. No kids crying, no toys strewn everywhere. That's what he likes. And this expected baby threatens to change everything—from a couple to a threesome, and from a luxury apartment to a house that looks horrible right now. I'd be nervous about the entire situation myself," Lianne said.

"So what do you suggest?" Annalise asked.

"Make a fuss over him. I'm trying to keep Tray happy and not feeling second place to the baby, though you know how much I want this child. But I want Tray as my husband as much—if not more. I never thought I'd fall so deeply in love, but I have and it's wonderful."

"Sounds as if I'd be acting with an ulterior motive—butter him up to get my way," Annalise said. She looked at her sister. "I asked him if he loved me. He never answered."

"Men aren't as open with their feelings. You know that."

"A simple *Yes, I love you* would work," Annalise said. "What if he doesn't love me?"

"Then it's time you found that out," her sister said candidly. "You need to come to an agreement as a couple on how you'll face the future. Especially if he's to come around about the baby." Lianne looked around the room and made a face. "But I'm not sure he'll come around about the house."

Annalise took offense. "It's going to be a showplace when it's renovated."

"You keep seeing this place when it's all renovated. The rest of us see it as it is today, and it's a dump. And if he lived in poverty as a kid, this probably brings flashbacks which he doesn't want or need. When I suggested you go ahead with a home, I had no idea it would take so much work."

"Okay, I'll grant that maybe everyone doesn't have my vision. But, trust me, this is going to be wonderful. The perfect family home."

"If you say so," Lianne replied dubiously

The two sisters spent the remainder of the afternoon cleaning the upstairs bedrooms and discussing ways for Annalise to recapture Dominic's devotion. The talk segued into about how they felt being pregnant and what to name their babies. Not surprisingly, they both wanted the same name if their babies were girls— Caroline, in honor of their grandmother Carrie.

"So first girl born gets it?" Annalise said.

"When are you due?" Lianne asked suspiciously.

"Early June."

Lianne looked at her. "This is so weird. I'm due the first week of June. I can't believe we got pregnant at the same time."

"Twins," Annalise said, and they both laughed.

By the time Lianne had to leave for home, the cleaning was complete. Now the renovations could begin.

After dropping Lianne at her apartment, Annalise

called the number for Randall Hawthorne. He answered after three rings, and knew instantly who she was when she identified herself.

"My brother Sean said you might be available to help me renovate an old house," she said.

"My hours at the construction site have been cut due to the weather, so I have several days a week free. When do you need me?"

"I'm arranging my time so I can work on the house Friday, Saturday and Sunday. I figured working a block of days at a time would be better than spreading things out over the week."

"Sounds like a plan. I can do that."

They discussed what she could pay, what she wanted done.

"How about I come over now and check out the place, give you my suggestions on what to start first?" he offered.

"That would be great. The sooner the better. I don't have lights in all the rooms, so you need to see them before dark."

In less than half an hour Randall Hawthorne knocked on the door.

Annalise opened it, surprised at the young man standing there. He was as tall as Dominic, with sandy blond hair and an engaging grin. He was muscular from his work, and wore faded blue jeans and a ski jacket over his shirt.

"Randy Hawthorne, at your service," he said with an easy smile.

"I'm Annalise Fulton. Come in."

"Great old place. Man, this could really be cool when it's fixed up," he said as he gazed around the foyer and then into the living room. Stepping inside, he wandered around, running his hands lightly over the mantel, gazing out the window over the front porch. "But it's going to take a lot of work."

"Not more than I can handle, I hope," she said.

He turned and grinned at her. "Hey, you and me together can do a lot. Let's see the rest of the place."

Annalise showed him around, telling him what she envisioned for each room, with colors and repairs or, in the case of the kitchen, complete renovation.

When they ended up back in the foyer after the tour, Randy said, "I'd say get started on the front rooms first. They will be some of the easiest to do and you won't get discouraged. Once we have a few redone, we can tackle the kitchen and the bathrooms. Those are going to be the hardest and the most expensive. Leave them until later, so you'll start enjoying part of your handiwork long before we get to them."

"Okay." Annalise was pleased with his suggestions. She knew how she wanted everything to look at the end, but wasn't sure of the steps to get there. "What do we do first?"

They discussed the renovation plan for a while, deciding to start with the living room and dining room—beginning with refinishing the floors, painting the walls, and then thinking about furnishings.

"So, next Friday, early?" she said.

"I can be here at six."

"Oh, maybe not that early," she said, remembering how hard it was for her to get up these days. "Seven will be early enough. And I'll have the floor sander by then, so we can start right away."

When Randy had left, Annalise debated not returning to the flat. She knew there wouldn't be a warm welcome. But she wasn't going to be the one to leave this marriage. She'd try some of the tactics she and Lianne had discussed regarding Dominic. If their marriage was shaky, she was going to do her best to strengthen it. With or without Dominic's help!

CHAPTER FIVE

IT WAS late by the time Annalise returned to the apartment. Dominic was in the den. She peeked in at him, but he was working on the computer and barely acknowledged her greeting. She went to take a shower and dressed in her sexiest nightie. It was a little cool in the apartment, but she hoped that would change. Slipping on a silky robe, she went to the kitchen and prepared some hot chocolate.

Carrying two mugs into the den, she set one down near Dominic on the desk.

"Hot chocolate. Take a break."

"Sounds good," he said, reaching for the mug. He glanced at her and his eyes held. Slowly he moved his gaze down her body, seeing the robe part slightly when she sat on the small chair near the desk, her slender legs revealed.

He looked away, taking a swallow of the hot beverage and then exclaiming when it burned his mouth.

"Careful—it's hot."

"So, it appears, are you," he said, looking back.

She could see desire in his eyes, the way they darkened and went so smoky. Her own pulse increased.

"I was when I got out of the shower, but it's cool in here."

He carefully sipped his chocolate. Annalise wanted to smile. She could almost see the calculations in his mind. Carefully, Dominic put down his mug and rose. He held out his hand for hers. She had not even had a sip, but gladly relinquished it.

"Come to bed," she said, rising.

"My pleasure," he said, leaning in to kiss her.

Pleasantly tired some time later, Annalise relished snuggling against her husband. She'd fall asleep in another moment, but she wanted to savor the afterglow. There was more to resolve, answers to get, but for the moment, she was with Dominic, and it was enough.

"Tell me about Phyllis," she said. Instantly she felt him tense.

"What's to tell?"

"Everything. You said you were high-school sweethearts?"

"We dated. Hung out together when I wasn't working. Even then I was trying to save enough for college. I had a scholarship to Penn, but knew I'd need more money to make it."

"Did she plan on college?"

"No."

"What was she going to do?"

"I don't remember," he said slowly. He was silent for a moment.

"What was she like?" Annalise asked.

"Small, dark. She changed after high school—after we were married."

"How?"

"Different ways. Before we seemed to get on okay. But once we were married, when she was pregnant, she became clingy. Never wanted me out of her sight. She used her condition to manipulate everything to go her way. We couldn't go to the movies because we had to save for the baby. Couldn't have friends in—our apartment was too small and crummy, and what could we serve them? She'd spend hours reading books about babies."

"Sounds as if she was scared."

"I never thought so then."

"What would you know? You weren't going to be a mother at eighteen," Annalise said softly.

"I knew I was scared we wouldn't make it. The dead-end job at the mill was boring and tedious, but it brought me a paycheck. God, I hated that job. Phyllis managed the money and did it well. We had no debts, managed to have food on the table every meal. But the thought of doing that for another fifty years about drove me insane."

"You were both too young to have a baby," Annalise said.

"Well, we didn't, did we?" he said, sitting up.

"Dominic, you did not cause that baby to be still-born," she said, sitting up, as well.

"You don't know everything, Annalise. Maybe thoughts *can* influence an outcome. The intensity of my desire to be free was almost tangible. How do you know it didn't penetrate Phyllis some way and end that baby's life."

"Come on—don't be like that. You did not do anything wrong."

"I did it all wrong." He stood and went to pull on a pair of jeans. Grabbing a shirt from the closet, he stormed out of the bedroom.

Annalise debated following him, but decided against it. She'd pushed a lot, and he'd responded. Now she'd brought it all to the forefront. What would he do next?

* * *

Dominic went to the kitchen and poured himself a drink. He usually only drank socially at parties, but tonight he wanted the burn of alcohol, the forgetfulness it could bring. He'd worked so hard to forget that year. Annalise couldn't understand how awful things had been. Phyllis had changed from the girl he'd gone out with throughout the last two years of high school to a whiny, clinging girl who wouldn't give him any space.

In retrospect, he hadn't handled it well. He'd been resentful of losing his chance at college, angry at finding only the job at the mill and scared as he'd told Annalise. He'd known nothing then about being a father, and he knew nothing now.

He stood in the dark and let the memories wash through him. Each one strengthened his resolve. He could not go through that again. He didn't want his feelings for his wife to turn into bitter resentment. He didn't want to see Annalise become clingy. He had come as far from that life as he could get. To be sucked down into a repeat was not in the cards.

Yet Annalise was right. Stay or go, he'd still be a father. What kind of man wasn't there for his child? Even his old man had always been there—complaining every moment, but there. Once again he'd do his duty. And count the years until he could be free.

The next morning, Annalise woke late and rushed getting dressed and dashing to the office. Dominic was already gone. She had appointments lined up all day and didn't have a moment to worry about her personal life.

Midafternoon, she took a break and called Dominic's cell.

"Fulton," he answered. As always, her heart skipped

a beat at just hearing his voice. How could he even suggest a trial separation? She wanted to be closer, not drift apart. Yet now that the specter had been raised she began to question every aspect of their marriage. Last night had been glorious, until she'd brought up his first wife. He had not returned to their bed after he'd left.

And she could not forget that he had not answered her question the other night.

"Hi," she said, wishing the breach between them could be miraculously healed.

"Hi, yourself." He sounded like the old Dominic.

"Want to meet for Chinese dinner?' she asked.

"What time?"

"My last showing is at four. So, unless they decide to buy on the spot, I could make it around six-thirty."

"See you then," he said.

As she hung up, she considered that maybe Lianne was right. She needed to show Dominic that nothing had changed as far as the two of them were concerned just because a baby was expected. She would always make time for her husband. They'd still eat out, go to a show, entertain. Maybe she should plan another party.

But when? She was guarding her weekends jealously. That was the only time she had to work on the house.

Thinking about that had her wanting to call Mary Margaret. Did her sister put her children first, to the detriment of her husband? But she couldn't call and ask— first of all it would insult her sister, and second no one knew about her pregnancy but Lianne. Maybe Annalise should call her parents and announce the news and have done with it.

But not until Dominic was reconciled to the idea.

Annalise arrived at their favorite Chinese restaurant

promptly at six-thirty. She entered, and saw Dominic lounging against the wall in the narrow entryway.

"Did I keep you waiting?" she asked, reaching up to kiss him.

"Just got here a minute ago." He turned and nodded to the hostess.

Annalise was a bit disappointed he hadn't returned her kiss with more fervor, but they were in a public place—though Dominic had never been that reticent when they'd first married. And usually he held her hand or flung an arm over her shoulder. Tonight they could pass for business colleagues going to dinner.

The waitress seated them in a booth near the front. It was quiet and dimly lit. Handing them menus, she went to get the hot tea.

"Let's get the same thing as always," she said, leaving the menu closed near the table's edge.

"Suits me," he said.

The same as always comprised Szechuan beef, kung pao chicken and pork chow mein. They had discovered early in their relationship that they had similar tastes in food.

"So how was your day?" Annalise asked brightly. She could have kicked herself. That sounded so first date-ish. Were they down to banalities? She wanted to establish their old rapport before demanding answers to questions about Phyllis and the life they'd led. Or finding out more about the child who had not lived.

Dominic's eyes flashed amusement. "Fine. How was your day?"

"Okay, that was dumb. What's going on at work?"

"We have a new client in Maryland. I may have to go up there later in the week, to get an overview of the computer setup. They are a startup security firm in Annapolis and are bidding for a contract with the Navy, so are beefing up their own security to show the Navy they are up to the task they're bidding for."

"I'd think you could tell that from dialing into their system."

"Most of it I can, but I want to check out the physical layout and see what security procedures they have to protect the mainframe. Backup measures, that kind of thing."

"What else?"

He smiled slightly. "I played games."

She nodded. When Dominic said he played games, he didn't mean the kind she played on computers. His firm had some of the brightest minds in the world as employees. They constantly tried to trip up one another through altered codes on existing programs. It kept them on their toes, devising problems and then solving them.

"What about you?" Dominic asked.

"I showed the Worthys two more houses. I swear, they have seen every house in the north-east section, the north-west and near the Capitol. Neither of these was quite right, either. I think they like looking at houses, but I'm beginning to think they are not seriously looking, and have no intention of buying."

"Do what you did with that other couple who only wanted to look. Get the credit report and the mortgage pre-approved before showing them any more."

"I think I will. That usually separates the men from the boys," she said.

The waitress showed up with their meal, and for the next few moments, they were quiet as they ate. Annalise was beginning to feel as if they'd regained their old footing. She looked up and feasted her gaze on Dominic for a moment. She still thought he was the best-looking man she'd ever seen. His dark eyes flicked up and met hers, holding her gaze for a moment. She could feel the quiver of anticipation shoot through her. Would they return to the flat and make love?

"So what does Lianne think of your house project?" he asked, as if deliberately thrusting a wedge between them.

Annalise's heart sank. Anytime the house or baby came up it widened the distance between them.

"She shares your opinion that it's a dump."

"Enlightened woman," he murmured.

"You both have no imagination. It's going to be beautiful. You'll see. And I'm starting on Friday. I've hired a construction worker to help me."

"Who?" Dominic went on the alert.

"The brother of the girl Sean is seeing. He came by the house on Sunday and I hired him. *He* thinks the house is going to be beautiful when it's done." And so far Randy was the only one besides her that did.

"What do you think you're doing? You shouldn't have had him out to the house with only you there," Dominic said, leaning closer and glaring at her. "He could have been a mass murderer or something."

"I told you, he's Bunny's brother."

Dominic looked at her for a moment. "Bunny?"

"Sean's latest. The vet. Her name is Bunny."

"And what's her brother's name? Doggie?"

Annalise wanted to giggle, but she was miffed Dominic had acted as if she didn't know what she was doing. She'd bought this house on her own. She was directing the renovations. She knew exactly what she was doing. And if the man had been anyone other than the brother of Sean's girlfriend, she *wouldn't* have had him at the house when she was there alone. Though she was constantly showing homes to strangers. Which Dominic also had a problem with. Maybe he was just being protective.

"His name is Randy and he works in construction, but not so much now that the weather is bad. He had some great ideas and we start on Friday." She kept her tone reasonable.

Dominic was quiet for a moment. "I thought I'd go to Annapolis on Friday and you could go with me. After I visit the new client we could find a bed and breakfast and stay the weekend. Wander around the old part of town."

She was torn. A trip to Annapolis sounded wonderful. And she'd have a chance to build a bridge over the chasm that seemed to grow wider each time they were together. But she'd already committed to Randy to start on the house. Time truly was not on her side. If the weather got too inclement they would have to delay some of the repairs to the windows, and wouldn't be able to paint and air out the place.

"I wish I had known earlier. I'm sorry, but I can't make it. I've reserved a floor sander, and Randy will be there early on Friday to start. The weekends are the only time I'll have to get this house in shape before the baby comes. I won't be able to go anywhere for a while."

She hated seeing the flash of anger in his eyes.

"Maybe I could take another day during the week," she offered. It would mean the possible loss of revenue, but there was no sure sale in the works, so she'd be glad to chance that.

"I'm busy until Friday," he said, sitting back and finishing the last of his tea. "Ready to leave?"

She nodded. So much for building bridges. Why

hadn't she been more amenable to his suggestion? Was it pride? Or resentment that he wouldn't see things her way? She was mad he seemed to make no effort to change.

When they returned home, Dominic closed himself in the den. Disappointed that the evening that had started so promising had turned out badly, Annalise pulled out her laptop and connected to the Internet, reading how-to articles on refinishing floors and woodwork. She wanted the knowledge if not the experience when she and Randy began work on Friday.

The next morning, Annalise overslept again. She hoped she would not be this tired all through her pregnancy. She scrambled to make it to her first appointment, and the day was hectic, with home tours from the office and two new listings to be signed. She had a strong clientele in the area, and word of mouth expanded it each year. She loved showing homes and making suggestions on creative financing. She had a solid base of happy homeowners who had bought through her. Some had become friends and they often saw each other.

Thinking about it, she should be planning another party for December. Would Dominic be available? She called him.

"I am already too late for a party in early November. And then we run into Thanksgiving. But what about a party that first weekend in December? Will you be here?" she asked as soon as he answered.

"Do you have time? What about your house?"

"Stop antagonizing me. I can't go with you this weekend because I made prior plans. But with enough notice I can do almost anything. We always have a party or two this time of year. But before I reserve caterers and all I want to make sure you'll be home."

"I'll mark down that first Saturday. Can't guarantee it, but I'll do my best."

"Perfect. We can review the guest list tonight and I'll start with invitations—December gets full really fast. We'll get a jump on the others."

Getting home a bit early, she prepared a nice dinner. They'd eat, plan the party, and fall back into their normal routine.

By seven, however, Annalise gave up on Dominic showing up. She'd called his cell, but it was inactive. Had he deliberately turned it off, or had the battery run down? That rarely happened, but it did once in a while if he was too involved with other things.

Was he playing his games again? She was constantly amazed at how he and his other computer coworkers could get lost for hours in tracing codes to find a problem. It sharpened their diagnostic skills. Dominic was a natural at it—with an intuitive concept of problems. She was fascinated with the way he thought.

She ate, and put Dominic's portion on a plate in the fridge to be heated when he got home. Going to the den when she'd finished, she drafted a list of friends and relatives she'd invite to the party. Knowing she'd have to cut down on entertainment for a while afterwards, she listed more people than she could handle with a buffet. So this one would be only a cocktail party, with hors d'oeuvres. Leaving the names on the desk for Dominic to review, she went to bed.

The next night when Dominic didn't come home before she was ready to go to bed, Annalise was fed up. She packed up a few items, left him a note and headed for the house. If he didn't want to spend time with her, she'd show him what a trial separation was really like. It might bring him to his senses.

It could backfire and she'd find he loved being on his own. But that was a chance she'd have to take. After making love so ardently earlier in the week, she knew there was still that spark of attraction between them. Maybe Dominic needed to pay more attention to that than dwell on the past.

He did not call on Thursday.

Friday, Annalise woke excited at finally beginning work on the house. She made coffee and heated bagels, and was eating the small meal when she heard Randy pull into the driveway.

It was cold, and threatening rain, but to Annalise the day was rosy with promise. She would begin actual renovations today! She hurried out to meet her new helper.

Annalise had rented the floor sander, which had been delivered yesterday afternoon. It sat in the center of the living room.

"Know how to work that?" she asked Randy when they entered that room.

"Sure."

In no time he was sanding the scarred wooden floors, while she hand-sanded the woodwork around the windows. By lunchtime her hand ached from holding the sander, and her shoulder hurt from the repetitive motion. But the windows were ready to be primed. She only had the mantel around the fireplace to finish and this room would be ready for paint. Randy was almost finished with the large floor in the living room.

"I'll make a sandwich run," she said, rotating her shoulders to try and ease the ache.

"Works for me. I'll be finished here soon, and ready to do the dining room after lunch. And then the entry hall. Stairs will have to wait."

"I think I'll carpet them, so we don't need to redo," she said, studying the stairs. Carpet would make it quieter, so not to hear the clatter of children running up and down. She planned to carpet the upstairs rooms for the same reason.

After a congenial lunch, they resumed their tasks. Once she finished the mantel, she vacuumed up the grit and washed everything down to minimize the dust. She wanted the floors to be silky smooth. Randy had told her they needed to get all the dust up and wait for it to settle out of the air. Then do another sweep with tacky cloth. Tomorrow they'd be able to begin staining.

Randy left around six, and Annalise ate another sandwich for dinner. She went shopping for more groceries afterward, and then watched a silly show on television before going to bed. She wondered how Dominic was enjoying Annapolis. She was hurt he hadn't called to see how she was doing. Maybe leaving had been a mistake.

Saturday, she had breakfast ready when Randy arrived. They ate quickly and she put the dishes in the sink, running hot water over them. She'd clean up later. Now they needed to get started on the final wipe-down and staining the wood. She was excited to see the room transformed. Randy had been right. It would be gratifying to have one completed so soon.

Randy showed her how to brush the stain on the wooden floor in the direction of the grain and then wipe off the excess, repeating until she got the perfect shade. When the stain dried, they'd seal it, and the floor would be beautiful for many years to come.

It was easier than Annalise had anticipated. She chatted with Randy, learning more about his sister. Did he believe Sean was serious? They discussed jobs he'd worked on, finding a house she'd sold a couple of years ago had been one he'd renovated.

When they were halfway through the living room, Annalise heard a car in the driveway.

"Who can that be?" she murmured. *Darn,* she didn't want to stop.

CHAPTER SIX

FOOTFALLS sounded on the porch, then the front door opened.

"Annalise?" Dominic called.

"Oh," she said, looking at the floor. She was on the left side of the room, with Randy on the right. They were half-way through, and wanted to complete it by lunchtime.

"Friend of yours?" Randy asked, still working.

"Husband. In here, Dominic," she called.

When he reached the archway, she sat back on her heels and looked at him. "Don't come in. We're staining."

He looked at Randy, then at the floor that had been stained.

"I thought you went to Annapolis," Annalise said. What was he doing here?

"I came home last night." He looked at Randy again.

"Randy, this is my husband, Dominic Fulton. Dominic, Randy Hawthorne. He and I are staining the floor," Annalise said, hoping to defuse the tension that seemed to be growing.

"I can see that," Dominic said, not taking his eyes off the construction worker.

"Hey, man," Randy said with an easy grin. "I'd get up to shake hands, but don't want to interrupt the rhythm."

"Annalise, can I see you a moment?" Dominic asked.

"I'm kind of busy right now. Can it wait another hour or so? We'll be finished by then."

Ignore her for three days and then expect her to jump when he said so? Not by a long shot, she thought, annoyed he'd shown up when she was in the middle of a project.

Dominic looked at his wife and the man, working diligently on their staining. They had accomplished a lot already. The trim around the windows had been stained the same color as the floor. The carved wooden mantel looked as new as it had eighty years ago. The floors would turn out nice. No slacker here.

But he didn't like the idea of Annalise working closely with this man. If he'd been fifty and balding, maybe. But Randy Hawthorne looked young and fit and too friendly by half.

"I'll wait," he said.

"We're doing the dining room after lunch," she said, carefully applying the brush and then wiping away the excess stain. Already ignoring him.

With another glance at Randy, Dominic asked, "Got coffee?"

"Some instant in the kitchen. We drank the other already."

He walked through the dining room, noting how nicely the floors had been sanded. Not Annalise's work, he knew; she wasn't skillful enough to sand a floor so evenly. He reached the kitchen and put on a kettle. Looking in the cupboard for coffee, he noticed the dishes in the sink. Two sets. How cozy.

Dammit, she was his *wife*. What was she doing eating meals with another man?

When he'd suggested a separation, he'd expected her to fight tooth and nail to stay together. Seemed as if she was doing just fine on her own. Didn't she miss him?

He missed her like crazy. He'd come here today to talk some sense into her. She had made her point. Now she could come home.

And not a moment too soon if she was taking her meals with some stranger.

Probably part of the pay for this construction worker. Whom she wouldn't have needed to hire if she hadn't bought the damn house.

Or if he had helped. He'd worked in construction for six summers, from high school through college. He knew enough about building to manage this place. And what he didn't know he could learn—a lot easier than Annalise.

But he didn't want to work on this house. If it hadn't been for the house she would have gone with him to Annapolis. It was as if she had a split personality—the woman he'd married, and a stranger bent on having babies and renovating old homes. He *wouldn't* encourage her to fix the house up. That would have her even more determined to live in it. Their flat had all they needed.

Except a nursery, came the unbidden thought.

He clenched his jaw at the reminder and gazed out the back window while the water heated. He did not like the yard. Sure, they could hire a gardener, but he still didn't like the idea of being responsible for a lawn and a garden.

He disliked the idea of his wife turning to someone else even more.

He fixed the coffee and wandered back to the archway. Annalise was on her knees, and when she leaned over her sweetly rounded rear rose in the air. Randy worked beside her, so he couldn't see, but Dominic didn't like their camaraderie, either.

Get used to seeing her with another man if you leave, he told himself. And hated the very idea. Annalise was *his*.

Randy was telling Annalise about a fishing trip he'd been on, and she was laughing at his story. She knew enough about the subject to discuss lures and flies with him. Dominic leaned against the doorjamb and grew more frustrated as the minutes ticked by.

"You do much fishing?" Randy asked over his shoulder to Dominic.

"Sea-fishing in the summer, sometimes."

"One of my brothers has a boat, and we go out with him," Annalise explained.

The man nodded. He was almost finished with his portion of the floor, and undoubtedly would be helping with Annalise's side when he'd done.

They bumped into each other. Dominic could tell it wasn't intentional, but it still made him want to reach out and grab the man.

"I have some vacation time coming. I could help here," he said. Almost as soon as the words were out he wished he could recall them. He did not *want* to work on this house—he would be giving mixed messages if he did. Annalise would think he was softening in his stance against the place. But he sure wouldn't tell her it was because he was jealous of the smiles she gave that man.

Randy looked up and grinned. "Hey, man, that's cool. With three of us working we can get this place fixed up in no time. I was telling Annalise her ideas are terrific. This is going to be a showplace. I can't wait to see it, can you?"

"I can't wait," Dominic said. So Randy had bought into Annalise's scheme. Or was he just saying what his employer wanted to hear?

Annalise rocked back on her heels and looked at Dominic. "I thought you didn't want anything to do with this place."

"Well, I changed my mind." His look challenged her to argue. She was so pretty, even in old clothes and with brown stain on her fingers. He wanted to snatch her up and take her to the bed upstairs. Hardly likely with Randy around.

"Fine. We can use the help." She resumed the staining.

"I'll go home and change clothes and be back this afternoon," he said a moment later. "Shall I pick up lunch?"

"Get yourself something. I have enough for me and Randy," she said.

Dominic almost told her Randy could go out and find his own food, but he held back. Things were too tenuous between them to give vent to how he really felt.

Driving back to the flat, Dominic acknowledged he was jealous of the man working so well with his wife. He'd never minded her colleagues at the real-estate office or the men she knew in finance and banking. But none of those had ever represented a threat in Dominic's mind. Randy liked her idea of the house. That was heady stuff when her own husband was so against it.

Randy was also young and good-looking. Dominic suppressed the anger that rose at the thought of him coming on to Annalise. She wasn't going to be distracted by some guy, even if he *was* good-looking. Unless she felt neglected by her own husband. Which of course, she did. She'd made overtures last week and he'd rebuffed them. Now it was his turn. He hoped she would be more generous.

But he couldn't seem to get by his feeling of history repeating itself. And he did not want that. He didn't know what he wanted. That was the problem. Being in San Francisco without her had made him realize how much she was a part of his life. They enjoyed the same shows, books, movies. They liked to wander around historic parts of different cities. Their taste in food was similar. They had a good marriage. Two people who liked the same things.

Do you love me? The thought came unexpectedly.

He'd tried to evade the question, but it echoed in his mind. What was love?

Two people, two good friends, doing things together—only more? They had so much in common. He wouldn't give up their intimacy for anything. Yet wasn't he suggesting that very thing with a trial separation?

What was love? A yearning to be with a special person? He could ask her the same question. Only she hadn't been the one to suggest separation.

When Dominic returned an hour later, wearing old jeans and a shirt that had seen better days, he heard laughter from the kitchen and walked through the now empty dining room to find Randy and Annalise sitting at the small table.

She looked up at Dominic, the smile lingering in her eyes.

He felt the flare of desire he always had around her. And a curious hunger for more. To know her thoughts, her fears, her hopes and dreams. And where he fit in each of them.

"I'm finished, if you want to sit at the table," Annalise said. There were only two chairs.

"No, I ate as I drove. What's scheduled for this afternoon?" He'd find a way to get her alone for a serious discussion. If he helped with the renovations, she wouldn't need to hire another man.

"We're going to stain the dining-room-window trim and the floor." She held up her hands, dark brown from the color they were using. "I hope that's the end of it. I'll have to soak my hands in bleach for a month to get them clean again."

"Naw, I've some stuff in the truck that'll take that right off," Randy said.

"Good. I'd hate to have walnut-brown hands the rest of my life." She grinned at him.

Dominic drew in a sharp breath. He wanted his wife smiling at *him* like that again.

"Should you be working around these fumes?" he asked. He walked closer, put his hand on her shoulder. "She's pregnant, you know," he told Randy. It was primitive—like he was staking his claim. Which he was.

"No? Really? Bunny didn't say. Cool. Congrats to you both. Wow, a little rug rat. Your first?" Randy seemed genuinely pleased with the news.

Annalise nodded, smiling. She threw a wary glance at Dominic.

Another notch against the man. He was as excited about the news as Annalise's family was going to be. Obviously he didn't have any of his own, Dominic thought cynically. Nor did he know what havoc babies could cause in people's lives.

"I'm due next summer. I'm hoping to have the house finished by then," she said.

"Cool. We'll do it. Especially with your husband's help. Annalise has bragged on you, man. Said you worked years in construction. Between us we should knock it out in no time," Randy said.

"Cool," Annalise repeated.

Dominic wanted to grind his back teeth. He put his hands in his jeans pockets and faced Randy. "I thought I could do Annalise's shift on the staining, and she could do something easier, away from the fumes," he said. He'd rather be paired with Randy-the-friendly than have his wife working with him all afternoon.

"I'll get started upstairs," she said, jumping up and taking the remnants of her lunch to the trash. She put the dish in the sink. "First I'll do these dishes and start the crockpot for dinner." She looked at Dominic uncertainly. "Will you be here for dinner?"

"Of course," he said, before Randy could say a word. He was going to make sure the man knew his wife was off-limits.

Annalise looked at her husband in surprise. There was no *of course* about anything he did anymore. And nothing could have surprised her more than having him show up today and volunteer to work on the project. And announce her pregnancy to Randy. She looked between the two men and wondered if something was going on that she was unaware of.

She grabbed some more sandpaper and walked up the stairs, wondering how long this offer of extra help would last. She'd take all she could get. But it was odd he'd waited until Randy had started.

It couldn't be because he was jealous. Dominic knew he would never have reason to be jealous of anyone. She had loved him since she'd first met him. Even now, when he was being infuriating. She wished Randy would leave and Dominic would come up to the bedroom with the bed in it. Dreaming the afternoon away, she sanded until her arm was numb.

When she could do no more, she sat on the floor and dialed her sister Bridget's phone.

"How would you like the wonderful opportunity to design a garden from beginning to end—design to planting?" she said, when Bridget answered.

"What's the catch?" her sister asked.

"None. I've bought a house that has a disaster of a yard. I envision a lush lawn and colorful flowers, but haven't a clue even where to start. You have always loved gardens. How many hours have you spent in Grandma Carrie's garden? And your own? Here's your chance to design one however you like—the only caveat is to keep it easy to maintain."

"I heard you bought a house. When can I see it?"

"Anytime. I'm here this weekend, and as many weekends as I can manage."

"I'll come by tomorrow around noon—that work?"

"Perfect."

"So what's up with the parents?" Bridget asked.

"Nothing that I know of. Why?"

"Mom called earlier to see if I was free next weekend. I'm home, and she said she'd call back when they'd firmed things up. So I asked her what, but she just blew me off."

"She hasn't said anything to me. Maybe it's something special for you."

"It's not my birthday, so what else could it be?"

"Any promotion at work that deserves a celebration or something?"

"*Nada*. Well, if she calls you, let me know. See you tomorrow."

Annalise finished sanding the trim in the front bedroom and then went to the room in the back that held
the bed. She'd lie down just for a minute. Her entire
right side ached now. She needed to work into fixing this
place up gradually. There was no need to attempt to do
everything this weekend.

On that thought she promptly fell asleep.

"Annalise?" Dominic shook her gently.

She opened her eyes. It was dark outside. The faint
illumination from the hall light showed her husband
leaning over her.

"Are you all right?" he asked.

"Just tired. And my arm hurts from sanding so much
these last two days. No wonder Randy is in such good
condition. This is hard physical work!"

"Yeah, well, you shouldn't push yourself so much."

"Pace myself? Good idea. Only there's so much to
do, and I'm anxious to have it all completed."

"Dinner's ready. Your construction friend left. He
had a date," Dominic said.

"Oh? How late is it?"

"After seven."

She groaned and sat up, still feeling as if she could
sleep a week.

"I can dish up the dinner and bring it up, if you'd rather
stay here," he said, stepping back to give her space to rise.

"No, I'll be right there." She hated to move. Truthfully, there was nothing she'd like more than to roll over
and go back to sleep. But she needed to eat.

Walking down the stairs, she surveyed the floors of
the main level.

"They look beautiful," she said, stepping gingerly on
the foyer portion.

"They're dry. Tomorrow we'll seal them and let that dry for a week, then give a second coat next Sunday. But you can walk on them carefully in the meantime."

"Thank you for your help. I know the work will go faster with the two of you in charge. I lack your experience."

Dominic made a noncommittal sound and led the way into the kitchen. The aroma of the stew in the crockpot filled the air. She was instantly starving. Using the few plates and utensils she'd brought, they soon began eating.

"This tastes so good," she said, watching in satisfaction as her husband gave every appearance of enjoying his meal. The old adage came to mind. The way to a man's heart is through his stomach. Maybe this was a way to remind him of all they had? He wasn't much of a cook. Before they'd married he had made do with fast food and hamburgers—typical college fare. Her mother had taught her how to prepare meals of all kinds, and Dominic liked the food she made. Obviously including tonight.

"What's up for tomorrow?" she asked.

"We'll tackle that little room behind the living room, and then seal the floors. Once that's done, no walking on them for at least twenty-four hours."

"Bridget's coming over at noon to see the yard. I asked her to landscape. How long will it take you and Randy to seal the floors?"

"A couple of hours, max."

"Next weekend I can paint the living and dining room walls, right?"

He nodded.

She took another bite. If she couldn't walk on the floors while the top coat dried, where would she go?

Glancing at him, she considered returning home. Then promptly vetoed the idea. First of all, she wanted him to ask her back. She needed that. It wouldn't be much of a statement if she headed for home the first time something came up. She didn't need Dominic. She wanted him—as husband, lover, father to her baby. But if that was not to be, she could manage on her own. Time her husband realized that.

It didn't take long to do the dishes when they'd finished.

"Ready to go home?" he asked casually, hanging up the drying towel.

"I am home," she said, turning to face him. "You wanted a trial separation, you've got it."

"Okay, we tried it. I don't like it."

She shrugged, holding his gaze.

"What do you want?" he asked.

"Some assurance we are going to make it," she said.

"There are no guarantees in life."

"That's reassuring," she replied dryly.

"Look, I know we're stuck with the baby. I have to make the best of it."

"Get out, Dominic. Wrong answer, wrong attitude— wrong, wrong, wrong *everything*."

She pushed past him and headed upstairs, slamming the bedroom door when she'd entered the room. She held her breath, waiting for some indication he wasn't going to let the situation remain as it was.

The sound of his car gave her the answer. Not the one she wanted.

She flipped open her phone and called Lianne.

"Can I stay with you this week?" she asked, when her sister answered the phone.

"Oh-oh—trouble in river city?"

"Maybe, maybe not." Annalise explained about moving out, and then about Dominic showing up to help her today. "I think he's surprised I'm not like his first wife."

"And how is that?"

"Dependent."

Lianne laughed. "That does not sound like you. He's known you for years—does he really think you'll become dependent?"

"Apparently his first wife did when she became pregnant." Annalise could say the words *first wife* without a pang. She was accepting the past, growing used to it. Maybe she'd never know the full story about their relationship, but as long as it remained in the past she would not dwell on it. What had happened before she met him went into making him the man he was today—hang-ups and all.

"So what's the plan?"

"I'm living in the house until further notice. Only, they are sealing the floors on the main part of the house tomorrow, and I can't walk on them for a while. So I'd need to stay with you for several nights."

"You are always welcome here, sis, you know that," Lianne said. "And I want to hear more about Dominic's first wife."

"I'll tell you all I know—which still is hardly anything."

"See you when you get here," Lianne said.

Annalise went to bed more content than she'd been in days. Dominic had come to help on the house. That meant a lot.

By the time Bridget arrived the next day, Annalise was glad to escape to the yard. She'd tried to help with the flooring, but Dominic didn't want her around the fumes. Randy and Dominic seemed to have an armed truce between them. They were cordial enough, but neither seemed to like the other much. Were they disagreeing on how to do the job?

It was her house, and she wanted to make sure things got done the way she wanted, but at one point even Randy said they'd do more faster if she'd get out of their way.

She was sitting on the front porch, imagining what the garden could look like, when her sister turned into the driveway. There was scarcely room for her vehicle with their own two cars and Randy's truck. Bridget climbed out of her low-slung sports car and headed up the crumbling walkway.

"Wow, this is fantastic," she called, when she spotted Annalise. "And I get to do whatever I want?"

"As long as I can afford it," Annalise said, coming down the steps to give her sister a hug. Another one in her camp. "I want it to be a showplace."

"It kind of reminds me of Grandma Carrie's garden. You already have roses growing." Bridget examined the sprawling branches. "But not so good. I can fix that."

"And there are more in the back," Annalise said.

"With a little care these old bushes will be full of blooms next summer. I bet they're the old-fashioned fragrant kind. We'll have to see." Bridget walked around the expanse of yard, examining former flowerbeds, kicking at the brown grass, studying the tall trees.

"Let's see the back," she said, completing her circle.

She was just as pleased with the backyard—large by city standards, and full of old trees and shrubs. She and Annalise discussed what could be done, and Bridget was even more excited than Annalise about the possibilities.

Randy came around the side of the house. "Anyone here own that car behind my truck?" he asked.

"I do," Bridget said, turning. She smiled brightly. "Hello, I don't think we've met."

"Bridget, this is Randy Hawthorne. My sister Bridget. Randy's helping me renovate the inside of the place."

"And I'm finished for the day. See you next Friday?"

"Yes—as we arranged."

"Wasn't sure we were going to continue in light of Dominic now helping."

Annalise wanted to say *that* was the arrangement she was uncertain about, but she wouldn't say it aloud. "Dominic may have to go out of town on business at a moment's notice. I want some assurance this project will continue on track. You're hired for the duration."

"Works for me," Randy said, with an easy grin.

"I'll move my car," Bridget said, walking over to Randy and falling in step as they both headed for the driveway.

Annalise sat on the back steps, waiting for her sister. She liked the ideas Bridget had proposed, and couldn't wait until spring, when she would see the flowers in bloom.

Bridget returned a few moments later. "Wow—what a hunk. What does Dominic think of you working with that guy?" She sat on the steps beside Annalise.

"He hasn't said anything, but he sure volunteered to help quickly enough when he got a good look at Randy."

Bridget laughed. "Not that he'd ever have to worry about you. I never saw two people so in tune with each other. You can practically finish each other's sentences."

Annalise wanted to confide in her sister, but until she made her announcement to the whole family about her pregnancy, she had to keep quiet. Except…

"He doesn't think much of my remodeling project. He likes the flat we own."

"I do, too. It's so elegant, and yet comfortable." She looked around. "This is going to be a lot of work compared to no yard at all. You don't even have a balcony with flowers now. Are you sure you're up to it? You two travel so much. Though I wouldn't mind coming over to keep an eye on things."

"We may not be traveling as much in the future. And I figure we can always hire a gardener."

"I guess. Nothing like getting your fingers in the soil, however. Or talking to your plants as you prune them and water them," Bridget said.

"Is that the secret to your green thumb? You talk to the plants?"

"And encourage them to be all they can be. It works. Grandma Carrie taught me that."

Dominic came around from the side of the house. "I thought I heard voices. Hi, Bridget. What's your verdict about the jungle?"

"Hi, Dominic. You have a huge challenge here, but I'm up to it. Leave everything in my capable hands and you'll have a showplace in spring."

He looked at the tangled and overgrown yard and shook his head. "I can't picture it."

"Annalise said to make it low maintenance, so I'll install sprinklers and get only plants that require minimum care. With maybe a couple of flowering ones that might take a bit more."

"A gardener will take care of it all," Annalise repeated, with a glance at Dominic. "I want a big lawn area."

"Umm, you may change your mind," Bridget said. "Can I see the inside now?"

"Sorry—we just sealed the wood floors on the ground level. Can't go in for forty-eight hours," Dominic said.

"Come back next weekend. I'll give you the grand tour," Annalise said.

Her cell rang. She answered, looking at Bridget as she said, "Hi, Mom."

Her mother asked if she and Dominic were available next weekend, to meet with the rest of the family at the sea cottage.

"What day?" she asked, already wondering what she could rearrange with the tasks on the house to accommodate her mother's request.

"Sunday. I haven't confirmed that day with everyone yet, but so far everyone I have talked with has the weekend free," Helen said.

"I'm available Sunday." She raised her eyebrows, looking at Dominic, and he paused a moment, then nodded. It would still give her two days for renovation work.

"Is Dominic in town?"

"Dominic's available, too, as far as I know. He's right here. As is Bridget. Do you want to talk to her?"

"Yes. Plan to arrive midmorning. We'll have lunch, and then everyone can leave before dark."

"What's up, Mom?"

"Tell you on Sunday. Let me speak to your sister."

Annalise handed the phone to Bridget and walked over to Dominic. "Mom is gathering the entire family at the sea cottage next Sunday. But she won't say why. Nothing awful, do you think?"

"I'm sure she'd tell you right away if something awful was up."

She glanced at her sister, who was still talking on the phone.

"So, can you go with me?" She hated to ask, but if

he didn't go it would raise more questions than she wanted to answer.

"Of course."

Annalise wished he'd take her in his arms and kiss away the estrangement. But before she could even ask him to hold her, Bridget rose and crossed the distance to hand Annalise back her phone.

"Weird. Why won't she say why we're all meeting?" Bridget asked. "I think I'll go home and call the others. Maybe she let some clues drop and I can put them all together to find out why."

"Good luck. Mom doesn't let anyone know what she doesn't want them to know," Annalise said.

"See you next Sunday, then." Bridget hugged them both, and left.

"Nothing more to do inside?" Annalise asked. Did she have to worry about her parents on top of everything else going on in her life?

"I checked everything was turned off before we finished the floors. We worked our way to the front door. You can lock it, and we can leave. I have to go by the office. I'll be home later."

"Thanks for your help, Dominic."

"You don't need to pay for help, Annalise. If I'm not available, get one of your brothers."

"This way I can call the shots and not have to wait on someone's availability. Don't you think Randy's competent?"

"He seems to know his stuff. What I don't like is the idea of the two of you working so closely."

She shrugged.

Dominic turned and headed for his car. "I'll be home later."

"I'll be staying at Lianne's until the house is habitable again," she said.

He turned back and stared at her for a long moment. "As you like." In only moments, he was gone.

Annalise kept her days busy with clients and new listings. Evenings she spent with Lianne and Tray, trying to ignore the fact her husband had not called.

To Annalise's surprise, Dominic arrived at the house on Friday morning earlier than Randy. He told her he'd arranged for a few days off to help out, and that she should take advantage of the time while he had it.

She and the two men painted the front rooms and worked on the small room behind the living room. She was anxious to get started on the kitchen, but knew that would be such a monumental task it was best left until she had more energy. If she ever would while pregnant.

Nothing was said about their living arrangements. With Randy in earshot all day, it was hard to have any private conversation—which both suited Annalise and frustrated her.

Sunday, Dominic picked her up at the house to drive to the cottage together. Annalise watched the familiar scenery as they drove east, feeling awkward. She hadn't completely severed ties with Dominic. Yet she hoped the estrangement was showing him what he was missing with her gone. Glancing at him, she wondered if it was working. She was encouraged by his helping with the house. Yet yesterday, he could have been the hired help like Randy for all the special treatment he'd given her.

Dominic hadn't said much since he picked her up and she didn't know how to open the topic closest to her heart—literally. She wanted to tell her family about the baby. Yet the last thing she wanted was for him to tell everyone how against having a baby he was. No one would understand. She, who knew him best, didn't fully understand. She knew the past held a tremendous hold on him even today. Would anything get through that barrier?

They were not the last to arrive, but more than half the family was there when they pulled in. The day was beautiful, cold, but sunny with no wind. Children ran on the beach, staying back from the waves, but tempting fate by running up to the water's edge and dashing away when the water advanced.

"We did that as kids," Annalise said, watching them for a moment. She couldn't wait until her own son or daughter dared the water. And got scolded when they got wet against instructions to the contrary.

Her brother-in-law, Sam, was watching the kids. No one let the children on the beach without adult supervision.

Dominic looked at him when he got out of the car.

"Sam got kid duty."

"Until someone switches with him. Didn't you watch them last summer for a while when Grandpa Paul wanted a break?"

Dominic nodded.

"And was it so awful?"

"Annalise, watching your nieces and nephews for a few hours at the shore is nothing like raising a child. A few hours' duty is not a life sentence."

"Having a child is not a life sentence. You make it sound like a crime," she said, annoyed he still held that view. She walked into the house and was immediately surrounded by brothers and sisters and grandparents and parents. She hugged everyone, so grateful to have such a loving family. Dominic entered a moment later and was swept up into greetings, as well. How could he not want some of this for himself with his own child?

Everyone arrived before lunch. The food was set out on the porch, deli trays for making sandwiches, an assortment of salads, cut up fruit, chips and a variety of beverages. It was buffet-style. Chairs were brought from the house, from the storage shed and soon everyone was eating and catching up on news. Since they'd all been together just a few weeks ago when celebrating Lianne's news, there wasn't as much to catch up on. But conversations were lively and full of laughter.

Once everyone had eaten, Patrick O'Mallory rose. His wife crossed the porch to join him and beamed at the group. The silence was sudden. Siblings exchanged glances. Annalise reached for Dominic's hand. If it was bad news, she needed his support.

"You mother and I have an announcement."

"You're not pregnant!" one of her brothers called.

Everyone laughed.

"No, we did that enough times," Helen said. She smiled up at Patrick.

"Since we are having a new grandbaby in the family come next summer," he smiled at Lianne, "time to do something extravagant right now. We are going on an archeological dig in the Yucatan. We leave just before Christmas and will be gone for five months. So no delivering that baby before we return," he said, with another smile at Lianne.

The group broke out in questions and comments. Annalise sat back, feeling oddly bereft. Her parents didn't even know about her baby—and they were leaving in a few weeks for months. She had to tell them before then. She glanced at Dominic, he was studying the group's reaction.

"We'll tell you all about it," Patrick said. And he began to relate how they decided to try something new, how they researched opportunities for amateurs to help, how he was taking a sabbatical from his practice. They had been planning this for months and no one in the family had had a clue.

Dominic leaned closer to Annalise and said softly, "You are not the only one who can keep a secret."

She nodded, holding back tears. Once again she had to keep silent. She would not take away from her parents' glow of excitement. She'd tell them before they left, but not today.

She pulled her hand from Dominic's and balled it into a fist. If not for his reaction, everyone would have learned of her pregnancy weeks ago, and be celebrating it like Lianne's. If he had acted like this around Phyllis, no wonder the woman had become clingy, she wanted to make sure he'd stick around.

When her father finished talking, she stood and went to give her parents a hug.

"I'm excited for you both. What a fun adventure. Next maybe you can go to Egypt or something," she said, careful to keep her voice excited.

"We may not like it, sounds like a lot of work," her mother said. But the happiness shining in her eyes belied her true belief.

Annalise stepped aside for her brother Declan to hug her parents. She slipped off the porch and walked to the water's edge. Maybe a walk along the beach would help. She felt all mixed up, happy for her parents, annoyed with Dominic, feeling a bit sorry for herself.

"Hey, wait up," Lianne called and then came hurrying after Annalise.

"I thought I'd take a walk along the beach," she said when her twin caught up.

"I'll go with you," Lianne said, turning to head north.

Glancing over her shoulder, she waved. "I think Tray will join us, unless you want a private time."

"Doesn't much matter, does it, don't you tell him everything," Annalise said.

"Pretty much," Lianne admitted. "Unless you told me in confidence, then I'd never say a word."

"I'm not much company. Sometimes I get so angry at Dominic I want to slap him or something. Everyone's rejoicing in your pregnancy. Now Mom and Dad are doing something fun and exciting and we're all happy for them. I haven't told anyone but you about my baby, and soon my parents will be a thousand miles away and they may not know even then." To her horror, she burst into tears. "Oh, great, now they'll think I don't want them to go," she said, brushing the tears away.

Lianne put her arm across her sister's shoulders. "No one can see, they are too far away. Come on, a walk will put things into prospective. You can always march back there right now and tell them you're pregnant."

"And spoil Mom and Dad's announcement day? I don't think so. Besides, I've held off because I don't know what Dominic's going to say or do."

"So press him for some answers, wait a weekend or two and then have another gathering, another announcement."

"And if Dominic isn't on board by then?"

"What if he never is?" Lianne asked gently.

"I don't want to have to choose between a baby or my husband."

Dominic watched as Annalise went to the water's edge. Her sister went after her and the two headed up the beach, just out of the reach of the waves. She had pulled away from him after her parents' announcement. Was she upset over their plans? Maybe. She had them around all her life. And as far as he could tell, they certainly reacted differently to their children than his father had to him.

A few minutes later, Patrick walked over. Dominic smiled and reached out to shake hands. "Congratulations—sounds like the adventure of a lifetime."

"Hopefully the first of a few."

"Your children are all grown, even though Kelly and Shea are still in college. It's time to do what you want at last," Dominic said.

Patrick looked at him oddly. "I've always done what I wanted. Sometimes I feel very selfish, having my life go just the way I planned."

"Didn't having eleven children tie you down?" Dominic asked.

"Maybe having so many limited what we could do, but I wouldn't trade any one of them for anything else in the world. Helen and I knew when we were still dating that if we got married we wanted a large family. How could a man ask for better children?"

"You did great with Annalise," Dominic said, trying to ease the seriousness of the conversation. "Have you always wanted to be part of an archeology dig?"

"No—in fact, I didn't even enjoy history that much

when I was in school. I always knew I wanted to practice medicine, so science classes caught me every time. But in the last few years, I've discovered how much I enjoy learning about the past. When Helen first suggested we try a dig, I jumped at the idea. Now we'll see how much we really like it. Digging in the dirt and uncovering artifacts from five hundred years ago should prove interesting. Maybe we'll love it. Or maybe we'll long for home and the kids. This'll be the longest I've been away from them all."

Dominic thought about his father, who hadn't been able to wait until Dominic was out of the house. He thought of his own dreams when he'd been sitting on the ratty sofa he and Phyllis had owned, wishing his life were different.

And of the guilt when his wish came true.

He shook his head, still not understanding the O'Mallorys.

He and his father went years without seeing each other. Every visit was a duty on Dominic's part. In memory of his mother more than anything. She would have encouraged him to visit had she lived.

"And our first Christmas away," Helen said, joining them. She linked arms with her husband and smiled at Dominic. "My parents are hosting Christmas this year. They'll have Patrick's folks to help out, so all you children can plan to get together. If we can, we'll call that morning. But who knows what the conditions at the dig will be like?" She squeezed Patrick's arm. "I can't wait to find out."

"At least winter there should be halfway tolerable," he said.

"Dad?" Declan called from across the porch.

"We'll see you before you go," Dominic said. He stepped to the top of the stairs, looking up the beach.

"Want to go find them?" Tray asked, coming up beside him. "I could use a break from the crowd."

"Sure," Dominic said, starting down the stairs. When they were out of earshot from the porch, he glanced at Tray. "Overwhelming?"

"Do you know Lianne worked for me for five years and I never even knew she had a twin—much less ten brothers and sisters. Add that to the older generations and you have the makings of a small town. I still don't know who is who and who is married to whom."

"It takes a while. I had the advantage of knowing the siblings before their marriages started. We've been married the second longest after Mary Margaret and Sam."

They reached the hard-packed sand and turned to follow the pair of footprints heading north. The women could be seen in the distance.

"Heard you and Annalise bought a house," Tray said.

"She bought it. I'm helping refurbish it, but I don't want to live in it," Dominic said.

"We're in negotiations to buy a place out here. I have a house in Richmond where my uncle and I lived. Now that he's dead, I debated keeping it for the future, but I know Lianne would be happier with her own cottage here at the shore."

"You lived with your uncle?" Dominic asked.

"He raised me. He was my mother's brother. She died when I was two weeks old and he stepped in. He never married. I figure one kid was enough for him and he was afraid if he married, he'd end up with a bunch."

"Must have been hard to raise a child that was not even his own," Dominic said. "What happened to your father?"

"He took off when my mother died. I was kidding about Uncle Hal not wanting more children. He said he never found the right woman. I think he would have been thrilled to learn Lianne and I are expecting a baby. He was the best father a kid could have had."

"He didn't resent having to raise you?"

"I don't think so." Tray looked at him. "Should he have?"

Dominic shrugged. "Having a baby ties a man down. Keeps him from doing what he wants." He knew he was parroting his father, and that other men did not appear to resent family life. Tray's uncle had been a single man who took on another's child. Surely he'd felt there was more he could have done on his own, with the freedom to choose?

Tray laughed. "Sure it can. But only if the man lets it. Otherwise, what a grand opportunity to shape some of the future. I'll teach our child about my family history, and Lianne has a lot to share about hers. We'll take trips, educate him or her to be a responsible, contributing member of society. And get a boatload of love in return. I'm overwhelmed by Lianne's family, but I recognize the love and devotion evident in all of them. Do you think Patrick resented having so many children? He's a doctor—he certainly could have prevented any of those pregnancies if he'd wanted."

"Some men are better suited to be fathers," Dominic said.

Ahead of them his wife and her twin had turned and were walking back.

"I hope I'm one of them," Tray said quietly.

"How will you know? What if two years into it you wish you were free again?"

"I can't imagine ever wishing to be free of Lianne. And this baby is part of her. So I will always love it, no matter what."

The baby Annalise carried was part of both of them. She seemed happy enough about the situation. It was only he who wasn't. She saw it like Tray, while he kept hearing echoes of his father. He would make a terrible father. He needed to step away, let Annalise find some man who wanted children, who would make a good father for her baby.

For *his* baby. Could he step aside and let her walk out of his life?

CHAPTER SEVEN

LIANNE smiled as they drew closer. Dominic compared the twins. Despite their different attire, they looked identical. Even to the way their hair blew in the breeze. The only difference evident today was it looked as if Annalise had been crying. That hurt. Was it the thought of her parents being gone for several months? As her father had said, they'd never been apart that long.

"Are you okay?" he asked when they met.

"Fine," she said, still walking. He turned and fell into step with her.

"Upset about your parents leaving?"

"Partly. Partly about us." She slowed her pace, and soon Lianne and Tray were ahead of them. "I want to go home now," she said.

"You could still tell your parents today," he said.

Maybe he should just acknowledge he was tied for the next eighteen years, do the best he could and then be free again.

Or he could choose to end his marriage and continue with life much as it had been this past week. Long lonely nights. Eating fast food or makeshift meals. No one to talk to, to laugh with. Who was he trying to fool? He missed his wife. Only, he didn't believe he could give her what she needed.

Ending their marriage would be impossible to deal with. They'd been together since college. Shouldn't the fear of parting be stronger than his fear of the baby? Maybe there wasn't love between them? The fault lay with him. He had not loved Phyllis in the end. Was history repeating?

When they reached the cottage, Annalise ran in to get her purse and bid everyone goodbye. Dominic heard her give the excuse of being tired from working on the house. Which brought a new round of conversation as people asked her how things were going. Sean asked after Randy. Bridget told them about the garden. Dominic felt like a fifth wheel, standing on the periphery, listening to the interested discussion and wishing nothing more than that the house would burn to the ground and end Annalise's interest forever.

When they reached the outskirts of Washington, Dominic asked where she wanted to go.

"To the house," she replied.

Nothing had changed—except an added wrinkle with her parents leaving. She wasn't giving in one bit. Dominic was annoyed at her decision. Yet one part of him admired her for her stand. He had thought a night or two away would have her returning home. Or at least calling. Instead, she acted as if she didn't have a husband to consider.

"Let's have dinner first," he suggested.

"No, I'm tired. I just want to go home."

"Your home is with me, at our flat," he said tightly.

She gazed out the side window. "I'm not up to it tonight, Dominic."

Working on the house was too much. She'd mentioned how tired she was, being pregnant. She should be taking better care of herself, not adding additional chores on top of an already heavy workload.

Which she wouldn't have to do if *he* would step up to the plate. He should be supportive of his wife—offering extra help instead of adding to the stress of the entire situation.

He should.

He would.

Dominic poured himself a tall drink when he reached the empty apartment. He had no desire to go to bed this early. He wasn't sure he'd sleep when he *did* go to bed. He usually lay awake late into the night, trying to decide what to do with his life. He'd set himself goals years ago and had met most of them. Now he had another thirty or forty years of work before retirement. Who knew how long after that? Could he really see the years ahead without Annalise? Work was fascinating, but not all-consuming. He liked traveling with her. Entertaining with her. Sleeping with her. He'd never thought of the future in those terms before.

He took a long pull of the whiskey. He should end this separation, admit defeat and implore her to come back.

What if she said no?

Do you love me?

He woke early, and after a quick breakfast headed for work. At least there he knew what to expect and how he felt about things.

Around ten, Bill Patton came into his office.

"Bill," Dominic greeted him, automatically disengaging his monitor so it went black. Not that he needed to keep anything secret from Bill. He was the general manager of the security firm and kept his finger on the pulse of all assignments. But old habits were hard to break.

"We need someone in Rome, ASAP. An Italian pharmaceutical company bought an American program, have had it for four years, and now suspect someone has infiltrated and is stealing research information."

Dominic leaned back in his chair, looking at Bill. "How long?"

"Depends on how long it takes to debug it. The program may or may not have been infiltrated, but a thorough check will be needed. And if you find a link they'll probably want you to trace it out so they can apprehend the thieves. I'd plan on a week at least. Maybe longer."

"Can you get Bart?" Dominic asked. A second later, he wasn't sure who was more astonished—Bill or him. He *never* turned down assignments. The major perk of his job was the constant traveling. Yet the thought of being in Rome alone was unappealing. What if Annalise needed something?

While in Hong Kong he'd gone to the client's office and then to his hotel, with a stop at a restaurant some evenings. Other nights he'd just ordered room service. The fun of travel was seeing the sights of each place. But after five years, he'd visited most of the major cities of the world with Annalise. When he went back a second or third time, or even more, the visits were flat unless she was there with him.

"I could ask him," Bill said carefully. "Something I should know about?" he asked.

"My wife's pregnant. I think I should stick close to

home for a while." This was the second person Dominic had told, but the most important one.

"Hey—great news. Congratulations! Lucky man. I'll see what I can do to rearrange the schedules for the next few months. When's she due?"

Dominic didn't even know that basic fact. Quickly he tried to calculate nine months from when he thought she'd become pregnant. "June," he guessed.

"Then I suppose you'll want to stick close to home for another year or so, right?"

Bill rose and offered his hand. Dominic rose also, and took it, feeling like a fraud.

"I can still take trips if needed." He didn't want to cut off travel completely. But the timing wasn't right for Rome.

"Right. But only if no one else is available. Glad you told me. Give Annalise my best," Bill said, turning to leave.

Dominic watched him depart and almost called him back to change his answer. It was starting. He was going to end up staying home out of duty, envying the other men in the firm who traveled to exotic locations.

Only, the feeling he had at the moment was more of relief than resentment. He'd been gone a lot in the last few months. It'd be good to stay home for a while. There was plenty to do in the office, several projects he'd like to be a part of. And he could make quick trips around the East Coast. Was he becoming jaded about travel?

He closed his door and went back to the desk, sitting on the edge and dialing his father's phone.

"Hello."

"Dad, it's Dominic."

"Something wrong?" his father asked.

"No." It was a poor commentary on their relationship that the old man thought Dominic would only call if something was wrong. Yet how often *did* he call his father? "I thought I'd come up and see you." Time to tell his father about the baby. Dominic remembered his earlier telling about a baby, and how badly that had gone. He hoped this announcement would be better received.

"Why?"

"Do I need a reason beyond I want to see you?" Dominic could feel the tension begin. His father never made anything easy. Maybe he should forget the entire harebrained plan.

"I guess not. But I don't hear from you for months on end and then, *pow,* out of the blue you want to come visit. For how long?"

"A weekend."

"Sure—you've got that fancy job of yours that you can't leave for long. Going someplace soon?"

"Just Pennsylvania to see you," Dominic said. "I won't stay there. I'll get a hotel room. Take you to dinner." That would be one complaint less to listen to.

"You bringing that wife of yours?"

"Probably not." Annalise would want to spend time on her house, not take a weekend off to visit his father. Dominic wasn't sure himself why *he* was going. To lay ghosts, perhaps?

"Next weekend's fine. Or the one after that, too, I reckon. I don't get out much."

"I'll see you Saturday, then," Dominic said. He bade his father goodbye and hung up, already annoyed with his father's attitude. But he'd be shocked if the man ever showed any genuine delight in his only child.

* * *

Annalise felt more energetic than she'd had in a while on Monday. She was glad of her long night's sleep. And the news from her parents was more exciting the more she thought about it. She was delighted they were doing things outside the norm.

"Like mother, like daughter," she said aloud at one point, thinking of her house renovation.

She whipped through her paperwork and then scheduled two homes to be shown that afternoon. Later she worked with another real-estate agent to schedule an open house for one of the lovely homes in the north-east section of Washington that they were hoping would appeal to someone in one of the embassies. It was too large for most American families, but would be perfect for someone who had to entertain a great deal.

Her mother called to check on her, and Annalise was happy she could reassure her a good night's sleep had been enough to put her back on top of things.

"I'm worried about that house," her mother said.

"You haven't seen it. Come next weekend. We've painted the two front rooms and redone the floors and it's gorgeous."

"But at what price? I think it's too much for you. You seem tired all the time."

Annalise hesitated. She *was* tired most of the time. But not from working on the house. Should she tell her mother now?

"Anyway, the reason I called is we decided after you and Dominic left that we'd all go down to Tray's house next weekend to work on it, and if you and Dominic can join us we'll have such a crew we can complete anything he needs done. Then he can sell the house and buy the one he and Lianne want at the shore."

Annalise was torn. She wanted to help out. She loved family work days, with everyone pitching in. But that would mean lost time on her own project. She'd already missed last Sunday, and told Randy not to work without her.

"Let me check with Dominic," she stalled. No one in the family but Lianne knew she was operating under a tight deadline for renovating. It would be odd if she didn't pitch in.

"Of course. Don't you think Lianne looks great being pregnant? She's just radiant."

"Some of that is being in love with Tray and having him in love with her," Annalise said. Surely she should have the same radiant look? She was about as far along as her sister.

"True. They look like you and Dominic..." Her mother trailed off. "Annalise, is everything all right?"

"Of course."

"I was just thinking how you and Dominic used to look like Lianne and Tray. Lately there seems to be something different between you two."

"He's been working a lot—as I have. We're fine, Mom." She hoped that was true. How sad her parents would be for her if Dominic decided having a child was more than he could deal with and he left. In fact, the shock would ripple through her entire family.

"Well, then, call me after you talk with him and let me know if you can make next weekend."

"Okay—will do."

Annalise called Dominic after speaking with her mother. He was in a meeting, so she left a message.

But her afternoon was hectic and she missed his return call.

When she reached the house, it still smelled of fresh paint, and she left the door open to air the place out. She loved the cream color she'd chosen for the walls. Standing in the sparkling living room, she wanted to buy furniture right away, to furnish it as she wanted and have a sanctuary to retreat to every time she needed it while working on the rest of the place.

But, mindful of her sister's suggestion, she wouldn't make any rash purchases. If Dominic wanted furniture like they had in the apartment, maybe the living room could be that room. The little room behind the living room backed onto the pantry. Could that be opened up to the kitchen? Like a family room, where she could watch their baby while he or she played when she prepared meals?

Excited about that idea, she hurried to take measurements. She'd talk it over with Randy next time she saw him. She thought it would work. And the kitchen was so large the missing pantry wouldn't bother her at all. There was still loads of storage.

Later, when Annalise had prepared herself a light supper, she did sketches of how she envisioned the expanded room. It would open up the kitchen and give her a family room, while the living room could be like the one at their apartment.

That room make her feel serene every time she entered. There was no clutter. The paintings on the wall were beautiful, in rich jewel colors, instantly giving her a feeling of peace. The comfortable sofa looked modern, but the feel was pure comfort. The sheers at the windows filtered the light but could be opened at night to see the view. She'd miss that view, living here.

The phone rang. It was Dominic.

"My mom called today. The whole family is going down to Tray's next weekend to fix up his uncle's house so they can sell it. We're invited. Feel free to decline. It'll be a lot of work."

Dominic hesitated a moment. Annalise had expected him to say, *Sure, no problem.*

"Are you going somewhere? Not another trip!" she exclaimed. He could push away their situation by traveling. If he wasn't home, he wouldn't notice she wasn't, either.

"I'm going to see my dad," he said at last.

"You are? Since when?"

"Since this morning. I called him, and in his usual ungracious way he said I could come next weekend."

"Why do you want to see him?"

"You sound like him. Can't I want to see my father?"

"You can, but you usually don't," she said.

"Maybe I need to get some answers to the questions I have." He hesitated a moment, and then spoke again. "I may look up Phyllis."

Annalise swallowed. The anguish that hit her surprised her. She'd thought she'd become reconciled to the little she knew about Dominic's past, but this showed her how wrong she was.

"Why?" she asked.

"To see how her life is going."

She didn't like the thought, but she could come up with no reason for him not to see her. Was it just to tie up loose ends, or more? Phyllis had been his high-school sweetheart. His first wife. Was he going back to see if there were any feelings between them?

She pressed against the ache in her chest. She wanted

to tell him not to go. Had she been reading more into his help these last two weekends than was warranted?

She rose and crossed to the window over the sink, looking out into the black night.

"When are you going?"

"Friday night after work. I'll stay until Sunday."

"I'll go with my family, then." She wanted to say something—get him to invite her to go with him. Something to show there was a bond between them. Why did he need to see his ex-wife? To her uncertain knowledge he hadn't seen her in all the years Annalise had known him. Why now?

To see if he'd made a mistake in walking out on that marriage? Or to reassure himself that if Phyllis had moved on with her life, there was every reason to expect Annalise would if he walked out on this marriage? The thought made her feel sick.

"This will probably be your last family work weekend until after the archeological adventure," he said.

"I was hoping some of them would want to come to our house and help," she said slowly. "Once we're down to painting and things like that, a huge crew could sweep through it in a weekend."

She stood leaning against the sink, trying to maintain some semblance of coherency while all she could think about was Dominic going to see his first wife. And the fact he had not invited her on the trip.

"Are you okay?" he asked.

"No, I'm not. I'm scared, Dominic. We are not like we were. I think we may never be. You don't talk to me, and I don't know how you feel or what you want to do. What does that say about our marriage?"

"It's not you, it's me."

"Great—thanks for that."

She clicked off the cell phone and then turned it off.

"Go and see your first love—maybe you can rekindle old flames," she said to the empty kitchen. She'd go and help at Tray's old home, and then invite the entire family to help at hers.

Taking a deep breath, she ignored the ache in her heart and returned to the table, to try and make some sense out of the drawings she'd done.

Dominic tried her number again. Not in service. Blast it! Yet what could he say? She was right. She didn't know how he felt—he didn't know himself. How uncertain he was about this baby. How he didn't want his life to change. How he longed for her to be there for him no matter what. And how she was slipping away no matter what he did.

He wished he had the words to change things back to the way they were. But more than a baby was at stake. Their entire way of marriage was on the line. Could he change—open up about his past and offer more to his lovely wife?

Yet how could he stay in their marriage? She'd voiced what he feared—he was not man enough to be her husband. He'd never make a good father.

Next weekend he was going to his home town alone. Maybe it was a state he should get used to.

She would go with her family. It would give her a chance to spend some time with her parents before they left. And to see the house Tray had grown up in. She'd never seen the one Dominic talked about. He hoped she never did. The truth was he wanted to hide *all* the sordid past. Pretend he came from a family as loving and functional as hers. Never let her learn the full truth.

* * *

Annalise called Randy the next day to tell him she wouldn't be at the house that next weekend, either. "We're having a family work weekend in Richmond. My sister's husband has a home there he wants to put on the market. If we all pitch in together for one weekend, it'll be ready to be listed."

"I can work there, as well as at your house, if you like. No charge. I know Bunny is tied up, but Sean has already told her about the weekend. That way it'll go faster, and the following weekend we'll be back at your place," he offered.

"The house is in Richmond."

"I heard. It's not that far away," he returned.

It was tempting. Randy had true construction experience, so if anything major needed to be done he could probably do it. "Okay, but it's for Saturday and Sunday only."

"So I'll catch up on things around here on Friday, and meet you in Richmond on Saturday morning. How early?"

"How about nine?" She expected they'd all get an early start on Saturday, drive to Richmond and be ready to go. She did enjoy family work weekends, and one brother or another was always bringing extra friends to help. "Bring all your tools," she added.

"I always travel with them. Give me the address."

Once she'd hung up from talking with Randy, she called Lianne.

"Mom told me about the work weekend. When are *you* going down?"

"Friday afternoon. We'll have everything noted that needs to be done, and be ready to start first thing Saturday as people arrive."

"Can I ride down with you?"

"Isn't Dominic coming?"

"No, he's going to see his father."

"Is he sick?"

"Who? His father? No, but for some reason Dominic is going to see him." She did not mention his proposed visit to see Phyllis. "Randy volunteered to come. He's really knowledgeable in building, and I'm sure will be a great help."

"Good—the more the merrier. We're leaving after lunch on Friday."

"I'll be ready. What can I bring?"

They chatted for a few more minutes, with Lianne referring to one of her innumerable lists. Annalise knew there would be lists posted everywhere in the house, of all the tasks needing to be done. Her sister was super-organized.

When they arrived at Tray's house in Richmond, Friday afternoon, Annalise was intrigued. This was the place her brother-in-law had grown up. It looked so homey. He struck her as being tough as nails. To think of him coming from a regular home seemed odd. She wondered about the house Dominic had grown up in.

She got out and followed Lianne and Tray into the house. "I wish I had a real-estate license in Virginia. I'd love to sell this home," she said when she took in the room. It was spacious, and bright with sunshine. "You won't have any trouble getting it sold."

"There's so much to be done, however, to get top dollar," Lianne said.

Annalise grinned at her sister. "Nothing the O'Mallorys can't handle."

They went out for dinner and then stayed in a motel,

as Tray had already removed most of the furnishings from the house to ease the preparation. They would show the house empty and hope prospective buyers could use their imagination to see their own furniture in it.

After picking up bagels and doughnuts and coffee the next morning, they reached the house before the first of the many cars of the O'Mallorys arrived. The day was balmy and beautiful. Opening windows to air out paint fumes would not be a problem. For November, it was almost springlike weather.

Bridget arrived first. She claimed the yard, which matched with Lianne's plan. Then Declan and Sean arrived, followed almost instantly by Patrick and Helen O'Mallory and Helen's parents, Carrie and Paul. Within twenty minutes, cars were jamming the driveway and parked all along the quiet street. When Randy's pickup turned onto the street, he got the last space, two doors down.

"I guess I came to the right place," he said, walking up the front steps to where people were congregated, listening to Tray and Lianne assign rooms to work on.

There was a moment of silence until Annalise came from the house and recognized him. She quickly made introductions. Everyone was glad to have his help and expertise. Sean greeted him warmly. Randy made a comment about his sister and they both laughed.

Enthusiasm was high as everyone got started on the update. Rooms were being painted. Hardwood floors installed. The bathroom was to be renovated, with new fixtures and lights. Randy took that on, with Sean helping. Annalise drew kitchen detail, cleaning each cupboard and preparing for paint. She worked with her brother Declan and her father. Grandpa Paul was unfastening each door, marking it and carrying it outside for sanding in preparation for paint.

Lunch was boisterous, with her brothers easily accepting Randy into their camaraderie. Everyone was bubbling with enthusiasm over the speed at which the house was taking shape. By the end of the next day, the place would be ready to be listed for sale.

"I thought we could rotate tasks in the afternoon, so no one has to do one thing all the time," Lianne said. "Sean, you get to work with Grandpa Paul on the kitchen cabinets. Bridget, you and Grandma Carrie stick with the yard. Get someone else to help you. Who do you want?"

"Declan. We have some major pruning we want done; he'll be up to it."

"Annalise can help. She'll need to come up to speed to learn how to care for her own house."

"But don't have her doing anything heavy—not good for a pregnant woman," Randy said.

The silence was sudden. All eyes looked at him, and then at Annalise.

Her heart dropped. This was not how she'd wanted to tell her family. Everyone was staring, and her parents looked concerned.

"Pregnant?" her mother asked carefully.

Randy picked up on the stunned silence. "Did I let the cat out of the bag? Man, I'm sorry, Annalise. I thought your family knew."

"How do *you* know?" Bridget asked.

"Dominic told me," he said.

The crowd erupted in congratulations and why-didn't-you-tell-us comments.

"Trust the twins to do things together again—even have babies together," Declan said.

Annalise smiled and looked at her mother.

"Lianne's known for a while, but I was just waiting for the right time to tell the rest of you. Then you gave your news, and I didn't want to take away from your excitement."

"Honey, this is cause to celebrate—and it would never take anything away from anyone else, just add to the joy in the family." She quickly gave Annalise a hug, beaming. "I'm so thrilled. Another grandbaby! When are you due?"

"June."

"We'll be back by then," her dad said, giving her a hug. "Dominic's a lucky man."

Annalise nodded, but the look in her eyes betrayed her.

"What's wrong, honey?" her mother asked.

"He doesn't want the baby," she said, and burst into tears.

Dominic turned onto the familiar road where the house in which he'd grown up stood. Slowing down, he stopped the car when he drew even with it. Staring at the place, he was surprised to see it had been refurbished, complete with lush green lawn and a flowerbed beneath the front windows. It looked nothing like it had during his childhood. A tricycle was overturned on the grass near the front steps, and a late-model car was parked in the driveway. Whoever lived in the home now had changed it completely.

How much work would it have taken to make a green lawn? His mother would have loved a garden. She'd had a small vegetable plot in back, which she'd tended faithfully each summer, but Dominic knew she'd loved flowers. Hadn't he brought in his share of dandelions he'd picked? She'd always made a big fuss over his gifts. How pitiful in retrospect.

For a long time he just stared, remembering. The harsh words of his father echoed. He'd forgotten how soft his mother's voice had been. What had she wanted from life? More children? A loving husband? Or had she mourned a lost career? She had died long before Dominic had matured enough to wonder—to even see her as a person in her own right. To him, she had been Mom.

She and his father had once loved each other enough to create him. Or had it only been a one-night stand? Another fact he'd never questioned. He felt the guilt of his own failed marriage. The obsession he'd had about getting out of this town. The despair when Phyllis had become pregnant and he'd known he had to do the right thing. But the crushing blow had been the birth of their stillborn baby. Freedom mixed with remorse. Accepting the truth, regretting the longing for freedom that had been answered at a terrible cost.

Finally he started the car again and drove to his father's apartment.

The building looked old and shabby. Was this a pattern for his old man? A little effort would have gone a long way when they'd lived at the house on Stanton Street. Dominic knew his father wasn't in charge of this apartment complex, but it looked as run-down as the former residence of Steve Fulton.

Dominic parked and entered, smelling the stale scent of meals gone by. He took the elevator to the third floor, and soon knocked on his father's door.

Steve opened it, and stared at him for a moment. "Come on in," he said, turning.

Dominic took a deep breath and entered. His father looked older than he remembered. And smaller. He followed him into the living room, where Steve sat down on a recliner in front of the dark television.

Dominic sat on the sofa that Steve had bought after his wife's death. It was brown, fading a little where the sunlight hit it each day.

"How are you?" Dominic asked. For a moment, he contrasted the greeting with the ones he received from Patrick O'Mallory. As a son-in-law he received more affection than his own father offered.

"Still hanging in," his father said. He frowned. "You doing okay? Don't need anything, do you?"

"I'm doing well," Dominic said. What would his father do if he asked for help—like he had when he'd been eighteen. Probably tell him to act like a man and find his own way out of any difficulty. He had never asked his father for a single thing after that.

"Still traveling?" the older man asked.

Dominic nodded, glancing around. The entire room looked drab. There was little color in it beyond the brown furniture and the faded yellow curtains. After all the years his father had worked, surely his salary would cover a few luxuries? He had only himself to care for.

"Where have you been lately?" the older man asked.

"Got back from Hong Kong and the West Coast a few weeks ago. Before that Annalise and I were in London."

His father raised his eyebrows, then lowered them. "I never get out of town."

"And why is that?" Dominic asked. Not for the first time he wondered why his father hadn't taken off after he'd left home. His mother had died years earlier. His departure had left his father free—which was what he'd constantly said he wanted to be all along.

"Too late. I was tied down since I was just a kid. I had a family to support, remember? Didn't have money to go tooling around the world like you do."

"It's part of my job. You could have gotten another job, one that involved travel."

"Didn't have some fancy education like you."

"I put myself through university, Dad. You could have gone back to school. Face it, you had lots of opportunities and for some unknown reason you turned them all down. You're not all that old now—not even fifty. You still have time to explore new options. Why don't you?"

It was the first time he'd challenged his father on this issue. But he was tired of hearing the same old story, tired of being the scapegoat for all his father's problems.

"Didn't know how to do anything but work in the mill."

"Ten years ago, when I left, you were even younger. You could have learned some new skills, tried something different. Why haven't you done something else? You don't have to work at the mill your entire life."

"Too late. I'm too old to change."

Dominic rose and walked to the window, gazing out at the quiet street, feeling the turmoil roil inside him. "Truth to tell, Dad, you never do anything but complain. Was it so bad being a father?" Maybe he needed to get some straight answers.

"Fatherhood ties a man down. Gives him no options."

Dominic turned and glared at his father. "I don't buy that. I did for a long time, thinking everything you said was the truth. But now I'm really looking at other families, and I'm seeing that no one is grumbling all the time. They make their lives conform to their ideas, with kids fitting in." The words were hardly said before he realized it was the truth. He and Annalise did not have to end up like his parents. She'd been right. They could make their lives as they wanted *and* fit in a baby. A precious new life to keep their family going.

"You try it—you'll see. Seems to me you don't know what you are talking about. You don't have any children."

"I will soon. Annalise is pregnant. That's why I came up today—to tell you in person you're going to be a grandfather."

Steve blinked. Then a slow smile spread across his face. "So now you'll know what I meant. You'll be tied down to walking the floor at night, running to the doctor the first time the kid cries funny. Your wife will be too tired to do anything with you. So all your fancy degrees and traveling days will mean nothing."

Dominic shook his head. "And you'd like that, wouldn't you?"

"Naw, I wouldn't wish it on any man. But you come talk to me about options when that kid is in school. Needing shoes all the time—some for gym, some for Sunday best. Kids grow out of their clothes before they wear them out. You come back then and tell me if I'm wrong."

"You'll be the child's grandfather. You want to even know him?"

Steve thought about it for a moment. "Shows how old I'm getting—now I'm a grandfather."

"Time to think about the future, Dad. Go for what you want. Maybe you'll take a chance and try for a job in New York, like you always talked about."

Steve rubbed his jaw, looking away.

"What?" Dominic asked, picking up on the sign.

"Tried it once. They turned me down," Steve said slowly.

"Sometimes it takes more than one try," Dominic said, surprised by the response. But maybe it helped him understand his father's bitterness better. The one job he'd talked about, to him the golden dream, was being a set designer in New York. It hurt to hear he'd been turned down.

"Too old now."

"So try another avenue. You've always said you wanted to work behind the scenes in plays. There are plays given all over—in legitimate theater and little theater. Summer stock. Hell, school plays for that. Lots of different avenues to explore."

Steve looked at Dominic. "Now that you're going to be a father you're some smart man, eh?"

Dominic laughed. "I've always been smart, Dad. Time you acknowledged it. And me, too."

"You weren't so smart with that Phyllis girl."

The amusement died. "You're right. That was down-right stupid. I want to see her while I'm here. Know where she lives?"

There were a few more things to for him settle. But for the first time Dominic began to believe that having a child would not be the end of life as he knew it. He had some serious thinking to do. Marriage wasn't only for partying and good times. It meant sticking with his partner through all life threw their way. He'd forgotten that bit. And he'd acted like a fool these last few weeks. Fish or cut bait. Stay married or end up lonely and alone—like his father. If he was so smart, that would be a no-brainer.

* * *

Saturday afternoon, Dominic pulled in front of a neat ranch-style home and parked. Climbing out of his car, he drew in a deep breath. This would be hard, but he had to do it. He walked up the path and knocked on the door.

In only a moment Phyllis opened it. He stared at her for a moment without saying a word. She looked better than he'd ever seen her. Her hair was short, curling. She wore jeans and a sweater and looked younger than she had the last time he'd seen her.

"Good grief—Dominic!" she exclaimed. Her expression was one of delight. "I never expected to see you again in this life. My, you are still the best-looking guy I ever knew. Come on in."

"Hi, Phyllis." He smiled at her exuberance. What a change from the sad, dependent girl who had clung so hard.

A toddler looked up when they entered the living room. The furniture was serviceable, comfortable. The carpet was cluttered with toys.

The little boy looked at Dominic, then stood up and brought his truck for Dominic to see.

"Not now, honey. This nice man has come to visit Mommy. Go back and play." Phyllis looked at Dominic. "I can fix coffee if you'd like?"

"No, I won't be here long. Just wanted to see you again. I'm visiting my dad this weekend."

"Sit down. I wish Ray were home. Do you remember him from school? He was a year ahead of us— Ray Stoddard?"

"I remember him. Played on the basketball team, didn't he?"

"Yes. He has an insurance business, and he stays open on Saturday for his customers. He takes Mondays off. What are you doing these days? I saw your father ages ago. He's not the friendliest of men, so I didn't ask after you."

She sat on the sofa, glanced at her son, then smiled back at Dominic.

"Nice boy," he said, studying the toddler.

"I have a baby girl napping. I hope you get a chance to see her before you go."

He looked back to Phyllis. "You're looking really good. Happy."

"Oh, I am. Lordy, I am so blessed." She tilted her head slightly. "It didn't work with us, did it? We were too young, Dominic. I was crazy about you in high school, but we were too young to have a baby, to set up house. I have never been so unhappy in my life. Now I'm so happy I worry something will happen."

"Why, you deserve to be happy. It seems everything is going your way."

"Oh, it is. I love my husband, my kids. Are you married?"

He nodded.

"Kids?"

He took a breath. "One on the way, our first." Where had that come from? First? Only, more like it.

She smiled again, then grew pensive. "It's not likely to happen again, you know," she said.

"What?"

"Being pregnant and then not delivering a healthy baby. I was so afraid when I was pregnant with Tyler. Afraid history would repeat itself and I couldn't deliver a healthy baby. But he came out perfect in every way. The second time was easier. I guess I won't ever forget our baby, Dominic. But don't let the past interfere with the present."

"I remember how hard it was being married," he said.

"I know it was." She looked around her home. "We wanted this kind of life, but we weren't ready. You had that awful job at the mill, I had the killer job at the five and dime. God, my feet ached at night. If we'd taken better precautions, we would never have been in that situation. I'm so sorry that baby died, but in the way life has turned out, maybe it was a hard lesson we both needed to learn. I won't ever entirely get over it, but I sure appreciate what I have that much more."

"Not fair on that baby, never to have drawn a breath."

"I used to think I wished it away," she said slowly.

Dominic gave a small start. "I thought I had," he replied.

Sadly, she shook her head. "We can't wish things like that. Once I got over the initial shock and grief, I knew better. Still, we could have made something work if she'd lived."

"But not the lives we each have now," he said.

"No, but something fine, I'm sure. You were always destined for great things. Tell me what you're doing now and about your wife."

Dominic spent a surprisingly friendly half hour with his former wife. Some of the guilt from the past faded as her happiness shone in every word she said. And before he left, her baby girl woke and he got to see her, as well.

He felt a wave of affection for Phyllis.

"I'm glad you stopped by. Come some time to see Ray," she said when he said he had to leave.

"I'm glad I came, too. You've made things easier for me."

She held her baby in one arm and reached out with

her free hand to touch his arm. "You were a good husband to me, Dominic. It wasn't easy. I wasn't easy to live with. You never blamed me for getting pregnant, or for losing the baby. I'll always be grateful for that. Tell Annalise how lucky she is to have you. You're still the best-looking guy I know."

He smiled at that. Leaning over he kissed her cheek. "Have a long and happy life, Phyllis."

One more stop and then he'd head for home.

He turned into the open gates of the old cemetery and drove along, hoping he could remember where the stones were. He had not been back since the day they'd buried their daughter. She was next to his mother, the only family either of them had in the cemetery. There, he remembered that tree. He parked and walked over to the stones he remembered. His mother's and his daughter's. He stood there for a long moment, studying the words on each, the small lamb that rested on top of his daughter's. Her birth had not been the cause of celebration as it should have been. Was Phyllis right, a hard lesson to cause him to appreciate what he had now.

Which was what exactly? A wife he'd driven from home. An empty apartment to return to?

"I think I've made a mess of my life," he told the cold stones. His mother would not be proud of his reaction to Annalise's news. Nor would his daughter had she lived.

"Maybe I can change it."

He thought what Annalise had said once, he was not his father. He was not a clone of Steve Fulton. He had his mother's genes in him, as well. And genes from her family. Who had given him his drive and determination?

Who had passed along the brains that enabled him to understand and troubleshoot complex software problems?

What would he pass on to his child?

Annalise sat in the living room of her sister's apartment. The weekend had been hectic. And emotionally draining from the family's discovery of her pregnancy to her stupid burst into tears. She still felt embarrassed to have had her entire family witness that. But her mother and sisters had whisked her away to semiprivacy to learn the entire story. Later she gave an abbreviated version to the others. To a person, they were surprised to learn Dominic had been married before—and no one understood his reason for not telling her years ago.

Her father took her aside on Sunday and asked if she was certain she knew what she wanted from the future. If staying married was not an option, she could always come back home to regroup.

His offer had touched her. For the first time she really considered a future without Dominic. While living for the moment, she'd always assumed they'd be together until old age. Now she wondered if that was to be. She loved her husband—or the man she'd built him up to be. He was showing flaws. Did she love the person he really was? Or did she only want the dashing man who took her around the world; who bought her beautiful things; and partnered her to parties and plays?

What did that say about her? It was the first time she spent thinking about what she wanted from the future. How she saw herself with a child to raise. What were the values she wanted to pass on? What philosophies and beliefs to share and hope her child would embrace? Could she be a part-time mother, sharing the child with a father who lived elsewhere? Or would he ignore their baby entirely, leaving the child to Annalise to raise alone?

The trip to Richmond had been well worth it from many aspects. She felt relief her secret was out and that her family had rallied around her so strongly. She'd spent some time with Lianne alone and discussed options. She'd picked up a few more pointers about renovation and had another idea for one of her bedrooms. But tonight she was not in the mood to think about all the work facing her. Her family had agreed to come for a work weekend in a couple of weeks. She'd have to list all that needed doing to utilize their labor. Lianne was a pro at that. Maybe she could get her sister to do it for her house?

It wasn't the remodeling that her thoughts dwelled on, but Dominic. What had he done all weekend? She'd called the apartment when they reached Washington, but there'd been no answer. She had not tried his cell. Was he still in Pennsylvania? Had the meeting with his father gone well?

She didn't care a bit about that—she was more worried about his meeting Phyllis again, and the results of that encounter. Why had he wanted to see her after all these years? Just when she'd begun to think he would come around, he'd surprised her and taken off to see a woman she had had no knowledge of only a few weeks ago.

Rising, she paced the living room impatiently. It was stupid to think her future rested in the hands of some woman she'd never met, but she couldn't help but worry that seeing her would change Dominic even more. They had a history together—a child who had died. Their bond was at least as strong as hers and Dominic's, maybe more—they'd shared their teenage years together. Had a similar background.

"Here we are." Lianne entered, carrying a tray with

tea and the ice cream she'd dished up. "Tray called the office and there's a slight problem, so he's gone in," she added, setting the tray on the coffee table. "I thought you'd be resting, not pacing. I'm so tired I'm going to bed after this. What's up?"

"I'm thinking about Dominic's visit to Pennsylvania. Why does he need to visit Phyllis? As far as I know he hasn't seen her since they separated, more than a decade ago. Why now?"

"You're going to have to accept that there is a portion of Dominic's life you won't ever share—his first marriage. He told you it wasn't happy. It ended soon enough when the baby died. Let it go, sis."

"He feels he's to blame. But a person can't wish circumstances into being. Heaven knows I'd wish for things to come right between us if that would work."

"Intellectually he knows that. But a baby—one he resented…" Lianne shook her head. "Imagine when things turned out the way they did. He remembered all that anger and resentment. He projected his father's complaints about life onto his own. And it all came down to a stillborn baby. I can see the guilt. Even if he and Phyllis had stayed married, I think Dominic has too much drive and determination to have remained in that town. He would have found other work, maybe ending up eventually where he is today."

"A baby changes all that again," Annalise said. "There's nothing I could have done differently. I didn't expect to get pregnant. But I'm adapting. Why can't he?"

"Personally, I'm thrilled to death about both our babies. They'll be close cousins, being practically the same age and all. I wonder what we'll have? I want a little girl, do you? Sit—eat." Lianne handed her a cup of tea.

Annalise sat down and took the cup and saucer. She sipped, placing them on the table and reaching for the dish of ice cream nearest her. "I want a healthy child. I don't much care about its gender."

She took a spoonful of the butter pecan ice cream, letting it melt in her mouth, crunching the nuts.

"Are you two moving soon?" she asked, glancing around.

Lianne looked surprised. "No. Why would we? I just moved into Tray's apartment when we married. Mine is history. But this place is large enough for us. And I love having a doorman downstairs."

"What about when the baby comes?" Annalise asked, licking another spoonful.

"We'll fix up the second bedroom as a nursery. We're buying a house at the shore. That'll be our escape when things get hectic," Lianne said.

"You'd raise a child *here?*" Annalise looked around.

Tray's apartment was nicely furnished, but looked nothing like her image of a family home. Surely Lianne had the same image?

"What's wrong with here?"

"No yard, for one thing. No family room separate from the living room, where kids' clutter could stay even if guests came over. Don't you want a dog?"

"You're thinking of our home when we were growing up. It was perfect for our family—but not, I think, for me and Tray."

Annalise looked at her twin. "Why not?"

"I like this place. There's a park nearby, and whenever we want the feel of nature we'll head for the shore. And, no, I do not want a dog. Maybe when the baby is older we'll get a cat—who can stay by itself when we go places, or come with us to the shore. But that's for the future. In the meantime, I'm just working on having this baby."

"You go to the shore all the time, year-round. Is that why you want a house there?"

"Tray and I are buying a house a few doors down from the one the grandparents own. We can stay in our own place when everyone's up, and yet visit as much as we want. And whenever I want to get away I'll have my own place, and won't have to make sure no one else will be using it," Lianne explained.

"Nice. Only two of you for the bathroom," Annalise said, remembering the long lines sometimes at her grandparents' cottage—even after the second bathroom had been installed.

Lianne laughed. "I know. That's the best part—no more standing in line. If you're really nice to me, you and Dominic can come over and use our bathroom, too."

The lightheartedness vanished. Annalise stirred her melting ice cream. "If there is still a Dominic and me. He's not the man I thought I married."

"So what other secrets can he be hiding?"

"Don't even suggest he might be," Annalise said. She put her bowl down and finished her tea. "I'm ready to leave when you are ready to take me."

"Stay the night. Tray may not be back for hours, and I'm tired. Would it be a hardship to stay here?"

"Not at all. You'll have to lend me a nightgown, but I'll stay."

The two sisters changed for bed, then settled in front of the television to watch an old movie. Having seen it a dozen times before, Annalise didn't need to pay strict attention to keep up with the storyline. Her thoughts revolved around Dominic and her fear for their uncertain future.

When Dominic arrived at the house Annalise had bought, she was not there. Her car was in the driveway, so she must have gotten a ride to Richmond with Lianne. Shouldn't they be back by now? It was after eleven. Frustrated, he left the front door and went back to his car. Turning on his phone, he saw the message indicator light and listened to his calls. Three calls: two from Annalise's brothers, and one from Tray. None sounded friendly. She had told them everything, obviously. *Damn.*

He was physically tired from the long drive, and emotionally drained from the weekend. He'd deal with the calls tomorrow. It was late. He'd wait here until midnight. If she weren't back by then, he'd head for home.

It was twelve-thirty when he entered their flat. It was dark and quiet. For a moment, he'd hoped she'd returned here after the Richmond trip, but the empty bedroom showed how vain that hope had been.

The bedroom seemed oddly empty as he discarded his clothes. In the old days, he could remember only a very few nights when Annalise hadn't been home when he was. Usually when she and Lianne went to the beach. When that happened, he missed her. Tonight he missed her more than usual.

After this weekend he had a different perspective on things. Was it too late?

CHAPTER EIGHT

ANNALISE WENT to the house early next morning, to shower and dress for work. The office would be hectic and her workload heavier than normal, with trying to squeeze in five days for every four.

She felt buoyed up by the promise from her family to help at her new house in two weeks. She hoped for good weather so they could accomplish as much that weekend as they had in Richmond.

Around ten, Dominic called her.

"You didn't come home last night," he said when she answered.

"I stayed at Lianne's. How did you know?"

There was silence for a moment.

"I went by the house when I got back from Pennsylvania. Can I pick you up for lunch?" Dominic asked.

"Why?"

"Can't a husband ask his wife out?"

Sure, but he usually didn't do it so formally. "I guess so. I don't have any appointments today."

When she'd hung up, Annalise wondered if she should have asked about his trip. She deliberately had not. At least they'd have something to talk about at lunch. She didn't want a repeat of the awkward silence of their last meal out together.

Shortly thereafter a large bouquet of fall flowers arrived for Annalise. The receptionist brought them in and several coworkers crowded around to see who they were from. The card said simply, *Love, Dominic*.

"I wish my husband would send *me* flowers," Margo said, touching one of the bronze chrysanthemums.

"Is it a special occasion?" another coworker asked.

Annalise shook her head, curious as to the reason for the flowers. She'd used to receive them a lot in years past. Lately the deliveries had tapered off. Were they a gesture of courting, or an appeasement for the weekend? What had gone down in Pennsylvania?

Dominic arrived at her work right at noon. When she met him in the lobby of the real-estate agency, he looked the same as always, and as usual her heart rate kicked up a notch. His hair was getting to the stage of needing a trim. She liked it a bit longer than he normally wore it. His dark eyes were grave. She wanted to fling herself into his arms and cling for life. But he didn't like clingy women, and she wasn't going to put herself in the category of his first wife.

"I thought we'd eat at Bacchigalupia's," he said, mentioning a favorite Italian place.

"Nice." Warily she tried to gauge Dominic's mood. He seemed reserved. Was he going to tell her something she wouldn't like? Was he trying to make it easier by going to a public place? No scene that way.

They spoke little on the way to the restaurant. Since it was a Monday lunch, it was crowded. They had to wait twenty minutes for a table. The crowded entry to the restaurant was not conducive to personal discussions.

Once they were seated, they quickly ordered, and then Annalise looked at him across the table.

"So," she began brightly, "how was your weekend?" She would not get upset, no matter what he said.

"Interesting," he responded. "I saw my father and then Phyllis."

She kept the pleasant smile plastered on her face with effort. She so did not want to hear about his visiting the woman he'd married before her.

"And?" she said when he paused.

He moved his fork an inch to the left, and then looked up at her. "It went well enough. Do you have to return to work this afternoon?"

"I planned to."

"Take time off and come with me."

"Where?" she asked.

"I thought we'd go to the National Gallery of Art. They have a traveling exhibit of Monet. The gardens at Giverny. I know you love those."

She nodded. They visited the National Gallery several times a year—usually in winter, when the weather was bad. How had she missed hearing about a Monet exhibit? He was her favorite Impressionist.

"I would enjoy that," she said.

"Then we'll go after lunch, and I'll tell you more about my weekend. I assume from the phone calls I've been getting from your brothers and father that you told your family I wasn't exactly thrilled with the pregnancy."

She was astonished. "They've called you?"

"I had three messages last night, and today Sean and Patrick left messages. Even Tray joined in."

Annalise didn't know whether to laugh at the thought of all the males in her family rallying round, or be outraged that they didn't think she could handle things on her own. She decided she needed to have a talk with a few of them—but later. Right now she was intrigued.

"Did you talk to any of them?" she asked.

"No. I'm smarter than that. But I can't dodge them forever." He moved his fork back an inch.

Annalise had never seen her husband nervous before. Her heart sank. He probably didn't know how to tell her he'd decided their marriage wasn't what he wanted, with the new baby coming. She was not going to make things easy for him. If he wanted out of the marriage he'd have to flat out tell her so.

The waiter served their order with a flourish. She glanced around at businessmen having lunch meetings, a table of women celebrating someone's birthday. She wished she could be as carefree as the rest of the patrons looked.

She picked at her linguine. Normally she loved the dish, but today she was too churned with nerves to enjoy it. Dominic seemed to have no difficulty finishing his food.

When they were done, they headed for the National Gallery. Annalise knew if he didn't say something soon, she'd explode. Even walking into the huge halls with their quiet atmosphere and lovely paintings did not soothe her as it normally did.

They followed the signs for the Monet exhibit, and soon stood before one of her favorite paintings—*The Water-Lily Pond*. The tranquil colors delighted her senses. She wished she could visit Giverny and see the settings herself.

Dominic stood beside her, studying the painting. "It's beautiful and calming at the same time."

"That's what I think." She looked at him. How many times had they walked around the gallery discussing paintings but never sharing more personal insights?

"Can you see children running across the bridge, tossing pebbles into the pond?" she asked, letting her imagination soar. One day she'd have a little boy or girl who would run and play.

"No. I see a quiet garden—a place a man comes at evening time to contemplate and think over the day. To count his blessings and vow to do better."

She blinked. "Tell me about your weekend," she said softly, her gaze still on the lovely painting.

He glanced around. There was another couple across the hall, studying another painting. He reached out to link his hands with hers and gently drew her to a different water-lily painting.

"It turned out to be more interesting than I expected. First I went by the house I was raised in. I didn't recognize the place. Nothing stays the same. Then I went to my dad's. I took a long hard look at my father. We talked, and as we did, I realized he has chosen a different way. The choices he made over the years are not the ones I've made. He says he wants out of that small town, but he's made little effort to get out. Though he surprised me by telling me he tried once for a position in a theater in New York."

"But didn't get a job?" she guessed.

"Right—and he didn't try again."

"That's too bad. I bet given time someone would have hired him."

Dominic shrugged. "I think it was easier for him to

blame circumstances than the fact he wasn't aggressive enough, diligent enough, to get what he said he wanted."

"Easier to blame everything on having a child?" she said carefully.

He nodded. "It's hard for me to talk about this, Annalise. But I'm going to. I made a vow and I plan to keep it. To me and to you. As a kid, it was hard for me to get beyond hearing him talk like that every day. It's only now that I realize my being there had nothing to do with the way he lived his life. It was just a convenient excuse. I wonder what he would have used if he and my mother had not had me."

Annalise didn't know where this was leading. Did it mean Dominic was not going to resent a child, like his father had? She studied the painting, her heart beating faster. She tightened her fingers slightly and he squeezed her hand in return. They were connected. She hoped they always would be.

"I should have told you about Phyllis and our marriage when I first met you. I apologize for not doing so," he said.

Annalise turned to gaze up at him. "Why didn't you? When we first met, it wouldn't have meant much. Even if you'd told me before we married I wouldn't have cared. But to keep it hidden all these years only makes me wonder if we are as close as we should be as a married couple."

He looked up at the painting for a moment, then back at her. "I wanted to forget. To pretend that year had never happened. Erase twelve months and act as if I came from as uncomplicated a background as everyone else at university. Back then it was important to me to fit in. To be as carefree as the other students. I didn't want anything to remind me of what had happened and how I got there."

"The death of your baby?" she said, understanding how fresh the wound would have been when he'd been at university.

He nodded. "Can you understand?"

"I can see you starting university with that attitude. But, if not when we first met, at least after we were engaged you could have found a moment to tell me."

"You were young and enthusiastic, and full of optimism. I didn't want anything from my past to dim that. And then we forged a good life together. It was what I'd always dreamed of and more. Once we began, there was never a good time to say anything—and less and less reason for it. The past was over."

"Until my getting pregnant resurrected it?" she said.

He nodded, and led her to yet another painting. They both ignored it to gaze at each other.

"Right. The minute I learned about it, I immediately remembered how much I railed against fate before. And how awful I felt about the outcome. How could anyone resent a baby? What kind of monster did that make me?"

"Not a monster. Just a teenager who was given too much to deal with before he was ready," she said, understanding how he must have felt. It didn't mitigate her own feelings of hurt that he'd never confided in her, but she could understand his emotions after the baby was delivered. "You're human. Let it go, Dominic," she said. "Forgive yourself. You did not cause your baby to be born dead."

"I went to see Phyllis this weekend," he said.

"So you said." She did not want to hear about his first wife. If he truly was over her, why resurrect the past? And if not, she didn't want to hear it. Ostriches had the right idea.

Yet one small part of her wondered at the girl who had captured his interest when he'd been younger. Was she anything like Phyllis?

"She's married and has two children. She's happy," he said.

The other couple came up to the picture. Dominic raised an eyebrow at Annalise and they moved to another room. This one held only a lone, elderly man, studying another Monet.

Annalise moved across the room from the man and lowered her voice. "You sound surprised. If you'd asked me two months ago, I'd have said *you* were happy," Annalise said. "Why shouldn't she be?"

"The funny thing is, the man she's married to I knew in high school. He always had a thing for her, apparently, only we never knew it before we got divorced. He hadn't said anything, but when she was free again, and aching over the loss of her baby, he stepped in. They were married a year later. Before you and I got married, even. Her oldest child is a two-year-old boy. She has a baby girl, too."

"Why did you go to see her?"

"I'm not sure—to get closure, maybe? To see if I remembered the past accurately? To get forgiveness for my thoughts?"

"And did the meeting give you all you wanted?" she asked. She felt left out. Not a part of this portion of Dominic's life. As Lianne had said, she had to accept that and let go of the hurt.

"More, actually. It was odd to see her so happy. I only remembered the months we were married, and how unhappy she was. She's so happy it almost made me envious. Until I remembered how happy you and I were.

After that, I ended up going to the cemetery. I'd never seen the headstone. It wasn't anyone's fault our baby died. It was just the way things happened. Phyllis was afraid with her other pregnancies that the same thing would happen, but she has two healthy children." He took a deep breath. "She didn't blame me."

Annalise felt her heart warm to hear that. She knew Dominic was harder on himself than anyone else could be. Again she squeezed his hand. "But you knew there was nothing you had done. You may feel differently, but you *know* you weren't to blame."

"I could have stood by her longer."

"Did she want you there?"

He shook his head. "She's the one who asked for the divorce. Said I had places to go that she didn't want to. Things to do so far from her comfort level she'd always feel out of step. She's happy living in the same neighborhood she grew up in. Her children will go to the same schools we did."

"And did this visit change how you feel about our baby? Are you still wishing I had never gotten pregnant?" Annalise asked, wanting everything out in the open.

"We decided long ago not to have children. Now that's changed. I'm feeling my way, here. I don't know what kind of father I'll make. But I'm willing to try and be the best one I can be."

Hope began to blossom.

"I know one thing," he continued, tightening his grip. "We need to find a way to keep our marriage going."

Annalise looked at their joined hands and wondered if they could do that. "How? It seems we have different goals."

"So we work on meshing them until we share the

same goal. I want a healthy baby. I'm sure you do. That's a start, isn't it?"

"Yes. But is that enough? When we have another crisis, are you going to freak again?"

"I know I'm not the best communicator in the world. That is going to change. This talk today is my first attempt. In the future, I want you to know how I feel, why I think the way I do about things, and for us to work through any crisis or problem that comes our way."

"I think that's what married folks do," she said.

"You asked me a question a few weeks ago. I should have answered instantly. I do love you, Annalise. I love you now more than ever. I appreciate what we have more than I have ever done. When I thought of leaving—really imagined what it would be like to live without you—I panicked. I can't do it. You are a part of my life. Without you I'm just an empty shell, like my father. He didn't have a love in his life like I do. It makes a difference."

Her heart beat faster. "I have loved you since we met. Oh, Dominic, I love you so much."

He pulled her into his arms and kissed her. The embrace went on for long moments before he remembered where they were. When he lifted his head, he was pleased to note they were alone. Had their display sent the other viewer fleeing? No matter—he'd take advantage of it. Again he kissed her.

The sound of voices coming in from the adjacent room had them breaking apart.

Annalise had a rosy glow as she smiled up at Dominic. "I was so afraid. Especially when you took off for Pennsylvania and didn't want me along. I couldn't understand why you would want to see Phyllis after all this time."

"I haven't had any contact with her since our divorce. I wanted to see how she was."

"And?"

"She's happy, like I said."

"And you are, too, right?"

"Yes. I'm happiest when I'm with you." He kissed her softly. "It wasn't right between Phyllis and me. It's perfect between you and me."

"So you'll be okay with the baby?" She wanted everything cleared up. Her heart was brimming. She loved him so much, to have him tell her was wonderful.

"I will be. I hope. I'm still worried about how I'll be as a father."

"I've never worried about that. And if you ever need any suggestions, ask my dad—he raised eleven. We're just having one."

"Maybe."

Her eyes widened. "Twins, you think?"

"They run in your family."

She frowned. "Good grief. I hadn't thought about that. I'll be huge before I know it if I'm carrying twins."

"Let's go home," Dominic said.

They turned to leave. Annalise linked her arm with his, leaning slightly. "It's okay if I lean a bit. That's not too clingy, is it?"

He laughed. "You would never be clingy. That was pure panic talking."

"Speaking of home—which? Your place or mine?" she asked flirtatiously.

Dominic smoothed her hair back from her cheek, tucking it behind her ear. "In light of my being frank and open with you, maybe you should consider that we don't *have* to have a house when we have a baby.

Lianne and Tray haven't said anything about moving into a house, have they? Our flat is large enough to expand our family."

"They're staying in Tray's apartment, but they are buying a place at the shore."

"And planning to stay in their flat here in the city?"

"Yes. Fixing up their spare room as a nursery."

"Couldn't we do that?" he asked.

Annalise pictured her house as it would be when completely renovated. And then pictured a jumble of baby things in their flat. She knew there was an inordinate amount of work to be done to make the house as she envisioned it. And Dominic had never shown any interest. How important *was* the place? It was just a building.

Not as important as her husband. Not as important as harmony and love in her marriage.

"The house is larger than the flat…" she said slowly. She hated to let the dream go.

"The flat suits us. Our friends know how to find us. We know almost everyone in the building, in the neighboring shops. We like going out to dinner on the spur of the moment, walking around the area. That house is isolated. We'd need to drive to go anywhere. We won't know all the neighbors, and the houses are far enough apart it won't be easy to get to meet everyone. And I really do not want yard work. In that I guess I'm like my dad. We talked about our house. He moved there for my mother's sake. He's happy in his apartment. I'm happy in ours—aren't you?"

"Don't you see our lifestyle changing when the baby is born?" she asked.

"To a degree. But, Annalise, think about it. We've established our routines as we like them. Travel, visiting and partying with friends. Going to the beach. A baby needs to fit into *our* lives. We are not supposed to rearrange everything for an infant."

"I think my parents did."

"They did what suited them. Do you seriously want to quit work and stay home, like your mother?"

She shook her head. "I have thought about that. I love my job. I could cut back on my hours, but still keep involved. Once the child's in school, I can work full-time again."

"So you don't want to do all your parents did? As they did it?"

She tilted her head in thought. "No." Actually, there were lots of things she'd do differently with her child than her parents had. Take him or her with them when they traveled, for one thing.

"So why it is so important to have a house? We can make our place perfect for a family of three."

The pang of not finishing the house, of never living in the rooms she'd already renovated, struck. But was a house more important than her future with Dominic?

"I love you, Annalise. I want to be there when our child is born. I'm going to do my best to always be there, though there will be times I have to travel. But I see no reason you can't accompany me. Traveling is educational. And it's one thing you regret about being part of such a large family—never time or money enough to take the entire family on trips anyplace but the shore."

She nodded, her heart beginning to ease. She squeezed his hand.

"Tell me the I-love-you part again," she said.

"I love you. Only you. What I had with Phyllis was only a teenage infatuation. I know the difference—can feel it inside. And it's stronger than ever. I will never let you down again. This has shown me that we need to continually work to stay together, no matter what life throws our way. If there weren't people around, I'd kiss you again."

"I love you, Dominic. We were still young when we married, arrogantly thinking we could determine our future. I'm not sorry we're going to have a baby. Who knows? We may even decide to have a second one sometime along the way. But if not, we'll be a happy family of three."

"So when we throw the next party for our closest friends, we'll share the good news of the baby?" he asked.

Her heart blossomed. He'd called it good news. "Just you make sure you're there for the party."

"Actually, I told Bill to keep me close to home for the next few months," he said.

"You did?" Annalise was astonished. Then she smiled broadly. "You really do plan to change."

"Anything for you, my love. With you, the past no longer has a hold on me."

"Then let's go home."

Dominic took his wife to their beautiful flat, to show her once again how much he loved her.

EPILOGUE

Twenty months later...

ANNALISE sat on the grass, leaning against Dominic. She glanced around, smiling in delight at the flowers blooming in profusion. Hyde Park was beautiful in summer. All of London was in bloom.

"How far can he get?" Dominic asked, watching as their toddling son took his first steps on grass, heading determinedly for the bank of blossoms that beckoned.

"You can still outrun him," she said, laughing. Then a thought struck her. "You know, this is like my vision." She looked around again.

"What vision?" Dominic asked.

"When I was working on the house, and I wanted Bridget to fix up the yard, I kept seeing you and me sitting on the grass and watching our baby take steps. I thought it was the backyard of that house, but it was anyplace that had grass. Here in London, back in Washington—even at the beach, if we find a lawn."

"No regrets at not living in the house?"

"Maybe one or two. I do love our flat, you know. The house turned out to be beautiful, though, didn't it?" she said proudly.

"It did. Bridget and your grandmother worked miracles in the garden. It was the prettiest place on the block when you sold it. But you are the one who worked miracles in that house."

"I drove by a couple of weeks ago. The owners have children, and they were playing in the yard. Bicycles strewn on the lawn. A dog was barking." She smiled in remembrance. It wasn't *her* family filling the home with love and laughter, but the house held another. And that was enough for her. She had enough happiness to wish it on the whole world.

Dominic took her hand, lacing his fingers with hers, keeping a sharp eye on their toddling son. "Maybe we'll get a house one day."

"If we do, let's make it at the beach, like Lianne and Tray."

"Twin thing?"

"No, I think Grandpa Paul's place is bursting at the seams now whenever the family gets together. What with Mary Margaret's new one, and our own Dylan. Plus I love staying with Lianne—no long wait for the bathroom."

"Think they are as happy as we are?" Dominic asked.

"Yes, I do. Lianne and Tray were made for each other."

"Lucky?"

"Just the infinite wisdom we twins share in finding perfect husbands."

Dominic kept a close watch on Dylan as he made his way with utmost concentration to the bank of flowers.

"Sorry we didn't have twins?" he asked.

"Good Lord, no. Lianne and Tray are run ragged with those little girls. Though they are adorable, aren't they? And it's a good thing we had Dylan. I had dibs on the name Caroline and would have been mad when Lianne delivered four days before me."

"So maybe we'll try for a girl next time."

Annalise smiled, hugging her secret just a little longer. She knew she would not get the same response from her husband when she told him this time.

"Sean and Bunny will have a new one before long. So when Lianne and Tray come with the twins for meals at the sea cottage, and everyone else is there, we'll have to eat buffet-style on the porch. Soon we'll have to eat in shifts," she said.

"Ready to buy that house?" Dominic asked.

She turned to look fully at him. "Actually, I'd rather consider the penthouse in our building. I hear it's coming up for sale. It has three bedrooms and a den, and that lovely terrace on the roof. Think of the view we'd have from there."

"No grass?"

She ran her hands across the green lawn. "This is grass enough for me. Next week, we'll be in Rome. We'll have to find a park there for Dylan to run in."

Dominic leaped to his feet and hurried after his son, who was now some ten feet away, reaching out to grasp one of the blossoms. It would go right in his mouth if Dominic didn't get there first.

Annalise smiled. All her fears were long gone. Her husband was a wonderful father, who cherished their son in a manner that warmed her heart every time she saw them together. His fears he'd be like his father had been dispelled. Dominic loved Dylan as much as he loved her.

They had not planned on children, but now they couldn't imagine their lives without Dylan. Or each other.

Their marriage had become stronger than ever. Their

quiet time at night after Dylan was in bed was especially close. They talked about feelings and hopes and problems. Dominic had kept his vow to make their marriage work. It was blissful. She was the happiest she'd ever been.

Annalise watched the two men in her life return. When Dominic sat on the grass, she leaned over and kissed him, her heart bursting with love.

"What's that for?" he asked, keeping an eye on Dylan.

"For being you. For loving me." For the secret she'd tell him tonight, when the two of them were snuggled together in bed.

"Ah, sweetheart, you have erased the bad memories of my past and brought me the best future possible. I love you, Annalise."

She never tired of hearing him say the words.

"I love you."

Their happiness would last a lifetime.

* * * * *

HER PREGNANCY SURPRISE

BY
SUSAN MEIER

Susan Meier spent most of her twenties thinking she was a job-hopper—until she began to write, and realized everything that came before was only research! One of eleven children, with twenty-four nieces and nephews and three kids of her own, Susan has had plenty of real-life experience watching romance blossom in unexpected ways. She lives in western Pennsylvania with her wonderful husband, Mike, her three children and her two overfed, well-cuddled cats, Sophie and Fluffy. You can visit Susan's website at www.susanmeier.com.

Susan says: "The beautiful beach house my family rented for vacation last summer was the inspiration for Danny's Virginia Beach house. I took a few liberties with the decorating—I've always wanted red leather sofas—but the ocean view and the wonderful deck are very real, making that house the perfect getaway for Danny and Grace!"

I'd like to thank my editors, Katinka Proudfoot
and Suzy Harding, and also
Senior Editor Kim Young, for helping me
turn Grace and Danny's story into a real keeper.

CHAPTER ONE

"YOU AREN'T planning on driving back to Pittsburgh tonight, are you?"

Danny Carson walked into the third floor office of his Virginia Beach beach house talking to Grace McCartney, his newest employee, who stood behind his desk, hunched over her laptop. A tall brunette with bright violet eyes and a smile that lit the room, Grace was smart, but more than that she was likable and she genuinely liked people. Both of those qualities had helped enormously with the work they'd had to do that weekend.

Grace looked up. "Would you like me to stay?"

"Call it a debriefing."

She tilted her head to one side, considering the suggestion, then smiled. "Okay."

This was her real charm. She'd been working every waking minute for three days, forced to spend her entire weekend assisting Danny as he persuaded Orlando Riggs—a poor kid who parlayed a basketball scholarship into a thirty-million-dollar NBA deal—to use Carson Services as his financial management firm. Not only was she away from her home in Pittsburgh and her friends, but she hadn't gotten to relax on her days off. She could be annoyed that he'd asked her to stay another night. Instead she smiled. Nothing ruffled her feathers.

"Why don't you go to your room to freshen up? I'll tell Mrs. Higgins we'll have dinner in about an hour."

"Sounds great."

After Grace left the office, Danny called his housekeeper on the intercom. He checked his e-mail, checked on dinner, walked on the beach and ended up on the deck with a glass of Scotch. Grace took so long that by the time Danny heard the sound of the sliding glass door opening behind him, Mrs. Higgins had already left their salads on the umbrella table and their entrées on the serving cart, and gone for the day. Exhausted from the long weekend of work, and belatedly realizing Grace probably was, too, Danny nearly suggested they forget about dinner and talk in the morning, until he turned and saw Grace.

Wearing a pretty pink sundress that showed off the tan she'd acquired walking on the beach with Orlando, she looked young, fresh-faced and wholesome. He'd already noticed she was pretty, of course. A man would have to be blind not to notice how attractive she was. But this evening, with the rays of the setting sun glistening on her shoulder-length sable-colored hair and the breeze off the ocean lightly ruffling her full skirt, she looked amazing.

Unable to stop himself he said, "Wow."

She smiled sheepishly. "Thanks. I felt a little like celebrating Orlando signing with Carson Services, and though this isn't exactly Prada, it's the best of what I brought."

Danny walked to her place at the table and pulled out her chair. "It's perfect." He thought about his khaki trousers, simple short-sleeved shirt and windblown black hair as he seated her, then wondered why he had. This wasn't a date. She was an employee. He'd asked her to stay so he could give her a bonus for the good job she'd done that week, and to talk to her long enough to ascertain the position into which he should promote her—also to thank her for doing a good job. What he wore should be of no consequence. The fact that it even entered his head nearly made him laugh.

He seated himself. "Mrs. Higgins has already served dinner."

"I see." She frowned, looking at the silver covers on the plates on the serving cart beside the table, then the salads that sat in front of them. "I'm sorry. I didn't realize I had stayed in the tub so long." She smiled sheepishly again. "I was a little more tired than I thought."

"Then I'm glad you took the extra time." Even as the words tumbled out of his mouth, Danny couldn't believe he was saying them. Yes, he was grateful to her for being so generous and kind with Orlando, making the athlete feel comfortable, but the way Danny had excused her lateness sounded personal, when he hardly knew this woman.

She laughed lightly. "I really liked Orlando. I think

he's a wonderful person. But we were still here to do a job. Both of us had to be on our toes 24/7."

When she smiled and Danny's nerve endings crackled to life, he realized he was behaving out of character for a boss because he was attracted to her. He almost shook his head. He was so slow on the uptake that he'd needed an entire weekend to recognize that.

But he didn't shake his head. He didn't react at all. He was her boss and he'd already slipped twice. His "wow" when he'd seen her in the dress was inappropriate. His comment about the extra time that she'd taken had been too personal. He excused himself for those because he was tired. But now that he saw what was happening, he could stop it. He didn't date employees, but also this particular employee had proven herself too valuable to risk losing.

Grace picked up her salad fork. "I'm starved and this looks great."

"Mrs. Higgins is a gem. I'm lucky to have her."

"She told me that she enjoys working for you because you're not here every day. She likes working part-time, even if it is usually weekends."

"That's my good fortune," Danny agreed, then the conversation died as they ate their salads. Oddly something inside of Danny missed the more personal chitchat. It was unusual for him to want to get friendly with an employee, but more than that, this dinner had to stay professional because he had things to discuss with her. Yet he couldn't stop the surge of disappointment, as if he were missing an unexpected opportunity.

When they finished their salads, he rose to serve the main course. "I hope you like fettuccini alfredo."

"I love it."

"Great." He removed the silver covers. Pushing past the exhaustion that had caused him to wish he could give in and speak openly with her, he served their dinners and immediately got down to business. "Grace, you did an exceptional job this weekend."

"Thanks. I appreciate the compliment."

"I intend to do more than compliment you. Your work secured an enormous account for Carson Services. Not only are you getting a bonus, but I would like to promote you."

She gaped at him. "Are you kidding?"

Pleased with her happy surprise, Danny laughed. "No. Right now you and I need to talk a bit about what you can do and where in the organization you would like to serve. Once we're clear, I'll write up the necessary paperwork."

She continued to stare at him slightly openmouthed, then she said, "You're going to promote me anywhere I want to go?"

"There is a condition. If a situation like Orlando's ever comes up again, where we have to do more than our general push to get a client to sign, I want you in on the persuading."

She frowned. "I'm happy to spend time helping a reluctant investor see the benefits of using your firm, but you don't need to promote me for that."

"The promotion is part of my thank-you for your assistance with Orlando."

She shook her head. "I don't want it."

Positive he'd heard wrong, Danny chuckled. "What?"

"I've been with your company two weeks. Yet I was the one chosen for a weekend at your beach house with Orlando Riggs—a superstar client most of the men and half of the women on staff were dying to meet. You've already given me a perk beyond what employees who have been with you for years have gotten. If there's an empty position somewhere in the firm, promote Bobby Zapf. He has a wife and three kids and they're saving for a house. He could use the money, and the boost in confidence from you."

Danny studied her for a second, then he laughed. "I get it. You're joking."

"I'm serious." She took a deep breath. "Look, everybody understood that you chose me to come with you this weekend because I'm new. I hadn't worked with you long enough to adopt your opinions, so Orlando knew that when I agreed with just about everything you said I wasn't spouting the company party line. I hadn't yet heard the party line. So I was a good choice for this. But I don't want to be promoted over everybody's head."

"You're worried about jealousy?"

She shook her head. "No! I don't want to take a job that should go to someone else. Someone who's worked for you for years."

"Like Bobby Zapf."

"In the two weeks I spent at the office, I watched

Bobby work harder than anybody else you employ. If you want to promote somebody he's the one."

Danny leaned back in his chair. "Okay. Bobby it is." He paused, toyed with his silverware, then glanced up at her, holding back a smile. He'd never had an employee turn down a promotion—especially not to make sure another person got it. Grace was certainly unique.

"Can I at least give you a bonus?"

She laughed. "Yes! I worked hard for an entire weekend. A bonus is absolutely in order."

Continuing to hold back a chuckle, Danny cleared his throat. "Okay. Bonus, but no promotion."

"You could promise to watch my performance over the next year and then promote me because I'd had enough time to prove myself."

"I could." He took a bite of his dinner, more pleased with her than anybody he'd ever met. She was right. In his gratitude for a weekend's work, he had jumped the gun on the promotion. She reeled him in and reminded him of the person who really deserved it. If he hadn't already been convinced she was a special person, her actions just now would have shown him.

Grace smiled. "Okay. It's settled. I get a bonus and you'll watch how well I work." Then as quickly as she'd recapped their agreement, she changed the subject. "It's beautiful here."

Danny glanced around. Darkness had descended. A million stars twinkled overhead. The moon shone like a silver dollar. Water hit the shore in white-foamed waves.

"I like it. I get a lot of work done here because it's so quiet. But at the end of the day I can also relax."

"You don't relax much, do you?"

Lulled by the sounds of the waves and her calming personality, Danny said, "No. I have the fate of a company that's been around for decades on my shoulders. If I fail the company fails and the legacy my great-grandfather sweated to create crumbles into nothing. So I'm focused on work. Unless relaxation happens naturally, it doesn't happen."

"I don't relax much, either." She picked up her fork again. "You already heard me tell Orlando I grew up the same way he did. Dirt poor. And in the same away he used his talent to make a place for himself, I intend to make a place for myself, too."

"Here's a tip. Maybe you shouldn't talk your bosses out of promotions?"

"I can't take what I don't deserve." She wiggled her eyebrows comically. "I'll just have to make my millions the old-fashioned way. I'll have to earn them."

Danny laughed and said, "I hate to tell you this, but people who work for someone else rarely get rich. So if you want to make millions, what are you doing working for me?"

"Learning about investing. When I was young I heard the theory that your money should work as hard for you as you work for it. Growing up, I didn't get any experience seeing how to make money work, so I figured the best place to get the scoop on investing was at an investment firm." She smiled, then asked, "What about you?"

"What about me?"

She shrugged. "I don't know. Anything. Did you want your family's business? Were you a happy child? Are you happy now?" She shrugged again. "Anything."

She asked the questions then took a bite of her dinner, making her inquiry into his life seem casual, offhand. But she'd nonetheless taken the conversation away from herself and to him. Still, she didn't seem as if she were prying. She seemed genuinely curious, but not like a bloodhound, like someone trying to become a friend.

He licked his suddenly dry lips and his heart rate accelerated as he actually considered answering her. A part of him really wanted to talk. A part of him *needed* to talk. Two years had passed. So much had happened.

He took a breath, amazed that he contemplated confiding in her, yet knowing he wouldn't. Though he couldn't ignore her, he wouldn't confide. He'd never confide. Not to her. Not to anyone.

He had to take the conversation back where it belonged. To business.

"What you see is who I am. Chairman of the Board and CEO of Carson Services. There isn't anything to talk about."

She blinked. "Really?"

"From the time I was six or eight I knew I would take over the company my great-grandfather started. I didn't have to travel or experiment to figure out what I wanted. My life was pretty much mapped out for me and I simply followed the steps. That's why there's not a lot to talk about."

"You started training as a kid?"

"Not really training, more or less being included in on conversations my dad and grandfather thought were relevant."

"What if you didn't like investing?"

"But I did."

"It just sounds weird." She flushed. "Sorry. Really. It's none of my business."

"Don't be sorry." Her honesty made him laugh. More comfortable than he could remember being in years, he picked up his fork and said, "I see what you're saying. I was lucky that I loved investing. I walked into the job as if it were made for me, but when my son—"

He stopped. His chest tightened. His heart rate kicked into overdrive. He couldn't believe that had slipped out.

"But your son what?"

"But when my son began to show artistic talent," he said, thinking quickly because once again the conversation had inadvertently turned too personal. And this time it was *his* fault. "I suddenly saw that another person might not want to be CEO of our company, might not have the ability to handle the responsibility, or might have gifts and talents that steer him or her in a different direction. Then the company would have to hire someone, and hiring someone of the caliber we would require would involve paying out a huge salary and profit sharing. The family fortune would ultimately deplete."

She studied him for a second, her gaze so intense Danny knew the mention of his son had her curious. But he wouldn't say any more about Cory. That part of his life was so far off-limits that he didn't even let himself think about it. It would be such a cold, frosty day in hell that he'd discuss Cory with another person that he knew that day would never come.

Finally Grace sighed. "I guess you were lucky then—" she turned her attention back to her food "—that you wanted the job."

Danny relaxed. Once again she'd read him perfectly. She'd seen that though he'd mentioned his son, he hadn't gone into detail about Cory, and instead had brought the discussion back to Carson Services, so she knew to let the topic go.

They finished their dinner in companionable conversation because Grace began talking about remodeling the small house she'd bought when she got her first job two years before. As they spoke about choosing hardwood and deciding on countertops, Danny acknowledged to himself that she was probably the most sensitive person he'd met. She could read a mood or a situation so well that he didn't have to worry about what he said in front of her. A person who so easily knew not to pry would never break a confidence.

For that reason alone an intense urge to confide in her bubbled up in him, shocking him. Why the hell would he want to talk about the past? And why would he think that any woman would want to hear her boss's marital horror stories? No woman would. No *person* would. Except maybe a gossip. And Grace wasn't a gossip.

After dinner, they went inside for a drink, but Danny paused beside the stairway that led to his third-floor office suite.

"Bonuses don't pass through our normal accounting. I write those checks myself. It's a way to keep them completely between me and the employees who get them. The checkbook's upstairs. Why don't we just go up now and give you your bonus?"

Grace grinned. "Sounds good to me."

Danny motioned for Grace to precede him up the steps. Too late, he realized that was a mistake. Her perfect bottom was directly in his line of vision. He paused, letting her get a few steps ahead of him, only to discover that from this angle he had a view of her shapely calves.

He finished the walk up the stairs with his head down, gaze firmly fixed on the Oriental carpet runner on the steps. When he reached the third floor, she was waiting for him. Moonlight came in through the three tall windows in the back wall of the semidark loft that led to his office, surrounding her with pale light, causing her to look like an angel.

Mesmerized, Danny stared at her. He knew she was a nice person. A *good* person. He also knew that was why he had the quick mental picture of her as an angel and such a strong sense of companionship for her. But she was an employee. He was her boss. He needed to keep his distance.

He motioned toward his office suite and again she preceded him. Inside, he sat behind the desk and she gingerly sat on the chair in front of it.

"I think Orlando Riggs is the salt of the earth," Danny said as he pulled out the checkbook he held for the business. "You made him feel very comfortable."

"I felt very comfortable with him." She grimaced. "A lot of guys who had just signed a thirty-million-dollar deal with an NBA team would be a little cocky."

"A little cocky?" Danny said with a laugh. "I've met people with a lot less talent than Orlando has and a lot less cash who were total jerks."

"Orlando seems unaffected."

"Except that he wants to make sure his family has everything they need." Danny began writing out the check. "I didn't even realize he was married."

"And has two kids."

Kids.

Danny blinked at the unexpected avalanche of memory just the word kids brought. He remembered how eager he'd been to marry Lydia and have a family. He remembered his naive idea of marital bliss, and his chest swelled from the horrible empty feeling he got every time he realized how close he'd been to fulfilling that dream and how easily it had all been snatched away.

But tonight, with beautiful, sweet-tempered, sincere Grace sitting across the desk, Danny had a surprising moment of clarity. He'd always blamed himself for the breakdown of his marriage, but what if it had been Lydia's fault? He'd wanted to go to counseling. Lydia had simply wanted to *go*. Away from him. If he looked at the breakdown of his marriage from that very thin perspective, then the divorce wasn't his fault.

That almost made him laugh. If he genuinely believed the divorce wasn't his fault then—

Then he'd wasted years?

No. He'd wasted his life. He didn't merely feel empty the way he'd been told most people felt when they lost a mate; he felt wholly empty. Almost nonexistent. As if he didn't have a life. As if every day since his marriage had imploded two years ago, he hadn't really lived. He hadn't even really existed. He'd simply expended time.

Finished writing the check, Danny rose from his seat. It seemed odd to think about feeling empty when across the desk, eager, happy Grace radiated life and energy.

"Thank you for your help this weekend."

As he walked toward her, Grace also rose. He handed her the check. She glanced down at the amount he'd written, then looked up at him. Her beautiful violet eyes filled with shock. Her tongue came out to moisten her lips before she said, "This is too much."

Caught in the gaze of her hypnotic eyes, seeing the genuine appreciation, Danny could have sworn he felt some of her energy arch to him. If nothing else, he experienced a strong sense of connection. A rightness. Or maybe a purpose. As if there was a reason she was here.

The feeling of connection and intimacy could be nothing more than the result of spending every waking minute from Friday afternoon to Sunday night together, but that didn't lessen its intensity. It was so strong that his voice softened when he said, "No. It isn't too much. You deserve it."

She took a breath that caused her chest to rise and fall, calling his attention to the cleavage peeking out of the pink lace of her dress. She looked soft and feminine, yet she was also smart and sensitive. Which was why she attracted him, tempted him, when in the past two years no other woman had penetrated the pain that had held him hostage. Grace treated him like a person. Not like her rich boss. Not like a good catch. Not even like a guy so far out of her social standing that she should be nervous to spend so much one-on-one time. But just like a man.

"Thanks." She raised her gaze to his again. This time when Danny experienced the sense of intimacy, he almost couldn't argue himself out of it because he finally understood it. *She* felt it, too. He could see it in her eyes. And he didn't want to walk away from it. He *needed* her.

But then he saw the check in her hands and he remembered she was an employee. An affair between them had consequences. Especially when it ended. Office gossip would make him look foolish, but it could ruin her. Undoubtedly it would cost her her job. He might be willing to take a risk because his future wasn't at stake, but he couldn't make the decision for her.

CHAPTER TWO

DANNY cleared his throat. "You're welcome. I very much appreciated your help this weekend." He stepped away and walked toward the office door. "I'm going downstairs to have a drink before I turn in. I'll see you in the morning."

Grace watched Danny go, completely confused by what was happening between them. For a few seconds, she could have sworn he was going to kiss her and the whole heck of it was she would have let him.

Let him? She was so attracted to him she darned near kissed him first, and that puzzled her. She should have reminded herself that he was her boss and so wealthy they were barely on the same planet. Forget about being in the same social circle. But thoughts of their different worlds hadn't even entered her head, and, thinking about them now, Grace couldn't muster a reason they mattered.

Laughing softly, she combed her fingers through her hair. Whatever the reason, she couldn't deny the spark between her and Danny. When Orlando left that afternoon, Grace had been disappointed that their weekend together had come to an end. But Danny had asked her to stay one more night, and she couldn't resist the urge to dress up and hope that he would notice her the way she'd been noticing him. He'd nearly ruined everything by offering her a promotion she didn't deserve, but he showed her that he trusted her opinion by taking her advice about Bobby Zapf.

The real turning point came when he mentioned his son. He hadn't wanted to talk about him, but once Danny slipped him into the conversation he hadn't pretended he hadn't. She had seen the sadness in his eyes and knew there was a story there. But she also recognized that this wasn't the time to ask questions. She'd heard the rumor that Danny had gone through an ugly divorce but no report had mentioned a child from his failed marriage. Nasty divorces frequently resulted in child custody battles and his ex-wife could very well make him fight to see his son, which was undoubtedly why he didn't want to talk about him.

But tonight wasn't the night for probing into a past that probably only reminded him of unhappy times. Tonight, she had to figure out if he felt for her what she was beginning to feel for him. The last thing she wanted was to be one of those employees who got a crush on her boss and then pined for him for the rest of her career.

And she wouldn't get any answers standing in his third floor office when he was downstairs!

She ran down the steps and found him in the great room, behind the bar, pouring Scotch into a glass.

He glanced up when she walked over. Though he seemed surprised she hadn't gone to her room as he'd more or less ordered her to, he said, "Drink?"

Wanting to be sharp and alert so she didn't misinterpret anything he said or did, Grace smiled and said, "No. Thanks."

She slid onto one of the three red leather bar stools that matched the red leather sofas that sat parallel to each other in front of the wall of windows that provided a magnificent view of the Atlantic Ocean. A black, red and tan Oriental rug between the sofas protected the sand-colored hardwood floors. White-bowled lights connected to thin chrome poles suspended from the vaulted ceiling, illuminating the huge room.

Danny took a swallow of his Scotch, then set the glass on the bar. "Can't sleep?"

She shrugged. "Still too keyed up from the weekend I guess."

"What would you normally do on a Sunday night?"

She thought for a second, then laughed. "Probably play rummy with my mother. She's a cardaholic. Loves any game. But she's especially wicked with rummy."

"Can't beat her?"

"Every once in a while I get lucky. But when it comes to pure skill the woman is evilly blessed."

Danny laughed. "My mother likes cards, too."

Grace's eyes lit. "Really? How good is she?"

"Exceptional."

"We should get them together."

Danny took a long breath, then said, "We should."

And Grace suddenly saw it. The thing that had tickled her brain all weekend but had never really surfaced. In spite of her impoverished roots and his obviously privileged upbringing, she and Danny had a lot in common. Not childhood memories, but adult things like goals and commitments. He ran his family's business. She was determined to help her parents out of poverty because she loved them. Even the way they viewed Orlando proved they had approximately the same beliefs about life and people.

If Danny hadn't asked for her help this weekend, eventually they would have been alone together long enough to see that they clicked. They matched. She knew he realized it, too, if only because he'd nearly slipped into personal conversation with her four times at dinner, but he had stopped himself. Probably because she was an employee.

It was both of their loss if they weren't mature enough to handle an office relationship. But she thought they were. Her difficult childhood and his difficult divorce had strengthened each of them. They weren't flip. They were cautious. Smart. If any two people could have an office relationship without it affecting their work, she and Danny were the two. And she wasn't going to miss out on something good because, as her boss, Danny wouldn't be the first to make a move.

She raised her eyes until she caught his gaze. "You know what? Though you're trying to fight it, I think you like me. Would it help if I told you I really like you, too?"

* * *

For several seconds, Danny didn't answer. He couldn't. He'd never met a woman so honest, so he wasn't surprised that she spoke her mind. Even better, she hadn't played coy and tried to pretend she didn't see what was going on. She saw it, and she wanted to like him as much as he wanted to like her.

And that was the key. The final answer. She wanted to like him as much as he wanted to like her and he suddenly couldn't understand why he was fighting it.

"It helps enormously." He bent across the bar and kissed her, partly to make sure they were on the same page with their intentions, and partly to see if their chemistry was as strong as the emotions that seemed to ricochet between them.

It was. Just the slight brush of their lips knocked him for a loop. He felt the explosion the whole way to his toes.

She didn't protest the kiss, so he took the few steps that brought him from behind the bar and in front of the stool on which she sat. He put his hands on her shoulders and kissed her deeply this time, his mouth opening over hers.

White-hot desire slammed through him and his control began slipping. He wanted to touch her, to taste her, to feel all the things he'd denied himself for the past two years.

But it was one thing to kiss her. It was quite another to make love. But when he shifted away, Grace slid her hand around his neck and brought his lips back to hers.

Relief swamped him. He'd never had this kind of an all-consuming desire to make love. Yet, the yearning he felt wasn't for sexual gratification. It was to be with Grace herself. She was sweet and fun and wonderful…and beautiful. Having her slide her arms around him and return his kisses with a passion equal to his own filled him with an emotion so strong and complete he dared not even try to name it.

Instead he broke the kiss, lifted her into his arms and took her to his bed.

The next morning when Grace awoke, she inhaled a long breath as she stretched. When her hand connected with warm, naked skin, her eyes popped open and she remembered she'd spent the night making love with her boss.

Reliving every detail, she blinked twice, waiting for a sense of embarrassment or maybe guilt. When none came she smiled. She couldn't believe it, but it was true. She'd fallen in love with Danny Carson in about forty-eight hours.

She should feel foolish for tumbling in over her head so fast. She could even worry that he'd seen her feelings for him and taken advantage of her purely for sexual gratification. But she wasn't anything but happy. Nobody had ever made love to her the way he had. And she was sure their feelings were equal.

She yawned and stretched, then went downstairs to the room she'd used on Friday and Saturday nights. After brushing her teeth and combing her hair, she ran back to Danny's room and found he was still sleeping, so she slid into bed again.

Her movements caused Danny to stir. As Grace

thanked her lucky stars that she had a chance to fix up
a bit before he awoke, he turned on his pillow. Ready,
she smiled and caught his gaze but the eyes that met
hers were not the warm brown eyes of the man who had
made love to her the night before. They were the dark,
almost black eyes of her boss.

She remembered again the way he'd made love to her
and told herself to stop being a worrying loser. Yes, the
guy who ran Carson Services could sometimes be a
real grouch, but the guy who lived in this beach house
was much nicer. And she was absolutely positive that
was the real Danny.

Holding his gaze, she whispered, "Good morning."

He stared at her. After a few seconds, he closed his
eyes. "Tell me we didn't make a mistake."

"We did not make a mistake."

He opened his eyes. "Always an optimist."

She scooted closer so she could rest her head on his
outstretched arm. "We like each other. A lot. Something
pretty special happened between us."

He was silent for a few seconds then he said, "Okay."

She twisted so she could look at him. "Okay? I
thought we were fantastic!"

His face transformed. The caution slipped from
his dark eyes and was replaced by amusement. "You
make me laugh."

"It's a dirty job but somebody's got to do it."

Chuckling, he caught her around the waist and
reversed their positions. But gazing into her eyes, he

softened his expression again and said, "Thanks," before he lowered his head and kissed her.

They made love and then Danny rolled out of bed, suggesting they take a shower. Gloriously naked, he walked to the adjoining bathroom and began to run the water. Not quite as comfortable as he, Grace needed a minute to skew her courage to join him, and in the end wrapped a bedsheet around herself to walk to the bathroom.

But though she faltered before dropping the sheet, when she stepped into the shower, she suddenly felt bold. Knowing his trust was shaky because of his awful divorce, she stretched to her tiptoes and kissed him. He let her take the lead and she began a slow exploration of his body until he seemed unable to handle her simple ministrations anymore and he turned the tables.

They made love quickly, covered with soap and sometimes even pausing to laugh, and Grace knew from that moment on, she was his. She would never feel about any man the way she felt about Danny.

CHAPTER THREE

WHEN Grace and Danny stood in the circular driveway of his beach house, both about to get into their cars to drive back to Pittsburgh, she could read the displeasure in his face as he told her about the "client hopping" he had scheduled for the next week. He wanted to be with her but these meetings had been on the books for months and he couldn't get out of them. So she kissed him and told him she would be waiting when he returned.

They got into their vehicles and headed home. He was a faster driver, so she lost him on I-64, but she didn't care. Her heart was light and she had the kind of butterflies in her tummy that made a woman want to sing for joy. Though time would tell, she genuinely believed she'd found Mr. Right. She'd only known Danny for two weeks, and hadn't actually spent a lot of that time with him since he was so far above her on the company organizational chart. But the weekend had told her everything she needed to know about the real Danny Carson.

To the world, he was an ambitious, demanding, highly successful man. In private, he was a loving, caring, normal man, who liked her. A lot.

Yes, they would probably experience some problems because he owned the company she worked for. He'd hesitated at the bar before kissing her. He'd asked her that morning if they'd made a mistake. But she forced herself not to worry about it. She had no doubt that once they spent enough time together, and he saw the way she lived her beliefs, his worries about dating an employee would vanish.

What they had was worth a few months of getting to know each other. Or maybe the answer would be to quit her job?

The first two days of his trip sped by. He called Wednesday morning, and the mere sound of his voice made her breathless. Though he talked about clients, meetings, business dinners and never-ending handshaking, his deep voice reminded her of his whispered endearments during their night together and that conjured the memory of how he tasted, the firmness of his skin, the pleasure of being held in his arms. Before he disconnected the call, he whispered that he missed her and couldn't wait to see her and she'd all but fainted with happiness.

The next day he didn't call, but Grace knew he was busy. He also didn't call on Friday or Saturday.

Flying back to Pittsburgh Sunday, Danny nervously paced his Gulfstream, fighting a case of doubt and second thoughts about what had happened between him and Grace. In the week that had passed, he hadn't had a spare minute to think about her, and hadn't spoken with her except for one quick phone call a few days into the trip. The call had ended too soon and left him longing to see her, but after three days of having no contact, the negatives of the situation came crowding in on him, and there were plenty of them.

First, he didn't really know her. Second, even if she were the perfect woman, they'd gone too far too fast. Third, they worked together. If they dated it would be all over the office. When they broke up, he would be the object of the same gossip that had nearly ruined his reputation when his marriage ended.

He took a breath and blew it out on a puff. He couldn't tell if distance was giving him perspective or calling up all his demons. But he did know that he should have thought this through before making love to her.

Worse, he couldn't properly analyze their situation because he couldn't recall specifics. All he remembered from their Sunday night and Monday morning together were emotions so intense that he'd found the courage to simply be himself. But with the emotions gone, he couldn't summon a solid memory of the substance of what had happened between them. He couldn't remember anything specific she'd said to make him like her—like? Did he say like? He didn't just like Grace. That Sunday night his feelings had run more along the lines of a breathless longing, uncontrollable desire, and total bewitching. A man in that condition could easily be seduced into seeing traits in a woman that weren't there and that meant he had made a horrible mistake.

He told himself not to think that way. But the logical side of his brain called him a sap. He'd met Grace two weeks before when she'd come to work for his company, but he didn't really know her because he didn't work with new employees. He worked with their bosses. He said hello to new employees in the hall. But otherwise, he ignored them. So he hadn't "known" her for two weeks. He'd glimpsed her.

Plus, she'd been on her best behavior for Orlando. She had been at the beach house to demonstrate to Orlando that Carson Services employed people in the know. Yes, she'd gone above and beyond the call of duty in her time with Orlando, making him feel comfortable, sharing personal insights—but, really, wasn't that her job?

Danny took a long breath. Had he fallen in love with a well polished persona she'd pulled out to impress Orlando and simply never disengaged when the basketball star left?

Oh Lord!

He sat, rubbed his hands down his face and held back a groan. Bits and pieces of their Sunday night dinner conversation flitted through his brain. She'd grown up poor. Could only afford a house that needed remodeling. She wanted to be rich. She'd gone into investing to understand money.

He *had* money.

Technically he was a shortcut to all her goals.

He swallowed hard. It wasn't fair to judge her when she wasn't there to defend herself.

He had to see her. Then he would know. After five minutes of conversation she would either relieve all his fears or prove that he'd gone too fast, told her too much and set himself up for a huge disappointment.

The second his plane taxied to a stop, he pulled out his cell phone and called her, but she didn't answer. He left a message but she didn't return his call and Danny's apprehensions hitched a notch. Not that he thought she should be home, waiting for him, but she knew when he got in. He'd told her he would call. He'd said it at the end of a very emotional phone conversation in which he'd told her that crazy as it sounded, he missed her. She'd breathlessly told him she missed him, too.

Now she wasn't home?

If he hadn't given her the time he would be landing, if he hadn't told her he would be calling, if he hadn't been so sappy about saying how much he missed her, it wouldn't seem so strange that she wasn't home. But, having told her all those things, he had the uncontrollable suspicion that something was wrong.

Unless she'd come to the same conclusions he had. Starting a relationship had been a mistake.

That had to be it.

Relief swamped him. He didn't want another relationship. Ever. And Grace was too nice a girl to have the kind of fling that ended when their sexual feelings for each other fizzled and they both eagerly walked away.

It was better for it to end now.

Content that not only had Grace nicely disengaged their relationship, but also that he probably wouldn't run into her in the halls because their positions in the company and the building were so far apart, he went to work happy. But his secretary buzzed him around ten-thirty, telling him Grace was in the outer office, asking if he had time for her.

Sure. Why not? Now that he'd settled everything in his head, he could handle a debriefing. They'd probably both laugh about the mistake.

He tossed his pencil to the stack of papers in front of him. "Send her in."

He steeled himself, knowing that even though his brain had easily resolved their situation, his body might not so easily agree. Seeing her would undoubtedly evoke lots of physical response, if only because she was beautiful. He remembered that part very, very well.

His office door opened and she stepped inside. Danny almost groaned at his loss. She was every bit as stunning as he remembered. Her dark hair framed her face and complemented her skin tone. Her little pink suit showed off her great legs. But he wasn't meant for relationships and she wasn't meant for affairs. Getting out now while they could get out without too much dif-ficulty was the right thing to do.

"Good morning, Grace."

She smiled. "Good morning."

He pointed at the chair in front of his desk, indicat-ing she should sit. "Look, I know what you're going to say. Being away for a week gave me some perspective, too, and I agree we made a mistake the night we slept together."

"What?"

Confused, he cocked his head. "I thought you were here to tell me we'd made a mistake."

Holding the arms of the captain's chair in front of his desk, she finally sat. "I came in to invite you to dinner."

He sat back on his chair, knowing this could potentially be one of the worst conversations of his life. "I'm sorry. When you weren't home last night when I called, I just assumed you'd changed your mind."

"I was at my mother's."

"I called your cell phone."

She took a breath. "And by the time I realized I'd hadn't turned it on after I took it off the charger, it was too late for me to call you back." She took another breath and smiled hopefully. "That's why I came to your office."

He picked up his pencil again. Nervously tapped it on the desk. "I'm sorry. Really. But—" This time he took the breath, giving himself a chance to organize his thoughts. "I genuinely believe we shouldn't have slept together, and I really don't want to see you anymore. I don't have relationships with employees."

He caught her gaze. "I'm sorry."

That seemed to catch her off guard. She blinked several times, but her face didn't crumble as he expected it would if she were about to cry. To his great relief, her chin lifted. "That's fine."

Pleased that she seemed to be taking this well—

probably because his point was a valid one—bosses and employees shouldn't date—he rose. "Do you want the day off or something?"

She swallowed and wouldn't meet his gaze. She said, "I'm fine," then turned and walked out of his office.

Danny fell to his seat, feeling like a class-A heel. He had hurt her and she was going to cry.

Grace managed to get through the day with only one crying spurt in the bathroom right after coming out of Danny's office. She didn't see him the next day or the next or at all for the next two weeks. Just when she had accepted that her world hadn't been destroyed because he didn't want her or because she'd slept with him, she realized something awful. Her female cycle was as regular as clockwork, so when things didn't happen on the day they were supposed to happen, she knew something was wrong.

Though she and Danny had used condoms, they weren't perfect. She bought an early pregnancy test and discovered her intuition had been correct. She had gotten pregnant.

She sat on the bed in the master suite of her little house. The room was awash with warm colors: cognac, paprika, butter-yellow in satin pillows, lush drapes and a smooth silk bedspread. But she didn't feel any warmth as she stared at the results of the EPT. She had just gotten pregnant by a man who had told her he wanted nothing to do with her.

She swallowed hard and began to pace the honey-yellow hardwood floors of the bedroom she'd scrimped, saved and labored to refinish. Technically she had a great job and a good enough income that she could raise a child alone. Money wasn't her problem. And neither was becoming a mother. She was twenty-four, ready to be a mom. Excited actually.

Except Danny didn't want her. She might survive telling him, but she still worked for him. Soon everybody at his company would know she was pregnant. Anybody with a memory could do the math and realize when she'd gotten pregnant and speculate the baby might be Danny's since they'd spent a weekend together.

He couldn't run away from this and neither could she.

She took a deep breath, then another, and another, to calm herself.

Everything would be fine if she didn't panic and handled this properly. She didn't have to tell Danny right away that she was pregnant. She could wait until enough time had passed that he would see she wasn't trying to force anything from him. Plus, until her pregnancy was showing, she didn't have to tell anybody but Danny. In six or seven months the people she worked with wouldn't necessarily connect her pregnancy with the weekend she and Danny together. They could get out of this with a minimum of fuss.

That made so much sense that Grace easily fell asleep that night, but the next morning she woke up dizzy, still exhausted and with an unholy urge to vomit. On Saturday morning, she did vomit. Sunday morning, she couldn't get out of bed. Tired, nauseated and dizzy beyond belief, she couldn't hide her symptoms from anybody. Which meant that by Monday afternoon, everybody would guess something was up, and she had no choice but to tell Danny first thing in the morning that she was pregnant. If she didn't, he would find out by way of a rumor, and she couldn't let that happen.

Grace arrived at work an hour early on Monday. Danny was already in his office but his secretary had not yet arrived. As soon as he was settled, she knocked on the frame of his open door.

He looked up. "Grace?"

"Do you have a minute?"

"Not really, I have a meeting—"

"This won't take long." She drank a huge gulp of air and pushed forward because there was no point in dilly-dallying. "I'm pregnant."

For thirty seconds, Danny sat motionless. Grace felt every breath she drew as the tension in the room increased with each second that passed.

Finally he very quietly said, "Get out."

"We need to talk about this."

"Talk about this? Oh, no! I won't give credence to your scheme by even gracing you with ten minutes to try to convince me you're pregnant!"

"Scheme?"

"Don't play innocent with me. Telling the man who

broke up with you that you're pregnant is the oldest trick in the book. If you think I'm falling for it, you're insane."

Grace hadn't expected this would be an easy conversation, but for some reason or another she had expected it to be fair. The Danny she remembered from the beach house might have been shocked, but he would have at least given her a chance to talk.

"I'm not insane. I am pregnant."

"I told you to get out."

"This isn't going to go away because you don't believe me."

"Grace, I said leave."

His voice was hard and cold and his office fell deadly silent. Knowing there was no talking to him in that state and hoping that after she gave him a few hours for her announcement to sink in he might be more amenable to discussing it, Grace did as he asked. She left his office with her head high, controlling the tears that welled behind her eyelids.

The insult of his reaction tightened her chest and she marched straight to her desk. She yanked open the side drawer, withdrew her purse and walked out of the building as if it were the most natural thing in the world for her to do. When she got into her car, she dropped her head to her steering wheel and let the tears fall.

Eventually it would be obvious she hadn't lied. But having Danny call her a schemer was the absolute worst experience she'd ever had.

Partially because he believed it. He believed she would trick him.

Grace's cheeks heated from a sudden rush of indignation.

It was as if he didn't know her at all—or she didn't know him at all.

Or maybe they didn't know each other.

She started her car and headed home. She needed the day to recover from that scene, but also as sick as she was she couldn't go back to work until she and Danny had talked this out. Pretty soon everybody would guess what had happened. If nothing else, they had to do damage control. There were lots of decisions that had to be made. So when she got home she would call her supervisor, explain she'd gotten sick and that she might be out a few days. Then she and Danny would resolve this *away* from the office.

Because she had written down his home number and cell number when he left the message on her answering machine the Sunday night he'd returned from his business trip, Grace called both his house and his cell that night.

He didn't answer.

She gave him forty-eight hours and called Thursday morning before he would leave for work. Again, no answer.

A little more nervous now, she gave him another forty-eight hours and called Saturday morning. No answer.

She called Monday night. No answer.

And she got the message. He wasn't going to pick up her calls.

But by that time she had something a little more serious to handle. She couldn't get well. Amazed that she'd even been able to go to work the Monday of her encounter with Danny, she spent her days in bed, until, desperate for help and advice, she told her mother that she was pregnant and sicker than she believed was normal. They made a quick gynecologist appointment and her doctor told her that she was simply enduring extreme morning sickness.

Too worried about her baby to risk the stress of dealing with Danny, Grace put off calling him. Her life settled into a simple routine of forcing herself out of bed, at least to the couch in her living room, but that was as far as she got, and watching TV all day, as her mother fussed over her.

Knowing the bonus she'd received for her weekend with Orlando would support her through her pregnancy if she were frugal, she quit her job. Swearing her immediate supervisor to secrecy in their final phone conversation, she confided that she was pregnant and having troubles, though she didn't name the baby's father. And she slid out of Carson Services as if she'd never been there.

She nearly called Danny in March, right before the baby was born, but, again, didn't have the strength to handle the complexities of their situation. Even though he would be forced to believe she hadn't lied, he might still see her as a cheat. Someone who had tricked him. She didn't know how to explain that she hadn't, and after nine months of "morning sickness" she didn't give a damn. A man who behaved the way he had wasn't her perfect partner. His money didn't make him the special prize he seemed to believe he was. It was smarter to focus on the joy of becoming a mother, the joy of having a child, than to think about a guy so hurt by his divorce that he couldn't believe anything anyone told him.

When Sarah was born everything suddenly changed. No longer sick and now responsible for a child, Grace focused on finding a job. Happily she found one that paid nearly double what she'd been making at Carson Services. Because her parents had moved into her house to help while she was pregnant, she surprised them by buying the little bungalow down the street. Her mother wanted to baby-sit while Grace worked. Her dad could keep up both lawns. And the mortgage on the new house for her parents was small.

Busy and happy, Grace didn't really think about Danny and before she knew it, it was September and Sarah was six months old. Everything from baby-sitting to pediatrician appointments was taken care of. Everyone in her little family was very happy.

And Grace wondered why she would want to tell Danny at all.

But holding Sarah that night she realized that this situation wasn't about her and Danny anymore. It was about Sarah. Every little girl had a right to know her daddy.

The following Saturday evening, Grace found herself craning her neck, straining to read the small sophisticated street signs in the development that contained Danny's house. It hadn't been hard to find his address. Convincing herself to get in the car and drive over had been harder. Ultimately she'd come to terms with it not for Danny's sake, but for Sarah's. If Grace didn't at least give Danny the chance to be a dad, then she was no better than he was.

She located his street, turned onto it and immediately saw his house. Simple stone, accented by huge multi-paned windows, his house boasted a three-car garage and space. Not only was the structure itself huge, but beyond the fence that Grace assumed protected a swimming pool, beautiful green grass seemed to stretch forever before it met a wall of trees. Compared to her tiny bungalow, his home was a palace.

She parked her little red car in his driveway, got out and reached into the back seat to unbuckle Sarah. Opting not to put her in a baby carrier, Grace pulled her from the car and settled her on her arm.

Holding her squirming baby and bulky diaper bag, she strode up the stone front walk to Danny's door, once again noting the differences in their lifestyles personified by decorative black lantern light fixtures and perfect landscaping.

Grace shook her head, trying to stop the obvious conclusion from forming, but she couldn't. She and Danny were different. Too difference to be together. Why hadn't she recognized that? He probably had. That's why he'd told her he didn't want to see her. They *weren't* made for each other. Not even close. And he'd now had fifteen months to forget her. She could have to explain the entire situation again, and then face another horrible scene.

Still, as much as she dreaded this meeting, and as much as she would prefer to raise Sarah on her own, she knew it wasn't fair for Sarah to never know her father. She also knew Danny should have the option to be part of his daughter's life. If he again chose not to believe Grace when she told him Sarah was his child, then so be it. She wouldn't beg him to be a father to their baby. She wouldn't demand DNA testing to force him in. If he wanted a DNA test, she would comply, but as far as she was concerned, she was the one doing him the favor. If he didn't wish to acknowledge his child or be a part of Sarah's life that was his decision. She wasn't going to get upset or let him hurt her again. If he said he wanted no part of her or her baby, this time Grace and Sarah would leave him alone for good.

Again without giving herself a chance to think, she rang the doorbell. Waiting for someone to answer, she glanced around at his massive home, then wished she hadn't. How could she have ever thought she belonged with someone who lived in this part of the city?

The door opened and suddenly she was face-to-face with the father of her child. Though it was Saturday he wore dress slacks and a white shirt, but his collar was unbuttoned and his tie loosened. He looked relaxed and comfortable and was even smiling.

Then his eyes darkened, his smile disappeared and

his gaze dropped to Sarah, and Grace realized he remembered who she was.

She took a breath. "Can we come in?"

The expression in his eyes changed, darkening even more, reminding Grace of a building storm cloud. For the twenty seconds that he remained stonily silent, she was positive he would turn her away. For those same twenty seconds, with his dark eyes condemning her, she fervently wished he would.

But without saying a word, he pulled open his door and stepped aside so she could enter.

"Thank you." She walked into the echoing foyer of his big house, fully expecting this to be the worst evening of her life.

CHAPTER FOUR

AS GRACE brushed by Danny, a band of pain tightened his chest. At first he thought the contraction was a result of his anger with Grace, fury that she'd continued with her pregnancy scheme. He wondered how she intended to get around DNA since he would most certainly require the test, then he actually looked at the baby in her arms, a little girl if the pink one-piece pajamas were any indication. She appeared to be about six months old—the age their baby would be if he had gotten Grace pregnant that Sunday night at his beach house. More than that, though, the baby looked exactly as Cory had when he was six months old.

Danny stood frozen, unable to do anything but stare at the chubby child in Grace's arms. Suddenly the baby smiled at him. Her plump lips lifted. Her round blue eyes filled with laughter. She made a happy gurgling sound that caused playful spit bubbles to gather at the corners of her mouth. She looked so much like Cory it was as if Danny had been unceremoniously flung back in time.

Feeling faint, he pointed down the corridor. "There's a den at the end of the hall. Would you please wait for me there?"

Grace caught his gaze with her pretty violet eyes and everything inside of Danny stilled. In a hodgepodge of pictures and words, he remembered bits and pieces of both the weekend they'd spent together with Orlando and the morning he'd kicked her out of his office—wrongly if his assumptions about the baby were correct. In his mind's eye, he saw Grace laughing with Orlando, working with him, making him comfortable. He remembered her soft and giving in his arms. He remembered her trembling when she told him she was pregnant, and then he remembered nothing but anger. He hadn't given her a chance to explain or even a sliver of benefit of the doubt. He'd instantly assumed her "pregnancy" was a ruse and wouldn't hear another word.

"I don't think we want to be interrupted," he said, grasping for any excuse that would give him two minutes to come to terms with some of this before he had to talk to her. "So I need to instruct my house-keeper that we're to be left alone."

She pressed her lips together, nodded and headed down the hall. Once Danny saw her turn into the den, he collapsed on the bottom step of the spiral staircase in his foyer and dropped his head to his hands.

They were shaking. His knees felt like rubber. Pain ricocheted through him and he squeezed his eyes shut. In vivid detail, he saw Cory's birth, his first birthday party, and every Christmas they'd had together. He remembered his giggle. He remembered his endless questions as he grew from a toddler into a little boy. He remembered how he loved garbage trucks and mailmen.

Pain overwhelmed him as he relived every second of the best and worst six years of his life and then realized he could very well go through it all again. The first birthday. Laughing, happy Christmases. Questions and curiosities. And pain. One day he was a doting dad and the next he was living alone, without even the possibility of seeing his son again.

He fought the anger that automatically surged up in him when the thought about his marriage, about Lydia. In the past year, his sense of fair play had compelled him to examine his marriage honestly and he had to admit that Lydia hadn't been a horrible shrew. *He* hadn't been a terrible husband. Their marriage hadn't ended because he and his ex-wife were bad people, but because they'd hit a crossroad that neither had anticipated. A crossroad where there had been no choice but to separate. They had once been the love of each other's life, yet when their marriage had begun to crumble, they'd both forgotten the eight good years, only remembered their horrible final year, and fought bitterly. They'd hurt each other. Used Cory as a weapon. And both of them had walked away damaged.

Remembering that only made his upcoming showdown with Grace more formidable. He and Grace didn't have two years of courtship and six years of marriage to look back on to potentially keep them from hurting each other. So how did he expect their confrontation to turn out any better than his fight with Lydia had?

He didn't.

He wouldn't shirk his responsibility to Grace's baby. But he had learned enough from the past that the key to survival was not being so in love with his daughter that she could turn into Grace's secret weapon.

Finally feeling that he knew what he had to do, Danny rose from the step, went to the kitchen and told his housekeeper he and Grace weren't to be disturbed, then he walked to the den.

Unfortunately he couldn't keep the displeasure out of his voice when he said, "Let me see her."

Grace faced him. "Save your anger, Danny. I was the one left to have this baby alone. I was so sick I had to quit my job and depend on my parents to basically nurse me for nine months. The bonus you gave me went to support me until I had Sarah and could go back to work. I was sick, exhausted and worried that if anything went wrong when she was born I wouldn't be able to pay for proper care. You could have helped me through all of that, but you never even followed up on me. So the way I see this, you don't have anything to complain about."

She was right, of course. It didn't matter that he was still hurting from the end of his marriage when she told him she was pregnant. He hadn't for two seconds considered Grace or her feelings. Still, he had no proof that she was the innocent victim she wanted him to believe she was. The weekend they'd spent together, he'd made himself an easy mark for a woman he really didn't know. He'd never wanted another relationship, let alone a child. And now he had one with a stranger. A woman he genuinely believed had tricked him.

"What made it all worse was wondering about your reaction when I did bring Sarah to you." She sat on the leather sofa in the conversation area, laid the gurgling baby on the cushion and pulled the bonnet ribbon beneath the little girl's chin, untying the bow.

Danny's breathing stuttered as he stared at the baby. *His daughter.* A perfect little pink bundle of joy. She punched and pedaled her legs as Grace removed her bonnet.

Grace's voice softly intruded into his thoughts. "I understood when you told me you didn't want to see me anymore. I had every intention of respecting that, if only because of pride. But this baby was both of our doing."

Sarah spit out her pacifier and began to cry.

Grace lifted the little girl from the sofa cushion and smoothed her lips across her forehead. "I know. I know," she singsonged. "You're hungry."

She rose and handed the baby to Danny. "Can you take her while I get her bottle?"

Panic skittered through him and he backed away. He hadn't held a baby since Cory.

To his surprise Grace laughed. "Come on. She won't bite. She doesn't have teeth yet."

"I've…I'm…I just—"

Realizing he was behaving like an idiot, Danny stopped stuttering. He wasn't an idiot. And he would always think of Cory every time he looked at Sarah, but there was no way he'd admit that to Grace. She already knew enough about him and he didn't know half as much about her. Seeing Cory every time he looked at Sarah would be his cross to bear in private.

He reached out to take the baby, but this time Grace pulled her back.

"Sit," she said as if she'd thought his hesitancy was uncertainty about how to hold the baby. "I'll hand her to you."

Deciding not to argue her assumption, Danny lowered himself to the sofa and Grace placed the baby in his arms. "Just set her bottom on your lap, and support her back with your left hand."

He did that and the baby blinked up at him, her crying becoming sniffles as she lost herself to confusion about the stranger holding her.

Staring at her mutely, Danny identified. The first time he'd seen Cory was immediately after he'd slid into the doctor's hands. He'd been purple and wrinkled and when the doctor slapped his tiny behind he'd shrieked like a banshee. The little girl on Danny's lap was clean and now quiet. The total opposite of her half brother.

Grace pulled a bottle from her diaper bag. Dripping formula onto her wrist, she checked the bottle's temperature and said, "Can I take this to your kitchen and warm it?"

"Go back to the foyer, then turn right. The door at the end of the hall leads to the kitchen. My housekeeper is there. She'll help you."

Grace nodded and left.

Danny glanced down at the blue-eyed, rather bald baby. He took a breath. She blinked at him again, as if still confused.

"I'm your father."

She cocked her head to the right. The same way Cory used to. Especially when Danny would tell him anything about Carson Services, about responsibility, about carrying on the family name, as if the idea of doing anything other than paint was absurd.

Remembering Cory's reaction tightened Danny's chest again, but this time it wasn't from the memory of how, even as a small child, Cory had seemed to reject the idea of taking over the family business. Danny suddenly realized this little girl was now the one in line to run Carson Services. Grace might not know it, but Danny did.

Grace ran to the kitchen and didn't find a housekeeper, but she did locate a microwave into which she quickly shoved the bottle. She'd never seen a person more uncomfortable with a baby than Danny appeared to be, which was surprising considering he had a son, but she wasn't so insensitive that she didn't realize that meeting Sarah hadn't been easy for him.

She'd been preoccupied with Sarah's needs and hadn't factored Danny's shock into the equation. But having watched his facial expression shift and change, she realized that though he might not have believed Grace when she told him she was pregnant he seemed to be accepting that Sarah was his.

When the timer bell rang, she grabbed the bottle and

headed back to his den. Walking down the hall she heard Danny's soft voice.

"And that's why mutual funds are better for some people."

Grace stopped just outside the door.

"Of course, there are times when it's more logical to put the money of a conservative investor in bonds. Especially a nervous investor. Somebody who can't afford to take much risk. So you always have to question your investor enough that you can determine the level of risk his portfolio and personality can handle."

Standing by the wall beside the door, Grace twisted so she could remain hidden as she peered inside. Sarah gripped Danny's finger and stared up at him. Her blue eyes sharp and alert. Danny appeared comfortable, too, holding the baby loosely on his lap, and Grace realized that talking about something familiar was how Danny had overcome his apprehensions. Still, stocks? Poor Sarah!

"It's all about the individual. Some people are afraid of the stock market. Which is another reason mutual funds are so great. They spread the risk over a bunch of stocks. If one fails, another stock in the fund could sky-rocket and balance everything out."

If it had been under any other circumstances, Grace would have burst out laughing. Danny looked up and saw her standing there. He grimaced. "Sorry. I didn't know what else to talk about."

She shrugged. "I guess it doesn't really matter. All a baby really cares about is hearing your voice." She walked into the room and lifted Sarah from Danny's lap.

Nestling the baby into the crook of her arm, she added, "When in doubt, make up something. Maybe a story about a bunny or a bear. Just a short little anything."

Danny didn't reply, but rose and walked to the window. "You should be the one to sit."

Not about to remind him that there was plenty of space for both of them on the leather sofa, Grace took the place he had vacated. With two silent parents, the sound of Sarah greedily sucking filled the room.

"I almost wish you hadn't brought her to me."

Grace hadn't forgotten that he'd broken up with her before she told him she was pregnant. Still, that was his tough luck. He'd created a child and she wasn't letting him pretend he hadn't.

"She's your child."

"Yes. And I know you think there are all kinds of reasons that's great, but you're not going to like the way this has to play out."

"The way this has to play out?"

"I have to raise my daughter."

Not expecting that, Grace stared at his stiff back. But rather than be offended by his defiant stance, she remembered the feeling of his corded muscles beneath her fingertips. The firmness of his skin. Her own shivers of delight from having his hands on her.

Reaction flared inside her but she quickly shook it off. She wouldn't let herself fall victim to his charm again. Too much was at stake. She didn't know the official definition of "raise his daughter," but it sounded as if he intended to get more than a Saturday afternoon with Sarah every other weekend. There was no way Grace would let him take Sarah and ignore her. He hadn't ever wanted her. If he took her now, it would probably be out of a sense of duty to his family.

Still, if Grace argued, if she didn't handle this situation with kid gloves, her reply could sound like an accusation and accusations only caused arguments. She did not want to argue. She wanted all this settled as quickly and amicably as possible.

"It's good that you want to be involved—"

Danny suddenly turned from the window and caught her gaze, but Grace couldn't read the expression in his eyes and fell silent. She didn't know what he was thinking because she didn't know him. Not at all. She hadn't worked with him long enough to even know him as a boss. With Orlando he had been fun and funny. But when she'd told him about being pregnant he'd been hard, cold, unyielding. As far as she knew he had two personalities. A good guy and a bad guy and she had a sneaking suspicion few people saw the good guy.

"I want my daughter to live with me."

"Live with you?" *Grace* would be the one getting a visit every other Saturday afternoon? He had to be joking. Or insane.

"I've got money enough and clout enough that if I take you to court I'll end up with custody."

Grace gaped at him. It had been difficult to bring her child to meet him. As far as she was concerned, he could have stayed out of their lives forever. She was only here for Sarah's sake. Trying to grasp that he wanted to take Sarah away from her was staggering. Could his money really put Grace in a position where she'd be forced to hand over her innocent, defenseless baby daughter to a complete stranger? A man who didn't even want her?

She pulled in a breath and said, "That's ridiculous."

"Not really. When I retire, the option to take over Carson Services will be Sarah's. She'll need to be prepared. Only I can prepare her."

"But your son—"

"Never wanted the job. It falls to Sarah."

Overwhelmed, Grace shook her head. "This is too much in one day. I never even considered the possibility that you wanted to know I'd had a baby. Yet the day you find out, you're suddenly demanding custody."

"I don't have any other choice."

Grace sat in stunned silence. The whole hell of it was he didn't want Sarah. He wasn't asking for any reason except to fulfill a duty. Which was just wonderful. Grace would lose the baby she adored to a man who didn't want her, a man who intended to *train* her for a job. Not to love and nurture her, but to assure there was someone to take over the family business.

The injustice of it suffocated Grace at the same time that she understood it. Danny might not want Sarah, but he had a responsibility to her and to his family.

She wondered if he really needed to live with Sarah to teach her, then unexpectedly understood his side again. Preparing to take over a family fortune required more than a formal education. It required knowledge of family history and traditions. It required social graces. It required building social relationships.

All of which Grace didn't have. Sarah had to live with him at least part of the time.

Part of the time.

Suddenly inspired, Grace said, "You know what? I think I have a compromise."

"I don't compromise."

No kidding.

"Okay, then maybe what I have is a deal to propose."

His eyes narrowed ominously. "I don't need a deal, either."

"Well, listen anyway. The problem I see is that you don't know Sarah—"

"Living together will take care of that."

"Just listen. You don't know Sarah. I don't think you really want her. You're asking for custody out of a sense of duty and responsibility not to her but to your family, and, as bad as it is for my cause, I understand it. But as Sarah's mother I can't let you take my baby when you don't want her. So what I'm going to propose is that you come to live with Sarah and me for the next two weeks."

His face scrunched in confusion. "How exactly would that help?"

"If nothing else, in two weeks, I'll get to know you and you'll get to know her. Especially since I don't have a housekeeper or nanny. You and I will be the ones to care for her."

His shrewd brown eyes studied her, as if he were

trying to think of the catch. Since there was no catch, Grace continued.

"The deal is if you can spend two weeks with us, learning to care for her, and if at the end of that two weeks I feel comfortable with you having her, I won't contest *shared* custody. Week about. I get her one week. You have her the next. That way, as she gets older, you can schedule the functions you think she needs to be involved in, and I won't have to give her over to you permanently."

Danny shook his head. "Grace—"

"I won't give her over to you permanently. Not for any reason. Not any way. The best you'll get from me is week about and only if I believe you can handle her."

"You're not in a position to name terms," Danny said, shaking his head. "I can beat you in court."

"And then what?" Grace asked barely holding onto her temper. This time yesterday he didn't know he had a daughter. This time last year he didn't want to even hear Grace was pregnant. He couldn't expect her to hand over their child. She'd spend every cent of money she had before she'd recklessly hand over her baby to a man who didn't want Sarah, a man who probably would keep his distance and never love her.

"Say you do beat me in court. What are you going to do? Pass off your daughter's care to nannies, and let her be raised by a stranger when she could be spending that time with her mother? Is that your idea of grooming her? Showing her how to walk all over people?"

He ran his hand along the back of his neck.

She had him. They might not have spent much time

together, but she'd noticed that when he rubbed the
back of his neck, he was thinking.

"It sure as hell isn't my idea of how to teach her,"
Grace said quietly, calming down so he would, too. "If
nothing else, admit you need some time to adjust to
being her dad."

He sighed. "You want *two* weeks?"

"If you can't handle her for two weeks, how do you
expect to have her permanently?"

Danny said nothing and Grace retraced her argument, trying to figure out why two weeks made him
hesitate. A person who wanted full custody couldn't
object to a mere two-week stay with the same baby he
was trying to get custody of —

Unless he wasn't worried about two weeks with
Sarah as much as he was worried about two weeks with
Grace. The last time they'd spent three *days* together
they'd ended up in bed.

The air suddenly filled with electricity, so much that
Grace could almost see the crackles and sparks.
Memories—not of his accusations when she told him
she was pregnant, but his soft caresses that Sunday
night and Monday morning—flooded her mind and the
attraction she'd felt the weekend they'd spent together
returned full force.

But she didn't want it. She did not want to be attracted to this man. He'd come right out and said he
didn't want a relationship with her. Plus, he had clout
that she didn't have. Grace needed all her facilities to
fight for Sarah's interests. She couldn't risk that he'd

push her around in court the way he'd steamrolled her when she told him she was pregnant.

The reminder of how he'd kicked her out of his office without hearing her out was all she needed. Her chin came up. Her spine stiffened. She would never, ever trust him again. She would never give in to the attraction again.

"You're perfectly safe with me. Our time together was a mistake. I wouldn't even speak to you were it not for Sarah."

He remained silent so long that Grace sighed with disgust. He hadn't had a clue how painful his words had been to her. He hadn't cared that she could have misinterpreted everything he'd said and drawn the conclusion that he'd had his fun with her but she wasn't good enough to really love. He'd been so wrapped up in his own wants and needs that he never considered hers.

Or anyone's as far as Grace knew.

Another reason to stay the hell away from him.

"I mean it, Danny. I want nothing to do with you and will fight tooth and nail before I let you take Sarah even for weekends if only because you're a virtual stranger."

Obviously controlling his anger, he looked at the ceiling then back at her. "If I spend two weeks with you and the baby you won't contest shared custody," he said, repeating what he believed to be their arrangement.

"*If* by the end of those two weeks I believe you'll be good to Sarah."

Sarah had stopped sucking. Grace glanced down to see the baby had fallen asleep in her arms. "If you wish, we can have our lawyers draw up papers."

"Oh, I *will* have my lawyer write an agreement."

"Great. Once we get it signed we can start."

"You'll have it tonight. Do you have an e-mail address?"

"Yes."

"Watch your computer. You'll have the agreement before you go to bed. You can e-mail me directions to your house and I'll be there tomorrow."

CHAPTER FIVE

WHEN GRACE received Danny's e-mail with their agreement as an attachment, she realized that no matter how simple and straightforward, she couldn't sign any legal document without the advice of counsel. She replied saying she wanted her own lawyer to review the agreement before she signed it, expecting him to be angry at the delay. Instead he was surprisingly accommodating of her request.

She spoke with a lawyer Monday morning, who gave her the go-ahead to sign, and e-mailed Danny that she had executed the agreement and he could sign it that evening when he arrived at her house.

Busy at work, she didn't give Danny or the agreement another thought until she walked into the foyer of her little bungalow and saw something she hadn't considered.

The downstairs of her house had an open floor plan. Pale orange ceramic tile ran from the foyer to the back door. An oatmeal-colored Berber area rug sat beneath the burnt-orange tweed sofa and the matching love seat, delineating that space. Similarly the tan, brown and black print rug beneath the oak table and chairs marked off the dining area. A black-and-tan granite-topped breakfast bar separated the living room from the kitchen, but because there were no cabinets above it, people in the kitchen were clearly visible from any point downstairs.

Grace wasn't afraid that Danny wouldn't like her home. She didn't give a damn if he liked it or not. What troubled her was that with the exception of the two bedrooms, both upstairs, there was nowhere to hide. Anytime they were downstairs they would technically be together.

"Well, Sarah," she said, sliding the baby out of her carrier seat and giving her a quick kiss on the cheek. In her yellow one-piece outfit, Sarah looked like a ray of sunshine. "I guess it's too late to worry about that now."

As the words came out of her mouth, the doorbell rang, and Grace winced. If that was Danny, it really was too late to worry about the close quarters of her house now.

Angling the baby on her hip, Grace walked to the door and opened it. Danny stood on her small porch, holding a garment bag, with a duffel bag sitting beside his feet. Dressed in jeans and a loose-fitting sport shirt, he looked comfortable and relaxed, reminding her of their time together at his beach house.

A sudden avalanche of emotion overtook her. She had really fallen hard for him that weekend. Not just because he was sexy, though he was. He had an air of power and strength that—combined with his shiny black hair, piercing black eyes and fabulous body—

made him one of the sexiest men Grace had ever met. Staring into his eyes, she remembered the way he made love to her. She remembered their pillow talk and their one phone conversation. He had definitely felt something for her that weekend, too, but in the one short week he was out of town he'd lost it. He hadn't believed her when she told him she was pregnant. He'd kicked her out of his office. And now they were here. Fighting over custody of a baby he hadn't wanted.

"This house doesn't look big enough for two people, let alone three."

"It's got more space than you think," Grace said, opening the door a little wider so he could enter, as she reminded herself she had to do this because she couldn't beat him in court. "It looks like a ranch, but it isn't. There are two bedrooms upstairs."

"Yeah, they're probably no bigger than closets."

Grace told herself she could do this. She'd dealt with grouchy Danny every time she'd spoken to him—except for that one weekend. The person she'd met that weekend was more likely the exception and grouchy Danny was the rule. She wasn't about to let their two weeks begin with her apologizing.

Ignoring his closet comment, she said, "Let's take your bags upstairs and get them out of the way."

Grace turned and began walking up the steps, and, following after her, Danny got a flashback of following her up the steps of his beach house. It intensified when he glanced down at the steps to avoid looking at her shapely legs. The memory was so clear it made him dizzy, as if he were stepping back in time.

But he wasn't. They were here and now, fifteen months later. She'd had his child. She might have done it without him, but ultimately she'd brought the baby to him. And why not? As far as Grace knew little Sarah could inherit a fortune—even before Danny was dead if she became the CEO of Carson Services when Danny retired.

He didn't want even a portion of the family fortune to go to an opportunist, but his threat of taking Grace to court to get full custody had been empty. An attempt to pressure her into giving him their daughter. Then Grace had come up with a compromise and to Danny's surprise it really did suit him. He could train Sarah without paying off her mother.

Plus, he no longer had the worry that a custody battle gave her reason to dig into his past.

All he had to do was spend two weeks with Grace, a woman who he believed tricked him.

At the top of the steps, Grace turned to the right, opened a door, and stepped back so he could enter the room. To his surprise, Grace was correct, the bedroom was more spacious than he'd thought from the outward appearance of the house. Even with a double bed in the center of the room, a knotty pine armoire and dresser, and a small desk in the corner, there was plenty of space to walk.

He hesitantly said, "This is nice."

"We have to share the bathroom."

He faced her. She'd taken a few steps into the room, as if wanting to be available to answer questions, but not exactly thrilled to be in the same room with him. Especially not a bedroom.

Her soft voice triggered another batch of beach house memories. Grace telling him to promote someone else. Grace looking like an angel in front of the upstairs widows. Grace ready to accept his kiss…

He shoved the memories out of his brain, reminding himself that woman probably didn't exist. "I'll keep my things in a shaving kit. I won't take up any room."

She turned away from him with a shrug. Walking to the door, she said, "It doesn't matter one way or the other to me."

He couldn't tell if she intended to insult him or prove to him that his being there had no meaning to her beyond their reaching an accord about custody, but the indifference he heard in her voice was just fine with him. He didn't want to be involved with her any more than she wanted to be involved with him.

Which should make for a fabulous two weeks.

He tossed his duffel bag on the bed and walked the garment bag to the closet before going downstairs. At the bottom of the steps, he realized that the entire first floor of the house was open. He could see Grace puttering in the compact kitchen and Sarah swinging contentedly in the baby swing sitting in the space between the dining area and living room.

Walking to the kitchen, he said, "Anything I can help you with?"

"You're here for Sarah. So why don't you amuse her, while I make dinner?"

"Okay." Her cool tone of voice didn't affect him because she was correct. He was here for Sarah. Not for Grace. Not to make small talk or plans or, God forbid, even to become friendly.

He glanced at the cooing baby. A trip to the department store that morning to arrange for baby furniture to be delivered to his house had shown him just how behind the times he had become in the nine years that had passed since Cory was a baby. Playpens were now play yards. Car seats had become downright challenging. He didn't have to be a genius to know that if the equipment had changed, so had the rules. He wouldn't do anything with Sarah without asking.

"Should I take her out of the seat?"

Pulling a salad bowl from a cabinet, Grace said, "Not when she's happy. Just sit on the floor in front of her and chat."

Chat. With a baby. He'd tried that the day Grace brought Sarah to his house and hadn't known what to say. Obviously he had to think of something to talk about other than investing. But he wasn't sitting on the floor. After a quick look around, he grabbed one of the oak ladder-back chairs from the table in the dining room section and set it in front of the swing.

"Hey, Sarah."

She pulled the blue plastic teething ring from her mouth and cooed at him. He smiled and settled more comfortably on the chair as he studied her, trying to think of something to say. Nothing came. She gurgled contently as she waved her arms, sending the scent of baby powder through the air to his nose. That brought a burst of memories of Cory.

He'd been so proud of that kid. So smitten. So enamored with the fun of having a baby that he'd thought his life was perfect. Then Cory had shown artistic ability and Lydia wanted to send him to special school. Danny had thought she was jumping the gun, making a decision that didn't need to be made until Cory was older.

Taking a breath, Danny forced himself back to the present. He had to stop thinking of Cory. He had to focus on Sarah. He had to create an amicable relationship so their time together would be happy and not a horrible strain.

Then he noticed that the one-piece yellow thing she wore made her hair appear reddish brown. "I think somebody's going to be a redhead."

The baby gooed. Danny smiled. Curious, he turned toward the kitchen. "My parents are French and English. So I don't think the red hair comes from my side of the family. How about yours?"

Grace grudgingly said, "Both of my parents are Scottish."

"Well, that explains it."

Danny's comment fell on total silence. Though he was here for Sarah, he and Grace had two long weeks to spend together. He might not want to be her friend, but he didn't want to be miserable, either. Studying Grace as she ripped lettuce and tossed it into a bowl, he swore he could see waves of anger emanate from her.

It might have been her idea to share custody, but she clearly didn't want to spend two weeks with him any more than he wanted to spend two weeks with her. He'd forced her hand with the threat of taking her baby away.

Taking her baby away.

He hadn't really looked at what he was doing from her perspective and suddenly realized how selfish he must seem to her.

"Had I gone for full custody, I wouldn't have shut you out of her life completely."

"No, but you would have demanded that she live with you and I'd be the one with visitation."

She walked over to him and displayed a plate with two steaks. "I'm going to the back deck to the grill." She waited a heartbeat, then said, "You're not afraid to be alone with her, are you?"

As if any man would ever admit to being afraid of anything. "No. But I'm guessing you're a better choice to stay inside with her, which means I should grill the steaks."

"Great." She handed him the plate. "I'll finish the salad."

She pivoted and returned to the kitchen without waiting for his reply. Danny rose from his seat and walked out to the deck. He agreed with her nonconversation policy. There was no point in talking. She didn't like him. And, well, frankly, he didn't like her.

He dropped the plate of steaks on a small table and set the temperature on the grill. Still, whether he agreed with her or not, not talking guaranteed that the next two weeks would be two of the longest of his life. Torture really. Maybe payback for his not believing her? He slapped the steaks on the grill rack.

That was probably it. Payback. But what Grace didn't realize was that the way she treated him was also proof that she wasn't the sweet innocent she'd pretended to be.

He almost laughed. What a mess. All because he couldn't keep his hands off a woman. He'd never make *that* mistake again.

He closed the lid and looked out over the expanse of backyard. Grace didn't have a huge space but what she had was well tended. Her bungalow was neat and clean, newly remodeled. Her yard was well kept. He hoped that was an indicator that Grace would take good care of Sarah during the weeks she had her.

He heard a giggle from inside the house. Turning, he saw he hadn't shut the French doors. He ambled over and was just about to push them closed when he heard Grace talking. "So, somebody needs to go upstairs and get a fresh diaper."

She lifted the baby from the swing and rubbed noses with her. "I swear, Sarah, there's got to be a better system."

The baby laughed. Danny sort of chuckled himself. A person would think that after all the generations of babies, somebody, somewhere would have thought of a better system than diapers.

"Let's take care of that. Then we'll feed you something yummy for dinner."

The baby giggled and cooed and Danny felt a quick

sting of conscience for worrying about Sarah when she was in Grace's care. Grace obviously loved the baby.

He took a quick breath. She might love the baby but there was a lot more to consider in child rearing than just love. Grace was on trial these next two weeks every bit as much as he was. He wouldn't be convinced she was a good mom, just because she was sweet. She wasn't sweet. As far as he knew she was a conniver. She could have seen the French doors were open and put on a show with the baby for him to see.

He closed the doors and checked the steaks. They were progressing nicely. He sat on one of the deck chairs. The thick red, yellow and tan striped padding felt good to his tired back and he let his eyelids droop. He didn't raise them again until he heard the French doors open.

"How's it going?" Grace asked quietly. Sarah sat on her forearm, once again chewing the blue teething ring.

Danny sat up. "Fine. I was just about to peek at the steaks." He poked and prodded the steaks, closed the lid and chucked Sarah under the chin. "You're just about the cutest kid in the world, aren't you?"

Sarah giggled and cooed and Grace regretted her decision to bring the baby with her when she checked on him. When she least expected it, he would say or do something that would remind her that she'd genuinely believed he was a nice, normal guy the weekend they'd spent at the beach house. Volunteering to help her in the kitchen when he first came downstairs hadn't been expected. His wanting to know Sarah's heritage had struck her as adorable. And now he looked perfectly natural, perfectly comfortable on her back deck.

But he was also here to convince Grace that he would be able to care for Sarah. Technically he was on good behavior. She refused to get sucked in again as she had at the beach house.

She turned to go back into the house, but he said, "Grace?" And every nerve ending she had went on red alert. He had a sexy quality to his voice that was magnified when he spoke softly. Of course, that took her back to their pillow talk the night they had slept together and that made her all quivery inside.

Scowling because she didn't want to like him and did want to let him know that if he thought he could charm her he was wrong, she faced him. "Yes?"

"You never told me how you wanted your steak."

Feeling embarrassment heat her cheeks, she quickly turned to the door again. "Medium is fine."

With that she walked into the house. She put Sarah in her high chair and rummaged through the cupboards for a jar of baby food, which she heated. By the time she was done feeding Sarah, had her face cleaned and the rubber teething ring back in her chubby hands, Danny brought in the steaks.

"Salad is on the counter," she said, as she laid plates and silverware on the table. "Could you bring that in, too?" Her new strategy was to put him to work before he could volunteer. This way, he wouldn't seem nice, he would only be following orders.

He did as she asked and they sat down at the table,

across from each other, just as they had been sitting that Sunday night at his beach house. She'd dressed up, hoping he would notice her. But tonight, on the trip upstairs to change Sarah's diaper, she'd put on her worst jeans, her ugliest T-shirt. What a difference fifteen months made.

"Your house is nice."

"Thank you."

Silence reigned for another minute, before Danny said, "So, did you buy it remodeled like this?"

She bit back a sigh, loath to tell him anything about herself. More than that, though, they'd discussed this that night at the beach house. He'd forgotten. So much for thinking she'd made any kind of impression on him

"It was a wreck when I bought it."

"Oh, so you did the remodeling—I mean with a contractor, right?"

"No. My cousin and I remodeled it." And she'd told him that, too.

He smiled. "Really?"

Grace rose from her seat. "You know what? I'm really not all that hungry and it's time for me to get Sarah bathed and ready for bed." She smiled stiffly. "If you'll excuse me."

Alone at the table Danny quietly finished his steak. If Grace was going to continually take Sarah and leave the room, maybe he shouldn't cancel tomorrow's dinner engagement? He drew in a breath, then expelled it quickly. He couldn't dodge or fudge this commitment. He wanted at least shared custody of his daughter, and Grace had handed him the way to get it without a custody battle that would result in her investigating his past and probably result in him losing all but scant visitation rights. So he couldn't leave. He had to be here every minute he could for the next two weeks.

The problem was he and Grace also had to be together. He'd thought they could be at least cordial, but this was what he got for his positive attitude. The silent treatment. Well, she could save herself the trouble if she intended to insult him. His ex-wife had been the ultimate professional when it came to the silent treatment. Grace would have to go a long way to match that.

But when he'd not only finished eating his dinner and stacking the dishes in the dishwasher and Grace still hadn't come downstairs, he wondered if maybe she couldn't give Lydia a tip or two in the silent treatment department. Angry, because the whole point of his being here was to spend time with his daughter, Danny stormed up the steps. He stopped outside Grace's bedroom door because it was ajar and what he saw compelled him to rethink everything.

Though Grace's bedroom was pretty, decorated in warm colors like reds, yellows and taupe, a big white crib, white changing table and two white dressers took up most of the space. Still, there was enough adult furniture pushed into the room's corners that Danny could almost envision how she probably had her room before the baby was born. When she met him, she had had a pretty house, a sanctuary bedroom and a budding career. When she got pregnant, she'd lost her job. When she actually had Sarah, most of her pretty house had become a nursery.

"Oh, now, you can't be sleepy yet."

Grace's soft voice drifted out into the hallway.

"You still need to spend some time with your daddy."

Danny swallowed when he heard himself referred to again as a daddy. He was only getting used to that.

"I know you're tired, but just stay awake long enough to say good-night."

She lifted Sarah from the changing table and brushed her cheek across the baby's little cheek. Mesmerized, Danny watched. He'd forgotten how stirring it was to watch a mother with her baby.

"Come on," Grace said, turning to the door. Danny jumped back, out of her line of vision.

Thinking fast, he leaped into his room and quickly closed the door. He counted to fifty, hoping that gave her enough time to get downstairs, then opened the door a crack and peered out into the hall. When he found it empty, he walked downstairs, too. Grace sat on the sofa, Sarah on her lap.

"Can I hold her before she goes to bed?"

"Sure."

She made a move to rise, but Danny stopped her. "I'll take her from your lap."

Grace nodded and Danny reached down to get Sarah. Lifting her, he let his eyes wander over to Grace and their gazes caught. Except now he knew why he was no longer dealing with the sweet, innocent woman he'd slept with at the beach house. Her life had changed so much that even if she hadn't tricked him, she couldn't be the same woman. She'd gotten pregnant to a stranger. He'd rejected her. She'd lost her job and was too sick to get another. She'd had her baby alone. Any of those would have toughened her. Made her cynical. Maybe even made her angry.

No. She was no longer the woman he knew from the beach house.

CHAPTER SIX

DANNY awakened to the sounds of the shower. Grace was up before him and already started on her day. He waited until the shower stopped, then listened for the sounds of the bathroom door opening before he got out of bed, slipped on a robe and grabbed his shaving kit.

In the hall he heard the melodious sounds of Grace's voice as she spoke to Sarah and laughed with her. He stopped. Her soft laughter took him back to their weekend at the beach house. He shook his head and walked into the bathroom. He had to stop remembering. As he'd realized last night, that Grace no longer existed. Plus, they had a child. Sarah's future was in their hands. He didn't take that responsibility lightly anymore.

After a quick shower, Danny dressed in a navy suit, ready for a long day of business meetings. He jogged down the stairs and was immediately enfolded in the scent of breakfast.

Walking to the small dining area, he said, "Good morning."

Grace breezed away from the table and strode into the kitchen. "Good morning."

Sarah grinned up at him toothlessly. He smiled down at her. "And how are you today?"

Sarah giggled. Danny took a seat at the table. Grace set a dish containing an omelet, two slices of toast and some applesauce in front of him. Suddenly her coolness made sense. He'd forced her to have their baby alone, yet she'd nonetheless suggested shared custody, allowing him into her home to give him the opportunity to prove himself. Even if the Grace who'd seduced him that night no longer existed, the woman who'd taken her place had her sense of generosity. Even to her detriment. She wouldn't cheat him out of time with her daughter. Or use Sarah as a weapon. She was fair and it cost her.

Grace set her dish at the place opposite Danny and sat down. She immediately grabbed her napkin, opened it on her lap and picked up her fork.

Sarah shrieked.

Grace shook her head. "You already ate."

Sarah pounded her teething ring on the high chair tray.

"A tantrum will do you no good," Grace said to Sarah, but Danny was painfully aware that she didn't speak to him. She didn't even look at him.

His chest tightened. She'd been such a fun, bubbly, lively person. Now she was cautious and withdrawn. And he had done this to her.

Grace all but gobbled her breakfast. She noticed that Danny had become quiet as she drank a cup of coffee, but she didn't have time to care. She wasn't entirely sure she would care even if she had time. He'd basically accused her of lying. He clearly believed she'd tricked him. And if both of those weren't enough, he intended to take her child every other week. She didn't want to be his friend. He was only in her house because she couldn't risk that he'd get full custody, and she also wouldn't risk her child's happiness with a grouch. So he was here to prove himself. She didn't have to entertain him.

He was lucky she'd made him breakfast. That was why she was late, and rushing, so if he expected a little morning chitchat, that was his problem.

Having eaten enough food to sustain herself until lunch, Grace rose from her seat and took her dish to the kitchen. To her surprise Danny was right behind her when she turned from the dishwasher. Her heart thudded in her chest, half from surprise, half from being so close to him. He radiated warmth or energy, or something, that made being near him intoxicating. And trouble. His being irresistible was what had caused her to let her guard down in the first place.

He handed her his plate, though most of his food hadn't been eaten.

She took a quick gulp of air to try to rid herself of the breathless feeling and looked up at him. His eyes mirrored an emotion she couldn't quite read, except that he was unsure of what he was supposed to be doing.

"I'm rushing because I'm late. You can stay and finish. Just rinse your plate when you're through and put it in the dishwasher."

"I've had enough," Danny said and as Grace turned away from the dishwasher she saw him glance around her small kitchen. "Since I'm the boss I don't have to worry about being late, so if you'd like I could clean up in here."

In his neat navy blue suit, white shirt and blue print tie, he might look like the guy who ran Carson Services, but he behaved like the Danny Grace had met at the beach house, and that wasn't right. Being attracted to him wasn't right. Even being friendly wasn't right, if only because they were on opposite ends of a custody battle.

"No, thank you," she coolly replied. "It will take me only a minute or two to wipe the skillet and stove. You go on ahead. I'm fine."

"Grace," he said with a chuckle. "It's not a big deal."

"Really?" Try as she might, she couldn't keep the sarcasm out of her voice. "I'm surprised a rich guy like you even knows how to clean a skillet."

He laughed. The sound danced along her nerve endings, reminding her again of how he'd been the night they'd made love. She fought the happy memories by recalling the scene in his office. The one where he'd called her pregnancy a scheme.

"I couldn't exactly take a maid to university. My parents might have gotten me an apartment, but unless I wanted to live in squalor I had to do at least a little straightening up."

Grace felt herself softening to him and squeezed her eyes shut. It was much easier dealing with mean Danny. No expectations were better than unmet expectations.

Opening her eyes, she faced him. "Look, I don't want you to be nice to me. I don't need you to be nice."

"Helping clean up isn't nice. It's common courtesy."

"Well, save it. You're here to prove yourself with Sarah. And you did fine this morning just by saying good morning. You noticed her. You didn't ignore her. You're on the right track."

"I'm not going to let you wait on me while I'm here."

Grace removed her apron and set it on the counter. She didn't have time or the inclination to argue. She also couldn't give a damn what he did. That only tripped memories of a man she was absolutely positive didn't exist. She couldn't get into arguments that tempted her to believe otherwise.

"Fine. Dishcloths are in the bottom drawer."

She walked out of the kitchen and over to the high chair, where she lifted Sarah into her arms before she headed for the stairway.

But from the corner of her eye she could see Danny standing in the kitchen, plate in hand, watching her. He looked totally out of place and equally confused and Grace again fought against emotions she couldn't afford to have.

How could he make her feel like the one in the wrong when he had done such terrible things to her?

After a horrifically long day, Danny finally had ten minutes alone in his office. Though he tried to make a few phone calls before leaving he couldn't. Being with Grace at her house and yet not really being with Grace was driving him crazy. He could not live with someone for two whole weeks who barely spoke to him. Not that he wanted lively conversation, but he couldn't handle being ignored, either. Plus, if they didn't at least discuss Sarah and her care, especially her likes and dislikes, how were these two weeks supposed to prove to Grace that she could relax when Sarah was with him?

Knowing it wouldn't help matters if he were late for dinner that night, Danny stuffed a few files into a briefcase and left early. At her front door, he hesitated. He felt so ill at ease just walking inside that he should ring the bell. But he was living here. The next two weeks this was his home. And maybe walking in would jar Grace into realizing she had to deal with him.

He opened the door and saw Grace on the floor with Sarah, playing peekaboo.

"Hey."

Sarah squealed her delight at seeing him. Grace glanced over. "Hey."

He didn't smell anything cooking and finally, finally saw a golden opportunity. "I was thinking this afternoon that things might go easier if we just went out to dinner." He paused, but she didn't say anything. "On me, of course."

She sighed, lifted Sarah into her arms and rose from the floor. "It's not practical to go out to a restaurant with a baby every night." She walked into the kitchen, Sarah on her hip.

With Grace's reply ringing in his head, Danny looked around again. Two bears sat on the sofa. A baby swing was angled in such a way that the baby inside could be seen from the kitchen, dining room or living room. A high chair sat by the dining table. Blocks were stacked on the buffet. The room smelled of baby powder.

He remembered this now. For the first few years of a baby's life everything revolved around the baby. That had been a difficult enough adjustment for a married couple. But it had to be all-consuming for a single mom. Not just because she didn't have assistance with Sarah, but because it affected everything.

He walked into the kitchen. "Can I help with dinner?"

She pulled a package of hamburger from the refrigerator. "Do you want to grill the hamburgers?"

Eager to do his share, Danny said, "Sure."

He reached for the hamburger, but Grace pointed at his jacket and tie. "You can't cook in that."

He grimaced. "Right."

After changing into jeans and a T-shirt, he took the hamburger from the refrigerator and headed for the back deck and the grill. Grace was nowhere around, but he assumed she and the baby were in her room. Maybe because the baby needed a diaper change.

Gazing out over the short backyard Danny studied the houses near Grace's. Realizing none was as well kept as hers, he remembered her telling him about remodeling her home the night they spent at his beach house. That was why her comments about wanting to be rich hadn't struck him oddly that night. He knew she was a hard worker. But three weeks later when she told him she was pregnant, he'd forgotten how eager she was to earn her way in life. He only remembered that she'd wanted to be rich and he'd assumed the worst.

He'd seduced her, left her for a week, said he didn't want to see her again when he returned, refused to believe her when she told him she was pregnant and then threatened to file for full custody of their baby. While he'd acted on inaccurate "interpretations" of things she'd done, he'd given her five very real reasons to hate him.

It was no wonder she was cool to him. He'd not only misjudged her. He'd behaved like a horrible person.

The sound of a car pulling into her driveway brought him out of his thoughts. He strode to the far end of the deck and glanced around the side of the house just in time to see Grace pulling Sarah from the car seat. With a grocery bag hooked over her arm and Sarah perched on the other, she walked, head down, into the house.

Danny's heart squeezed in his chest. Would he ever stop hurting people?

Grace stepped into her house at the same time that Danny walked in from the deck. "Where did you go?"

"I needed milk and hamburger buns." Carrying Sarah, she went to the kitchen to deposit her purchases.

Danny grabbed the gallon jug that dangled from her hand and put it in the refrigerator. "I could have gone to the store."

"Well, I did."

He sighed. "Grace, I want to help but I can't do things that I don't know need done."

"I didn't ask you to do anything."

But even as the words were coming out of her mouth, Grace regretted them. She slid Sarah into the high chair and turned to face Danny. He might be a difficult person, but she wasn't. And she refused to let him turn her into one.

"Here's the deal. I'm accustomed to being on my own. There's no point in breaking that habit because you'll only be here for another twelve days. So don't worry about it. Okay?"

He nodded, but he kept looking at her oddly as if she'd just discovered the secret to life. He continued to steal peeks at her all through dinner, making her nervous enough that she chattered to Sarah as they ate their hamburgers and salads, if only to bring some sound into the room.

When she could legitimately slip away to feed Sarah a bottle and put her to bed, she felt as if she were escaping a prison. She extended her alone time with a long, soothing shower, but rather than slip into her usual nightgown and robe she put on sweatpants and a T-shirt and shuffled downstairs to watch a little TV to unwind before trying to sleep.

She had just turned off all the lights and settled on the sofa with a cup of cocoa, when Danny came down the steps.

Seeing her curled up on the couch, he paused. "Sorry."

He pivoted to go back upstairs and Grace said, "Wait." She didn't want to be his friend. She didn't want to like him. She most certainly didn't want to get romantically involved with him. But she couldn't take the silence anymore and she suspected he couldn't, either.

"You don't have to leave. For the next two weeks this is your home. We might as well get accustomed to each other."

At first he hesitated, but then he slowly made his way down the steps and into the sitting area.

"Would you like some cocoa?"

As he lowered himself to the love seat, he chuckled softly. "I haven't had cocoa in—"

He stopped. Grace suspected that the last time he'd had cocoa it had been with his son, but she was also tired of tiptoeing around his life. He'd told her very little about himself the night they had dinner at the beach house and she'd not pushed him. But if she had to accept him into her house and Sarah's life, then he had to accept her into his. They couldn't pretend his other life didn't exist.

"In?" Grace prompted, forcing him to talk about his son.

"In years." He took a breath and caught her gaze. "Since I had cocoa with my son."

The words hung in the room. Danny kept his gaze locked with Grace's, as if daring her to go further. But she had no intention of delving into every corner of his world. She only wanted them to begin having normal conversations, so the tension between them would ease.

"See. We can talk about both of your children." She rose from the sofa. "Let me make you a cup of cocoa."

Without waiting for his reply, she walked into the
kitchen, pulled a small pot from the cupboard by the
stove and set it on a burner. Danny lowered himself to
one of the stools by the counter, reminding Grace of
how she had sat at the beach house bar while he poured
himself a glass of Scotch.

Danny suddenly bounced from the seat, as if he'd
had the memory, too, and didn't want it. He strode into
the kitchen and reached for the refrigerator door handle.
"I'll help you."

Removing the cocoa from a cupboard, Grace turned
so quickly that she and Danny nearly ran into each other
in the compact kitchen.

He caught her elbows to steady her, and tingles of
awareness skipped along her skin. This close she could
feel the heat of his body. Memories of making love, of
how different he had been that night and how happy she
had been, flipped through her brain. The sizzle between
them was so intense she suddenly wondered what might
have happened if they hadn't made love that night.
Would the nice guy she'd met at the beach house have
pursued her? Would he have remained nice? Would
they have discovered differences and gone their separate
ways or lived happily ever after?

Pulling her arms away, she turned toward the stove.
What might have been wasn't an issue. If she thought
about what might have been for too long she might get
starry-eyed again and that would be insane. The guy had
hurt her and now he wanted her child. She wouldn't be
reckless with him again.

"Hand me the milk."

He did.

"Thanks." Exaggerating the task of pouring it into the pan so she didn't have to look at him, she said, "How are things at Carson Services?"

He walked back to the counter, but didn't sit. Instead he leaned against it. "Fine."

"How's Orlando?"

Danny laughed. "Great. He's a dream client. Because he does his homework, we're always on the same page when I suggest he move his money."

"That's so good to hear. I liked him."

"He's asked about you."

Dumping three scoops of cocoa on top of the milk, she grimaced. "What did you tell him?"

Danny shifted uncomfortably. "That you'd moved on."

She heard the stirring of guilt in his voice. Though part of her found it fitting, she couldn't pretend she was innocent. She'd recognized from the beginning that losing her job was one of the potential consequences of a failed relationship between them. So she wouldn't pretend. She would discuss this like an adult.

She faced him. "So you told him the truth."

"Excuse me?"

"What you told him was the truth. I *had* moved on."

He barked a laugh. "Yeah."

Grace walked over to him and stood in front of him, holding his gaze. "We won't survive twelve more days of living together if we don't admit here and now that we both made mistakes that weekend. We don't need to dissect our sleeping together and place blame. But we do need to admit that we *both* made mistakes."

"Okay."

"It is okay because we both moved on."

"Bet you wish you had stayed moved on."

She might be willing to agree to be polite and even friendly, but she didn't intend to discuss nebulous things like regrets. So she fell back on humor to get her out of the conversation. Batting her hand in dismissal, she said, "Nah. What fun is having a nice, quiet life with no one pestering you for custody of your child?"

He laughed again. She turned to leave, but he caught her fingers and stopped her. Her gaze swung back to his.

"You're one of only a few people who make me laugh."

Memory thrummed through her. Her being able to make him laugh had been their first connection. But the touch of his fingers reminded her that they'd taken that connection so much further that night. She remembered the way his hands had skimmed her body, remembered how he'd held her, remembered the intensity of the fire of passion between them.

But in the end, passion had failed them. The only thing they had between them now was Sarah. And everything they did had to be for Sarah.

Grace cleared her throat and stepped back. "We'll work on getting you to laugh more often for Sarah." She pulled her hand away from his, walked to the stove and poured Danny's cocoa into a mug. "So what do you like to watch?"

"Watch?"

"On TV."

He took the mug she handed to him. "Actually I don't watch TV."

"Then you're in for a treat because you get to watch everything I like."

That made him laugh again, and Grace's heart lightened before she could stop it, just as it had their weekend together. But she reminded herself that things at the beach house had not turned out well. And she didn't intend to make the same mistake twice. He needed to be comfortable and relaxed for Sarah. She and Danny also needed to be reasonably decent to each other to share custody. But that was all the further she could let things between them go.

They spent two hours watching crime dramas on television. Danny was oddly amused by them. The conversation remained neutral, quiet, until at the end of the second show the eleven o'clock news was announced and Grace said she was going to bed.

"Ripped from the headline is right," he said, when Grace hit the off button on the remote and rose from the sofa. "That program couldn't have been more specific unless they'd named names."

"That's the show's gimmick. The writers take actual situations and fictionalize them. It's a way to give curious, gossip-hungry viewers a chance to see what might have happened, and how it would play out in court."

Danny said, "Right," then followed her up the stairs. In the little hallway between their closed bedroom doors, Danny put his hand on his doorknob, but he couldn't quite open the door. It didn't seem right to leave her just yet. And that spurred another beach house memory. He hadn't wanted to leave her after he'd given her her bonus. He'd tried to ignore the feeling, but Grace had followed him down to the bar in his great room.

That made him smile. The hall in which they stood was far from great. It was a little square. Only a bit wider than the bar that had separated them at the beach house. He'd closed that gap by leaning forward and kissing her, and he'd experienced one of the most wonderful nights of his life.

And he'd ruined even the pleasant memories he could hold onto and enjoy by not believing her. Not appreciating her.

"Thanks for the cocoa."

She faced him with a smile. "You're welcome."

He took a step away from his door and toward hers. He might not have appreciated her the weekend at the beach house, but tonight he was beginning to understand that she probably had been the woman he'd believed her to be when he seduced her. Everything that had happened between them was his fault. Especially their misunderstandings.

He caught her gaze. "I'm glad you moved on."

He took another step toward her, catching her hand and lifting it, studying the smooth skin, her delicate fingers. He recalled her fingers skimming his back, tunneling through his hair, driving him crazy with desire, and felt it all again, as if it were yesterday.

"I'm a lot stronger than I look."

Her words came out as a breathy whisper. The same force of attraction that swam through his veins seemed to be affecting her. In the quiet house, the only sound Danny heard was the pounding of his heart. The only thought in his mind was that he should kiss her.

Slowly, holding her gaze, watching for reaction, he lowered his head. Closing his eyes, he touched his lips to hers. They were smooth and sweet, just as he remembered. Warmth and familiarity collided with sexual hunger that would have happily overruled common sense. Their chemistry caused him to forget everything except how much he wanted her. How happy she made him. How natural it was to hold her.

But just when he would have deepened the kiss, she stepped away.

"This is what got us into trouble the last time." She caught his gaze. "Good night, Danny."

And before he could form the words to stop her, she was behind her closed bedroom door.

CHAPTER SEVEN

DANNY awoke feeling oddly refreshed. He opened his eyes, saw the sunny yellow bedroom around him and was disoriented until he remembered he was living with Grace.

Grace.

He'd kissed her, but she'd reminded him that was what had gotten them into trouble the last time. And he didn't think she was talking about creating Sarah. Sarah wasn't trouble. Sarah was a joy. Their "trouble" was that they had slept together when they didn't know each other, which was why he hadn't trusted her enough to continue the relationship, and why he hadn't believed Grace when she told him she was pregnant. He'd thought she was lying to him. Tricking him. Because he didn't know her well enough to realize Grace would never do something like that.

He now knew his accusations were the product of an overly suspicious mind, but he also had to admit to himself that he hadn't changed much from the man who had dismissed her as a liar. Yes, he'd gotten past the tragedies of his life and to the outside world he appeared normal. And he really could be normal at work, normal with friends, normal with a woman only looking for an evening of entertainment. But his divorce had soured him on commitment. He wasn't marriage material. He wasn't even a good date for anyone who wanted anything other than a fun night out or no-strings-attached sex. Forget about being the right guy for someone as wonderful as Grace. She deserved better. Even he knew it.

She needed a husband. A mate. Someone to share her life. He was not that guy.

He rolled out of bed and tugged on his robe. But once the slash belt was secured, he stopped again. He'd nearly forgotten he was sharing a bathroom.

Sharing a bathroom.

Watching TV.

And happy.

How long had it been since he could say he was happy? Years. He'd accustomed himself to settling for surface emotions, convinced that if he loved anything, life would yank it away. But though he might not believe he could make a commitment to a woman, living with Grace made him consider that he could love Sarah and he could be a real dad. Especially since Grace was kind enough, honest enough, fair enough that she was willing to share custody. Not as adversaries, but as two friends. Both having the best interests of their little girl at heart. And without a hearing that would air his less-than-perfect past.

He grabbed his shaving kit, opened his bedroom door and glanced down the short hall. The bathroom door was open and Grace wasn't anywhere to be seen. Good. He didn't want to bump into Grace dressed only in a robe. As she'd reminded him last night, kissing— or more appropriately runaway emotions and hor- mones—had gotten them into trouble the last time. He wasn't going to make the same mistake twice. Getting romantically involved had cost them. He'd lost a good employee and someone who probably would have turned into a friend.

And he'd hurt her.

He wouldn't let himself forget that. He also wouldn't let himself hurt her again. He could say that with absolute certainty because he wouldn't get involved with her again. That was a promise he was making to himself.

He showered and shaved and was back in his bedroom before he heard the sound of Grace's alarm. Removing a suit from the garment bag he'd hung in the closet, he heard Sarah's wailing and Grace's words of comfort. He put the suit back in the closet, and yanked on jeans and a T-shirt, listening to Grace soothing Sarah as she carried her downstairs. He heard Grace quietly return upstairs and knew that the lack of crying meant Sarah was sucking her bottle.

He listened for the sound of Grace's door closing and then sneaked downstairs. It had been years since he'd made his "world famous" blueberry pancakes, but if anybody ever deserved a little treat, it was Grace.

After taking a last peek to be sure her black skirt and print blouse were in the proper position, Grace shifted away from her full-length mirror to lift already-dressed Sarah from her crib. But as she turned, the scent of something sweet stopped her.

Whatever it was it smelled like pure heaven.

Her mouth watered.

She grabbed Sarah and rushed down the steps. In the kitchen, dressed in jeans and a T-shirt and wearing a bib apron, stood Danny.

"What is that smell?"

He turned with a smile. "Pancakes. My one and only specialty."

"If they taste as good as they smell, they are absolutely your specialty."

"Oh, they do."

The ringing endorsement—combined with the growling of Grace's tummy—had her scampering into the dining area. She slid Sarah into her high chair and went to the kitchen to retrieve plates from the cupboard. "More stuff you learned while at school?"

He winced. "Not really. These are the only thing I can cook. Unless you count canned soup and fried eggs."

Avoiding her eyes, he set two fluffy blueberry pancakes on each of the two plates she held. Grace took them to the table. She set her dish at the seat beside the high chair and the second across the table from her.

The night before he'd kissed her and just the memory of that brought a warm fuzzy somersault feeling to her empty tummy. She hadn't let the kiss go too far. But there was something between them.

Something special. Something sharp and sexual. It wasn't something that would go away with the press of a button, or just because it complicated things. And today he'd made her breakfast. Though she appreciated it, she also knew she had to tread lightly. She didn't want to get involved with him again and he was tempting her.

Danny brought the syrup to the table and sat across from her. "I think there are some things you and I need to discuss."

Her stomach flip-flopped again. The last thing she wanted was to talk about their one-night stand. Or whatever it was that had happened between them. But disliking him hadn't worked to keep them apart. So maybe it was best to talk?

"Okay."

He took a breath. "All right. Here's the deal. That kiss last night was wrong and I don't want you to have to worry about it happening again."

She looked across the table at him, her heart in her throat, and praying her eyes weren't revealing the pain that brought. She also didn't think getting involved was a good idea, but he hadn't needed to say the words.

"The truth is I know you deserve better than me."

Grace blinked. That wasn't at all what she was expecting and she had absolutely no idea how to reply.

"The night we slept together, I was going through a bad time," he said, glancing down at his pancake before catching her gaze again. "Not that that makes what happened right, but I think it might help you to understand that now that I'm past those personal problems, I can see I misjudged you and I'm sorrier than I can ever say."

Grace took a breath. Once again he was talking about himself, but not really about anything. Still his apology was a big step for them. "Okay."

"Okay you understand or okay you accept my apology?"

She took another breath. Her gut reaction was to accept his apology, but she simply didn't trust him. He had a powerful personality. He might say that she needn't worry about him kissing her again, but she didn't believe either of them could say that with absolute certainty. There was something between them. Chemistry, probably. Hormones that didn't listen to reason. She was afraid that if she accepted his apology and told him she understood it would open the door to things she couldn't control. Things neither one of them could control.

Before she could answer, Danny said, "I hate excuses for bad behavior, but sometimes there are valid reasons people do all the wrong things." He took a breath. "Because that weekend was the two-year anniversary of my son's death, I wasn't myself."

Grace blinked. "What?"

"Cory had died two years before. Six months after his accident my wife and I divorced. I spent the next year and a half just going through the motions of living."

Shocked into silence, Grace only stared at him.

"That weekend you reminded me of happiness." He combed his fingers through his hair. "I don't know.

Watching you with Orlando and hearing the two of you make jokes and have a good time, I remembered how it felt to be happy and I began to feel as if I were coming around." He caught her gaze. "You know…as if I were ready to live again."

Stuck in the dark place of trying to imagine the crushing blow of the death of a child and feeling over-whelmed at even the thought, Grace only nodded.

"But I'd always believed you and I had gone too far too fast by making love the very first weekend we really even spoke, and when I went away for that week of client hopping my doubts haunted me. I started imagin-ing all kinds of reasons you'd sleep with me without really knowing me, and some of them weren't very flat-tering." He took a breath. "When you told me you were pregnant it just seemed as if every bad thing I had conjured had come true." He held her gaze steadily. "I was wrong and I am sorry."

Grace swallowed hard. She'd left the beach house happy, thinking she'd found Mr. Right and believing all things good would happen for them. But Danny had left the beach house worried about the potential bad. It was no wonder neither of them had seen the other's perspec-tive. They were at two ends of a very broad spectrum.

"I'm sorry, too. I was so happy I didn't think things through. Had I known—"

Sarah pounded on her tray with a squeal. Grace grimaced. "I forgot to feed her."

Danny calmly rose. "I can get that."

Grace's first instinct was to tell him to sit back down.

Their discussion wasn't really over. But wasn't it? What else was there to say? He was sorry. She was sorry. But they couldn't change the past. She didn't want a relationship. He'd hurt her and she rightfully didn't trust him. And he didn't want a relationship. Otherwise he wouldn't have promised not to kiss her again. There was nothing more to say. The discussion really was over.

"Do you remember how to make cereal?" Grace asked.

"The stuff in the box with a little milk, right?"

She nodded.

"I can handle it."

He strode into the kitchen and Grace took several long, steadying breaths.

His child had died.

She had always believed that nothing he could say would excuse the way he treated her when she told him she was pregnant.

But this did.

It didn't mean she would trust her heart to him, but it did mean she could forgive him.

That night Grace had dinner nearly prepared when Danny arrived. She directed him upstairs to change while she fed Sarah some baby food and by the time Sarah had eaten, Danny returned wearing jeans and a T-shirt. He looked as relaxed as he had their night at the beach house. Confession, apparently, had done him a world of good.

Incredibly nervous, Grace fussed over the salads.

Now that she knew about Danny's son everything was different. She almost didn't know how to treat him. His admissions had opened the door to their being friends, and being friendly would work the best for Sarah's sake. But could two people with their chemistry really be friends?

While Grace brought their salads to the table, Danny took his seat.

"You know, we never have gotten around to discussing a lot of things about Sarah."

Glad for the neutral topic, Grace said, "Like what?"

"For one, child support."

"Since we'll each have Sarah two weeks a month, I don't think either one of us should be entitled to child support. So don't even think of filing for any."

He laughed. "Very funny."

A tingle of accomplishment raced through her at his laughter, but she didn't show any outward sign of her pleasure. Instead she shrugged casually. "Hey, I make a decent salary. How do I know it wasn't your intention to file?"

"You never did tell me where you got a job."

"I work for a small accounting firm. Johnson and O'Hara."

"So you do okay financially?"

"Yeah." Grace smiled. "Actually they pay me double what your firm did."

He chuckled. "You got lucky."

"Yes, I did."

He glanced into the kitchen, then behind himself at

the living room. "And you seem to know how to use your money wisely."

"I bought this house the day I got my first job."

"The night I was grilling, I remembered you told me about remodeling your house while we ate that Sunday night at the beach house." He smiled across the table at her, and Grace's stomach flip-flopped. Lord, he was handsome. And nice. And considerate. And smart. And now she knew he wasn't mean-spirited or selfish, but wounded. Life had hurt him and he needed somebody like her to make him laugh.

Oh God, she was in trouble!

"You did a good job on the remodel."

"My cousin did most of it." Shifting lettuce on her dish, Grace avoided looking at him. "I was the grunt. He would put something in place, tack it with a nail or two then give me the nail gun to finish."

"It looks great." He took another bite of salad.

But Grace was too nervous to eat. She couldn't hate him anymore. But she couldn't really like him, either.

Or could she?

By telling her about his son, he'd both explained his behavior and proved he trusted her.

But he'd also said she didn't need to worry about him kissing her anymore.

Of course, he might have said that because she'd pushed him away the night before, reminding him that kissing only got them in trouble.

They finished their salads and Grace brought the roast beef, mashed potatoes and peas to the table. Unhappy with being ignored, Sarah pounded her teething ring on her high chair tray and screeched noisily.

"What's the matter, Sarah Bear," Grace crooned, as she poured gravy onto her mashed potatoes. Sarah screeched again and Grace laughed. "Oh, you want to sit on somebody's lap? Well, you can't."

She glanced at Danny. "Unless your daddy wants to hold you?"

Danny said, "Sure, I'll—"

But Grace stopped him. "No. You can't hold a baby in front of a plate with gravy on it. You would be wearing the gravy in about twenty seconds."

"If you want to eat your dinner in peace, I could take her into the living room, then eat when you're done."

He was so darned eager to please that Grace stared at him, drawing conclusions that made her heart tremble with hope. There was only one reason a man wanted to please a woman. He liked her. Which meant maybe Danny had only promised not to kiss her again because she'd stopped him, not because he didn't want to kiss her anymore.

Or she could be drawing conclusions that had absolutely no basis in fact.

"I'm fine. I like having Sarah at the table. When I said you might want to hold her I was just teasing her."

"Oh, okay."

Determined to keep her perspective and keep things light and friendly, Grace turned to the high chair. "So, Miss Sarah, you stay where you are."

"What's that thing your mother's got you wearing?"

Danny asked, pointing at the fuzzy swatch of material in the shape of a stuffed bear that had been sewn onto Sarah's shirt.

"It's a bear shirt."

Danny's fork stopped halfway to his mouth and he gave Grace a confused look. "What?"

"A bear shirt." Grace laughed. "From the day she was born, my dad called her Sarah Boo Beara…then Sarah Bear. Because the name sort of took, my parents buy her all kinds of bear things." She angled her fork at the bear on Sarah's shirt. "Push it."

"Push it?"

"The bear. Push it and see what happens."

Danny reached over and pushed the bear on Sarah's shirt. It squeaked. Sarah grinned toothlessly.

Danny jumped as if somebody had bitten him. "Very funny."

"It makes Sarah laugh and some days that's not merely a good thing. It's a necessity."

"I remember."

Of course, he remembered. He'd had a son. Undoubtedly lots of things he did for Sarah or things Sarah did would bring back memories for him. If he needed anything from Grace it might not be a relationship as much as a friend to listen to him. Just listen.

"Would you like to talk about it?"

Danny shook his head. "Not really."

Okay. She'd read that wrong. She took a quiet breath, realizing she'd been off base about him a lot, and maybe the smart thing here would be to stop trying to guess what he thought and only believe what he said. Including that he wouldn't be kissing her anymore. So she should stop romanticizing.

"If you ever do want to talk, I'm here."

"I know." He toyed with his fork then he glanced over at her with a wistful smile. "I sort of wonder what might have happened between us if I'd told you everything the morning after we'd slept together, as I had intended to."

Her heart thudded to a stop. "You were going to tell me?"

He nodded. "Instead the only thing I managed to get out was that I had to go away for a week." He paused, glancing down at the half-eaten food on his plate. "I really shouldn't have slept with you that night. I was still raw, but fighting it, telling myself it was time to move on. And I made a mistake."

"You don't get sole blame for that. I was the one who went down to the bar."

"Yeah, but I was the one who knew I wasn't entirely healed from my son's death and my divorce. The whole disaster was my fault."

"It takes two—"

"Grace, stop. Please."

His tone brooked no argument—as if she'd been pushing him to talk, when she hadn't—and Grace bristled. Though he'd said he didn't want to talk about this, he'd been the one to dip their toes into the conversation. Still, because it was his trouble, his life, they were discussing, he also had to be the one with the right to end it. "Okay."

He blew his breath out on a long sigh. "I'm not trying to hide things or run from things, but I just plain don't want to remember anymore. I'm tired of the past and don't like to remember it, let alone talk about it. I like living in the present."

"I can understand that."

"Good." He set his fork on his dish. "So do you want help with the dishes?"

She almost automatically said no, but stopped herself. Giving him something to do made life easier for both of them. "Sure."

He rose, gathering the plates. She lifted the meat platter and walked it to the refrigerator. The oppressive tension of the silence between them pressed on her chest. If the quiet was difficult for her, she couldn't even imagine how hard it was on Danny. Knowing he didn't want to think, to remember, she plunged them into the solace of chitchat.

"So what did you do at work today?"

Danny turned on the faucet to rinse their dishes. "The same old stuff. What did you do?"

"I'm in the process of reviewing the books for a company that wants to incorporate."

That caught his interest. "Oh, an IPO."

Grace winced at the excitement in his voice. "No, a small family business. The corporation will be privately held. The principals are basically doling out shares of stock to the family members who made the company successful, as a way to ensure ownership as well as appropriate distribution of profits."

"Ah."

"Not nearly as exciting as investing the fortunes of famous athletes, but it's good work. Interesting."

"Have you begun to do any investing for yourself?"

His question triggered an unexpected memory of telling him she'd gone to work for his investment firm because she wanted to learn about investing to be rich. The heat of embarrassment began to crawl up her neck. She'd meant what she said, but given everything that had happened between them, her enthusiastic pronouncement had probably fed the fire of his suspicions about her.

They'd really made a mess of things that night.

She walked back to the dining room table and retrieved the mashed potato bowl. "I'm working on getting the house paid off. So I haven't had a lot of spare cash."

"Since we'll be splitting expenses for Sarah, you should have some extra money then, right?"

She shrugged. "Maybe."

"Grace, I want to pay my fair share. And I can be pretty stubborn. So no maybes or probablys or whatevers. Let's really be honest about the money."

"Okay."

He stacked the dishes in the dishwasher. "Okay. So once we get everything straightened out I would like to open an account for you at Carson Services."

Grace laughed. "Right. Danny, even if I have spare cash from our sharing expenses for Sarah, I'm not sure I'll have more than a hundred dollars a month or so."

"A hundred dollars a month is good."

"Oh, really? You're going to open an investment account with a hundred dollars?"

He winced. "I thought I'd open it with a few thousand dollars of my own money. You know, to make up for what you've spent to date and you could add to it."

Grace sighed. "You told me to stop talking about the past and I did. So now I'm going to tell you to stop fretting about the money."

"But I—"

"Just stop. I don't want your money. I never did. When I said I wanted to be rich that night at the beach house, I was actually saying that I wanted my parents and me to be comfortable." She motioned around her downstairs. "Like this. This is enough. I am happy. I do not want your money. Can you accept that?"

He held her gaze for several seconds. Grace didn't even flinch, so that he would see from her expression that this was as important to her as no longer discussing the past was for him.

"Yes, I accept that."

"Okay."

Sliding under the covers that night, Grace was still annoyed by their money discussion. Not because he wanted to pay his fair share, and not even because she had brought his suspicions about her on herself, but because that one memory opened the door to a hundred more.

She remembered what it felt like to be with him. He'd made her feel so special. Wonderful. Perfect.

Warmth immediately filled her. So did the sense that she'd had during their weekend together. That they fit. That they were right for each other. She had been so happy that weekend, but she also remembered that *he'd* been happy too.

Was she so wrong to think *she* brought out the nice guy in him? And was it so wrong to believe that there was a chance that the nice guy could come out and stay out forever? And was it so wrong to think that maybe— just maybe—if the nice guy stayed out forever they could fall in love for real? Not fall into bed because they were sexually attracted. But fall in love. For real. To genuinely care about each other.

She didn't know, and she couldn't even clearly analyze the situation because they'd slept together and that one wonderful memory clouded her judgment.

Plus she'd already decided she wouldn't be second-guessing him anymore. He'd said she didn't have to worry about him kissing her again.

He didn't want her. She had to remember that.

CHAPTER EIGHT

GRACE awakened to the scent of pancakes and the sound of Sarah slapping her chubby hands against the bars of her crib.

"I'm coming."

She groggily pulled herself out of bed and lifted Sarah into her arms. Rain softly pitter-pattered on the roof. The scent of blueberry pancakes wafted through the air. It would have been a perfect morning except Grace had tossed and turned so much the night before that she'd slept in.

Though she had said she didn't want to get accustomed to having Danny around, after dressing Sarah for the day, she padded downstairs and into the kitchen area.

"Hey."

Danny looked up from the newspaper he was reading at the kitchen counter. "Good morning."

"I'm sorry, but I slept in. Could you take her?"

"And feed her?"

Grace nodded.

"Sure. Come on, Sarah Bear."

Sarah easily went to Danny and Grace turned and walked back though the living room, but at the stairs she paused, watching Danny as he held Sarah with one arm and prepared her cereal with the other. Rain continued to tap against the roof, making the house cozy and warm. Breakfast was made. She would have privacy to dress. It all seemed so perfect that Grace had a moment of pure, unadulterated sadness, realizing that *this* was what sleeping together too soon had cost them.

She drew in a breath and ran upstairs. There was no point crying over spilled milk. No point wishing for what might have been. And no way she could jeopardize the comfort level they had by yearning for a romance. Particularly with a man who so desperately needed to do things at his own pace, in his own way.

She showered, dressed and returned downstairs. Sarah sat in her high chair and cooed when Grace approached. Danny rose from the dining room table and walked into the kitchen.

"I'll microwave your pancakes. Just to warm them up."

"Thanks."

"Want some coffee?"

"Yes, but I'll get it." She laughed. "I told you, I don't want to get too accustomed to having help."

He leaned against the counter and crossed his arms on his chest. "We could share the nanny I hire."

She held up her hands to stop him. "Don't tempt me."

"Why not? What else is she going to do during the weeks you have Sarah?"

"Take yoga."

He burst out laughing. "Come on, Grace, at least think about it."

She poured herself a cup of coffee, then grabbed the cream from the refrigerator. "The part of me that wants help is being overruled by the part of me that loves the one-on-one time with Sarah."

He nodded. "Okay. Makes sense."

She turned and smiled at him. "Thanks."

He returned her smile. "You're welcome."

For a few seconds, they stood smiling at each other, then Grace's smile faded and she quickly turned away. She really liked him, and that triggered more phero-mones than a thousand bulging biceps. They were better off when she had disliked him, before his explanation and apology. Now instead of disagreeing and keeping their distance they were becoming friends, getting close, and she was wishing for things she couldn't have.

"By the way, my lawyer called this morning."

Brought back to the present by a very timely re-minder, Grace faced him. "Oh, yeah?"

Danny winced. "Yeah. The guy's a nut. He called me while he was shaving. He actually woke me." The mi-crowave buzzer rang. Unfolding his arms, Danny pushed away from the counter. "He asked about the progress on our agreement. I told him that you had told me you contacted a lawyer, and that lawyer had told you it was okay to sign, so you signed it, right?"

The casual, cozy atmosphere of Grace's little house shifted. Tension seeped into the space between them with words left unsaid. He hadn't signed their agreement. She had. But he hadn't. And it worried his lawyer. Or maybe it worried *him* and he used the call from his lawyer as a cover?

She swallowed, calling herself crazy for being suspicious. Shared custody was *her* idea. "I signed it."

"Great. Give it to me and I'll sign it, then we'll be set. According to my lawyer, once we have that in place we won't even need a hearing." Plate of warm pancakes in his hand, he faced her. "We simply begin sharing custody."

His pancakes suddenly looked like a bribe, and Grace froze, unable to take them from his hand. Until she reminded herself that Danny had nothing to gain by being nice to her. If anything *she* benefited from any agreement that kept them out of court.

She forced a smile and took the plate from his hands. "Sounds good. It's upstairs. I'll get it."

He glanced at his watch, then grimaced. "I have an early meeting today so unless you want your pancakes to get cold again, how about if you get it for me tonight. Tomorrow's Saturday, but I can take it to work on Monday and sign it in front of my secretary who can witness it. Then we'll make copies."

Calling herself every sort of fool for being suspicious, Grace walked to the table. "That sounds good." Eager to make up for her few seconds of doubt, she added, "But it's on top of my dresser. You could get it."

He waved a hand in dismissal. "We'll handle it tomorrow."

Grace drove to work, feeling like an idiot for mistrusting him. But walking from the parking garage, she reminded herself that it wasn't out of line for her to be suspicious of him. She might be prone to a little too much second-guessing about him, but he hadn't really told her a lot about his life. And he stopped the discussion any time they began to edge beyond surface facts.

Plus, *they* had a past. An unusual, unhappy past. He mistrusted her. When she told him she was pregnant, he kicked her out of his office. After that, she never tried to contact him again because she hadn't trusted him. She only took the baby to him for Sarah's sake. She hadn't expected him to want visitation, let alone have a hand in raising their daughter. But he did. He wanted full custody and had agreed to shared custody. To get Grace to give him that, he had to prove himself. Everything they'd done had been a negotiation of a sort.

She shouldn't magically feel that things between them had been patched up.

Except that he'd trusted her enough to tell him about his son.

Didn't that count as at least a step toward mended fences?

Yes, it did. Yet even knowing that he had good reason to be off his game something bothered her. Something in her gut said that Danny was too eager about their agreement and accepting shared custody, and she had no idea why.

Grace couldn't come up with a solid answer, even though the question popped into her head a million times that day. She returned home that evening edgy and annoyed, tired of running this scenario through her brain. Shared custody and the agreement had been *her* idea. She'd already signed the agreement. Week about with Sarah was the fair thing to do in their circumstance. The man had offered her the use of his nanny. He'd told her about his son. Yet something still nagged at her.

It didn't help that Sarah was grouchy. After a quiet and somewhat strained dinner, Danny excused himself to go to his room to work on a project that needed to be completed on Monday morning. Grace tried to stack the dishes in the dishwasher with Sarah crying in her high chair, but her patience quickly ran out. She lifted the baby and carried her up to Danny's room.

"Can you watch her while I finish clearing the kitchen?"

Looking too big for the little corner desk Grace had in her spare room more for decorative purposes than actual use, Danny faced her. "Grace, I—"

"Please." Grace marched into the room. "I know you have to get this project done for Monday morning, but I had a miserable day and I just need a few minutes to clean up." She dropped Sarah onto his lap. "When the dishes are done, I'll take her again."

With that she walked out, closing Danny's bedroom door behind her, leaving nothing but silence in her wake.

Danny glanced down at the little girl on his lap. "One of us made her angry and since I've been up here and you were the one with her in the kitchen, I'm blaming you."

Sarah screeched at him.

"Right. You can argue all you want but the fact remains that I was up here and you were down there with her."

He rose from the little desk chair and walked to the door, intending to take the baby to the living room where he and Sarah could watch TV or maybe play on the floor. But even before his hand closed around the knob, he had second thoughts. Grace said she wanted to clean the kitchen, but maybe what she needed was some peace and quiet. He glanced around, unsure of what to do. The room wasn't tiny, but it wasn't a center of entertainment, either.

"Any suggestions for how we can amuse ourselves for the next hour or so?" he asked Sarah as he shifted her into his arms so that he could look down at her. She smiled up at him and his heart did a crazy flip-flop. From this angle he didn't see as much of Cory in her features as he saw Grace. Were he to guess, he would say Sarah's eyes would some day be the same shade of violet that Grace's were.

She rubbed her little fist across her nose, then her right eye, the sign babies used when they were sleepy. Danny instinctively kissed the top of her head.

She peeked up and grinned at him and this time Danny's heart expanded with love. Not only had Sarah grown accustomed to him, but also he was falling in love with her. He was falling in love with the baby, happy living in Grace's home and having feelings for Grace he didn't dare identify. He knew she deserved a better man than he was. He'd made a promise to himself not to hurt her and he intended to keep it.

He looked down at Sarah, who yawned. "On, no, Sarah! You can't fall asleep this early. You'll wake up before dawn, probably ready to play and tomorrow's Saturday, the only day your mom gets to sleep in—"

He stopped talking because inspiration struck him. The thing to do would be to get Sarah ready for bed. That way she wouldn't fall asleep for at least another half hour and who knew? Maybe a bath would revive her? Plus he might make a few brownie points with Grace by keeping them so busy she could relax.

Pleased with that idea, he held Sarah against his shoulder, quietly opened his bedroom door and looked down the hall. Grace was nowhere in sight, and he could still hear the sounds of pots and pans in her kitchen.

He sneaked across the little hall and into her room. Inside he was immediately enfolded in a warm, sheltered feeling, the sense a man got when he felt at home. He squeezed his eyes shut, telling himself not to get so attached to Grace and her things that he again did something they'd both regret. He took a breath, then another and then another, reminding himself of all the reasons being too cozy with her was wrong.

Sarah wiped her nose in his shirt and snuggled into his shoulder, bringing him back to reality.

"No. No," he said, manipulating her into a different position before she could get too comfortable. "You'll be able to go to sleep soon enough if you let your daddy get you ready for bed."

He searched around the room for her baby tub, but

realized it was probably in the bathroom. Remembering that preparation was a parent's best trick when caring for a baby, he decided to get everything ready before he brought his sopping wet baby from the bathroom. He laid a clean blanket on the changing table, then pulled open the top draw of a white chest of drawers that had bears painted on the knobs. Inside were undershirts and socks so tiny they looked about thumb-size. Knowing those were too small, he closed the drawer, and opened the next one, seeking pajamas. He found them, then located the stash of disposable diapers, and arranged them on the changing table.

With everything ready he took Sarah to the bathroom. Holding her with one arm, he filled the baby tub he'd placed inside the regular bathtub, found her soap and shampoo and the baby towel that hung on the rack.

That was when he realized she was fully dressed and he was still wearing his suit trousers. In an executive decision, he pronounced it too late to do anything about his trousers and laid her on the fluffy carpet in front of the tub to remove her clothes.

She giggled and cooed and he shook his head. "Let's just hope you're this happy after I put you in the water."

She grinned at him.

Returning her smile, he lifted her to eye level. "Ready?"

She laughed and patted his cheeks.

"Okay, then." He dipped her into the tub and when she didn't howl or stiffen up, he figured she was one of the babies who loved to sit in water. Grateful, he kept one hand at her back as he wet a washcloth and squeezed a few drops of liquid soap on it, amazed by how quickly baby care was coming back to him.

"So you like the water?" Danny said, entertaining Sarah with chitchat as he washed her, just in case any part of bathtime had the potential to freak her out. She merely gooed and cooed at him, even when he washed her hair. Pleased by his success, he rinsed off all the soapsuds, rolled her in the soft terry-cloth baby towel and carried her back to Grace's room.

Not in the slightest uncomfortable, Sarah chewed a blue rubber teething ring while Danny put on her diaper and slid her into pajamas.

When she was completely dressed, he took her out into the hallway. He heard the sounds of the television—indicating Grace was done filling the dishwasher and probably waiting for the cycle to be complete so she could put everything away—and turned to the stairs, but his conscience tweaked. He'd been here five days and he hadn't done anything more than make pancakes, help with dishes and grill a few things. This was the first time he'd really helped with the baby. It seemed totally wrong to take Sarah downstairs and disturb the only private moments he'd allowed Grace.

He turned and walked back into Grace's bedroom. "So what do we do?"

Sarah rubbed her eyes again.

Danny frowned. He didn't have a bottle for her, but she didn't seem hungry. Or fussy. All she appeared to be was sleepy. Now that they'd wasted almost an hour getting her ready for bed, it didn't seem too early to let her fall asleep. The only question was, could she fall asleep without a bottle?

He remembered a comment Grace had made about making up stories for Sarah, and walked to the bed. If he laid Sarah in her crib, he ran the risk that she'd cry and Grace's private time would be disturbed. It seemed smarter to sit on the bed and tell Sarah a story and see if she'd fall asleep naturally.

He sat. Sarah snuggled against his chest. But sitting on the edge of Grace's bed was incredibly uncomfortable, so he scooted back until he was leaning against the headboard.

"This is better."

Sarah blinked up at him sleepily.

"Okay. Let's see. You clearly like bears since your grandfather blended a bear into your name, so let's make up a story about a bear."

She blinked again. Heavier this time. He scooted down a little further, then decided he might as well lie down, too.

Two hours later, Grace awoke on the sofa. She'd fallen asleep! Danny was going to kill her.

She ran up the steps and to Danny's room, but it was empty. Panicked, she raced across the hall and without turning on the light saw his shadowy form on her bed. She tiptoed into the room and peered down to discover he was not only sleeping on her bed with Sarah, he'd also put the baby in her pajamas for the night.

Both the baby and her daddy slept deeply, comfortably. Little Sarah lay in the space between his chest and his arm, snuggled against him in a pose of trust. Danny looked naturally capable. Grace wished she had a camera.

Careful not to disturb Danny, she reached down and lifted Sarah from his arms. The baby sniffled and stretched, but Grace "Shhed," her back to sleep and laid her in her crib.

Then she turned to her bed, her heart in her throat. Danny looked so comfortable and so relaxed that she didn't want to disturb him. The peaceful repose of his face reminded her of the morning she'd awakened in his bed in the beach house, and she involuntarily sat down beside him.

Unable to help herself, she lovingly brushed a lock of hair from his forehead. She wasn't going to fall into her black pit of recriminations again about sleeping together. She already knew that had been a mistake. No need to continue berating herself. Life had handled their punishment for prematurely sleeping together by using it to keep them apart. What she wanted right now was just a couple of seconds, maybe a minute, to look at him, to be happy he was here, to enjoy the fact that he loved their daughter so she wouldn't have to worry when Sarah was in his care.

She scooted a little closer on the bed, remembered waking up that morning at the beach house, laughed softly at how glad she had been that she'd had the chance to sneak away and brush her teeth before he woke up, and then sighed as she recalled making love in the shower.

She remembered thinking that she'd never love

another man the way she loved Danny and realized it was still true. He had her heart and she wasn't even sure how he'd done it. Except that he was cute, and sweet, and nice, and she desperately wanted to fill the aching need that she could now see he had.

But he wouldn't let her.

And that was what was bothering her. That was why she grabbed onto her suspicions like a lifeline. As long as she mistrusted him, she could hold herself back. But now that he'd told her about his son, explaining his irrational behavior, she had forgiven him. And once she'd forgive him, she'd begun falling in love again.

But he didn't love her. He didn't want to love her. If she didn't stop her runaway feelings, she was going to get hurt again.

After another breath, she lightly shook his shoulder and whispered, "Danny?"

He grumbled something unintelligible and she smiled. Damn he was cute. It really didn't seem fair that she had to resist him.

"Danny, if you don't want to get up, I can sleep in your room, but you'll have to wake up with Sarah when she cries for her two o'clock feeding."

The threat of being responsible for Sarah must have penetrated, because he took a long breath, then groggily sat up.

"Want help getting across the hall?"

He stared at her, as if needing to focus, and reached for her hand, which was still on his shoulder. His fingers were warm and his touch gentle, sending reaction from

Grace's fingertips to her toes. She remembered how sweet his kisses had been. She remembered how giving, yet bold he was as a lover. She remembered how safe she'd felt with him, how loved.

In the silence of the dark night, their gazes stayed locked for what felt like forever, then he put his hands on her shoulders and ran them down her back, along the curve of her waist and up again.

Grace swallowed and closed her eyes, savoring the feeling that she remembered from that summer night. Not sexual attraction, but emotional connection, expressed through physical attraction. Whatever was between them was powerful, but it was also sweet. By caring for Sarah tonight he'd shown her what she'd instinctively understood about him. That deep down he was a good guy. He'd kept Sarah beyond the time he'd needed to for Grace to get her work done, dressed her in pajamas and fallen asleep with the baby in his arms.

He might dismiss it or downplay it, but he couldn't deny it and that meant they were at a crossroad. He liked her enough to do something kind for her. It might be too soon for him to fall in love again. Or he might not want to fall in love again. But he was falling. And she didn't have to tell him she was falling, too. He could surely see it in her eyes.

Gazing into his dark eyes, Grace held her breath, hoping, almost praying he was thinking the same thing she was and that he had the courage to act on it.

CHAPTER NINE

IN THE dark, quiet bedroom that radiated warmth and the comfort of home, Danny stared at Grace. All he wanted to do was crawl under the covers of her bed with her. Not to make love but to sleep. He was tired, but also he simply needed the succor of this night. The peaceful feeling a man got when his baby was tucked away in her crib, sleeping like an angel, and the mother of his baby was tucked under his arm. The desire was instinctive, nearly primal, and so natural he hadn't thought it. It had overtaken him. Almost as if it wasn't something he could stop or change.

But every time he'd given in to his instincts, he'd failed somebody. He'd failed Lydia, he'd failed Cory, and he'd even failed Grace by not believing her when she told him she was pregnant. Did he really want to fail her again?

No.

He backed away from the temptation of Grace, his hands sliding off her in a slow, sad way, savoring every second of her softness for as long as he could before it was gone.

He hadn't said anything foolish like how beautiful she was or how much he had missed her or how the instant closeness they had shared was coming back to him. He hadn't done anything he couldn't take back like kiss her. He could get out of this simply by saying goodnight and leaving the room.

"Good night."

She swallowed. "Good night."

And Danny walked out of the room.

Grace sat on the bed. It was still warm from where he lay. She could smell the subtle hint of his aftershave.

She dropped her head to her hands. If she'd needed any more reason to stay away from Danny, he'd given it to her tonight. She'd watched the play of emotions on his face display the battle going on in his brain as he'd stared at her, wanting her, yet denying himself. She could have been insulted or hurt; instead she saw just how strong he was. How determined he could be to deny himself what he wanted, even when it was probably clear to him that she wanted it, too.

And it was her loss. She knew it the whole way to her soul.

For the second time since he'd moved in with Grace, Danny awakened happy. The night before he'd spent time with Sarah and had very successfully cared for her, proving to himself that he didn't need to be afraid about the weeks he would spend with his daughter. He'd also successfully stepped away from temptation with Grace.

He wanted her, but he didn't want to hurt her. Some day she would thank him.

As he dressed, he heard the sounds of Sarah awakening and Grace walking down the stairs to get her a bottle. When he was sure she had returned to her room to dress and get the baby ready for the day, he rushed downstairs, strode into the kitchen and retrieved the ingredients for pancakes.

Twenty minutes later she came down the stairs and he turned from the stove. "Good morning."

Wearing jeans and a pale blue top that made her eyes seem iridescent, Grace carried the baby to her high chair.

"Good morning."

She was beautiful in an unassuming, yet naturally feminine way that always caused everything male in Danny to sit up and take notice. But he didn't mind that. In fact, now that he knew he could control the emotional side of their relationship, he actually liked noticing Grace. What man didn't want to appreciate a beautiful woman?

As she puttered, getting the baby settled in the high chair with a teething ring, Danny looked his fill at the way her T-shirt hugged her full breasts and her blue jeans caressed her bottom. But what really drew him was her face. Her violet eyes sparkled with laughter and her full lips lifted in a smile. If his walking away the night before had affected her, she didn't show it. She was one of the most accepting, accommodating people he'd ever met.

He took a stack of pancakes to the table and she sniffed the air. "Blueberry again."

He winced. "They're my only specialty."

She surprised him by laughing. "You say that as if you'd like to learn to cook."

His reaction to that was so unexpected that he stopped halfway to the kitchen and he faced her again. "I think I do."

She took her seat at the table. "I don't know why that seems so novel to you. Lots of men cook."

But Danny didn't want to cook. He wanted to please Grace. Not in a ridiculous, out-of-control way, but in a way that fulfilled his part of the responsibility. Still, with only a week left in their deal to live together it was too late now to find a class.

Grace plopped a pancake on her plate as Sarah pounded her high chair tray. "You could get a cookbook."

Now that idea had merit.

"Or I could teach you."

And that idea had even more merit. He would get the knowledge he needed to do his part, and he'd have a perfect opportunity to spend time with Grace. Normal time. Not fighting a middle-of-the-night attraction. Not wishing for things he couldn't have. But time to get even more adjusted to having her in his world without giving in to every whim, sexual craving or desire for her softness.

"I'd like that."

She smiled at him. "Great. This morning we'll go shopping for groceries."

Reaching into the cupboard for syrup, he said, "Shopping?"

"Shopping is the first step in cooking. You can't

make what you don't have. If you'd tried to prepare these pancakes tomorrow," she said, pointing at her dish, "you would have been sadly disappointed because the blueberries would have been gone. That's why we're going shopping today."

He didn't really want to go to a store, but she had a point. Unfortunately her suggestion also had a fatal flaw. "How am I going to know what to buy if I don't yet know how to cook anything?"

"I'm going to help you."

"Right."

Sarah screeched her displeasure at being left out of the conversation. Danny took his seat at the table and before Grace could turn to settle the baby, he broke off a small bite of pancake and set it in her open mouth.

She grinned at him.

And Danny felt his world slide into place. What he felt was beyond happiness. It was something more like purpose or place. That was it. He had a place. He had a child, and a friend in his child's mother. In a sense, Grace getting pregnant had given him back his life. As long as he didn't try to make this relationship any more than it was, he had a family of sorts.

In the grocery store, Grace had serious second thoughts about her idea of teaching Danny to cook. He wanted to learn to steam shrimp and prepare crème brûlée. Her expertise ran more along the lines of pizza rolls and brownies. And the brownies weren't even scratch brownies. They were from a boxed mix.

"How about prime rib?"

"I'm not exactly sure how that's made, either."

"We need a cookbook."

"Or we could start with less complex things like grilled steak and baked potatoes."

Standing by the spice counter, he slowly turned to face her, a smile spreading across his mouth. "You don't know how to cook, either."

"That's a matter of opinion. I know the main staples. I can bake a roast that melts in your mouth, fix just about any kind of potato you want and steam vegetables. My lasagna wins raves at reunions—"

"Reunions?"

"You know. Family reunions. Picnics. Where all the aunts and uncles and cousins get together and everybody brings his or her specialty dish, plays volleyball or softball, coos over each other's kids and the next morning wakes up with sore muscles because most of us only play sports that one day every year."

He laughed.

"You've never been to a family reunion?"

"I don't have much of a family. My dad was an only child, and though my mother had two siblings, her brother became a priest and her sister chose not to have kids."

She gaped at him. "You're kidding."

"Why are you so surprised. *Your* parents had only one child."

"My parents had one child because my dad was disabled in an automobile accident. He appears fine and he can do most things, but he never could go back to work. It's why my parents have so little money. We had to live on what my mother could make."

"Oh."

Seeing that he was processing that, Grace stepped over to the spices and pulled out a container of basil. She had to wonder if the reason Danny couldn't seem to love wasn't just the mistake of his marriage, but a result of his entire past. Could a person who'd only seen one marriage, then failed at his own, really believe in love?

"I can also make soup."

"What kind?"

"Vegetable and chicken and dumpling."

"Ah. A gourmet."

"Now, don't get snooty. I think you're really going to like the chicken and dumpling. I have to use a spaetzle maker."

"What the hell is a spaetzle maker?"

His confusion about a cooking utensil only served to confirm Grace's theory that Danny couldn't love because he knew so little about the simple, ordinary things other people took for granted. "It's a fancy word for a kitchen gadget that makes very small dumplings."

"Why don't you just call it that?"

"Because I'm not the one who decided what it's called. It's German or something. Besides, spaetzle maker sounds more official."

"Right."

Grace laughed. She was having fun. Lots of fun. The kind of fun they probably would have had if she and Danny had let their relationship develop slowly. They were so different that they'd desperately needed time to get to know each other, to become familiar with each other's worlds, and to integrate what worked and get rid of what didn't. From Danny's eagerness to learn and his curiosity, it was clear something was missing in his world. And from the way he reacted to the simplicity of her life it was obvious she wouldn't have been able to stay the same if they'd actually had a relationship. That was also why Sarah needed both of them. Neither one of them was *wrong* in the way they lived. It was all a matter of choices.

They spent over double what Grace normally allotted for food, but Danny paid the bill. When she tried to give him her share, he refused it, reminding her that she'd paid for the first week's groceries. Another proof that Danny was innately fair. A good man. Not the horrible man who tossed her out of his office when she told him she was pregnant. But a man trying to get his bearings after the loss of a child.

At two o'clock that afternoon, with Sarah napping and Danny standing about three inches behind her, Grace got out her soup pot.

"Could you watch from a few feet back?"

"I'm curious."

"Well, be curious over by the counter." He stepped away from her and to keep the conversation flowing so he didn't pout, Grace said, "Soup is good on a chilly fall day like this."

Danny leaned against the counter and crossed his arms on his chest. "I think you're showing off."

"Showing off?"

"I doubted your abilities, so you're about to dazzle me with your spaetzle maker."

She laughed. "The spaetzle maker doesn't come into play for a while yet. Plus, there's very little expertise to soup," she said, dropping the big pot on the burner. "First you get a pot."

He rolled his eyes.

"Then you fill it halfway with water." She filled a large bowl with water and dumped the water into the big pot on the stove. "You add an onion, one potato, a stalk of celery and a chicken."

He gaped at her. "You're putting that entire chicken into the pot?"

"Yes."

Now he looked horrified.

She laughed. "Come on. This is how my grandmother did it." While he stood gaping at her, looking afraid to comment, she reached for the chicken bouillion cubes.

His eyes widened. "You're cheating!"

"Not really. The only thing bouillion cubes accomplishes is to cut down on cooking time."

"It's still cheating."

"I'm starting to notice a trend here. You're against anything that saves time."

"I want to learn to cook correctly."

She shrugged. "I need to be able to save time." With everything in the pot, she washed her hands then dried them with a paper towel.

"Now what?"

"Now, I'm going to take advantage of the fact that Sarah's still napping and read."

"Really?"

"Even with the bouillion cubes, the soup needs to cook at least an hour. It's best if we give it two hours." She glanced at the clock on the stove. "So until Sarah wakes I'm going to read."

"What should I do?"

"Weren't you working on something last night?"

He pouted. "Yeah, but I can't go any further because I left an important file at my office."

She sighed. "So I have to entertain you?"

He actually thought about that. For a few seconds Grace was sure the strong man in him would say no. Instead he laughed and said, "Yes. Somebody's got to entertain me."

Grace only stared at him. The night before she would have sworn he was firmly against getting involved with her, but today he was happy to be in her company. It didn't make sense—

Actually it did. The night before they were both considering sleeping together. Today they were making soup. Laughing. Happy. Not facing a life choice. Just having fun in each other's company. No stress. No worries. And wasn't that her real goal? To make him comfortable enough that Sarah's stays with him would be pleasant?

That was exactly her goal. So she couldn't waste such a wonderful opportunity.

"Do you know anything about gardening?"

"No."

"Ever played UNO?"

He gave her a puzzled look. "What's an Uno?"

"Wow, either you've led dull life or I've been overly entertained." Deciding she'd been overly entertained by a dad who couldn't do much in the way of physical things, Grace had a sudden inspiration. "If your mother's an expert at rummy, I know you've played that."

He glanced down at his fingernails as if studying them. "A bit."

"Oh, you think you're pretty good, don't you?"

"I'm a slouch."

"Don't sucker me!"

"Would I sucker you?"

"To get me to let my guard down so you could beat me, yes." She paused, then headed to the dining room buffet and the cards. "If you think you have to sucker me, you must not be very good."

"I'm exceptional."

She grinned. "I knew it."

Just then, a whimper floated from the baby monitor on the counter.

Grace set the cards back in the drawer. "So much for rummy. I'll try to get her back to sleep but I'm betting she wants to come downstairs."

"Why did she wake up so soon?"

"She probably heard us talking. That's why she didn't roll over and go back to sleep. She wants to be in on the action."

"Great. We'll play rummy with her in the high chair."

She paused on her way to the steps. "We could, but wouldn't it be more fun to spend a few minutes with Sarah first?"

He nodded. "Yeah. You're right."

As Grace went up the steps Danny took a long breath. He, Grace and the baby had had a good time shopping. He and Grace had had fun putting away the groceries and getting the soup into the pot. Now they would spend even more time together, and no doubt it would be fun.

He rubbed his hand across the back of his neck. The whole morning had been so easy—so right—that he knew he was correct in thinking that a friendship between him and Grace gave him the family, the connection, he so desperately wanted. But he also knew he was getting too close to a line he shouldn't cross—unless he wanted to fall in love with her and make their family a real family. He didn't want to hurt her, but right now, in his gut, he had an optimistic sense that he wouldn't. And the night before he'd seen in her eyes that she wanted what he wanted. For them to fall in love. She didn't have to say the words for Danny to know that she trusted him. She believed in him. He'd hurt her once, yet she trusted that he wouldn't hurt her again.

She believed in him and maybe the trick to their situation wouldn't be to take this one step at a time, but to trust what Grace saw in him, rather than what he knew about himself.

He walked into the kitchen and lifted the lid from the

pot. He sniffed the steam that floated out and his mouth watered. Even if soup was simple fare and even though he absolutely believed Grace had cheated with the bouillion cube, it smelled heavenly. He'd trusted her about spending two weeks here with her and Sarah, and had acclimated to being in a family again, albeit a nontraditional one. He'd trusted Grace about the soup, and it appeared he would be getting a tasty dinner. He'd trusted her about relaxing with Sarah and he now had a relationship with his daughter.

Could he trust her instinct that he wouldn't hurt her? Or let her down the way he'd let Lydia down?

Grace came down the steps carrying smiling Sarah.

When the baby immediately zeroed in on him, he said, "Hey, kid."

She yelped and clapped her hands.

"She does a lot of screeching and yelping. We've got to teach her a few words."

"Eventually. Right now, I think playing with the blocks or maybe the cone and rings are a better use of our time."

Danny was about to ask what the cone and rings were, but he suddenly had a very vivid memory of them. He saw Cory on the floor, brightly colored rings in a semicircle in front of him. He remembered teaching Cory to pick up the rings in order of size and slide them onto the cone.

And the memory didn't hurt. In fact, it made him smile. Cory had always had an eye for color. Maybe Sarah did, too? Or maybe Danny didn't care how smart

Sarah was or where her gifts were? Maybe his being so concerned about Cory's gifts was part of what had pushed Lydia away from him?

Forcing himself into the present, Danny glanced around. "Where's the toy box?"

"I don't have one. Sarah's toys are in the bottom drawer of the buffet in the dining area."

He walked over to it. "Curse of a small house?"

"Yes. This is the other reason I hesitated to talk with you about opening an investment account for me. I definitely need something with more space and I'm considering buying another house, and if I have extra money that's probably where it will go."

He opened the bottom drawer, found the colorful cone and rings and pulled it out. Returning to the area that served as a living room, he handed Grace the cone and sat on the sofa.

As Grace dumped the multicolored rings on the floor in front of Sarah, Danny cautiously said, "You know, we've never made a firm decision about child support."

She glanced up at him with a smile. "Yes, we did. I told you I wouldn't pay you any."

Her comment made him laugh and suddenly Danny felt too far away. He slid off the sofa and positioned himself on the floor across from Grace with Sarah between them, using the baby as a buffer between him and the woman who—whether she knew it or not—was tempting him to try something he swore he'd never try again. Even the idea of *trying* was new. He was shaky at best about trusting himself, and Sarah's happiness also tied into their situation. He couldn't act hastily, or let his hormones have control.

"Actually I think if we went to court a judge would order me to pay you something. So, come on. Let's really talk about this."

Grace busied herself making sure all the rings were within Sarah's reach. "Okay, if you want to pay something every month, why don't you put a couple hundred dollars a month into a college fund for Sarah?"

"Because she doesn't need a college fund. I can afford to pay for schooling." He took a breath, remembering that the last time they'd broached this subject she'd made him stop—the same way he made her stop when they got too far into his past. But resolving child support for their daughter was different than rehashing a past he desperately needed to forget. They had to come to an agreement on support.

"Look, I know you don't want to talk about this. But we have to. I don't feel right not contributing to her day-to-day expenses."

"I already told you that we're going to be sharing custody," Grace said as she gently guided Sarah's hand to take the ring she was shoving into her mouth and loop it onto the cone. "I will have her one week, but you will have her the next. Technically that's the way we'll share her expenses."

"I'd still like to—"

"Danny, I have a job. My house is nearly paid off. When I sell it, the money I get will be my down payment for the new one. I have a plan. It works. We're fine."

"I know. I just—"

Though Danny had thought she was getting angry, she playfully slapped his knee. "Just for one afternoon will you please relax?"

He peered at her hand, then caught her gaze. "You slapped me."

She grinned. "A friendly tap to wake you up, so you'll finally catch on that I'm right."

This was what he liked about her. She didn't have to win every argument. She also knew when to pull back. *Before* either one of them said something they'd regret, rather than after. It was a skill or sixth sense he and Lydia had never acquired. Plus, she had wonderfully creative ways of stepping away and getting him to step away. Rather than slammed doors and cold shoulders, she teased him. And she let him tease her.

"Oh, yeah? So what you're saying is that friendly tapping between us is allowed?"

"Sure. Sometimes something physical is the only way to get someone's attention."

"You mean like this?" He leaped behind Sarah, caught Grace around the shoulders, and nudged her to the floor in one fluid movement, so he could tickle her.

"Hey!" she yelped, trying to get away from him when he tickled her ribs. "You *had* my attention."

"I had your attention, but you weren't getting my point, so I'm making sure you see how serious I am when I say you should take my money."

She wiggled away from him. "I don't need your money."

"I can see that," he said, catching her waist and dragging her back. "But I want to give it."

He tickled her again and she cried, "Uncle! I give up! Give me a thousand dollars and we'll call it even."

"I gave you more than that for helping with Orlando," he said, catching her gaze. When their eyes met, his breathing stopped. Reminded of the bonus and Orlando, vivid images of their weekend came to Danny. He stopped tickling. She stopped laughing. His throat worked.

In the year that had passed he'd all but forgotten she existed, convinced that she had lied about her pregnancy and left his employ because she was embarrassed that her scheme had been exposed. Now he knew she'd been sick, dependent upon the bonus that he'd given her for expenses and dependent upon her parents for emotional support that *he* should have given her.

"I'm so sorry about everything."

She whispered, "I know."

"I would give anything to make it up for the hurt I caused you."

"There's no need."

He remembered again how she had been that weekend. Happy, but also gracious. She wouldn't take a promotion she hadn't deserved. She wouldn't pry, was kind to Orlando, never overstepped her boundaries. And he'd hurt her. Chances were, he'd hurt her again.

Still, he wanted so much to kiss her that his chest ached and he couldn't seem to overrule the instinct that was as much emotional as it was physical. He liked her.

He just plain liked her. He liked being with her, being part of her life, having her in his life.

He lowered his head and touched his lips to hers, telling himself that if he slid them into a simple, uncomplicated romance with no expectation of grandeur, she wouldn't be hurt. He wouldn't be hurt. Both would get what they wanted.

His mouth slid across hers slowly at first, savoring every second of the physical connection that was a manifestation of the depth of his feelings for her. She answered, equally slowly, as if as hesitant as he was, but also as unable to resist the temptation. When the slight meeting of mouths wasn't enough her lips blossomed to life under his, meeting him, matching him, then oh so slowly opening.

It was all the invitation Danny needed. He deepened the kiss, awash with the pleasure of being close to someone as wonderful as Grace. Happiness virtually sang through his veins. Need thrummed through him. For the first time since she'd brought Sarah to him, his thoughts didn't automatically tumble back to their beach house weekend. They stayed in the present, on the moment, on the woman in his arms and the desire to make love. To touch her, to taste her, to cherish every wonderful second. To build a future.

But the second the future came into play, Danny knew he was only deluding himself. He'd tried this once and failed. He'd lost a child, broken his wife. Spent a year mourning his loss alone in the big house so hollow and empty it echoed around him. He knew the reality of loss. How it destroyed a person. Emptied a life. He couldn't go through it again, but more than that, he wouldn't force Grace to.

CHAPTER TEN

DANNY broke the kiss, quickly rose from the floor and extended his hand to Grace. When she was on her feet, he spun away and Grace's stomach knotted.

"Danny?"

He rubbed both hands down his face. "Grace, this is wrong."

"No, it isn't." Glad for the opportunity to finally discuss their feelings instead of guessing, she walked over and grabbed him by the upper arm, turning him to face her. "This is us. We like each other. Naturally. We're like toast and butter or salt and pepper. We fit."

He laughed harshly. "Fit? Are you sure you want to say you fit with me?"

She didn't hesitate. "Yes."

He shook his head. "Grace, please. Please, don't. Don't fit with me. Don't even *want* to fit with me. If you were smart you wouldn't even want to be my friend."

At that her chin came up. If he was going to turn her away again, to deny her his love, or even the chance to be part of his life, this time she would make him explain. "Why?"

"Because I'm not good for you. I'm not good for anybody."

"Why?"

He raked his fingers through his short black hair. "Stop!"

"No. You say you're not good for me. I say you are. And I will not stop pursuing you."

"Then I'll leave."

"Great. Run. If that's your answer to everything, then you run."

He groaned and walked away as if annoyed that she wouldn't let him alone. "I'm not running. I'm saving you."

"I don't think you are. I also don't think you're a coward who runs. So just tell me what's wrong!"

He pivoted to face her so quickly that Grace flinched. "Tell you? Tell you what? That I failed at my marriage and hurt the woman I adored? Tell you that I don't want to do it again?"

His obsidian eyes were bright with pain. His voice seemed to echo from a dark, sacred place. A place of scars and black memories and wounds. A place he rarely visited and never took another person. Still, broken marriages were common. And though she understood his had hurt him, she also suspected even *he* knew it was time to get beyond his.

Her heart breaking for him, Grace whispered, "How do you know that you'll fail?"

Stiff with resistance, he angrily countered, "How do you know that I won't?"

"Because you're good. You may not know it but I see it every day in how you treat me and how you treat Sarah."

"Grace, you are wrong. I use people. Just ask my ex-wife. She'll tell you I'm a workaholic. If you called her right now, she'd probably even accurately guess that I'm only here because I need to raise my daughter because I need an heir. Carson Services needs an heir."

"Well, she'd be wrong. If you only wanted to raise Sarah because Carson Services needs an heir you could take me to court."

"Unless I didn't want you digging into my past."

That stopped her.

"What if this is all about me not wanting you to take me to court?" he asked, stepping close. "What if there is something so bad in my past that I know even you couldn't forgive it?"

She swallowed. Possibilities overwhelmed her. Not only did having a hidden sin in his past explain why he agreed to live with her and their daughter when letting his lawyers handle their situation would have been much easier, but it also explained why he always stepped back, always denied himself and her.

Still, she couldn't imagine what he could have done. He wasn't gentle and retiring by any means. But he also wasn't cruel or vindictive. He wasn't the kind to take risks or live on the edge. She might have told herself to stop guessing, to quit ascribing characteristics to him he didn't deserve, but she'd also lived with him for a week. Almost fifteen hours a day. She'd seen him *choose* to make breakfast, *choose* to bathe Sarah, *choose* to give Grace breaks. She didn't believe he could be cruel or do something so horrible it couldn't be forgiven.

She took a breath, then another. "I don't think there is something in your past that can't be forgiven."

"What if I told you that I killed my son?"

Her heart in her throat, more aware of the pain that would cause him than any sort of ramification it would have on their relationship, she said, "You couldn't have killed your son."

"It was an accident, but the accident was my fault."

Grace squeezed her eyes shut. An accident that was his fault. Of course. That accounted for so many things in his life and how he had treated her that before this hadn't added up.

But accidents were circumstances that somehow got out of someone's control. He hadn't deliberately killed his child. He couldn't deliberately kill his child. That was why he was so tortured now.

"Danny, it wasn't your fault."

His eyes blazed. "Don't you forgive me! And don't brush it off as if my son's life was of no consequence. I was in charge of him that morning. *I* knew he was in the mood to push me. He wanted to remove the training wheels from his bike and I refused, but he kept arguing, begging, pleading. When my cell phone rang, I should have ignored it. But my natural reaction kicked in, I grabbed it, answered it and gave him the chance to prove to me how good he was on his bike by darting out into the street right into the path of an SUV."

He paused, raked his fingers through his hair again and his voice dropped to a feather-light whisper. "A neighbor hit him. She doesn't come out of her house now. I ruined a lot of lives that morning."

The tick of the clock was the only sound in the room. Grace stood frozen, steeped in his pain, hurting for him.

"Not quite as sure of me now, are you?"

She swallowed. "It wasn't your fault."

He ran his hands down his face. "It was my fault. And I live with it every day. And I miss my son and I remember the look on my wife's face." Seeming to be getting his bearings, he blew his breath out on a long gust and faced her. "And I won't do that to you."

He headed for the stairway. Panicked, knowing they were only at the tip of this discussion, Grace said, "What if I—"

He stopped at the bottom of the steps. His face bore the hard, cold expression she remembered from the day she told him she was pregnant.

"You don't get a choice. You don't get a say. This pain is mine."

He ran up the steps and Grace collapsed on her sofa. Bending forward, she lifted Sarah from the floor and squeezed her to her chest, suddenly understanding why he didn't want her digging into his past. It could give her plenty of grounds to keep him from getting custody—even shared. But it also gave her a foot in the door to keep the baby away from him completely.

And she hated to admit she was considering it. Not because of what had happened with his son, but because he couldn't seem to get beyond it. What did it mean for Sarah that her father wouldn't let himself love again?

She took a breath, knowing her fears were premature because they had another week to live together, another week for him to recognize that though he didn't want to forget his son, he also had a daughter who needed him. She shouldn't jump to conclusions.

But twenty minutes later he came downstairs, suitcases in hand.

"We have another week to live together."

"Grace, I'm done." He shrugged into his jacket. "Besides, I never signed the agreement. This was a mistake anyway."

With that he opened the door, and stepped out, but he turned one final time and looked at Sarah, then his gaze slowly rose to catch Grace's. She saw the regret, the pain, the need. Then she watched him quickly erase it as determination filled his dark eyes. He stepped out into the September afternoon, closing the door behind him with a soft click.

Danny walked into the empty foyer of his huge house and listened to the echo his suitcase made as he set it on the floor, knowing this was the rest of his life, and for the first time totally, honestly, unemotionally committed to accepting it. He wouldn't risk hurting Grace. Telling his story that afternoon, he remembered in vivid detail how unworthy he was to drag another person into

his life. Now that Grace knew his mistake, he didn't
expect to even get visitation with Sarah. He expected
to live his life alone, the perfect candidate to serve
Carson Services and pass on the family legacy.

To Sarah. A little girl who wouldn't know him, probably wouldn't know about Carson Services, but who
shared his bloodline. When she came of age, Danny
would offer her the chance to train to take over the
family business, but would Grace let her? No mother
would sentence her daughter to even a few hours a week
with a cold, distant father.

Walking up the ornate curved stairway of the huge
home that went to the next Carson, Danny had to
wonder if that wasn't a good thing.

CHAPTER ELEVEN

A MONTH later, seated at the slim wooden table in the hearing room in the courthouse, Danny wasn't entirely sure why he had come to this proceeding. Grace's reasons for being here were a no-brainer. She'd had her lawyer set the hearing to make her case for Danny not getting custody. She could probably get enough reasons on the record to preclude him from even *seeing* their baby again.

But he knew she wouldn't do that. After his confession to her, and a week of wallowing in misery in his lonely house, he'd pulled himself up by his bootstraps and gone back to work like the sharp CEO he was, and his life had fallen into a strong, comfortable routine. Once he'd gotten his bearings and stopped feeling sorry for himself, he'd recognized that *all* was not lost. Grace wouldn't keep Sarah from him. She would be kind enough—or maybe fair enough to Sarah—to let him have visitation, even though she probably hated him.

Some days he hated himself. Blamed himself for the pain he'd caused both him and Grace by letting her believe in him—even if it was for one short week. Had he told Grace right from the beginning that his son was not only dead, but Danny himself was responsible for Cory's accident, Grace would have happily kept her distance. She wouldn't have mourned the loss of his love, as he'd pictured her doing. He wouldn't have again felt the sting of living alone in his big, hollow house, torturously reminded of how it felt to be whole, to be wanted, to have people in his life and a purpose beyond perpetuating the family business.

But if nothing else had come from the week he'd spent with Grace and Sarah, Danny knew Grace would be fair. He thoroughly loved his daughter. He wanted to be part of her life, not just to assure she'd be ready to make a choice about Carson Services, but because he loved having her around. He loved being with her. And she was Danny's last chance at a family. He might never have the good fortune to share his life with Sarah's mother, but he could at least have a daughter.

So he supposed he'd come to this hearing as a show of good faith, proof that if Grace intended to let him have visitation, he wanted it. He suspected that any visitation she granted him would be supervised. He'd been the one in charge when Cory was killed. Grace's lawyer would undoubtedly drop that fact into the proceeding as a way to demonstrate that Danny wasn't a good dad. But he'd take even supervised visitation. At this point, he'd take anything he could get.

Grace entered the hearing room. Wearing an electric-blue suit, with her dark shoulder-length hair swaying around her and her sexy violet eyes shining, she was pretty enough to stop his heart. Yet in spite of how gorgeous she was, Danny's real reaction to her was emotional rather than physical. He'd missed her. They'd spent a total of nine days together. Three at his beach house and six at her house and he missed her. Ached for her. Longed for everything he knew darned well they could have had together, if he hadn't looked away for one split second and changed his destiny.

Grace approached the table with her lawyer, young, handsome, Robby Malloy. The guy Danny's lawyer called pretty boy Malloy. Danny could see why. He had the face of a movie star and carried himself like a billionaire. Danny experienced a surge of jealousy so intense he had to fight to keep himself from jumping from behind the table and yanking Grace away from the sleazy ambulance chaser.

But he didn't jump and he didn't yank. Because as a father his first concern had to be assuring that he was part of his daughter's life. He'd never had the right to care about Grace, about who she dated, or even if she dated.

So why was his blood pressure rising and his chest tightening from just looking at her with another man? Her lawyer no less? A man who may not even be romantically interested, only earning his hourly fee for representing her?

The judge entered the room, his dark robe billowing around him with his every step. Danny followed the lead of his attorney, Art Brown, and rose.

Having not yet taken his seat, Malloy extended his hand to the judge. "Judge Antanazzo."

"Good morning, Mr. Malloy," Charlie Antanazzo boomed. "How's my favorite attorney today?"

Malloy laughed. "Well, I doubt that I'm your favorite attorney," he said, obviously charming the judge. "But I'm great, your honor. This is my client, Grace McCartney."

As Grace shook Judge Antanazzo's hand, he smiled. "It's a pleasure to meet you."

Danny would just bet it was. Not only did the judge smile like any man happy to meet a pretty girl, but also Danny hadn't missed the way the judge took a quick inventory that started with Grace's shiny sable hair and managed to skim her perfect figure and nice legs in under a second.

This time it was a bit harder to refrain from leaping over the desk and yanking her to him.

But that ship had sailed and Danny had to grow accustomed to watching men fawn over Grace. He'd had his chance and he'd blown it. Or maybe it wasn't so much that Danny had had his chance, as much as it was that Danny had destroyed his own life long before he met Grace.

Danny's lawyer finally spoke. "Good morning, your honor," Art said, then shook the judge's hand. "This is my client, Danny Carson."

The judge quickly shook the hand Danny extended and frowned as he looked down at the brown case file he'd brought into the hearing room with him.

"Yes, I know. Danny Carson. CEO of Carson

Services. Let's see," he said, skimming the words in front of him. "Ms. McCartney was in your employ at one time." He continued reading. "She told you she was pregnant. You didn't believe her. Circumstances, including her being sick during the pregnancy, kept her from pursuing the matter. Then she took the baby to you." He read some more. "There's no record of child support." He looked at Danny. "Do you pay child support?"

Danny's lawyer said, "No, your honor, but—"

The judge ignored him. "All right then. This case boils down to a few concise facts. Ms. McCartney told you she was pregnant, brought the child to you and you don't pay child support." He glanced from Danny to Grace and held Grace's gaze. "Am I up to speed?

"There's a little more, your honor," Grace's lawyer said. "Once the court reporter is ready, I'd like to go on the record."

Danny's heart sank. Great. Just great. From the scant information the judge had read, it was pretty clear whose side he was on. Once Danny's past came out, the judge might not even let him have supervised visitation. The urge to defend himself rose up in Danny and this time rather than fight it, he let it take root. All the facts that the judge had read had made him look bad. But he wasn't. Everything he'd done wrong wasn't really a deliberate misdeed. Every one of his "bad" things were explainable—defendable.

He'd *misinterpreted* Grace's not answering the phone the night he'd flown home after his week of client hopping. As a result of that he broke off with her. So, when she came in to tell him she was pregnant, he'd thought it was a ruse to get him back, and he hadn't believed her. And when she left his employ, Danny had thought it was because her scheme had been exposed. He wasn't bad. He wasn't a schmuck. He had made some mistakes. Very defendable mistakes. Technically he could even defend himself about Cory's death.

He took a breath. That wasn't at issue right now. Sarah's custody was.

The lawyers and judge made preliminary statements for the record. Danny studiously avoided looking at Grace by tapping the eraser of his pencil on the desk. Eventually the judge said, "Mr. Malloy, ball's in your court."

"Thank you, your honor. My client would like to testify first."

Danny's lawyer had warned him that preliminary hearings could sometimes seem unofficial, but Danny shouldn't take it lightly because a court reporter would be recording the proceedings. He sat up a little straighter.

Though Grace stayed in her seat at the table, she was sworn in.

Her lawyer said, "Okay, Ms. McCartney, there is no argument between you and Mr. Carson about paternity?"

"No. And if there were we'd get a DNA test. We've agreed to that."

"But there's no need because you know Mr. Carson is the father?"

"Yes. I didn't—hadn't—" She paused, stumbling

over her explanation and Danny frowned, not sure what she was getting at.

"You hadn't had relations," Robbie prompted and Grace nodded.

"—I hadn't had relations with anybody for several months before Danny—Mr. Carson—and I spent a weekend at his beach house."

Danny damned near groaned. Not because it sounded as if he'd taken her to his private hideaway to seduce her, but because for the first time since that weekend he realized how important sleeping with him must have been in her life. She didn't sleep around. Hell, she apparently barely slept with anybody. But she'd been with him that night. She'd smiled at him, made him laugh, made him feel really alive—

Robbie Malloy said, "So why are you here today, Ms. McCartney?" bringing Danny back to the present.

"I'm here today because Mr. Carson and I had a shared custody agreement."

"Briefly, what does the agreement say?"

"That if he could stay at my house for two weeks, basically to learn how to care for Sarah, I would agree to shared custody."

"Did Mr. Carson want shared custody?"

"No. At first he wanted full custody. The agreement we made about shared custody was drafted to prevent us from fighting over Sarah. Shared custody seemed like the fair way to handle things."

"But—"

Grace took a breath. Danny raised his gaze to hers

and she looked directly at him. Which was exactly what he'd intended to make her do. If she wanted to testify against him, then let her do it looking into his eyes.

"But he didn't stay the two weeks."

Danny's eyes hardened.

"Ms. McCartney, is it also correct that he didn't sign the agreement?"

"No, he did not."

"And is that why we're here?"

"Well, I can't speak for Mr. Carson, but the reason I am here is to get it on the record that even though he didn't sign the agreement, or stay the two weeks, I believe Mr. Carson fulfilled its spirit and intent and I feel we should honor it."

"Which means you believe you and Mr. Carson should have shared custody?"

She held Danny's gaze. "Yes."

"You want me to have Sarah every other week?" Danny said, forgetting they were on the record.

"Yes. Danny, you proved yourself."

"I left."

"I know." She smiled slightly. "It doesn't matter. You showed me you can care for Sarah."

Robbie said, "Your honor, that's what we wanted to get on the record. No further questions."

The judge turned to Art. "Do you want to question Ms. McCartney?"

Art raised his hands. "Actually I think we'll let Ms. McCartney's testimony stand as is."

"Does Mr. Carson want to testify?"

Without consulting Danny, Art said, "No."

The judge quickly glanced down at his notes. "Technically you have a custody agreement in place. It's simply not executed. But Ms. McCartney still wants to honor it." He looked at Danny. "Mr. Carson? Do you want to honor the agreement?"

Danny nodded as Art said, "Yes."

The judge made a sound of strained patience, then said, "You're a very lucky man, Mr. Carson. Very lucky indeed."

Staring at Grace, who had begun casually gathering her purse as if what she had just said hadn't been of monumental significance, Danny didn't know what to say. Art spoke for him. "Your honor, when parents share custody it's frequently considered that each is taking his or her share of the financial burden when the child is with him—or her."

The judge closed the file. "Right. As if these two people have equal financial means." He faced Danny. "Don't screw this up." He left the room in a flurry or robes and promises about writing up an order.

Art began gathering his files. "Well, that went much better than expected," he said with a laugh, but overwhelmed with too many emotions to name, Danny watched Grace and her lawyer heading for the door.

Just as Grace would have stepped over the threshold, emotion overruled common sense and he called, "Wait!"

Grace turned and smiled at him.

Danny's throat worked. She was incredibly beautiful and incredibly generous. And he was numb with gratitude. "Why didn't you—"

She tilted her head in question. "Why didn't I what?"

Go for the jugular? Fight? Tell the court about Cory?

"Why are you letting me have Sarah?"

"You're her dad."

"I —" He took a breath. "What if I can't handle her?"

To his amazement, Grace laughed. "You can handle her. I've seen you handle her. You'll be fine."

"I'll be fine," he repeated, annoyed with Grace for being so flip, when the safety of their daughter was at stake. "What kind of answer is that!"

"It's an honest one."

"How can you trust her with me!"

"Are you telling me you're going to put her in danger?"

He glared at her. "You know I won't."

"Then there's no reason you shouldn't have your daughter."

"You trust me?"

She smiled. "I trust you. But if you're nervous, hire a nanny. You've told me at least twice that you were going to do that. So hire somebody."

Danny's heart swelled with joy. He was getting a second chance. He would have something of a family. He swallowed hard. "Okay."

She took two steps closer to him and placed her hand on his forearm. "Or, if you don't want to hire a nanny, you could come home."

Home. Her house *was* home. Warm. Welcoming. He could remember nearly every detail of their six short days. Especially how tempted he was to take what they both wanted. Just as he was tempted now to take what she was offering. A complete second chance. Not just an opportunity to be Sarah's daddy, but a second chance at life. A real life.

But he also knew he was damaged. So damaged it wasn't fair to use Grace as a step up out of his particular hell. He smiled regretfully. "You know you deserve better."

"So you say, but I don't think so. I see the part of you that you're trying to hide, or forget, or punish. I don't see the past."

"You're lucky."

"No, Danny, I'm not lucky. It's time. Time for you to move on." She held out her hand. "Come home with me. Start again."

He stared at the hand she offered. Delicate fingers. Pretty pink fingernails. Feminine things. Soft things. Things that had been missing from his life for so long. A million possibilities entered his head. A million things he would do, *could* do, if he took that hand, took the steps that would put him in Grace's world again. He could teach Sarah to walk. Hear her first word. Hear the first time she called him daddy. Sleep with Grace. Use the spaezle maker. Steal kisses. Share dreams. Spend Christmas as part of a family.

None of which he deserved.

"I can't."

CHAPTER TWELVE

DANNY turned away and though Grace's gut reaction was to demand that he talk to her, she didn't. Tears filled her eyes. Tears for him as much as for the wonderful future he was denying both of them, and she turned around and walked out of the hearing room.

Robbie was waiting. "You okay?"

She managed a smile. "Yeah. I'm fine."

"You're awfully generous with him."

"That's because he's so hard on himself."

"Be careful, Grace," Robbie said, directing her to the stairway that led to the courthouse lobby. "Men like Danny Carson who have a reputation for taking what they want don't like to lose. You may think that by "granting" him shared custody you were doing him and your daughter a kindness, but you had him over a barrel and he knew it. He may have just played you like a Stradivarius. Made you feel sorry for him so that you'd give him what he wanted, since he knew he probably couldn't beat you in court."

"I don't think so. I know Danny better than you do. He wouldn't do something like that."

"You think you know Danny?"

"I *know* Danny."

"Well, you better hope so because what we got on the record today—you saying you believed he was capable of caring for Sarah—negated any possibility we had of using his son's death in future hearings."

Grace gasped. "I would never use his son's death!"

Robbie held up his hand in defense. "Hey, I'm okay with that. Actually I agree that it would be cruel to use his son's death against him. I'm just saying be careful. This whole thing could backfire and you could end up fighting for your own daughter."

"I won't."

Robbie shook his head. "God save me from clients in love."

"It's that obvious?"

"Yes." Holding open one of the two huge double doors of the courthouse entrance, Robbie added, "And if Danny's as smart as everyone claims he is, he'll use it. Better put my number on speed dial."

Reading to Sarah in the rocking chair that night, Grace thought about the look on Danny's face when she stated for the record that she wanted their shared custody agreement upheld.

She shouldn't have been surprised that he expected her to testify against him. He was angry with himself and nothing she said or did could change that. No matter how sad he appeared or how much she'd simply wanted to hug him, she couldn't. A man who couldn't forgive himself, especially for something so traumatic, wasn't ready for a relationship and he might never be. It had broken her heart when he refused her offer to return home. As much for him as for herself.

But at least she had her answer now.

With Sarah asleep in her arms, Grace set the storybook on a shelf of the changing table and rose from the rocker. She laid Sarah in her crib, covered her, kissed her forehead and walked down the steps.

It wasn't going to be easy sharing custody with a man she loved but who could never love her. But she intended to do it. Actually she intended to do the one thing she'd promised herself she wouldn't do the night she rushed down to his beach house bar to see if he felt about her the way she felt about him. She was going to pine for him. She intended to love him forever, quietly, without expectation of anything in return because the real bottom line to Danny's trouble was that nobody had ever really loved him. At least not without expectation of anything in return. His parents expected him to take over the family business. His ex-wife held him responsible for their child's death. The people who worked for him wanted a job. His investors, even investors he considered friends, like Orlando, needed his expertise. Nobody loved him without expectation of anything in return.

So she would be that person. She might never be his wife, but she would be there for him in all the right ways, so that he could see that he was okay and that life didn't always have to be about what he could give somebody.

Two Mondays later when Robbie called and told her that the judge's order had come down, Grace sat quietly and listened as her lawyer explained how she was to have Sarah ready at six o'clock that Friday night. With every word he said, her chest tightened. Her eyes filled with tears. It was easy to say she intended to love Danny without expectation of anything in return when the situation was abstract. But now that shared custody was a reality she suddenly realized loving Danny meant denying herself. At the very least, she would spend every other week without her daughter.

She hung up the phone, glad for four days to prepare herself to see him, and managed to greet him with a smile Friday evening. With Sarah's diaper bag packed and sitting by the door, she put Sarah into his arms.

"Hey, Sarah Bear," he said softly and the baby hit him on the cheek with her rattle. He laughed nervously. "I guess she's forgotten who I am."

"Maybe," Grace said, trying to sound strong and confident, but with Danny standing at her door, refusing to go beyond the foyer, wearing a topcoat and scarf because western Pennsylvania had had its first snowfall of the season, it seemed as if the Danny she loved no longer existed. The guy in jeans and a T-shirt who made pancakes seemed to have been replaced by the man who ran Carson Services.

"We won't need that," Danny said, nodding at the diaper bag, as he struggled to contain Sarah who had begun to wail in earnest and stretched away from Danny, reaching for Grace. "I have a nursery full of things." For the first time since he'd arrived, he met her gaze. "I also hired a nanny."

"Good." Tears clogged Grace's throat when Sarah squealed and reached for her. "Stay with Daddy, Sarah," she whispered, pushing the baby back in Danny's arms, then fussing with Sarah's jacket as she slowly pulled her hands way.

But with her mom this close, Sarah all but crawled out of Danny's arms again, with a squeal that renewed her crying.

Pain ricocheted through Grace. "Maybe we should have broken this up? Had her do an overnight visit or two before we forced her to spend an entire week."

"It's going to be hard no matter how we do it. Let's just get this over with."

He opened the door, not even sparing Grace a glance, taking her daughter.

"If she gives you any trouble, just call," Grace said, trying to keep her voice light and bright as he walked away, but it wobbled.

Already on the sidewalk, striding to his car, Danny said, "We're fine."

And he left.

Watching his car lights as they disappeared into the night, Grace stood on her stoop, with her lawyer's words ringing in her ears, suddenly wondering if Danny really hadn't tricked her.

Could he have put on jeans a few times, made a couple of pancakes and cruelly lured her into loving him, all to take her child?

* * *

Danny entered his home, sobbing Sarah on his arm. "Elise!" he called, summoning his nanny.

She strode into the foyer. Tall and sturdily build, Elise wore a brightly colored knit cardigan over a white blouse and gray skirt. She looked like she could have stepped out of a storybook, as the quintessential nanny.

"Oh, my. This little one's got a pair of lungs!" Elise said with a laugh, and reached out to take Sarah from his arms. But as Danny handed the baby to her nanny, he felt odd about giving over Sarah's care so easily. He remembered that Grace had told him that she didn't want to share his nanny because caring for Sarah was part of her quality time.

After shrugging out of his topcoat, he reached for Sarah again. "Tonight, I'll take care of her."

"But—"

"At least until she adjusts to being here."

Elise took a breath, gave him a confused smile and said, "As you wish."

Danny didn't care what she thought. All he cared about was Sarah. He'd thought hiring a nanny would be the perfect way to help ease Sarah into her new life, but seeing Elise with Sarah felt wrong. Sarah was his responsibility. His little girl. His daughter.

Carrying Sarah into the nursery, Danny thought of Grace. How tears had filled her eyes when Sarah had begun to cry. He'd left quickly, not to cause her pain, but to get all three of them accustomed to this every other Friday night ritual. But he'd hurt her.

Again.

It seemed he was always hurting Grace.

Still, with crying Sarah on his arm, it wasn't the time to think about that. He wrestled her out of her jacket, little black shoes, tiny jeans and T-shirt, then rolled her into a pair of pajamas.

She never stopped crying.

He put her on his shoulder and patted her back, as he walked downstairs and to the refrigerator where he extracted one of the bottles Elise had prepared. Sitting on the rocker in the nursery, he fed her the bottle and though she drank greedily, sniffled remnants of her crying jag accompanied her sucking. The second the bottle came out of her mouth, she began to cry again.

"I'm sorry. I know this is hard. I know you miss your mom, but this is the right thing. Trust me."

He paced the floor with her, trying to comfort her, but as he pivoted to make his third swipe across the room, he saw the books beside the rocker. The designer he'd hired to create the yellow and pink, bear-theme room had strategically stationed books on a low table within reach of the rocker. After sitting again, he took one of the books, opened it and began to read.

"Once upon a time, in a kingdom far away, there lived a princess. Her name was—" He paused, then smiled. "Sarah. Sarah bear."

Sarah's crying slowed.

"She was a beautiful child with blond—reddish-brown curls," he amended, matching the description of the little girl in the book to the little girl in his arms. "And blue eyes."

Her crying reduced to sniffles and she blinked, her confused expression taking him back to the first night he'd cared for her alone—the night Grace had been edgy. The memory caused him to smile. He hadn't wanted to be alone with Sarah. Wasn't sure he could handle her. He'd only kept the baby to please Grace.

He took a breath. This time he was caring for Sarah to *protect* Grace. From him. Adding a failed marriage to ignoring her pregnancy and taking her child wouldn't help anything. He had to remember that.

"The princess lived alone with her father, the king. Her mother had died when the princess was a baby and a governess had been hired. Mrs. Pickleberry had a face puckered in a perpetual frown and Sarah would pretend to be ill, rather than spend time with her when the king was out of the palace performing his royal duties. Each time, when Mrs. Pickleberry would leave her room, sufficiently convinced that Sarah should stay in bed for the day, Sarah would crawl into her window seat, her legs tucked beneath her, her thumb in her mouth, watching, alone, for her father to return."

Danny stopped reading. The king didn't have a choice about leaving his daughter in the care of her governess, but Danny had choices. Lots of them. In the argument they'd had the day Grace brought Sarah to him, Grace had asked if it was better for Sarah to be raised by strangers rather than her mother. Still, that wasn't what was happening here. Yes, Sarah would be stuck with a governess—uh, nanny—while Danny was at work, but he wasn't taking Sarah away from her mother. Not really. Just every other week.

He glanced down. Sarah was asleep.

Thank God. He didn't think he could take any more of the story's inadvertent accusations. He laid the baby in her crib and stood for several minutes, just watching Sarah, basking in the joy of being a dad, considering all the things he could do for Sarah, and convincing himself that while he had Sarah, Grace could also do so many things, things she otherwise didn't have time to do.

But the soft smile that had lit his face suddenly died. Grace might have time to do tons of different things, but she wouldn't. She would spend every hour he had custody worrying about Sarah. Not because Danny wasn't trustworthy, but because she would miss her. And only because she would miss her. In fact, right now, Grace was probably crying, or lonely. And he absolutely couldn't stand the thought of it.

He wasn't the kind of man to hurt people. But his reasoning this time went beyond his own image of himself. He couldn't stand the thought of Grace missing Sarah because he loved her. The last thing any man wanted to do was hurt the woman he loved most in this world. And yet that was what he always did with Grace. He hurt her. When he'd met her, he was a broken, empty man. She'd reminded him of life. That Sunday night at the beach house, she'd given him a glimpse of what they'd have together if he could open up. When he couldn't, she'd gracefully accepted that he didn't want to see her anymore. But when she'd gotten pregnant, she'd tried one more time. When he rejected her again, she didn't return until she had Sarah. Offering him something he truly didn't deserve: a place in their daughter's life. A place she hadn't snatched away. Even knowing his dark secret, she had faith in him when he had none in himself.

Danny gritted his teeth. He knew the solution to this problem. He knew it as well as he knew his own last name.

In order to save Grace, he had to let go of his guilt. He had to try again. In earnest.

Or he had to take Sarah back to Grace. For good. No more shared custody.

Halfway to the kitchen to make cocoa, Grace heard a knock on her door and peered at her watch. Who would be visiting after nine at night?

Expecting it to be her parents, who were undoubtedly worried about her because this was her first night without Sarah, she turned and headed for the door. When she looked through the peephole and saw Danny holding sleeping Sarah, she jumped back and yanked open the door.

Reaching for Sarah, she said, "What happened? What's wrong?"

He motioned inside her house. "Can we talk?"

Cradling Sarah on her arm, she looked down and

examined every exposed inch of her sleeping baby. Her gaze shooting to Danny, she said, "She's fine?"

He nodded. "Yeah. It's you and I who have the problem. We need to talk."

Grace's heart stopped. She'd nearly had herself convinced that Robbie was right. Danny had tricked her and he had gotten everything he wanted at Grace's expense. All because she'd fallen in love with him.

But he was back, saying they needed to talk, sounding like a man ready to give, rather than take. Still, this time she had to be strong, careful. She couldn't fall victim to the look in his beautiful dark eyes…or the hope in her heart.

She had to be strong.

"Danny, it's late and our lawyers said everything we needed to say—"

"Not mine. He hardly said anything. And there are a few things I need to say. Put Sarah to bed. In *her* bed."

The gentleness of his voice got to her. If nothing else, Grace knew with absolute certainty that Danny loved Sarah. Knowing her lawyer would probably be angry that she talked to Danny without counsel, Grace stepped aside so Danny could enter.

As she turned to walk up the steps with the baby, she saw Danny hesitate in her small entryway.

Remembering he was always more at ease in her home when she gave him something to do, she said, "I was just about to make cocoa. You could go in the kitchen and get mugs."

"Okay."

When she returned downstairs, Grace saw he had only gotten as far as the stools in front of the breakfast counter. Again noting his hesitation, Grace said, "Don't you want cocoa?"

"I'd love some."

He sounded so quiet and so unsteady that Grace didn't know what to say. She set the pan on the stove and poured in milk and cocoa, waiting for him to talk. When he didn't, she lowered the flame on the gas burner and walked to the breakfast bar.

"Did something happen with Sarah?"

"No. She was fine." He caught her gaze. "Why did you do this? Why are you letting me have her every other week?"

She shrugged. "You're Sarah's dad. She loves you. You love her."

He caught her gaze. "And that's it?"

"What else is there?"

"You didn't give Sarah to me to try to force my hand?"

"Force your hand?" She laughed. "Oh, my God, Danny, when have I ever gotten you to do anything? You didn't believe I slept with you because I liked you. You were sure I had an agenda. You didn't believe I was pregnant when I told you. You kicked me out of your office. You were so suspicious of me when I suggested shared custody that *you* insisted on the agreement. If there's one thing I know not to do it's try to force you to do anything."

"You didn't give me Sarah so that I'd be so grateful I'd fall in love with you?"

After a second to recover from the shock of that accusation, she shook her head sadly. He really did believe that people only did nice things when they wanted something from him. "Oh, Danny, I didn't give you time with Sarah to drag you into a relationship with me."

"Really?"

"Yes. I gave you time with Sarah because you're her dad."

"And you want nothing from me."

Grace debated lying to him. She *wanted* them to be a normal family. She wanted him to be the happy, laughing guy who'd made love to her at the beach house. She wanted him to want her. To welcome her into his life with open arms. She wanted a lot, but she didn't expect anything from him. The way she saw their lives unfolding, she would spend most of the time they had together just happy to see him unwind.

But if there was one thing she'd learned about Danny over the past weeks, it was that he valued honesty. So she took a breath and said, "I want a lot. But I'm also a realist. You won't fall in love again until you're ready. Nobody's going to push you."

He slid onto the stool. "I know." Pointing at the stove, he said, "I think your pot's boiling over."

"Eeek!" She spun away from the breakfast bar and ran to the stove, where hot milk bubbled over the sides of her aluminum pot. "Looks like I'll be starting over."

"I think we should both start over."

Not at all sure what he meant by that, Grace poured

out the burned milk and filled the dirty pot with water, her heart pounding at the possibilities. "And how do you propose we start over?"

"The first step is that I have to tell you everything."

She found a second pot, filled it with milk and poured in cocoa, again refusing to hurry him along or push him. This was his show. She would let him do whatever he wanted. She'd *never* misinterpret him again. "So tell me everything."

While she adjusted the gas burner, he said, "Tonight I really thought through the things that had had happened to me in the past several years, and I realized something I'd refused to see before this."

He paused again. Recognizing he might think she wasn't paying attention, Grace said, "And what was that?"

"My marriage to Lydia was over before Cory's accident."

At that Grace turned to face him. "What?"

"Tonight when I was caring for Sarah in my brand-new nursery and thinking about how sad you probably were here alone, I realized that you are very different from Lydia. She and I spent most of our married life fighting. First she didn't want children, then when we had Cory she wanted him enrolled in a school for gifted children in California. We didn't fight over my pushing him into taking over Carson Services. We fought because she kept pushing him away. She didn't want him around."

"Oh."

"I won't say I didn't love her when I married her, but I can now see that we were so different, especially in what we wanted out of life, that we were heading for divorce long before Cory's accident. Tonight, I finally saw that I needed to separate the two. Cory's accident didn't ruin my marriage. Lydia and I had handled that all by ourselves."

"I'm sorry."

He laughed lightly. "You know what? I knew you would be. And I think that's part of why I like you. Why I was drawn to you at the beach house. You really have a sixth sense about people. I saw how you were with Orlando and listened in sometimes on your conversations, and I knew you were somebody special. More than that, though, you respected the same things I did. Especially family and commitments. You and I had the thing Lydia and I lacked. Common beliefs. Sunday night when we were alone, I realized we also had more than our fair share of chemistry." He paused, then said, "But I panicked."

Since Grace couldn't dispute what he said—or add to it—she stayed silent, letting him talk.

"Tonight, rocking Sarah, thinking about you, hating that you had to give up your child, I was angry that life had forced us into this position, but I suddenly realized it wasn't life that forced us here. It was me because I didn't think I could love you without hurting you."

Too afraid to make a hopeful guess about the end of his conclusions, Grace held her breath.

"I guess thinking about my own marriage and Lydia

and Cory while holding Sarah, I finally saw something that made everything fall into place for me."

Grace whispered, "What's that?"

"That if you and I had been married, we would have weathered Cory's death. You might have honestly acknowledged my mistake in grabbing my cell phone, and even acknowledged that I would feel guilty, but you never would have let me take the blame. You and I would have survived. A marriage between us would have survived."

Grace pressed her hand to her chest. "That's quite a compliment."

"You're a very special person. Or maybe the strength of your love is special." He shook his head. "Or maybe you and I together are special. I don't know. I just know that through all this you'd been very patient. But I'm done running."

She smiled. "Thought you didn't run."

"Well, maybe I wasn't running. Maybe I was holding everybody back. Away. But I can't do that anymore."

She took a breath, her hope building, her heart pounding.

"Because I love you. I love you." He repeated, as if saying it seemed so amazing he needed to say it again. "I couldn't stand the thought of you here alone, and though I don't want to hurt you I finally saw that unless I took this step, I would always be hurting you."

Her voice a mere whisper, Grace said, "What step?"

"I want to love you. I want you to marry me."

She would have been content to hear him say he

wanted to try dating. His proposal was so far beyond what she'd been expecting that her breath stuttered in her chest. "What?"

"I love you and I want you to marry me."

Dumbstruck, Grace only stared at him.

"You could say you love me, too."

"I love you, too."

At that Danny laughed. The sound filled the small kitchen.

"And you want to marry me." He took a breath. "Grace, alone with Sarah I realized I had everything I needed and I could have talked myself into accepting only that. But I want you, too. Will you marry me?"

"And I want to marry you!" She made a move to launch herself into his arms, but remembered her cocoa and turned to flip off the burner. By the time she turned back, he was at her side, arms opened, ready for her to walk into them.

He wrapped his arms around her as his mouth met hers. Without a second of hesitation, Grace returned his kiss, opening her mouth when he nudged her to do so. Her heart pounded in her ears as her pulse began to scramble. He loved her. *He loved her and wanted to marry her.* It almost seemed too good to be true.

He pulled away. "Pot's probably boiling over."

"I thought I turned that off." She whirled away from him and saw the cooling pot. "I did turn that off."

"I have a better idea than cocoa anyway."

He pulled her to him and whispered something in her ear that should have made a new mother blush. But she laughed and countered something equally sexy in his ear and he kissed her deeply, reminding her of her thoughts driving up I-64 the Monday they left Virginia Beach. *She'd found Mr. Right.*

She *had* found Mr. Right, and they were about to live happily ever after.

EPILOGUE

RESTING UNDER the shade of a huge oak, on the bench seat of a weathered wooden picnic table, Grace watched Sarah as she played in the sandbox with the children of Grace's cousins. She could also see Danny standing in left field, participating in the married against the singles softball game at the annual McCartney reunion.

The CEO and chairman of the board of Carson Services didn't look out of place in his khaki shorts and T-shirt, as Grace expected he might. It wasn't even odd to see him punching his fist into the worn leather baseball mitt he found in his attic. Everything about this day seemed perfectly normal.

The batter hunkered down, preparing for a pitch thrown so hard Grace barely saw the ball as it sliced through the air toward the batter's box, but her cousin Mark had seen it. His bat connected at just the right time to send the ball sailing through the air, directly at Danny.

With a groan, she slapped her hands over her eyes, but unable to resist, spread her fingers and peeked through. The ball sped toward Danny like a comet.

He yelled, "No worries. I've got it." Punching his fist into his mitt twice before he held it up and the ball smacked into place with a crack.

Whoops of joy erupted from the married team because Danny had made the final out of the game. For the first time in almost twenty years, the married men had beaten the younger, more energetic singles.

Danny received a round of congratulations and praise. He was new blood. Exactly what the family needed. Grace sat a bit taller on the bench seat, glancing at eighteen-month-old Sarah, who happily shoveled sand into the empty bed of a plastic dump truck.

The married team disbursed to brag to their wives about the softball victory. The singles grumbled that Danny was a ringer. Danny jogged over to Grace looking like a man about to receive Olympic gold.

"Did you see that?"

"Yes. You were great."

"I was, wasn't I?"

Grace laughed. "Men." She took a quiet breath and he sat down on the bench seat beside her.

"Are you okay?"

"I'm fine."

"You're sure?"

"I'm sure."

"It's just that the last time you were pregnant you were sick—"

She put her hand over his mouth to shut him up. "For the one-hundred-and-twenty-seven-thousand-two-hundred-and-eighty-fourth time, all pregnancies are different. Yes, I was sick with Sarah. But I'm only a little bit queasy this time."

She pulled her hand away and he said, "Maybe you were sick because—"

She put her hand over his mouth again. "I was not sick because I went through that pregnancy alone. We've been over this, Danny." Because he was so funny, she laughed. "A million times."

"Or at least one-hundred-and-twenty-seven-thousand-two-hundred-and-eighty-four."

She laughed again and he glanced around the property. "This is a beautiful place."

"That's why we have the picnic here every year. There are no distractions. Just open space, trees for shade and a brick grill to make burgers and keep our side dishes warm. So everybody has time to talk, to catch up with what the family's been doing all year."

"It's great."

"It is great."

"And your family's very nice."

She smiled. "They like you, too."

He took a satisfied breath. "Do you want me to watch Sarah for a while?"

"No. It's okay. You keep mingling. We're fine."

"But this is your family."

"And I'm mingling. Women mingle more around the food and the sandbox. At one point or another I'll see everybody." She grinned. "Besides, this may be your last day out with people for a while. You should take advantage of it."

"What are you talking about? I have to go to work tomorrow."

"Right." She rolled her eyes with a chuckle. "Tomorrow you're going to be suffering. Every muscle in your body will be screaming. You'll need a hot shower just to be able to put on your suit jacket."

He straightened on the bench seat. "Hey, I will not be sore."

"Yes, you will."

"I am an athlete."

"You push papers for a living and work out at the gym a few nights a week." She caught his gaze, then pressed a quick kiss to his lips. "You are going to be in bed for days."

The idea seemed to please him because he grinned. "Will you stay in bed with me?"

"And let Sarah alone to fend for herself with Pickleberry?" They'd found Elise to be such a stickler for rules that Danny and Grace had nicknamed her after the governess in the storybook.

"Hey, you're the one who said to keep her."

"Only so we wouldn't be tempted to overuse her."

At that Danny laughed. He laughed long and hard and Grace smiled as she studied him. All traces of his guilt were gone. He remembered his son fondly now. He'd even visited the next-door neighbor who had been driving the SUV and they'd come to terms with the tragedy enough that Mrs. Oliver was a regular visitor at their home.

He'd also hired a new vice president and delegated

at least half of his responsibility to him, so they could spend the majority of their summer at the beach house in Virginia Beach. He loved Sarah. He wanted a big family and Grace was happy to oblige. Not to give him heirs, but because he loved her.

Completely. Honestly. And with a passion that hadn't died. Their intense love for each other seemed to grow every day. He had a home and she had a man who would walk to the ends of the earth for her.

Watching her other family members as they mingled and laughed, weaving around the big oak trees, sharing cobbler recipes and tales about their children, Grace suddenly saw that was the way it was meant to be.

That was the lesson she'd learned growing up among people who didn't hesitate to love.

Somewhere out there, there was somebody for everybody.

* * * * *

EXPECTING A MIRACLE

BY
JACKIE BRAUN

Jackie Braun is a three-time RITA® Award finalist, a three-time National Readers' Choice Award finalist and a past winner of the Rising Star Award. She worked as a copy editor and editorial writer for a daily newspaper before quitting her day job in 2004 to write fiction full-time. She lives in Michigan with her family. She loves to hear from readers and can be reached through her website at www.jackiebraun.com.

"There's something inordinately sexy about a man who is as good with his hands as he is quick with his mind."
—Jackie Braun, *Expecting a Miracle*.

For Will, our unexpected miracle

CHAPTER ONE

LAUREN Seville pulled her car to the side of the road and stepped out. The summer day was gorgeous, the sky impossibly blue and bright with sunshine. Standing in front of a picturesque pasture in rural Connecticut, she breathed in the mingled scents of wildflowers and listened as the birds chirped and chattered overhead. Then she bent at the waist and retched into the weeds.

The day might be gorgeous, but her life was as unsettled as her stomach at the moment. She was pregnant.

Long ago—long before she'd met and married investment broker Holden Seville and had embarked on a career as the Wife of a Very Important Man—doctors had informed Lauren that she would never conceive. Now, four years into a marriage that had proved as sterile as she'd believed herself to be, she had.

She straightened and stroked her still-flat stomach through the lightweight fabric of her sundress. The news, received just two weeks earlier, still filled her with elation, awe and a sense of anticipation. She was nearly three months into what she considered a miracle.

Her husband did not share her joy about the baby. In fact, quite the opposite.

"I don't want children."

She could still hear the cold dismissal in his tone, but his words were hardly a news flash. He'd made that fact perfectly clear when he'd proposed marriage one year to the day after their first date. Children were disruptive, messy and, most of all, needy, he'd said. They were an improper fit for the career-and-cocktails lifestyle Holden enjoyed and planned to continue enjoying.

Lauren didn't share his view, but she hadn't argued it at the time. Why bother when the point was moot? Or it had been.

A fresh wave of nausea had her bending over a second time.

"Oh, God," she moaned afterward, staggering back a few steps to lean against the passenger side of her car.

How foolish she'd been to hope that her husband's rigid opinion would soften now that the deed was done. It still came as a painful shock to discover that he wanted it *undone*.

"End your pregnancy," he'd told her. *Your pregnancy.* As if Lauren was solely responsible for her state. As if he had no tie—by blood or otherwise—to the new life growing inside of her.

He'd finished his ultimatum with: "If you don't, I'll end our marriage."

So, a mere twenty-four hours after refusing, Lauren found herself standing alone on the side of a country road gazing at a pasture, feeling queasy, exhausted and longing for the comfort of the king-size bed in their Manhattan apartment. She would go back eventually. She'd left with nothing but her purse and painful disillusionment. But she wasn't going to return until she had formulated a plan. When she faced Holden again she would do so with dignity, with her hormone-fueled emotions under check. This time she would offer him a few terms and conditions of her own.

"Hey, are you all right?"

The deep voice startled Lauren. She swung around in time to see a man jogging toward her from the farmhouse just down the road. Good Lord. Had he seen…everything? Embarrassment turned her cheeks hot and she couldn't quite meet his gaze.

"I'm fine," Lauren called.

She pasted on a smile and headed around the car's hood, all the while hoping he wouldn't come any closer. But he continued down the road in a long-legged stride that brought them face-to-face before she could open the driver's-side door of her Mercedes and get inside.

Doing so now would be rude. Lauren was never rude. So she remained standing, lips crooked up in the same polite smile that had gotten her through many a tedious dinner party with her husband's work associates.

"Are you sure?" the man asked. "You still look a little pale. Maybe you should sit down."

Lauren pegged him to be in his midthirties and physically fit, if the nice sculpting of his tanned arms was any indication. He was average height with tousled, mocha-colored hair that the breeze teased into further disarray.

"I've been sitting. Well, driving." She waved a hand down the road in the direction she'd come. "I just stopped to…to…to stretch my legs."

"Right." Kind eyes studied her a moment. "Are you sure I can't get you a glass of water or something?"

"Oh, no. But thank you for offering."

It was a programmed response and so it slipped easily from her lips. She was used to lying about her feelings, subjugating her needs and putting a positive spin on everything. She'd done that growing up so as not to upset her workaholic parents' hectic timetables. She'd done that as a wife, putting Holden and his demanding career first. But she'd been driving for more than two hours with no particular destination in mind. She had no idea how long it would be before she reached the next town. At the moment the undeniable truth was that she had to use the bathroom and would trade her Prada pumps for a good swish of mouthwash.

So, before she could change her mind—again—she said primly, "Actually, I would appreciate the use of your…facilities."

"Facilities." She thought he might grin. But he didn't. He swept a hand in the direction of his house and said, "Sure. Right this way."

As they walked toward the farmhouse, he rested his

hand on the small of her back, almost as if he knew she wasn't quite steady on her feet. The gesture struck her as old-fashioned, gentlemanly almost. It seemed a little odd coming from a guy who was wearing a T-shirt whose logo was too faded to be readable and a pair of jeans stained on the thighs with various hues of paint.

She chided herself for judging him based on appearances alone. Lauren knew better than anyone that looks could be deceiving. She'd met enough designer-dressed phonies over the years. People who said all the appropriate things, supported all the right causes and knew which fork to use for their salads, but it was for show. She could spot them easily enough. It took a fake to know one.

Did anyone know the real Lauren Seville?

That thought had her remembering her manners. "I'm Lauren, by the way."

He smiled and a pair of dimples dented his stubble-covered cheeks. "Nice to meet you. My name's Gavin."

When they reached the house, he guided her up the steps to the porch and held open the front door for her. Curiosity had her glancing around when she entered his house. Beyond the foyer, the living room was bare of furniture unless one counted the sawhorse set up next to the fireplace.

"Are you working here?"

"Why do you ask?" But he laughed then. "Actually, I own the place. I'm in the middle of some pretty aggressive renovations."

"So I see."

He settled his hands on his hips and glanced around, looking satisfied. "The kitchen's coming along nicely and the bedroom on this floor is done. I'm just finishing up the crown molding in here. I'm debating whether I should stain it or paint it white. Same goes for the mantel I made. What do you think?"

That threw her. Gavin barely knew her and yet he was asking her opinion. "You want to know what I think?"

He shrugged. "Sure. Fresh eyes. Besides, you look like someone with good taste." His gaze skimmed down momentarily, his expression frank and appreciative, but hardly leering. It left her feeling ridiculously flattered.

And flustered. "You built the mantel too, hmm? You're very good with your hands."

"So I've been told."

Heat prickled Lauren's skin. Hormones, she decided. Fatigue.

Gavin cleared his throat. "The bathroom is down that hall, first door on the right."

"Thanks."

As she walked away, he called, "Ignore the mess. I'm in the middle of rehabbing that room, too."

He wasn't kidding about the mess. Shattered tiles from the walls lay in a heap in one corner and the light fixture was a single bare bulb that hung from a wire protruding from the ceiling.

Lauren stepped to the pedestal sink and turned on the faucet, half expecting to see the water come out brown. But it was clear and cool and it felt gloriously refreshing when she splashed some of it on her face. Though she wasn't one to snoop, desperation had her opening his medicine cabinet in search of something to help rid her mouth of its foul taste. She sighed with relief when she found a tube of toothpaste. She squeezed some onto her index finger and used it as a makeshift brush. When she joined Gavin on the porch a few minutes later she felt almost human again.

He was seated on the swing at the far end, a bottle of water in each hand and a cell phone tucked between his shoulder and ear. When she stepped outside, he ended his call, maneuvered the bottles so he could clip the phone back onto his belt and stood.

"Feeling better?" he asked as he handed Lauren one of the waters.

"Yes. Thank you."

"Good. Have a seat." He swept a hand in the direction of the swing he'd just left.

It looked comfortable despite its worn cushion. Comfortable and inviting, much like the man himself. More than anything she wanted to sit. Lauren shook her head. "I really should be on my way."

"Why? Are you late for something?" he asked.

"No. I just…I don't want to put you out. I'm sure you have better things to do."

"Nothing pressing. Well, the house. There's *always* something to do here." Gavin laughed. "But it'll keep." When she hesitated, he added. "Come on, Lauren. Join me. Consider it your good deed for the day. Once you go I'll have to get back to work. I'd appreciate the break."

"Well, in that case…" She smiled, and though it wasn't like her at all to spend time with a strange man in the middle of nowhere, she sat on the swing.

It creaked softly under her weight. She allowed it to sway gently. Wind chimes tinkled in the breeze. The sound was pleasing, peaceful. It took all of her willpower not to sigh and close her eyes.

Gavin settled a hip on the porch railing, angled in her direction. "So, where are you headed, anyway? If you don't mind me asking."

Lauren uncapped the water and took a sip. "I don't have a destination, actually. I'm just out driving."

"It's a nice day for that."

"Yes." Because he was studying her again, she glanced away. "It's lovely around here."

"You should have seen it in the spring when my orchard was in bloom."

"Orchard?"

"Three acres of apple trees," he said, pointing behind her.

She turned for a better look and could just make out some of the golf-ball-size green apples that had taken the blooms' places. Lauren had always lived in the city, first in Los Angeles and now in New York. She'd never called the countryside home. Even vacations had been spent in urban settings…Paris, London, Venice, Rome. But something about this place was vastly appealing. Peace, she thought again. Ten minutes on Gavin's front porch had had the same effect as an hour with her masseur.

"Have you lived here long?" she asked.

"No. I bought the place last year." He sipped his water before adding, "After my divorce."

"Sorry."

"No need to be. I'm not."

The reply was quick and matter-of-fact, but Lauren thought she detected bitterness. She wasn't sure what else to say so she settled on, "I see."

Gavin didn't seem to be expecting any sort of response. In fact, he changed the subject. "I like challenges, which is one of the reasons I bought this place. A few months after I began working on it, though, I got tired of commuting out from the city on the weekends. So, I decided to take an extended break from my job and I moved here."

She couldn't imagine Holden taking a break, extended or otherwise, from his job. Her husband ate, slept and breathed the stock exchange. Even their vacations rarely saw him out of touch with his office. It struck her then that even if he changed his mind about the baby she'd still be a single parent for all intents and purposes.

"You're frowning," Gavin said.

"Oh, sorry. I was just thinking about…" She shook her head. "Nothing." Then, because he was still watching her, she said, "So, you lived in New York?"

He sipped his water. "For the past dozen years."

She couldn't quite picture him there amid the sky-scrapers, bustling pedestrians and heavy traffic. Though she barely knew him at all, he looked like a man who enjoyed wide-open spaces and the quiet that went with them. Places such as this. And though Lauren had always been an urbanite, she could understand why.

"I live in New York," she said.

"You're not from there originally, though, are you?"

She blinked. "No. I'm a West Coast transplant. Los Angeles. How could you tell?"

Gavin studied her. He hadn't expected that answer. Something about Lauren seemed too soft, too uncertain for city life. Her looks certainly fit, though. He allowed his gaze to take another discreet tour from her perfectly coiffed hair to the heels of her fashionable pumps. He'd seen plenty of women who looked just like Lauren parading into Manhattan's private Colony Club or exiting their stretch limousines in front of the posh apartment buildings on Park Avenue. Still…

"You don't seem like a New Yorker," he said at last.

She surprised him by replying, "I was just thinking the same thing about you."

"I'm not a native, either," he admitted. "I was born and raised in a little town just outside Buffalo. Does it still show?"

"Not really."

But he thought she was being polite. He supposed given the way he was dressed and where they were sitting, her opinion made perfect sense. Perhaps she would see him in a different light if he was wearing one of the suits he'd picked up on his last trip to Milan and they'd bumped into one another at the Met. For one strange moment he almost wished that were the case. It had been a long time since he'd enjoyed the company of a woman.

"Do you like New York?" she was asking.

It seemed an odd question, but Gavin answered it anyway. "I loved it at first." He sipped his water and allowed his mind to reel backward. The place had been so exciting in the beginning and he'd just made a killing with his first big real estate deal. "What about you? Do you like it?"

She seemed to hesitate, but then she replied, "Yes. Of course. What's not to like? It has all of those wonderful restaurants, endless entertainment opportunities and incredible cultural attractions."

The response struck him as something she'd read in a tourism brochure rather than a heartfelt assessment. He eyed her curiously for a moment before nodding in agreement.

The conversation lapsed, but the interim was peaceful rather than strained. The swing creaked rhythmically, helping to fill the silence, and the wind chimes offered an abstract melody as the breeze ruffled the leaves of the big oak trees that shaded the better part of the front lawn.

He thought he heard Lauren sigh, which he took as a good sign. The woman was wound tight and clearly in need of relaxation. Gavin knew the feeling. Not all that long ago, he'd been that way, too.

"So, what made you decide to move here?" she asked after a while.

"I was looking for a slower pace." Which was true enough. He'd been working sixty, sometimes even seventy hours a week. He'd been on fire and then. "I burned out, big-time."

He couldn't believe he'd just shared that with someone—and a virtual stranger no less. Hell, he'd glossed over the truth with most of his family.

"This is definitely slower," she said. "It's a good place to think."

Gavin had done plenty of that. "Exactly."

"There's no traffic at all, no blaring horns, no choking exhaust. No…urgency." Her tone sounded wistful and sincere, as if something about her current situation made her appreciate the bucolic setting and the sluggishness that went with it almost as much as he did.

It prompted him to ask, "So, are you looking for a place in the country?"

"Me? No. I…" She shook her head, but then asked, "Why? Do you know of a place nearby?"

"This one will be on the market when I finally finish with it. But at the rate I'm going now, it probably won't be ready for a good year or so."

Her brows shot up in surprise. "You're going to sell it?"

"Sure. That's what I do for a living, more or less." The more being that usually the real estate he acquired was much larger and worth millions of dollars. The less being that he delegated the physical restoration and remodeling work to others.

"So, this is just a job?" She sounded disappointed.

Gavin shrugged. "I guess you could say that."

Lauren flaked peeling paint off the armrest of the swing. She sounded wistful again when she said, "It seems more like a labor of love."

Labor of love? He'd considered the physical work to be therapeutic, wearing out his body so that his mind would shut down and take unpleasant memories with it. But now, as Gavin thought about the crown moldings, the mantel and the satisfaction he'd gleaned from crafting them, he decided that maybe Lauren was right. Still, he would be selling the house when he finished. He'd never planned to make this his permanent address. At some point he needed to return to New York and to Phoenix Brothers Development, the company he owned with his brother, Garrett. He couldn't hide in Connecticut forever, avoiding well-meaning friends and family, and foisting his responsibilities at Phoenix on others.

"So, you're not in the market for some real estate?" he asked.

Lauren frowned and her gaze slid away. "Actually, I am." She motioned toward the house. "But my needs are a little smaller than this house and a little more, well, immediate."

Smaller. The description was hardly what he'd

expected to hear. *More immediate.* An idea nudged him. An outrageous idea. Gavin ignored it.

"Are you…relocating?" He nearly said running. Why did that word seem a better fit?

"At least temporarily. Yes." Her head jerked in an emphatic nod as if she'd just reached a decision. "Do you know anything that might be available around here?"

"In Gabriel's Crossing, you mean?"

"Gabriel's Crossing." Her lips curved as she repeated the town's name, and Gavin got the feeling that before he'd said it Lauren hadn't actually known that's where she was.

That outrageous idea nudged him with a little more force. "Maybe."

"Is it nearby?" she asked.

"Very. There's a cottage about fifty yards behind the house. It's adjacent to the orchard, with great views out all of its windows. I lived in it myself before the rewiring of this place was complete."

"And it's for rent?"

It hadn't been. In fact, before this moment, Gavin had never entertained the idea of taking on a tenant. He certainly didn't need the income or, for that matter, the hassle. But he nodded. Then he felt compelled to point out, "It's not very big."

"It doesn't need to be big."

He glanced at Lauren's pricey clothes and Park Avenue appearance. The entire cottage could fit inside the master suite of his apartment back in New York.

He'd bet the same could be said for hers. And so he added, "There's not much closet space."

He was sure that bit of news would scuttle the deal. He almost hoped it would. He was being impulsive again. It was a trait that had all but doomed him in the past. But the lack of closets didn't appear to have any impact on Lauren's enthusiasm. Her expression remained a beguiling mix of hope and anticipation.

"Do you think I could see it?"

"You're interested?" Heaven help him, but Gavin knew he was, and it had nothing to do with a rental agreement. The woman was beautiful, enigmatic. He wouldn't mind unveiling some of her secrets.

For the first time since her arrival, his gaze detoured to her left hand. A set of rings encircled her third finger, and a whopper of a diamond was visible. *Married.* He nearly snorted out a laugh. *That's what I get for rushing ahead without thinking things through.*

Now if she took Gavin up on his hasty offer to rent the cottage, he would have a couple of lovebirds nesting within shouting distance of his house. Probably just as well, he decided, dismissing the spark of attraction. He wasn't in the market for a relationship. He hadn't been since his divorce. And although he missed certain aspects of female companionship, overall he didn't regret his decision one bit.

"I believe I am interested," Lauren said after a long pause. Her lips curved in a smile, and one of those aspects he had missed presented itself. "Do you think I could see it right now? I mean, if you can spare a little more of your time."

Gavin managed a grin as he straightened. "Sure. As I said, I've got nothing pressing at the moment."

Lauren stood in the middle of the cottage's main room. It was small—although the word *cozy* seemed a more apt description—and empty, except for some dusty storage boxes that Gavin assured her would be removed. She could picture an overstuffed chair and ottoman in front of the window that faced the orchard, and maybe a small writing desk in the vacant nook below the stairs. They'd already looked at the bedroom in the loft. It would be a tight fit, but it could accommodate a dresser and queen-size bed, as well as a changing table and crib.

"So, what do you think?" Gavin asked.

Lauren wasn't the spontaneous sort. Generally she thought things through carefully before making any decisions. Sometimes she even created lists, writing down the pros and cons of a situation and analyzing both columns in meticulous fashion before reaching a conclusion.

Not today.

Today was a day of firsts. Not only had she walked out on her husband, she was getting ready to lease a new home. A home for her and the baby.

"I'll take it." She swore she felt the leaden weight of recent events lift from her shoulders. "Maybe I should be spontaneous more often," she murmured.

"Excuse me?" Gavin said.

"Nothing. Just…thinking aloud. How much is the rent?"

Gavin scratched his chin thoughtfully before rattling off a sum that Lauren would have no problem affording. She'd hardly been a pauper coming into her marriage, and although she'd reluctantly quit her position six months before her wedding at Holden's request, she had a degree in advertising and prior work experience at one of the largest firms in Manhattan. She could always find a job if need be. For now, though, what she wanted was peace.

"Utilities are included," Gavin added as he waited for her answer.

She glanced around the room again, her gaze drawn to the windows and the outdoor beauty they framed. Another band of tension loosened. The peace she sought seemed included in the rent as well.

Turning to Gavin, she asked, "When can I move in?"

CHAPTER TWO

It was late afternoon by the time Lauren returned to the city. She unlocked the door to the apartment slowly, dreading the confrontation to come. She should have realized whatever was left to say would be said in a civilized manner—civilized to the point of being impersonal. Just as her parents had never believed in arguing, neither did her husband.

She found Holden in his study, sitting in his favorite leather chair next to the gas fireplace, which was flickering cheerfully, its heat competing with the air-conditioning. Little matters like high utility bills and energy conservation were beneath him. He had enough money to be wasteful. It was one of the perks of being wealthy, he'd once told Lauren when she'd gently chastised him for leaving the water running in the bathroom.

She studied him now. He was an attractive man—polished, sophisticated. It occurred to her that she'd never seen him in blue jeans, either the designer variety or the kind faded from wear. Nor could she imagine him operating power tools or smelling of sawdust and sweat. He considered himself above physical labor of any sort. The only calluses on his hands were the result of his weekly squash game, and his muscular build came courtesy of the workouts he scheduled with a personal trainer in their home gym.

She cleared her throat to gain his attention, breaking what had been her parents' cardinal rule: always wait to be spoken to first. It struck her then how much it bothered her that she always felt the need to maintain her silence around her husband, too.

Holden glanced over the top of the *Wall Street Journal*.

"I already ate dinner, since I wasn't sure when you'd be back," he said. "I think Maria might have left something warming in the oven for you."

Lauren's stomach gave a queasy roll that had nothing to do with the mention of food. "I'm not hungry. Aren't you even curious where I went?"

"I imagine you went to Bergdorf's to work off your irritation," he said dryly. "How much did you spend?"

Was that actually what he thought? If so, then he really didn't know her at all. Even so, for the sake of the baby, she decided to try one last time to salvage their marriage. "I'm not irritated, Holden. I'm…horrified by the solution you suggested. We need to talk about this."

He folded the paper and set it aside. He'd never been a terribly demonstrative man, but at the moment his expression was so damningly remote that it made her shiver. It matched his tone when he replied, "I believe we already have."

"We didn't really discuss anything," Lauren argued. "You issued an ultimatum."

One of his eyebrows rose in challenge. "Yes, and you did the same."

She had. And she'd meant it. She could not, she would not, destroy the miracle growing inside her. Lauren sucked in a breath and straightened her spine. This made twice in one day she wasn't going to back down. "I'll be moving out. I found a place to live this afternoon. A cottage in the country."

Just thinking about a skyline of leafy trees rather than steel, stone and glass made it easier to breathe.

Holden blinked twice in rapid succession. It was the only sign that her words might have surprised him. Then he inquired with maddening detachment, "Will you require any help packing? Maria's gone for the day, but Niles is still here."

Lauren's composure slipped a notch. "That's it? I'm leaving, our marriage…our marriage is *ending*, and that's all you have to say?"

"If you're expecting me to fall on my knees and beg you to stay, you've been watching too much daytime television." He steepled his fingers then. "Of course, if you've changed your mind about the situation…"

"It's not a situation. It's a baby, Holden. We're having a baby."

The tips of his fingers turned white. "*You're* having

a baby. I do not want children. You understood that. You agreed to that when we got engaged," he reminded her.

"I didn't think it was possible. The doctors had told me—"

"You agreed."

"So that's it?" Lauren said softly.

"Hardly, but the lawyers will have to figure out the rest."

Had she really expected him to change his mind? She swallowed as another, more unnerving question niggled. Had she *wanted* him to?

Their relationship had never included fireworks. Even at the beginning, when everything was new and should have been exciting, true sparks had been in short supply. What had it been based on? she wondered now. Mutual interests? Mutual respect? Gratitude for the fact that Holden had accepted her, reproductive defects and all?

Lauren frowned. "Why did you marry me, Holden? Do you love me? Did you ever?"

He studied her a long moment before tipping his hands in her direction. "Why don't you ask yourself those same questions?"

As she folded clothes and placed them in her suitcases, Lauren did. She didn't like the answers she came up with.

CHAPTER THREE

GAVIN noticed two things about his tenant: she went to bed early and she kept to herself.

She had been living in the little cottage for nearly a month. Her lights were always out by eleven and he'd only bumped into her twice, not including the day she'd moved in with only one small van full of belongings and a check to cover the rent for an entire year. He'd requested only the first month's amount, but she'd insisted on paying the remainder up front and signing a lease, which he'd hastily drawn up on his computer.

In truth, he hadn't expected her to return at all. He'd figured her trip to the country had been a fluke and she would reconsider her decision to move here. For all he knew, she'd had a spat with her husband and once they'd kissed and made up she would regret her impulsiveness. He knew he was regretting his. But two days after shaking his hand while standing in the dusty cottage, she had come back with her spine straight, her gaze direct and determined.

She'd been all business that day, although he thought he'd detected exhaustion and maybe a little desperation behind her polite smile and firm handshake. Both had him wondering, but he'd managed to keep his curiosity in check. Not my business, he told himself.

On their two subsequent meetings, both of which had occurred at the mailbox out by the road, they'd exchanged greetings and the expected pleasantries, but they hadn't lingered as they had that first day on his porch. Nor had they spoken at any length.

Gavin found that he wanted to.

He was only human, and the enigmatic Lauren Seville inspired a lot of questions. What was the real story? The bits and pieces he knew certainly didn't add up.

For starters, women who looked and dressed like Lauren didn't rent tiny cottages in the country. Gabriel's Crossing was quaint and its four-star inn and three bed-and-breakfasts attracted their fair share of tourists year-round, but the town was hardly a mecca for New York's wealthy. It had shops and restaurants, but it lacked the upscale boutiques, trendy eateries, day spas and high-end salons that a woman from Manhattan's Upper East Side would not only expect but require.

And then there was the not-so-little matter of a wedding ring. The gold band and Rock of Gibraltar he'd noticed that first day had been on her finger when Lauren had handed Gavin her check for the rent.

Seeing it had prompted him to ask, "Will anyone be joining you in the cottage?"

She'd answered with a cryptic "Eventually."

Gavin assumed that someone would be her husband. But a month later the man had yet to put in an appearance. Spat, he wondered again? Or something bigger and more permanent?

"Not my business," he muttered again and got back to work.

He'd long finished with the crown molding in the living room and had trimmed out the tall windows that faced the road. Per Lauren's suggestion, he'd opted to stain both them and the mantel a rich mahogany. The room was coming along nicely, needing only a few patches in the plaster, fresh paint and a refinished floor to complete its transformation. Those could wait. He still had plenty of other projects to keep him busy. Indeed, every room in the house except the master suite had something that still required his attention. If this were a company site, a bevy of contractors would be working off a master list with the various jobs prioritized and deadlines for completion penciled in. But this project was personal and, well, cathartic, so Gavin worked at his own pace and on whatever suited his mood.

Today, it was laying the floor in the secondary downstairs bathroom. He'd chosen a tumbled travertine marble imported from Mexico. The sandy color complemented the richer-hued tiles he'd used on the walls. He planned to grout that later in the day—assuming he hadn't succumbed to heatstroke by then.

He reached for his water bottle and, after taking a

swig, used the hem of his T-shirt to mop the perspiration from his brow. It was not quite noon but it was already pushing eighty degrees in the shade. The house didn't have working air-conditioning yet. The guys from Howard's Heating and Cooling had assured him a crew would be out later in the week. In the meantime, Gavin had to make do with a box fan and the meager breeze that could be coaxed through the home's opened windows. He put in the earpieces of his MP3 player and got back to tile laying. He liked to listen to music while he worked. He preferred up-tempo rock, the heavier on the bass the better.

"Hello?" Lauren's voice echoed down the hall, somehow managing to be heard over the music blaring in his ears.

He was on his hands and knees, having just laid another square, when he heard her. He tugged out the earpieces and levered backward so he could peer out the door.

"In here," he called.

She'd pulled her hair back into a tidy ponytail and was dressed in a sleeveless white linen blouse that she'd left untucked over a pair of pink linen shorts. On another woman the outfit would not have been all that sexy, but on Lauren… Gavin swallowed, and the heat that blasted through his system had nothing to do with the temperature outside. He didn't remember her being quite so curvy.

Tenant, he reminded himself. *Married* tenant.

Even so his mouth went dry. The woman had a classy set of legs. He'd caught a glimpse of them that first day when she'd been wearing a sundress, but this outfit did a much better job of showcasing them. They were as long as a model's, and slim without being skinny. She had smooth knees, nicely turned calves and those ankles… He made a little humming noise as he reached for his water, not sure whether he wanted to drink the stuff or dump it over his head. God help him. He had a thing about ankles. He downed the last of the water and forced himself to look elsewhere.

"I can't believe you're working today," she said.

He shrugged. "What can I say? I'm a glutton for punishment." His gaze veered to her ankles again. "H-how are you holding up?"

The cottage had no air-conditioning, either, and unlike the house, where Gavin's bedroom was on the main floor, the only sleeping quarters there were on the upper level.

"I'm fine."

It wasn't the answer he expected. He figured she had come to complain. If he were renting the cottage, he would.

"I'm having the air-conditioning here fixed and I'll also have a unit installed in the cottage if you'd like."

"Yes. I'll gladly pay for it."

"No need. Unfortunately, it won't be today. It probably won't be till the end of the week," he said.

"That's okay. I'm fine," she said again.

"Do you always say that?"

Her brow wrinkled. "Sorry?"

"Fine. It seems to be your stock response."

"Oh, sorry."

"That's another one."

She frowned again, clearly not knowing what to say. For one bizarre moment, Gavin found himself wishing she'd lose her temper. He'd bet she'd look incredible angry.

"The tile looks terrific." More politeness, but he let it pass. He wasn't sure why he'd goaded her in the first place. Most landlords would kill for such an easy-going tenant.

"Thanks."

"You've obviously done this before."

"A time or two." Although not recently.

For the past decade, Gavin had been in charge of the big picture. He and his brother paid other people to see to the details. Theirs was a rags-to-riches success story, or so the *New York Times* claimed in a feature story they'd done on him and Garrett a couple years back.

The article had made it seem as if Gavin O'Donnell, businessman and self-made millionaire, had it all. But even prior to his divorce, he'd felt something was missing, that some vital part of himself had been lost. Little by little he was getting it back.

Lauren's voice pulled him out of his introspection. "You must enjoy working with your hands."

Indeed he did and not just on houses. Though Gavin fought the urge, his gaze trailed to her trim ankles again. He'd bet he could encircle one with his hand. He rubbed his damp palms on his jean-clad thighs. "Yeah. I haven't done it for a while, though. I forgot how, um, satisfying it can be."

"I thought you were a builder."

"I'm more of a give-the-orders, sign-the-check sort these days."

"Ah." She nodded. "The boss."

That was true enough, but he'd never been the type to go around proclaiming himself as such. He knew too many people who'd gotten wrapped up in their own importance. If a year in self-prescribed exile had taught him nothing else, Gavin had conclusive proof that the world didn't stop turning just because he'd opted out as a cog.

He decided to change the subject. "So, what can I help you with?"

"Oh. Sorry," she said. He grimaced. There was that word again. "I…I was wondering if it would be all right if I made some changes to the cottage."

"Changes?"

She cleared her throat. "Nothing major. I'd like to paint the walls in the bedroom."

The entire place was done in a serviceable white that was little more than a primer coat.

"Got a color in mind?" he asked.

"I'm leaning toward sage green or something along those lines," she said.

He nodded and scratched his chin, thinking of his already lengthy to-do list. "It might be a little while yet before I can get to that. The new cabinets for the kitchen are due to arrive next week. I talked a friend of mine into coming out from the city to help me install them." He grinned. "He said he'd work for a prime rib dinner and beer. Obviously, that's not union scale."

"I'm an even better deal. I'll do the work for free."

"You want to paint it yourself?" His tone held enough incredulity that she looked insulted.

"Do I look helpless?" Her brows arched and she crossed her arms.

So, the woman had a spine after all. Gavin nearly smiled. "Ever done any painting?"

"Some."

"Really?"

Her answer surprised him until she added, "Okay, no. Unless my toenails count."

Gavin's gaze dipped to her feet. The flat sandals she wore offered an unrestricted view of ten cotton-candy-pink-tipped digits. His ankle fetish now had stiff competition.

"You do good work."

Her shoulders lifted slightly. "It's all in the wrist."

"That so?"

"I could teach you," she offered. "I'm sure it's a skill that would come in handy on your next job site."

The beginnings of a grin lurked around the corners of her mouth. He liked seeing it. He liked knowing he'd helped put it there.

"I think I'll pass. Maybe I could just watch you paint

your own instead." The prospect was a bigger turn-on than Gavin wanted it to be.

Hell, *she* was a turn-on, standing in front of him in pastel linen and looking sexier than most women could manage in skimpy black lace.

They studied each other. For Gavin, awareness sizzled like the business end of a firecracker. The way Lauren fidgeted with her wedding ring had him half hoping, half worrying, that she felt it, too.

"I've been watching the home improvement channel," she told him after a moment. "I think I've picked up some decent pointers."

It took a second for Gavin to remember what they had been talking about. Paint. Painting. The cottage. "Oh. Good. Some of it's common sense. A lot of it is elbow grease. Technique only counts if you're being paid by the hour."

She smiled. "So, you'll let me do it?"

"Sure. I've got nothing against free labor. And if you mess it up—" he shrugged. "—it's just paint. Another coat or two and the place will look as good as new."

"I won't mess it up," she assured him.

"A bit of a perfectionist, are we?"

He didn't get the feeling she was teasing when she replied, "If you're going to do something, why not do it well?"

"Too bad everyone doesn't share your philosophy. So, are you free around three o' clock?" he asked.

"Sure," she said slowly.

"Good. We'll drive into town and swing by the hardware store. I need a few things, anyway, and while we're there you can pick out a paint color."

Lauren waited for Gavin under one of the big oaks, making use of the shade. She was just far enough along in her pregnancy that she could no longer button the waistband of most of her fitted clothes, but she hadn't suffered from nausea in more than a week.

She was sleeping a lot, but she wasn't sure if that was because of her pregnancy, the result of depression over her pending divorce or flat-out boredom. She wasn't good at being idle. Back in the city she'd found a way to fill up her life, which of course was far different than being fulfilled. But here she had no luncheons to attend, no committees to help chair, no dinner parties to plan, shop for and execute. After staring at the blank white walls of the cottage for nearly a month, desperation had forced her hand and she'd decided to approach Gavin with her proposal to paint.

Somewhere in the midst of talking wall colors, though, she'd begun noticing the day's growth of beard that shaded his angular jaw and a sweaty T-shirt that was pulled tight over some seriously toned shoulders. She fanned herself now, blaming her heated skin on the mercury. It wasn't the man. No, it couldn't be the man. She was pregnant, newly separated and several months from a divorce. Besides, she'd never been the sort to fantasize. Yet for a moment there…

She groped for a tidy explanation to this curious tangle of emotions. The best she could come up with was that she was confused, lonely and alone in a new town, staring down not just one major life change, but two. Gavin was nice, good-natured, easy-going and friendly. So, she'd flirted with him a little. No law against that. As for this unprecedented attraction? It was a figment of her imagination, a figment likely fueled by her hopped-up hormones.

When Gavin joined her, Lauren noticed that he'd shaved and had changed into a pair of cargo shorts and a fresh shirt. She thought she caught a whiff of soap, and his hair appeared to be damp from a shower. Because she wanted to keep looking at him, she turned her attention to the tree.

"This oak would be perfect for a swing," she commented.

Gavin regarded the thick branches for a moment. "Or a fat tire on a rope."

She shook her head. "No. A swing. Definitely a swing. And the seat should be painted red."

"Reliving your childhood?"

Hardly, she thought. "I lived in Los Angeles, remember? But I worked on an advertising campaign for an airline once. The commercial started off with a little boy swinging and making airplane noises."

"'Our pilots have always been eager to soar.'" Gavin grinned as he supplied the text. "I remember that slogan.

I didn't realize it was yours. For that matter, I didn't realize you'd worked…in advertising."

She got the feeling he hadn't thought she'd worked at all. "I don't at the moment. I left my job at Danielson & Marx four years ago."

"Danielson & Marx." He whistled low. "That's the big-time. Do you miss it?"

"Sometimes," she replied. She hadn't shared that truth with anyone, even her closest friend. When others asked the same question, she told them how content she was and how busy with committees and her crowded social calendar. It was easy to tell Gavin the truth, so she continued. "I especially miss the creative process. It's not easy to sell consumers on an idea or product with only a few words or images."

"I'm betting you were good at it."

She smiled, thinking of the four Addys she'd racked up during her relatively brief career, and admitted, "I had my moments."

He tucked his hands into the front pockets of his cargo shorts. "So, why did you quit?"

She bent down and plucked a blade of grass. As she tore it into small pieces, she said, "Well, I was getting married and…and…"

She released the last shred of grass and dusted her hands together without having completed the thought.

"Priorities changed," he allowed.

Lauren nodded, although she could now admit she

hadn't been the one to change them. She'd gone along to get along. She wasn't proud of that now.

"Maybe you'll get back into it at some point," he said. "With a big agency like that on your résumé not many places would turn you away."

"I could do that." Her portfolio was anything but mediocre. Lauren had been good at her job and had taken pride in her work.

"But?" He smiled, as if he knew she had something else on her mind.

Once again she found herself baring her soul. "What I'd really like to do is start my own agency, something that specializes in causes rather than goods and services."

"There's not a lot of money in that, but then you probably know that. It sounds like you've given the idea some thought."

"I have. But it needs more," she conceded. The idea had been back-burnered for a couple of years now, growing stale as Lauren had grown more complacent.

"This is a good place for thinking. And when you're ready to start out, I'm sure you have enough contacts you could probably pull that off," he replied.

She'd almost expected him to shoot down the idea. She had little doubt her parents and Holden would have, which perhaps explained why she'd never shared her dream with any of them.

"Thanks."

Gavin's brow crinkled. "For what?"

"For…for letting me paint the cottage."

CHAPTER FOUR

LAUREN had never been in a hardware store. Neither her father nor her husband was the sort to attempt any kind of home repair. The one in Gabriel's Crossing, however, reminded her of something from a movie, complete with a couple of older men sitting on a bench in the shade of the porch. If they'd been chewing tobacco or whittling sticks she wouldn't have been surprised. It turned out they were eating sunflower seeds and helping each other with a crossword puzzle. One of them apparently was the owner. He stood and shook Gavin's hand.

"Haven't seen you in a while. I was beginning to wonder if you'd finally given up on that old house and moved back to the city." His eyes crinkled with a grin after he said it.

"Never. I finish what I start, Pat. Besides, someone has to keep you in business."

"And don't think I don't appreciate it."

Gavin turned toward Lauren then. "Lauren, this is Pat Montgomery."

"Nice to meet you, Mr. Montgomery."

"No need to stand on formality here. It's just Pat." He divided a speculative look between them. "So, will you be visiting the area for long?"

"Actually, I'm not visiting. I've moved here…at least temporarily."

"Lauren's renting the cottage on my property," Gavin supplied.

"You don't say." The man's woolly eyebrows inched up, and his mouth twitched with a grin.

Lauren felt her cheeks grow warm. She had a good idea what he was thinking, and her pregnancy hadn't become obvious yet. Thankfully Gavin came to her rescue.

"Lauren was looking for a retreat from the city. Her husband will be joining her."

She'd left Gavin with that impression, she realized. Lying wasn't in her nature, nor was omitting the truth. Still, it seemed the wisest course of action at the moment. So, when Pat said, "I'm sure you and your husband will enjoy Gabriel's Crossing. It's a nice place to get away to," she replied, "Yes, I'm sure we'll enjoy it here."

"Paint's down that first aisle," Gavin said, pointing to the far side of the store. "I'll load up the two-by-fours while you make your selection."

"Okay."

About twenty minutes passed as she pored over paint chips. Lauren knew the exact moment Gavin came up behind her. She didn't hear his footsteps. Rather, she smelled soap. And though she wasn't quite sure how, she felt his presence. She was probably being silly, but something about him was welcoming, comforting. She wouldn't allow herself to consider the other descriptions that came to mind.

"I've narrowed it down to these two shades," she said before turning. "I've read that green is a relaxing color, perfect for promoting a peaceful night's sleep."

"One of the walls in my bedroom is red. Well, officially, crimson. I wonder what that's supposed to promote." Humor danced in his eyes. Humor and something else.

She swallowed the other completely inappropriate answers that came to mind and said, "Insomnia."

Gavin laughed and pushed a hand through his hair, leaving it in its usual disarray. "I don't know about that. I sleep like a baby."

The mention of the word *baby* helped banish the last of Lauren's wayward thoughts. "Sea foam." She held the paint chip out in front of her as if she'd just drawn a dagger. "What do you think?"

He gave the square of color his full attention. "It's tranquil."

"Perfect."

His fingers brushed hers as he took the paint chip. "I'll have Pat mix up a couple gallons and we can be on our way."

"Don't forget, I owe you an ice cream cone."

"I haven't forgotten."

As she watched him walk away, Lauren was left with

the impression that Gavin O'Donnell was the sort of man who never forgot anything.

"This is a popular spot today," Gavin said when they arrived at the ice cream shop.

The place was small with no inside seating. People were lined up six deep in front of the two order windows, and every available picnic table was filled. Children of varying sizes, apparently immune to the heat index, ran around on the lawn in an impromptu game of tag.

As they made their way to the window, a boy of about five hurtled headlong into Gavin.

"Whoa, partner," Gavin said, steadying him.

Another child took the opportunity to tag the boy's back. "You're it!" he hollered in glee.

As the pair dashed away, Gavin glanced down at his shirt and grimaced at the mark that had been left behind. Lauren knew exactly what Holden's reaction would have been upon seeing a chocolate smudge decorating the fabric of one of his shirts. For that matter, the child would not have gotten off without hearing a stern reprimand. But Gavin was merely shaking his head and chuckling wryly.

"I guess I should have left my old clothes on." He sent Lauren a wink as he grabbed napkins from a nearby tabletop dispenser and swiped at his ruined shirtfront. "This is what I get for trying to impress you."

He said it lightly, clearly joking. But Lauren was impressed, and it had nothing to do with what the man was wearing.

"You're very…" She said finally, "patient."

"It's just a shirt and he's just a kid." He shrugged, as if that explained it all. Lauren supposed that in a way it did. Gavin's easy-going reaction to the mishap summed up his personality.

"You'd make a good dad." She hadn't meant to say that. At least not out loud. And certainly not on a sigh.

Hearing the words didn't send Gavin into panic mode. He nodded. "I hope to one day."

"You want children?"

He looked slightly surprised by the question. "Not right now. But sure, eventually. Don't you?"

Lauren swallowed. The dashed dreams of the past and the miracle of the present clogged her throat. Before she could respond, a woman of about thirty rushed over to where they stood in line. She looked hot, harassed and, given the dark circles under her eyes, exhausted. And no wonder. She had a baby on one hip and a sticky-faced toddler in tow.

"Gosh. I'm really sorry about that." She motioned to the mark on Gavin's shirt. "That was my son, Thomas, who ran into you."

Gavin chuckled easily. "He left a lasting impression."

The woman shifted the baby to her other hip and began to rummage through a large purse that did double duty as a diaper bag if the package of wipes peeking out the top was any indication. After pulling out a piece of paper and a pen, she said, "Here, let me give you my address. You can send me a bill for your dry-cleaning."

"Oh, there's no need for that. Really," Gavin assured her. "It will come out in the wash."

"You're sure?"

"Positive." He reached over then and tickled one of the baby's many chins, delighting a giggle out of the drooling infant. "Looks like someone's cutting teeth."

The woman jiggled the baby. "Yes and he's making us all pay for it, aren't you, pumpkin?"

"Three children," Lauren marveled. "You certainly have your hands full."

The other woman snorted out a laugh. "And to think I used to want four. Of course, that was before the first one came along and a sound night's sleep became a distant memory. Thomas had colic." Just then her toddler started off in the direction of an overflowing garbage can. "I'd better go. Thanks for being so understanding about the shirt," she said to Gavin. Her gaze included them both when she added, "You know how kids are."

Lauren's polite smile slipped. No, she didn't know. In fact, she didn't have a clue. A tsunami-size wave of panic grew inside her. She would be finding out in the not-so-distant future, and she would be doing so as a single parent without so much as prior babysitting experience.

With her knees threatening to buckle, she whispered, "Oh, God."

"Lauren?" Gavin grabbed her elbow. "You okay?"

"S-sure. It's just that this line is so long," she hedged.

He winked. "The wait will be over before you know it."

That's what she was afraid of.

At the window she and Gavin made their ice cream selections—a plain vanilla soft-serve cone for her, a double scoop of chocolate fudge for him—and looked around for a place to sit. The tables remained filled, but an older couple was leaving a shady spot on the lawn. Gavin handed Lauren his ice cream cone, and before she could guess what he intended to do, he'd tugged the shirt over his head and spread it out on the grass under the tree.

"No sense both of us going home with stains," he said when she glanced at him in question.

"Thank you." She folded herself onto his shirt without protesting, mostly because it gave her something to do other than stare at his bare chest. The man had the body of a god. He was tanned enough to suggest he went shirtless when he worked outdoors. And he was toned, the hard contours of his chest softened only by a light dusting of dark hair.

"Better watch out," Gavin warned.

"Wh-why?"

"That's going to drip."

When she continued to stare blankly at him, he leaned over and licked her cone. Lauren sucked in a breath as she watched his tongue swirl around the ice cream.

He glanced up. "Sorry. I just…" He laughed then, a combination of embarrassment and amusement. "I can't believe I did that."

She couldn't, either. Nor could she believe what his benign gesture had done to her pulse. "Th-that's okay."

"Want some of mine?" He held out his cone. "Go ahead."

"No, thanks."

"Sure? It's chocolate fudge," he coaxed with a bob of his eyebrows.

"I like chocolate," she said softly. His eyes were the color of the semisweet, dark variety.

"Who doesn't?" Then he frowned. "So, if you like it, why didn't you order it?"

"I don't know. I guess vanilla seemed the safer choice given how quickly it's melting today."

"Do you always do what's safe, Lauren?"

She licked her ice cream before it could drip and then wrapped a napkin around the base of the cone. "I'm afraid so."

"Boring," he murmured.

"That's me. Borin' Lauren."

He laughed. "Was that your nickname when you were a kid?"

"Unfortunately."

"So, what did you do to earn it?"

"Nothing," she insisted, slightly offended.

He lapped up a mouthful of ice cream from his cone. "Come on, Borin' Lauren. Your secret's safe with me."

"If you really must know, I wouldn't sneak out after curfew with the other girls." When he frowned in confusion, she explained, "Summer camp."

"Ah. How old were you?"

"Twelve." Her parents had gone to Europe for a month, sprinkling their vacation with assorted business seminars and workshops. Lauren had started her period while they were gone. She wrinkled her nose at the memory. She'd felt so awkward and out of sorts that summer. She'd had no one to confide in other than a sympathetic camp counselor.

"I bet you secretly wanted to sneak out."

"Maybe, but I've always been a rule follower."

He studied her a moment. "Well, here's an opportunity to take a walk on the wild side." He snatched the cone out of her hand and replaced it with his. "Go on. Indulge."

"Oh, no, really—"

Before she could finish her protest, he added, "Better be quick about it or you'll be wearing it." Dark brows rose over a pair of amused eyes. "And I'm not going to come to your rescue this time."

She had little choice but to comply. She tried dainty licks at first, but as a river of brown began to ooze toward her hand, she gave up the pretense of manners and got down to serious business. She finished the first scoop before Gavin had put much of a dent into her vanilla. The second scoop was gone just as he was biting into the rim of the cone.

"You've got a healthy appetite when you let yourself go," he commented on a laugh.

Because she felt ridiculous and just plain happy, she

replied, "You'd better finish that one before I get done with yours or I'm taking it back."

"Keep eating like that, kiddo, and you won't be fitting into those shorts much longer," he warned lightheartedly.

She opened her mouth, ready to protest. In the end, though, she merely smiled.

Lauren was quiet on the ride back to the house. Gavin glanced over at his passenger a couple of times. She'd stretched out her long legs, crossing them at those trim ankles. Her hands were clasped over her middle. He thought she might drift off to sleep in the comfort of the truck's air-conditioned cab, but when they pulled into the driveway, her eyes were still open and that same secretive smile was playing around the corners of her mouth.

He'd had a nice time today. He'd forgotten what it was like to enjoy a carefree afternoon with a beautiful woman. Lauren had a surprising sense of humor lurking behind those finishing-school manners of hers. Maybe he'd invite her to dinner this evening. He had a couple of juicy steaks they could throw on his new state-of-the-art stainless-steel grill. His sister had sent the grill to him for his birthday last month, but he had yet to try it out. It wouldn't be like a date or anything. Nope. It would just be two people having dinner. Nothing wrong with two people sharing a meal, even if one of them was married, Gavin assured himself when his conscience kicked up.

He stopped the truck at the side of the house, trying

to work out the wording for the invitation as he shifted into Park and they got out.

"I was wondering if you would—"

A car pulled into the driveway and stopped behind Gavin's work truck. It was a Mercedes, a pricy silver model that appeared to be showroom new. The man unfolding himself from behind the wheel looked like something out of a showroom, too. He wore designer sunglasses, a linen shirt that somehow managed to still look crisp and tan trousers. The expression on his face was one of supreme irritation.

Gavin figured he was lost. He'd probably missed the turnoff to the interstate and was now irked beyond measure to find himself in this seemingly primitive little backwater without access to five-star accommodations.

"Need directions?"

The man peeled off the sunglasses. The eyes behind them were bright with annoyance. "Yes. Perhaps you can tell me where I can find my wife?"

CHAPTER FIVE

HER husband.

Gavin knew she had one of those, but he still felt as if he'd taken a surprise punch to the gut. He looked at Lauren, trying to decipher her expression. She didn't appear overly happy to see the man, even though they had spent the better part of a month apart. She wasn't falling into his arms. For that matter, she wasn't even smiling.

She looked surprised, apprehensive and nervous. Or was she feeling guilty? But then, maybe Gavin was transferring that last emotion onto her since it was what he was experiencing at the moment. He'd been about to ask her to dinner, although it wouldn't have been a date, he reminded his conscience for a second time.

"Holden." She'd gone sheet white. "I wasn't expecting you."

"Obviously," the man said drily, and his gaze veered to Gavin.

They eyed each other stoically, each man taking the other's measure as Lauren performed the introductions.

"This is my…" She hesitated just long enough to make them both uncomfortable. Holden's eyebrows notched up. "Landlord," she said at last. "Gavin O'Donnell. Gavin, this is Holden."

As the two men shook hands, Holden's gaze drifted to the side of the house where the paint was peeling and the trim was missing from around a couple of the windows.

"Nice place you have here." The words were as insincere as his smile was insolent.

Gavin gritted his teeth and replied, "It will be when it's finished. These things take time."

"And money," Holden said.

Gavin neither liked nor appreciated the implication in Holden's words, but he managed an easy shrug. "That's not an issue for me."

Lauren's husband said nothing, but his gaze took in Gavin's stained and wrinkled shirt before moving to the truck. It was a work vehicle and as such it would never win any prizes for its looks. Gavin knew what the man was thinking but he resisted the urge to get into a debate over who had the bigger bank account. His financial status was nobody's damned business but his own.

Lauren broke the strained silence. "The cottage I'm renting is back this way." She sent Gavin a smile. "Thank you again for today."

He gave a curt nod. "No problem. I'll bring the paint and supplies by later."

"Okay. That'll be fine."

As Gavin watched them walk away, he doubted Holden was going to roll up his sleeves and help her out.

Lauren was as surprised as Gavin that her husband had shown up. And not surprised in a good way. She'd had a nice day, one of the most pleasant and relaxing in memory. Part of her hadn't wanted it to end. She'd even been thinking about asking Gavin to join her for dinner, although what she would have cooked, she wasn't sure. Then Holden had arrived. One look at his mordant smile and mocking eyes and she'd felt all of the tension of the past couple months return.

She waited until they were inside the cottage to say, "You didn't mention you were coming."

"I prefer the element of surprise."

She ignored the underlying accusation. She wouldn't feel guilty. And she damn well wouldn't offer an explanation. If anyone was owed an explanation, it was she. So, turning to face him, Lauren demanded, "Why are you here?"

"I came to see if you've come to your senses."

She folded her arms over her chest. "About what?"

"Come on, Lauren. You've made your point."

"My *point*. Do you really think that's what my moving out was about?"

He sighed heavily and fiddled briefly with the earpieces on his sunglasses before using one to hang the pricey lenses from the open collar of his shirt.

"I want you to come home."

Home. Their lovely Park Avenue apartment no longer felt like home. In truth, it never had. No place she'd lived, either before or after her marriage, had seemed the ideal location to settle in for the long haul.

Until now.

She had too much else on her plate to ponder the implications of such a thought, so she pushed it away and dealt with the matter at hand.

"I'm still pregnant, Holden. And I haven't changed my mind about the baby."

She'd felt a strange flutter in her abdomen today on the drive back to the house. It might have been nothing. It might have been the result of too much ice cream, but she wanted to believe it was the baby and as such it had made the new life growing inside her all the more real and vital.

"I have," he said quietly.

Holden's reply shocked her, so much so that she wasn't sure she'd heard him right. "You've changed your mind about the baby?"

"Yes. I have." He reached out and stroked her arm. "I want you to come home."

The contact was as surprising as his words. Lauren tried to convince herself that she was happy about his change of heart. Their child could have two parents now, two parents who would love him or her and take an active role in his or her life. But something seemed off. Holden's next words were proof.

"I've done some thinking. Our lives really needn't be

disrupted too much. We can hire a live-in nanny to see to the child's needs."

"A live-in nanny?" Her lips twisted on the words.

"Don't say it like that. I had a nanny as a child. You had one yourself."

Yes, she had. Her parents had hired an assortment of caregivers and sitters until she'd finally been old enough to ship off to summer camps and boarding schools. Even when her parents had been home from work, her care and keeping had been relegated to others. Of course, as a single mom Lauren would have to make arrangements for the baby while she was at work, but Holden was talking about more than that.

Lauren placed a protective hand over her belly. "*I* want to see to *my* child's needs as much as possible."

"But how can you do that and find time to attend to the many other important things in your schedule?" He sounded truly baffled.

She was baffled, too. "What other important things are you talking about? I no longer have a career," she reminded him. Of course, lately she'd been going through her portfolio with an eye on future employment. She'd forgotten how good it felt to have the creative juices flowing.

"You know what I mean." He waved a hand in impatience. "You sit on committees, chair some of them. You run our household and see to our social engagements." *Our* meaning *his*. Everything in their marriage had revolved around him. "I have a dinner party coming up next week or have you forgotten?"

"Is that why you've come here today? Are you looking for a hostess?"

"Don't be ridiculous," he chided, but his gaze slid away, and Lauren figured she had her answer.

Before her pregnancy, she had been foolish enough to stay in a loveless marriage, but she wouldn't subject her baby to that stark, chilly atmosphere, especially when she had little reason to believe the climate would warm up. Sure, Holden was asking her to come home, and claimed he wanted their baby, but he didn't appear excited or overjoyed about impending parenthood. Rather, his expression was one of resignation. The image of Gavin tickling the baby's chin earlier in the day popped into Lauren's head. He'd shown more interest in and enthusiasm for a stranger's child than Holden was showing for his own. You'll make a good dad, she'd told Gavin. What sort of father was Holden going to be?

Sadly, she knew the answer.

Holden shoved his hands into his trouser pockets and stalked to the window. It was open, but the air was heavy and still. The lightweight, café-style curtains didn't so much as twitch. "God, it's sweltering in here," he snapped irritably. "Can't you put on the air-conditioning or something?"

Lauren sighed. This was Holden, never happy, never satisfied. Over the years she'd grown used to his constant complaints, but they grated on her nerves now. "There isn't any air-conditioning." She didn't bother to add that Gavin had promised to have a unit installed soon.

He turned to face her, shaking his head as he swept a hand to encompass the room. "Lauren, you don't belong here. God, this place is barely habitable."

She glanced around and saw character, charm and coziness, which was far more than could be said for their Manhattan apartment. Oh, it was tastefully decorated, but Holden had vetoed her every attempt to stamp the place with personality…her personality. She'd had no such restrictions in the cottage. Gavin was even allowing her to paint.

"I disagree. I like it here. I wake up in the morning to the sound of birds singing."

He rolled his eyes, unimpressed. "You can get that on a compact disc. The sound of babbling brooks and rustling leaves, too, if that's what you want."

Until just recently, so much in Lauren's life had been artificial and her relationship with her husband had been utterly superficial.

"I want the real thing." She wasn't talking about bird songs.

He seemed to realize that, too. His voice held a note of desperation when he said, "I'd like you to move back into the apartment. I think we can put this misunderstanding behind us."

I'd like…

I think…

She shook her head slowly. "No, Holden, we can't."

"What more do you want from me, Lauren?" he asked in exasperation.

He placed his hands on his hips. The pose was reminiscent of her lecturing father. It only served to reinforce her decision.

What do I want? She wanted what he wasn't capable of giving her or their child. She wanted what, through his actions and words, he'd made abundantly clear he would never be capable of giving: unconditional love.

"I've made a horrible mistake," she whispered at last.

Not surprisingly, he took her words to mean something else entirely. "I'm glad you finally see that. I'll call the movers and have you out of here by the end of the day."

Lauren closed her eyes and expelled a ragged breath. She felt exhausted and yet unburdened. "That's not the mistake I was talking about."

His eyes narrowed, his gaze hardened. "What are you saying, Lauren?"

"I'm saying I want a divorce."

Lauren followed the sound of hammering up the stairs to the farmhouse's second level. The blows were interspersed with a great deal of cursing. She found Gavin in one of the bedrooms, using a long-handled sledgehammer to break through the plaster on an interior wall. He was stripped to the waist and the tanned skin on his back glistened with perspiration that had soaked the waistband of his shorts.

"What are you doing?" she asked, as he raised the sledgehammer over his head and prepared to batter the wall again.

He whipped around, nearly dropping the heavy tool. He looked surprised to see her, and not necessarily in a good way. But then his face softened with an easy smile.

"Lauren. Hey. I didn't realize that you were standing there." He cleared his throat. "Everything… okay?"

"Fine. Everything's fine." Or it would be. She motioned toward the wall and the pile of rubble on the floor in front of it. "What are you doing? Besides making a mess?"

"This?" His shoulders lifted. "Just taking care of a little demo work."

"It seems awfully hot to be doing that today. Especially up here."

"I'm working off that ice cream." He winked.

Lauren's gaze lowered to a pair of incredibly ripped abs. No need for that, she thought. Every inch of the man's body was rock solid and, at the moment, glistening like something ethereal. She realized she was staring. Embarrassed, she forced her gaze to the wall. It sported a hole big enough for a man to fit through. "I'd say you worked off the ice cream and then some."

"It's good for frustrations, too," he admitted. "So, your husband getting settled in okay?"

"Actually, he's not staying."

"Oh." Gavin set the head of the sledgehammer on the floor and leaned on the long handle.

"Holden and I…we've been having some problems."

"Sorry to hear that."

"Thanks." She fiddled with the hem of her blouse. "He came here today to ask me to move back to the city."

"So, you've worked things out, then?"

"In a manner of speaking." Lauren smoothed down her hem and looked up. "I've asked him for a divorce."

Gavin's eyelids flickered in surprise, but other than that she couldn't gauge his reaction—nor was she sure why she wanted to try.

In fact, Gavin was floored. He didn't know what to say or why he felt so damned elated by her news. He kept his smile in check, though. Sympathy was called for at the moment. He reached out and gave her arm a squeeze. With as much sincerity as he could muster, he said, "God, Lauren, I'm sorry to hear that."

"Thanks."

"Are you okay?"

"I think so." She nodded vigorously. To convince him? To convince herself? Then, she added, "Ultimately this is for the best."

Gavin had felt that way too when he'd divorced, but it hadn't made things any easier at the time. He'd still felt mule kicked. So, he meant it when he asked, "Do you want to talk about it?"

Lauren studied him. "A man who wants to talk? But will you listen, too?"

He frowned. "Sorry?"

She closed her eyes, shook her head and sighed. "No, *I'm* sorry. That comment was insufferably rude."

And telling, Gavin thought. Very telling. It made one of her husband's deficiencies very clear. "It's okay. The offer still stands. So?"

But she was shaking her head. "I'm touched by your concern. Truly, I am. But as tempting as it is to unload, I don't think you need to hear all of the sad details."

He should be grateful. He should be relieved. Why was it he wanted to disagree?

Lauren went on. "Let's just say that Holden and I have a fundamental difference of opinion on a certain vital matter, and leave it at that."

That vague description certainly piqued his curiosity, but she looked so sad and fragile that Gavin could only respect her wishes. He nodded, and then found himself admitting, "My wife and I had one of those, too."

"Oh?"

"Yeah. She wanted to continue having an affair and I felt that wasn't in our marriage's best interests." God, why had he told her that? He snatched his wadded-up shirt off the floor and swiped it across his damp forehead.

"Ah."

He tucked a corner of the shirt into his back pocket and leaned against the handle of the sledgehammer again. "I demoed an entire cinderblock wall by myself after I found out she was sleeping with a good friend of mine. They're both exes now."

"That must have been awful for you."

Awful? He'd felt as if his world had been tipped upside down. But he merely shrugged. "The wall looked like hell, too. Only about a third of it was supposed to come down."

"Well, Holden's not cheating on me. He...he doesn't

want—" Her eyes grew wide before filling, and she covered her mouth in a futile attempt to muffle a sob.

"Oh, God! Don't do that," Gavin pleaded, doing a poor job of camouflaging his panic.

Lauren waved a hand. "Sorry." But the tears continued to course down her cheeks.

He thought he was beyond begging, but he did so now with unabashed fervor. "Please, Lauren. Please, don't cry."

"Okay." She nodded, but the tears didn't stop. "S-s-sorry," she sobbed.

Gavin felt helpless, too. What should he do? What should he say? Finally he told her the only thing he knew with utter certainty: "He's not worth it."

She stopped crying. Watery blue eyes studied him. He had her attention.

"He's not worth it," he said again, this time with more conviction.

Gavin pulled the shirt from his back pocket, but a glance at it told him it was far too dirty to be used to dry her tears, so he tossed it to the floor and stepped forward.

"You deserve better, Lauren. You deserve so much more." Cupping her face in his rough palms, he used the pads of his thumbs to gently brush aside the evidence of her heartache.

"Gavin."

"That's right." And it seemed so perfectly logical to open his arms. "Come here."

He might as well have said come home, because

that's how Lauren felt when she stepped forward, stepped into his embrace. His loose hold was foreign yet familiar. Home and heaven wrapped into one.

With one big hand he stroked her back, murmuring words she couldn't quite decipher. She didn't need to. At that moment she knew all she needed to know. She was safe. Someone cared.

As the seconds ticked by, however, feelings that were a bit more disconcerting began to stir. Gavin turned his head and Lauren felt his hot breath stir her hair. She became aware that she was pressed against his body, which was partially bared, sweaty and unyielding.

The hand stroking her back stilled, settling just above the curve of her bottom and her pulse picked up speed.

"Lauren?"

She swore he sounded just as surprised and confused as she was. She took a step away, fussing once again with the hem of her blouse to occupy her unsteady hands.

When she glanced up, Gavin was watching her. She saw his throat work, but it was still a moment before he was able to form words. That fact stroked her battered ego.

"So, you've asked for a divorce?"

She nodded. "It was never a very good marriage." The admission stung, but it seemed important to be truthful. "I want it to be over."

"I'm glad." He stepped forward and she thought he might reach for her again. Would he hold her? Would he kiss her? He did neither. Instead he stepped back. "For you, that is."

* * *

Later that evening, as the sun lowered in the sky and the temperature dipped to the low eighties, Lauren dialed her parents' number. She hadn't told them about the baby yet or about her troubles with her husband. Nor had she given them her new address and telephone number since if they needed to reach her they had her cell. But she'd merely been putting off the inevitable. It was time to address that.

Her mother answered on the third ring.

"Hi, Mom, it's Lauren." She was an only child and so giving her name was completely unnecessary. Lauren didn't like what it said about the relationship she had with her parents that she always felt the need to point out their kinship.

"Lauren, hi." Camille sounded harried and pressed for time. Sure enough, she said, "I'm just on my way out the door to yoga and your father is still at the office." The words, as well as her tone, were intended to discourage a long conversation. Nothing unusual there.

"Sorry." Lauren grimaced after offering the apology. Gavin was right. Lauren forever seemed to be issuing one. Clearing her throat, she said, "This is important, Mom."

There was a sigh and then silence. Finally, "What is it? Is Holden all right?"

"I'm sure he's fine."

"You've had a fight," Camille surmised.

"A fight? No." It had been far too civilized for that. "I thought you and Dad should know, I've asked for a divorce."

"Oh, Lauren." It wasn't sympathy in Camille's tone,

but a mixture of exasperation and disapproval. "Why would you go and do something like that? You were so lucky to find someone like him."

Lucky. For a time that had been how Lauren had viewed the situation, too. But even before Gavin had told her she deserved better, she'd reached that conclusion, as well. "Our marriage hasn't been good for a long time, but now…I'm pregnant, Mom. I'm going to have a baby."

She smiled as she said the last word.

"A baby? But how is that possible? You've always been told… The doctors have always said that you wouldn't be able to have children."

Camille's disbelief was not quite the reaction Lauren had hoped for. Her smile faltered as it became clear why it had taken her well over a month to call and deliver this astounding good news. How ironic, how *sad*, that while Lauren's gynecologist had hugged her after reporting the results of the pregnancy test and the nurse had actually grown misty-eyed, her own mother seemed too hung up on the mechanics of this miracle to simply rejoice in it.

"Is that all you have to say, Mom?"

"No. Of course not. It's just that you've taken me by surprise." Still, instead of asking when the baby was due or how Lauren was feeling, Camille's next question was, "What does Holden think about this?"

Lauren closed her eyes, breathed through her mouth and counted to ten in an effort to defuse her anger and mask her disappointment. She'd read about the technique in a self-help book and had used it often in recent years when interacting with her parents. Interestingly, her mother was a therapist.

"What does Holden think? I've asked for a divorce. That should tell you what he thinks."

"Lauren—"

She broke another of her parents' rules by interrupting. "He doesn't want this baby. He doesn't want his own child."

Lauren expected a little sympathy or she hoped for it at any rate. She should have known better. Camille said matter-of-factly, "Not everyone desires children."

Lauren pinched her eyes shut and called herself a fool. "Not everyone desires children," she repeated half under her breath. As if she didn't know that. She'd been raised by two such people before foolishly marrying one.

Camille was saying, "You need to understand what Holden is going through. This has to be a very trying time for him."

What Holden was going through? What about what *she* was going through? This was a trying time for Lauren, too. Her tone turned a little sharp when she said, "Sorry, Mom, but I ran out of understanding when he asked me to end my pregnancy."

"You're being unfair."

One...two...three... "The point is moot," she managed in a civil tone. "I moved out a month ago and today I officially asked Holden for a divorce."

"Raising a child on your own will be difficult," her mother warned. "Children need two parents."

"I agree wholeheartedly." She jerked her head down

in an emphatic nod, even though her mother couldn't see her. "But I'd rather my child had no father at all than one who doesn't want his life disrupted and is too busy with work and social engagements to make it to school plays or honor banquets."

She was talking about Holden, but apparently she'd nicked a nerve. In her best therapist's voice, Camille said, "You're projecting."

Lauren was undeterred. "I'm not a patient, Mom. I'm your daughter. And I'm not projecting. I'm stating a fact."

"Your father and I must have done something right while raising you. You turned out well," Camille countered. Her tone bordered on insulted.

Lauren would have preferred that her mother feel wounded instead. That emotion was more personal and far closer to what Lauren felt. She started to count to ten again, but she only made it past one before the pain she'd kept bottled up inside for nearly thirty years burst its cork.

"You didn't raise me at all. You and Dad hired a bunch of people to do it for you. You were too busy fixing other people's lives and Dad was too busy climbing the corporate ladder to take an interest in me. Me! Your only child." Her voice broke on a sob and a tear leaked down her cheek.

In contrast, Camille's tone was sharp with impatience. "We worked, Lauren Elizabeth. We had careers. We still have careers. Lots of parents do, you know. Your circumstances were hardly unique. Lots of parents work outside the home, and, I might add, you certainly benefited from our dual incomes. They afforded you a lot of opportunities and advantages. Other children would be grateful."

"You've had my gratitude." But Lauren hadn't wanted opportunities. She'd wanted their affection, their time, their attention and their unfettered love.

Camille made a little harrumphing noise. "You know, it's easy to judge others without walking in their shoes. You'll need to return to the workforce yourself if you divorce Holden."

"When."

"Excuse me?"

"When I divorce Holden." She heard her mother sigh and decided not to give Camille another opportunity to argue. "I'd better let you go, Mom. I've taken up enough of your time and I know you're eager to get to yoga. Be sure to pass the news on to Dad."

She hung up without waiting for her mother's response. Lauren was tired, but she'd never felt more determined.

As she rubbed the small mound of her belly she promised, "I'm going to be a good mom."

Gavin wasn't the sort to eavesdrop on a private telephone conversation, but the cottage windows were open. He was standing outside and when he heard Lauren's voice, laced with such pain and disappointment, he hadn't been able to walk away. Curiosity and something else had kept him rooted in place for the duration of her brief talk with her mother.

He could only hear Lauren, but he didn't need to listen to both sides of the conversation to know that whatever her mother was saying to her wasn't what Lauren had hoped to hear. And no wonder, given all of the drama going on in her life.

Not only had she left her husband and planned to divorce him, she was pregnant.

Pregnant.

And he'd held her in his arms earlier. Gavin scrubbed a hand over his face. Honesty demanded he admit he wanted to do much more. He wasn't sure how he felt about that. Hell, he wasn't sure about anything when it came to Lauren Seville. Sure she was beautiful, smart, too, and sexy in an understated way that had engaged his interest from the first. But the woman's personal life was a huge, untidy knot of complications.

The question was: did he want to help her untangle it?

There'd been a time when Gavin would have barreled ahead, consequences be damned. He would have gone with whatever his heart told him to do, even if his head wasn't in complete agreement.

Well, he'd paid for such impulsiveness. He'd paid dearly. So he pondered the question carefully as Lauren ended her phone call, and because he wasn't sure of the answer, he retreated from the cottage doorstep without ever knocking.

CHAPTER SIX

A COUPLE of weeks passed as Lauren mulled her future. She couldn't live in the cottage forever, even if her lease was paid up for a year. Also at some point she would need to get a job, which would require her to find child care. Perhaps she could hire on somewhere that had more flexible hours than her previous position or that allowed her to work from home part of the time.

Thinking about all of that was too dizzying, though, so she put together a list of the things she needed to do in the interim. Finding an obstetrician in Gabriel's Crossing and hiring a good divorce attorney vied for the top spots. Interestingly, telling Gavin about the baby ranked high, as well.

It wasn't that he needed to know as much as Lauren needed to tell him. Why, exactly, she wasn't sure. She could say nothing, of course, and eventually he'd figure it out on his own. But that didn't seem right. Especially when she recalled the way he'd held her the other day after she'd started to cry. She rubbed her arms now, remembering.

She swore something had passed between them. Something innocent and sweet and yet still promising enough to steal her breath. She couldn't help wishing she'd met Gavin under vastly different circumstances. Then she would have been free and perhaps brave enough to explore her feelings. But not now. Not with her life in such turmoil and hormones churning up her already agitated emotions.

So she would tell Gavin about the baby and hope for his friendship.

He was a good man—kind and patient and surely no more in search of romance at the moment than she was, given the way his own marriage had ended. Oh, he hid the scars well enough, but Lauren knew they were there. Friendship. Yes, that would be enough. More than enough. How she longed to have someone close by to share her excitement about the new life growing inside her. Recalling the way Gavin had reacted to the children at the ice cream shop, Lauren decided he would be happy for her.

She didn't have many close friends. Acquaintances she had by the dozen back in the city. True friends were in awfully short supply. That was her fault. She'd never been very good at making them. She tended to be too quiet, too reserved.

Wait to be spoken to, Lauren Elizabeth.

It had been her parents' cardinal rule, and she'd

followed it so religiously that it had become a hard habit to break.

She had managed to now and again, though. She still kept in touch with some of the women she'd worked with at Danielson & Marx. They lunched together on occasion. And then there was Lilly Hamlin, the one close friendship she'd maintained since her teens. She and Lilly had attended the same prep academy and remained in touch despite living on opposite sides of the country. But Lilly was busy chasing after twin toddlers these days and running an older son to this activity and that, so the two women rarely managed a lengthy phone conversation much less a visit.

Even so, Lilly was the first person Lauren had told about her pregnancy. Her friend had been absolutely delighted about the news and, later, when Lauren called to tell her she'd left Holden, Lilly had been supportive and understanding. Bless her, she'd also resisted the urge to say, "I told you so."

Her friend had never thought Holden good enough. Lilly and Gavin had something in common, Lauren mused.

At some point before the baby came, she hoped to fly to California for a visit. In the meantime, she would do her best to make friends here—starting with Gavin.

It was barely eight o'clock, but the heat in the cottage was already cloying, so she showered in cool water and then dressed in a blouse whose empire waist camouflaged her pouchy middle and allowed her to leave the button on her shorts undone. She pulled her damp hair back into a simple ponytail, put on a minimal amount of makeup and, satisfied that she looked presentable, left the cottage. She decided she would take a walk along the road first and then, when the hour was more reasonable, she would knock on Gavin's door, maybe invite him to the cottage for a cup of coffee or iced tea.

When she rounded the side of his house, however, she spied him outside standing atop a ladder under one of the oak trees. He was leaning across a thick branch securing the ropes that held a swing—a swing with a bright-red seat. It looked just like the one in the airline advertisement she'd coordinated. The one she'd told him about.

Lauren's grin unfurled slowly. "Good morning," she called.

He returned the greeting as he finished the job.

"You're up early," she commented.

"I could say the same."

"Yes, but I haven't been nearly as productive." She motioned with her hand. "Nice swing."

"Thanks."

"It's like the one in the commercial," she said as he began to descend the ladder. It wobbled a bit and so she rushed forward to hold it for him.

"I know. Our conversation the other day got me thinking."

"Oh?"

"My sister and her family are stopping in on Saturday for a couple hours on their way to visit her husband's folks in Hartford. I'm hoping a swing will keep the kids occupied and out of trouble during their visit."

Now on the ground, Gavin rested an elbow on one of the ladder's steps. The T-shirt he wore fit snugly across his chest. She told herself the only reason she noticed was because bits of tree bark dotted the fabric. Dragging her gaze back to his face, she asked, "How many do they have?"

"Grace and Mitch have three under the age of seven. All boys." Dimples dented in his shadowed cheeks as he grinned. "I think it's God's way of paying my sister back for the way she treated her two younger brothers while we were growing up."

"She was that bad?"

"Worse," he assured her. "*The* worst."

"And you and your brother were angels, I suppose?"

"Absolutely."

They both chuckled then.

"I wish I'd had siblings to terrorize me," Lauren mused. She recalled how lonely her childhood had been. How utterly solitary.

"Yeah. No kid should be an only child." Gavin's gaze lowered to her waist, almost as if he knew her secret. She sucked in a breath, reasoning that either way the opening was there to make her announcement and so she took it.

"I agree with you, but at the moment I'm grateful to be having one." She rested a hand on her abdomen.

A pair of dark brows drew together in concern.

"Everything okay? You're not…you're not having trouble with the baby?"

"No." She tilted her head to one side. "How long have you known?"

"Not long." He flushed as he explained, "I came by in the evening to see how you were doing the day Holden stopped in and I…I overheard you talking on the phone to your mother."

"Oh." It was her turn to be embarrassed.

"I didn't mean to eavesdrop. Honest. But the windows were open and it was hard not to hear what you were saying."

"It's okay," she said, even though she felt mortified.

He swallowed and his voice dropped to an intimate whisper. "Why didn't you say something before?"

Before what? she almost asked, but then realized he wasn't referring to a specific event. And why would he be? She lifted her shoulders in a shrug. "I don't know. It just never came up in conversation."

"I guess not. It's really none of my business anyway." He cleared his throat, and gone was that moment of vulnerability that had made her want to confide all sorts of things. "I mean, I'm just your landlord."

Just her landlord? Even though they hadn't known each other for very long, the description was all wrong. Lauren laid a hand on his arm. "You've quickly become a lot more than that to me, Gavin. I count you as my friend, too."

Even that description seemed lacking.

His head jerked down in a nod. "Same goes for me." Afterward, his mouth crooked up with an easygoing grin, although his eyes never lost their intensity. "You can never have too many friends."

But you could have too few, as Lauren knew only too well. Friendship required an effort. It required a person to reach out. Her hand was still on his forearm, but that wasn't enough. And so she said, "Have you had breakfast yet? I've got enough eggs to make an omelet and a really ripe cantaloupe that's just begging to be sliced and eaten."

"That's a tempting offer, but I should be getting to work."

"Oh." She dropped her hand and forced aside her disappointment. "Another time then."

"Yeah, another time." He hefted the ladder and folded it. With it braced against one shoulder he started toward the garage, but then he stopped and turned. "What kind of cheese do you have for that omelet?"

"Feta. It's one of the things I've been craving lately. I was thinking about throwing in some black olives. You know, kind of a Greek omelet."

His nose wrinkled. "Feta?"

"I also have cheddar."

"I think that goes better with the cantaloupe. Have you been craving that, too?" he asked.

It was her turn to wrinkle her nose. "No, but it's healthy."

He chuckled. "Well, I'm not much on cantaloupe

either, but an omelet—one made with *cheddar cheese*—
now that sounds pretty tasty."

"Does that mean you've changed your mind?"

"It's a man's prerogative, too, you know."

She grinned. "I'm all for gender equality."

"Give me fifteen minutes to clean up and I'll be
over." A smile tipped up the corners of his mouth and
Lauren's pulse hitched. Friendship, she reminded her
wayward heart. This invitation was all about friendship.

In record time Gavin had showered, shaved and changed
into fresh clothes. When he arrived at the cottage his hair
was damp and his cheeks still stung from the aftershave
he'd slapped on. Lauren opened the door looking
nervous and as lovely as ever.

That made *him* nervous.

They stared at each other for an awkward moment
before she pointed to the package he held in one hand.
"Is that for me?"

"Of course. My mother told me never to show up
empty-handed. Besides, you can't have eggs without
bacon. They go together."

She took the package and studied it a moment. "I
can't say that a man has ever brought me a hostess gift
like this before."

Her deadpan delivery surprised him, and so he tucked
his tongue into his cheek and replied, "Well, flowers are
so overdone."

They both chuckled and some of the awkwardness dissipated.

"Come in, please."

She stepped back to allow him entry. It was the first time he'd been inside since her arrival, and he noticed just how cozy and inviting she'd made the place without overdoing it on the decorating. Maybe he'd ask her advice when he was ready to put the farmhouse on the market. Staging was important and she had a good eye. The main living area was furnished in a neutral palette with accent pillows and wall art providing splashes of vivid color. In addition to the belongings he'd seen movers unload the day she'd arrived, more furniture had been delivered just the week before, including a maple kitchen set.

She pulled out one of the chairs. "Why don't you have a seat while I get started?"

"Need any help?" he asked.

"No, thanks. Can I get you something to drink? I can make coffee, although as warm as it is maybe you would prefer iced tea. Or juice. Orange juice. I have orange juice." The words came out in a mortifying rush.

Gavin lowered himself onto a seat. "Whatever you're having is fine. Relax, Lauren. I'm easy to please."

"Sorry."

She should have the word trademarked, he thought, but said nothing.

"I'm a little rusty at this," she went on.

"Rusty at what?" The words came out slowly.

She wrung her hands. "Friendship."

"Ah." In addition to feeling disappointed—an emotion he wasn't quite ready to explore—her explanation left him baffled. "Why do you say that?"

"I just am. I can throw a dinner party for thirty of Holden's work associates and their spouses, and make small talk with perfect strangers for hours on end, but you're…different."

"Different," he repeated, not at all sure he liked her use of that adjective to describe him.

"You matter to me," she added softly.

Gavin swallowed, not sure he liked those words, either.

"I don't have a lot of close friends," Lauren continued. "I'm not very good at making them."

"I find that hard to believe." Sure, Lauren was quiet and could be too self-contained at times, but he would hardly consider her antisocial.

"No, it's true." She sat in the chair next to his and with heartbreaking sincerity confided, "I'm scared, Gavin. I'm really scared."

"Of me?" The thought had his blood running cold.

"Of course not." She reached for his hand on the tabletop and gave it a squeeze. That made twice in one morning that she'd touched him. Twice that such benign contact had zapped him with all the force of a lightning bolt. "I'm scared of what the future holds. If it were just me, I wouldn't worry so much. But with the baby?" She shook her head and her eyes turned bright.

"You're going to be fine. *Both* of you are going to

be fine," he stressed, turning his hand over so that he could hold hers.

"This is all so new to me and I'm terrified I'm going to screw it up. I…I didn't think I'd ever have children," she admitted.

"Why?" He coughed then. "Sorry. That's an awfully personal question."

And Lauren struck him as a private person. Even so, she replied with utter candor, "That's what the doctors had always told me. I have a couple of medical issues that, according to them, should have made conception impossible."

He snorted out a laugh, eager to lighten the mood. "Just goes to show you what they know."

"Yes. I suppose so." But she still looked worried.

He squeezed her hand again. "It's called 'practicing medicine' for a reason."

At long last a smile teased her lips. Impending motherhood, rather than his stale quip, had put it there, he was sure. Lauren looked radiant. She looked lovely. Sitting next to him wearing a pair of shorts that showed off her trim legs, she looked…sexy. He swallowed and felt his palms grow damp. Was it okay to think of a pregnant woman as sexy? A still-*married* pregnant woman, his conscience reminded him.

His thoughts turned to her husband then. "So, what does Holden think about the baby?" Even as he asked the question, he figured he knew, based on the telephone conversation he'd overheard.

Her gaze drifted away. Some of her radiance dimmed. "He didn't want children when we married. Actually, it was a condition of his."

Gavin frowned in disbelief. "What do you mean? Can you put something like that in a prenup?"

"No, of course not. But he made his wishes on the matter very clear."

He'd only met Holden once and briefly, but Gavin had little difficulty seeing the guy as the sort who preferred pristine designer clothes and a foreign two-seater to sticky faces and the many demands of parenthood. But Lauren?

"Why did you agree?"

"I didn't exactly. As I said, I didn't think I could have children, so the fact that he didn't want them…" She left the sentence unfinished and shrugged.

"Made him perfect for you."

At his words Lauren glanced up sharply. Her mouth fell open and she drew back her hand.

"I'm sorry," he said. "That was a rude and presumptuous thing to say."

She shook her head but said nothing. A flush stained her cheeks, but he didn't think anger had put it there. Guilt? Regret? Surprise that he knew and in a way could understand?

Gavin went on. "So, this is the fundamental difference you mentioned the other day when you told me you were divorcing."

"Yes."

Lauren's hands were in her lap now and she was studying them. He did so, too, noting that she'd taken off her wedding ring and had replaced it with one that had an amethyst stone. She may have had a sentimental attachment to the new ring, but he got the feeling that Lauren was merely old-fashioned enough that she didn't want to walk around with a naked third finger on her left hand during pregnancy.

"Holden feels raising children is incompatible with the lifestyle he prefers," she said after a moment. The words came out in a pained whisper.

Gavin wanted to curse loud and long. He wanted to break something with his sledgehammer. Forget that, with his fist. Even more, he wanted to take Lauren in his arms as he had the other day. He wanted to hold her, console her…kiss her. He banished the thought and in a matter-of-fact voice said, "I'm sure he's right. Kids change everything, or so my sister has told me enough times. But marriage is about compromise."

Lauren glanced up. "Were you willing to compromise?"

The question took him by surprise. "When I was married, you mean?"

"Yes."

He shifted his feet under the table, disconcerted to find himself on the receiving end of a query that forced him to re-examine his own union. He'd much rather talk about hers.

Now he wondered, had he compromised enough?

Had he made the right choices, especially before Helena's affair when he'd worked such long hours? He'd thought so at the time, eager to get ahead, but maybe…

"I wanted our marriage to work. Hell, I didn't want to admit I'd made a mistake."

"No one likes to admit that," Lauren agreed.

She made it easy to confess, "I jumped into things too quickly. Maybe if I'd waited, hadn't rushed things, I would have figured out that Helena and I were just too damned different to make it for the long haul. The signs were there."

Blaring, neon signs that his brother, Garrett, had tried to point out. They'd wound up fighting bitterly over it, their relationship and business partnership suffering until Gavin had finally admitted the truth of Garrett's words.

"How long did you know each other before you got engaged?"

"A couple months." It had seemed like plenty of time back then, but he grimaced now and shook his head. "Then we eloped."

She made a humming noise. "That is quick."

"Impulsive is another word." He shook his head, regretting such spontaneity now whereas at the time he'd viewed the quickie ceremony in a tacky chapel in Vegas as exciting despite the doubts that had nipped him before their I Do's.

"You don't strike me as the impulsive sort," Lauren said. She cocked her head to one side, studied him. "You seem so laid back, so thoughtful about things, if the farmhouse renovations are any indication."

"Ah, but this is the new and improved me. I've learned the value of slowing down and taking the time to evaluate a situation before going off half-cocked." He shook his head and chuckled wryly. "Garrett—he's my brother—claims I'm no fun anymore."

"I don't know about that. I like the new and improved you. Very much." Was it his imagination, or did her cheeks grow pink?

"Thanks." It seemed only fair to admit, "I like the new and improved you, too."

Lauren blinked in surprise. "How do you know I've changed?"

"Because you're here," he said simply.

She nodded slowly and in a quiet voice admitted, "I've always done what was expected of me. I've listened and followed the rules and…" She lifted her shoulders as her words trailed away.

He'd suspected as much. "Not this time, though."

"No. Not this time." She glanced away and he saw her swallow. "I couldn't this time."

He wondered if Lauren realized she'd squared her shoulders as she said it. The woman was a paradox. She seemed fragile in many ways, but he glimpsed steel now and then, too. He liked it. "Good for you."

"Thanks, but I'm embarrassed that it took me this long. My marriage hasn't been good in…well, ever. But I stayed."

"Some lessons take longer to learn than others," he said.

"I guess so." Lauren stood and walked to the counter, where she'd laid out the ingredients for their omelet. As she broke eggs into a bowl, she asked in a wry voice, "So, having been there and done that, can you recommend a good divorce attorney back in Manhattan?"

"Depends on what you want," he said slowly.

"I just want it to be over so the baby and I can move on with our lives."

She poured some milk into the bowl and balanced it against her torso as she picked up the whisk. Steel, he thought again as she began mixing the ingredients with surprising force. Steel wrapped in velvet. Still, he felt the need to point out, "Be careful what you wish for. I just wanted to move on with my life, too, and it wound up costing me plenty in the settlement."

"I don't care. Holden can have it all. The apartment, its furnishings, our stock portfolio and other investments. I only want what I came into our marriage with. I have some savings set aside and I can earn a living."

"I don't doubt that you can, but your child is entitled to financial support from both parents. Even if you don't feel that way now, you may not want to tip your hand early in the negotiations," Gavin advised, feeling like the voice of experience.

She frowned. "That makes it sound like a business deal."

"Sadly, in a way that's what divorce is." He cleared his throat. "Have you thought about custody and visitation?"

She stopped whisking. "Holden doesn't want this

baby. He won't seek custody. I can't imagine he'll want visitation."

"That could change." When the bowl she'd been holding clattered to the countertop, splattering the front of her shirt with eggs, Gavin added, "Sorry, Lauren. I'm not trying to scare you, but people do and say all sorts of unexpected things when a marriage ends. Holden strikes me as the sort of man who cares a great deal about his public image."

She blotted at the mess on her blouse with a damp dishcloth. "He does. He sees it as an asset to his career."

"Then he's not going to want to be known as the sort of man who divorced his wife because she got pregnant with his child and then abandoned both of them physically and financially."

"I hadn't thought about it that way." Lauren gave up trying to clean her shirtfront. She gripped the countertop with both hands, as if seeking balance. No wonder. Her face had turned sheet white. "God, do you think he will actually petition for custody, either full or joint?"

"I don't know. I just think you need to be prepared."

"But he doesn't want the baby," she insisted. She wrapped a protective arm over her belly as her eyes turned bright. "I can't even bring myself to repeat what his first 'solution' to my pregnancy was."

Gavin was on his feet before her first tear fell. Where other women's tears had sent him fleeing, Lauren's drew him.

"Hey, hey. Don't do that. Don't cry. It's going to be

okay." He patted her shoulder awkwardly at first and then, remembering what it had felt like to hold her in his arms, he gave up trying to keep his distance. She needed him. He needed something, as well. And though he wasn't ready to explore the depth and breadth of his feelings, he could admit that when he held Lauren it felt right. He felt right and oddly complete.

"He doesn't want our baby," she said. This time the words were mumbled against Gavin's shoulder.

"It's okay," he promised. He'd make sure it was.

Lauren wasn't listening. "I won't let him have it. My child deserves better than to be raised by someone who's too busy to care. I grew up like that. I know what it's like." A sob shook her then and he was helpless to do anything but hold her. "I won't let that happen to my baby," she vowed.

"I'm sorry, Lauren. I'm so sorry." The words weren't intended just to comfort. He truly was sorry—sorry for the lonely child she'd been, sorry that the man she'd married had disappointed her so badly. Gavin hoped to God he was right when he said, "Holden probably won't want custody and, given what you say, it's a good bet he won't exercise any visitation rights."

She stayed in his arms for several more minutes, her hands resting against his chest.

"Thank you," she said as she pulled away.

"No need to thank me." He kept his tone light and though the truth had always been exactly the opposite he claimed, "I'm a sucker for a crying woman."

"I've been doing that a lot lately. Hormones." She sniffled, but thankfully sounded more like herself when she added, "Just for the record, I don't usually go around busting into tears and blubbering like a baby. I'm stronger than that."

"Yes, you are," Gavin agreed. He leaned over, unable to resist brushing her lips with a light kiss. Though his words were whispered, they were nonetheless sincere. "But you don't always have to be, you know. At least not with me."

CHAPTER SEVEN

AUGUST gave way to September, and Lauren had a grand view of the changes from the windows in her small cottage. The apples on the trees in the orchard began to ripen even as summer's lush greenery faded to a more subdued hue. Splashes of red and orange began appearing, hinting at the fall spectacle to come. In the evenings, the air carried a new crispness and the scent of wood smoke.

Lauren and Gavin had gotten into the habit of taking a walk as the sun was setting. Then they would retire to his front porch, sway on the swing, talk or sometimes just sit in companionable silence until the first stars appeared in the sky. She'd never seen so many stars, living in the city as she had all of her life. Out in the country, with no artificial light to detract from their brightness, they simply dazzled.

When the moon rose and the night grew too cool for comfort, Gavin walked Lauren to the cottage. Standing on her doorstep, he always kissed her good-night. It was a friendly peck, sometimes on the cheek, sometimes on the corner of her mouth. Holden had kissed her like that. Other people in her life had, as well. But this was different, remarkable in a way she couldn't define, though she'd lain awake at night trying to figure out how.

As the weeks passed, Lauren looked forward to that kiss, anticipated it even. And sometimes, when she finally nodded off to sleep, she dreamed about the man in a way that made it difficult to maintain eye contact when she saw him the next day.

So much was happening in Lauren's life. So much was changing, not the least of which was her body. She marveled at the way her abdomen had begun to bulge and her breasts had grown larger, fuller, heavier. Thankfully, they were no longer so unbearably tender, although they remained sensitive.

Lauren had found a new doctor in town, but meetings with her divorce attorney required her to make the trip into New York. Last night, as she and Gavin had swayed on the swing and he pointed out the constellations, he'd offered to drive in to the city with her.

"I have business in Midtown. I can drop you at your appointment and we can meet up afterward. We can have dinner before heading back," he'd suggested.

His idea was practical and she supposed environmentally friendly, as it conserved gasoline and put one less vehicle on Manhattan's congested streets. They were carpooling, nothing more. Yet the next morning it took Lauren nearly an hour to decide what to wear.

She knocked on the rear door to the farmhouse and

waited. Her smile faltered when Gavin answered. She'd gotten used to seeing him in faded jeans and worn T-shirts, his jaw shadowed, his hair a sexy, tousled mess. Today, however, he was dressed in dark trousers with a suit coat draped over one arm and the tie loosened at his collar. His usually messy hair was tamed and his jaw was freshly shaved.

"Good morning." Dimples flashed with his grin.

For the first time in her life, Lauren knew what it felt like to have her knees go weak.

"You look…wow," she managed to say at last.

He laughed self-consciously. "Thanks. You look pretty wow yourself, but then you always do. New shirt?"

"This? It's a maternity blouse," she admitted, tugging at the ballooning hem.

"It looks good on you."

"Thanks. I just threw on the first thing my hand touched when I reached into my closet," she lied. Then she bobbed her eyebrows. "Talk about looking nice."

He shrugged and repeated, "It was the first thing my hand touched when I reached into my closet."

"I didn't realize you shared one with Armani." Her gaze trailed over a tailored shirt that was tucked into a pair of charcoal-colored trousers. Neither had come off a department store rack, of that Lauren was sure. "You have excellent taste in clothes."

"I have an appreciation for craftsmanship and quality in all its many forms," he agreed.

Such craftsmanship and quality, as he put it, did not

come cheaply. Yet, Gavin didn't strike her as the sort of man who lived beyond his means. She tilted her head to one side. "Why do I get the feeling that you do more than restore old farmhouses out in the middle of nowhere?"

"Because I do. My brother and I own a business together. We buy and rehabilitate buildings in Manhattan."

"Like historic sites?" she asked.

"We've done some preservation work, yes," he said. "But generally speaking we convert older buildings to new uses. For instance, we might buy a warehouse and turn it into trendy loft apartments or remake it into office space. That's what today's meeting is about. We've found a buyer for a site we rehabbed in the Village."

What he was talking about took money. A good deal of money. Yet he'd never flaunted his wealth. She liked him all the more for it. "What's the name of your company?"

"Phoenix Brothers Development."

Her mouth dropped open at that. Though she'd already ascertained that Gavin was no pauper, she hadn't expected this reply. "Oh my God."

"Heard of us?" he inquired with a casual lift of his brows.

Indeed she had. His company's distinctive fiery logo had been plastered on some of the most gorgeously restored buildings in New York.

"Is it okay to be impressed? I wouldn't want to make you uncomfortable by gushing over your obvious foresight and talent."

He grinned. "Go ahead. Gush."

"You do incredible work, but you already know that."

"We try," he said modestly. "If you're going to do something, why not do it well? That can take time and investment, but it usually pays off."

Time…investment…pay off. They were talking about his work, about buildings, but his words could be applied to so much more.

So she asked, "What if it doesn't? I mean, aren't you ever afraid that you're going to pour your heart and soul into something and wind up with nothing to show for it afterward?"

"Sometimes."

He stepped onto the porch and pulled the door shut behind him. The move brought him close enough that she could smell the tangy scent of his aftershave and see the pulse beating at the base of his throat. "And yet you still…go for it?" she asked.

"Are we talking about your advertising firm?"

Her gaze strayed to the door beyond him and she concentrated on the chipped paint when she replied, "Among other things."

"Life is all about risks."

Lauren swallowed. "Then I guess I'd better start working up my nerve."

They faced each other, the only sound the far-off yapping of a neighbor's dog.

"We should…we should…" she managed at last. He was watching her mouth.

"Exactly."

Without waiting to find out what he was agreeing to, Lauren turned and started for his truck.

Gavin reached for her hand and stopped her. She turned, startled and oddly expectant, until he pointed to the garage.

"For this trip I think we'll take my car."

"Car?"

"The ride will be smoother."

Lauren doubted that.

The garage was nearly as old as the house and in a similar state of disrepair, but when he pushed up the battered wooden door, a shiny black Porsche was parked inside.

Lauren whistled. "Nice car."

"It gets me from Point A to Point B," he replied blandly, but then he grinned with obvious male pride. "And it gets me there fast."

The meeting with her lawyer didn't go exactly as Lauren had hoped. Her divorce was not going to be a simple or quick matter, if what she'd learned today was any indication.

She was drained emotionally and physically and felt dead on her feet as she waited for Gavin. Of course, her choice in shoes didn't help matters. The three-inch heels had seemed a perfectly logical choice to go with the A-line maternity skirt and lace-edged smock. But Lauren hadn't worn heels of any height in a couple of months. Her arches ached and so did her lower back. She shifted her weight and glanced up Eighth Avenue, hoping Gavin would be there soon. She was tired, frustrated and eager to sit down so she could discreetly kick off her shoes.

The Porsche pulled to the curb a moment later and Gavin hopped out and came around the hood to open the passenger-side door.

"Sorry I'm late. I spied something in a store window on the way here and had to stop for it."

"Don't worry about it." She glanced inside the car. A huge, pink-tutu-wearing teddy bear was strapped to the seat. Laughter tickled her throat as she said, "I gather this is the something that you had to stop for."

"Yeah. It caught my eye." He rubbed the back of his neck sheepishly. "So, what do you think?"

She thought it was perfect. She thought *he* was perfect. He'd given her baby its very first gift. Well, other than a cute yellow sleeper that Lilly had sent with a note of congratulations. But this was different. She glanced up at Gavin and her smile faltered.

"You don't like it," he said.

"It's not that." Lauren made her tone light. "I just didn't realize you were into girly stuffed animals."

"Very funny. It's for the baby."

"And it's adorable," she assured him. "Thank you."

"You're welcome." Gavin grinned as he unbuckled the seat belt and removed the stuffed animal. Standing on the curb with the teddy bear in his arms as traffic and pedestrians bustled by, he looked both ridiculous and sweet.

"What if the baby's a boy?" she asked.

His brows tugged together as if that possibility had never occurred to him. But then he shrugged.

"My gut's telling me it's a girl, but if I'm wrong the bear can lose the tutu and we'll outfit it in something manly."

She laughed. "It sounds like you've thought of everything."

"I try." He maneuvered the bear into the small space behind her seat and helped Lauren into the car. "So, any requests for dinner?"

"I don't care where we go or what's on the menu. Just make sure the place has long tablecloths."

"Excuse me?"

"I'm dying to take off my shoes."

And Lauren did. He saw her kick them off in the car on their way to Cartwright's, a steakhouse located on Broadway in Midtown.

In the late 1800s, the area where the restaurant was located had been home to some of the city's most fashionable retailers, which is why it had been called the Ladies' Mile. But times changed, many of the retailers moved elsewhere and for years some of the buildings sat empty and neglected. Then the area enjoyed a renaissance. A good number of the structures had been restored now, including the one that housed Cartwright's on its main level.

The building was one of the Phoenix Brothers' shining successes, so much so that afterward they'd kept it, moved their offices to the top three floors and

rented out all of the others. Gavin had personally over-
seen the detail work on the facade. He was particularly
proud of the result and eager to gauge Lauren's reaction.

"I've never been here before," she said as they waited
for the valet to reach them.

"The restaurant opened last summer. The upper
floors of the building are office space. We're full up on
tenants at the moment, but maybe something will be
available when you're ready to start that advertising
firm. I'll cut you a sweet deal." He winked, even as the
breath backed up in his lungs.

Lauren's eyes rounded. "This is one of yours?"

He nodded.

"Oh, Gavin, it's gorgeous."

He accepted her compliment with a casual smile, but
he was beaming with pride inside. Then he gave up
acting nonchalant. "So you really like it?"

"I love it and I haven't even seen the inside yet. You
must be really proud."

"I am." And touched by her enthusiasm. "You should
have seen the before shot. It was in pretty rough shape
inside and out when we bought it and began work."

"That's hard to believe now."

The valet, a young man who looked to be of all
eighteen, arrived then. "Sweet ride," he said as Gavin
got out and he got in.

Gavin leaned down and, with a wink in Lauren's direction, confided, "It's got more than four hundred and
fifty ponies under the hood."

"Duuuude," was the valet's reverent reply.

Gavin knew just how the young man felt. "Take good care of her for me and there's an extra twenty in it for you."

"You got it."

While the valet climbed behind the wheel, Gavin came around to help Lauren out. She was trying to put her shoes back on and not having much success, partly because of the awkward angle. He crouched down in front of the open door.

"Here, let me give you a hand, Cinderella," he said on a chuckle.

He was merely being a gentleman, he told himself as he fished her shoes out from under the Porsche's low-slung dashboard. He would have performed the same service for his sister, for his mother. He would have done it for any woman, be she attractive or otherwise. It made no difference that Lauren was not related to him or that she had a face that would have made Helen of Troy seem plain.

He told himself that, but then Lauren shifted to swing her legs out of the vehicle. Her skirt hitched up, exposing her knees. He swallowed a groan and lowered his gaze in an effort to avoid temptation. That proved to be a huge mistake. There were her ankles, slim, inviting. He wanted to kiss them, then run his tongue over the silky skin. He sucked in a breath instead and let it hiss out slowly between his teeth.

"Gavin?" He glanced up. Lauren was watching him, and she wasn't the only one. Behind her, the valet was drumming his fingers on the leather-wrapped steering wheel, impatient to be off. "Are my feet swollen?" she asked.

Feet? He hadn't gotten that far down. He looked now. "Um, yeah. A little."

She nibbled her lip and peered at them. "I hope I can get them into my shoes."

"You're not the only one," he mumbled under his breath since the longer this went on the more likely he was to make a fool out of himself.

Cursing his nonsensical fetish, he got down to business, scooping up Lauren's right foot with one hand and the coordinating pump in the other. He mastered the task without incident, although when his fingers skimmed her ankle he slowed down and took a brief moment to enjoy the contact.

After straightening, he held out a hand to help her up. "Thanks, Gavin."

"My pleasure," he said with a little too much feeling.

He coughed, regretting his inflection and mentally kicking himself for his word choice when a blush stained her cheeks. Had he embarrassed her? He was embarrassed. And growing steadily more frustrated. He wasn't sure how to proceed with Lauren. They were friends, of course, but he was also attracted to her. He'd been from the start. Sometimes he was all but certain the feeling was mutual.

Gavin hadn't dated since his divorce. Before Lauren, he hadn't been tempted to get back into the game, but he was tempted now. He'd been tempted for weeks. If she were any other woman, he would simply ask her out. If the first date went well, he'd consider a second. Maybe a third and so on. But there would be no strings. He might be ready to date, but he wasn't ready for strings.

Lauren wasn't any other woman, though. That was both a blessing and curse in this case. She was smart, sensitive, caring, lovely. In other words, special.

She also was off-limits. Way off-limits.

As they walked into the restaurant, he mentally listed all of the reasons he couldn't get romantically involved with her: She was his tenant. She was pregnant. She was vulnerable. And, legally at least, she was still another man's wife.

He waited for one of those reasons to douse his desire. None of them did, though, perhaps because when Gavin glanced over at Lauren she was watching him, clear blue eyes taking his measure. She didn't look embarrassed. She looked…turned on?

Maybe I'd better start working up my nerve. She'd mentioned that earlier and he'd convinced himself she'd been referring to starting a business. But what if…

He glanced away. He had to be wrong. Did pregnant women get turned on? Should they? Maybe it wasn't good for them in their condition. It certainly wasn't good for *his* condition at the moment. He couldn't think about this now. Not the time and certainly not the place. He pulled his suit coat closed and buttoned it.

"Food's excellent here," he said, talking louder than normal. "They have some of the best prime rib in the city."

"Great. I'm starving."

It was both comforting and disconcerting that Lauren seemed to be nearly shouting, too.

By the time the waitress brought their dinner salads, Gavin had wrestled all sexual interest back into submission. The four glasses of ice water he'd had to drink helped. As did the fact he and Lauren were talking about her divorce, resurrecting unpleasant memories from his own.

"I didn't realize the grounds for divorce in New York were so limited. It's going to take a lot longer than I'd hoped," she admitted on a sigh.

Dismissing his own disappointment, Gavin kept his tone light, "No 'irreconcilable differences' here, I'm afraid."

"I know. My attorney drew up the papers to document a formal separation, but Holden and I have to live apart for at least a year before a divorce can be granted."

"What does Holden say to that?" Gavin asked.

"He's no more eager than I am to see the matter drag out. I agreed to let him be the plaintiff." When Gavin grimaced, she shook her head. "It's a salve to his ego and it lets him save face with his colleagues to make it look like he's the one who wants out. I can only imagine what he's telling them about me and my reasons for leaving." But she shrugged. "Frankly, I don't care."

Gavin had a pretty good idea what the guy was saying about Lauren to anyone who would listen. He'd bet his half of Phoenix Brothers that all of it was as unflattering as it was untrue. "So, what does your lawyer think of that strategy?"

"He isn't very pleased with the idea. In fact, when I hired him to represent me, he tried to talk me out of it. But Holden and I had already reached a verbal agreement." She sipped her water. "Can I ask you something personal?"

"Sure."

"How long did your divorce take?"

Gavin shifted in his seat. "Longer than our courtship, but less time than it appears yours will. Of course, I had grounds."

"Adultery."

He nodded, remembering with painful clarity the moment when he'd walked into their apartment and found his wife and his best friend together. "It also helped to speed things up that I was willing to give Helena just about anything she wanted to make her go away."

"Do you regret that now?"

Gavin snorted out a laugh. "I regret a lot of things when it comes to Helena. I probably could have given her half of what I did in the settlement. I was the injured party, after all. But, I don't know, in the end I got the better deal."

She set down her fork and studied him. "Why do you say that?"

Why *did* he say that? Gavin had expressed a similar sentiment to other people on numerous occasions in the past year, but this time he actually meant it. Oh, the wound from his wife and his friend's betrayal continued to ache, but it wasn't because he still loved Helena. His pride had been nicked, his ego battered. Both were rebounding, right along with his heart. He was healing.

"Well?" she asked softly.

In place of his usual flippant response, he chose his words with care. "Because I'm free and I'm heart whole."

"Do you think you'll ever marry again?"

"I'm not ready now, but yeah," he said slowly. "When both the time and the woman are right, I'll marry." His gaze lowered to her stomach and he added, "I want a family. And you? Will you remarry?"

"I think so. But I won't make the mistake of settling again."

"You shouldn't," he agreed.

"Whoever I marry the next time will have to love my child as much as he loves me," she said.

Gavin's chest felt tight and his stomach took an odd little tumble. He blamed it on heartburn and the vinaigrette dressing on his salad. "That much is a given. I mean, the guy wouldn't be good enough for you if he didn't."

The waiter came by to refill their water glasses, and the strangely intimate moment ended. Afterward, he said, "My ex remarried."

"Was the groom your former friend?"

"Yep." His tone turned wry. "It goes without saying that I didn't attend their wedding even though the money she walked off with probably helped pay for their fancy nuptials on Maui."

"Maui," she repeated, raising her brows.

"Mmm-hmm. Anyway, last I heard, a couple months into wedded bliss they'd already tired of each other and had hired attorneys." He grinned. "Turns out they both were having affairs."

Lauren shook her head. "I guess it's true what they say. What goes around comes around."

"You've got to love karma."

What goes around, comes around.

Three weeks later, Lauren was mulling over that saying again and finding it hard to believe she'd ever done anything to Holden to deserve the bomb he'd dropped on her via the legal papers with which she had just been served.

He was citing new grounds for divorce: adultery. He even claimed to have proof—photographs that documented the affair. Pictures of what? Of whom?

Lauren leafed through the papers a second time, sure she'd missed something. None of this made sense. She hadn't cheated on Holden and he damned well knew that. Just as he knew the baby she was carrying was his, yet he'd left the unmistakable impression that he was not the father with his request for a paternity test.

He was being cruel by making such claims. Holden could be distant and distressingly cool on occasion, but cruel? She'd never seen this side of him, though now that she thought back on it, the wives of some of his colleagues had sometimes let slip that her husband could be ruthless in his quest to get ahead. She'd chalked it up to professional jealousy at the time. Now, however, Lauren supposed it just went to show how little she really knew or understood the man she'd married, and how little he knew or understood her if he thought she was going to take this claim lying down. The old Lauren might have. The new Lauren had grown a spine.

Through the window she spied Gavin walking toward the cottage. Leaves swirled at his feet and the breeze had his dark hair dancing. He was dressed for the crisp weather in a leather-trimmed barn jacket. The collar was turned up and his hands were stuffed into the pockets. She opened the door before he reached it.

His smile helped chase away some of the chill she was feeling.

"Someone's eager," he said.

Lauren had an appointment with her obstetrician in Gabriel's Crossing, and Gavin had volunteered to drive her to it since he had things to pick up at the hardware store in town. She easily could have driven herself. It was barely fifteen minutes away. But she liked Gavin's company, and she figured he must like hers, too, since he kept making such offers. Indeed, they spent as much time together as most married couples, probably more since his work didn't take him away from the farmhouse often.

Since their trip into Manhattan, their evening ritual had expanded to include dinner before their walk. They took turns with cooking, although as of last week they had begun preparing all their meals in Gavin's kitchen, which was now completely refurbished. Not only was his kitchen much larger than the one in the cottage, it had commercial-grade appliances that would have made a gourmet chef weep with envy. Lauren had had fun helping him pick those out, as well as the paint color for the walls and the tile work on the backsplash.

"Just let me get my coat," she said.

She attempted to scoot past him, but Gavin, ever perceptive, grabbed her hand and gently tugged her back. "Hey, everything okay?"

It was so tempting to tell him no and then lay out all of her troubles. He would listen, Lauren knew, just as he always listened. And he would offer insight and suggestions, just as he always offered insight and suggestions. If she cried—and, God, it was a good bet she would, given her wayward emotions—she knew she could count on him to dry her tears and then hold her in his arms and stroke her back with those big calloused hands.

So tempting…but she needed to start standing on her own two feet for her own sake, as well as for her baby's.

She worked up a smile and lied. "Fine. I'm just… tired. I didn't sleep well last night."

"Oh." He nodded. "Glad to hear it's only that. I saw the car arrive earlier when I was out in the orchard. I noticed the guy coming to your door. He looked like the official sort and it looked like he was serving you with some papers. I thought maybe it was something to do with your divorce."

Lauren sighed as her head dipped down. "You don't miss anything, do you?"

"Not where you're concerned." Gavin used his index finger to raise her chin, forcing her to look at him. "Want to tell me about it?"

His dark eyes were full of compassion and something else that always made it difficult for Lauren to breathe normally. And so she admitted on a sigh, "I do, which is exactly why I shouldn't."

Dimples flashed in his freshly shaved cheeks. "I'm afraid I'm not following your logic."

"I've been leaning on you too much lately, Gavin. Way too much. Even today, I'm letting you drive me to my doctor appointment again."

He frowned. "It's no big deal. Have I complained?"

"Of course not." And he wouldn't, she knew. "You're too much of a gentleman for that."

To her shock, he muttered a curse and stepped away. With his back to her, he gazed out the window. "I'm not always a gentleman where you're concerned, Lauren. Believe me."

"Gavin?" She rested her hand on his shoulder.

When he turned, the intensity in his dark gaze stole her breath. "I'm sorry."

"For what?"

He said nothing for a full minute. He just watched her as some private battle waged. Then he stepped forward, framed her face in his hands.

Just before his mouth covered hers he whispered, "For this."

CHAPTER EIGHT

HE INTENDED to stop. For that matter, he'd never intended to stop. Off-limits, he reminded himself. Too many strings. The descriptions taunted him, because when Lauren's mouth opened in invitation beneath his, Gavin's intentions—right, wrong or otherwise—simply vanished. Need had no problem taking their place. Need so overwhelming, so intense and consuming, that it should have scared the hell out of him. It didn't. It excited him instead.

He stepped in closer and shifted the angle so that he could delve deeper. In response Lauren moaned softly and brought her arms up to his shoulders. Through the layers of his shirt and jacket, he swore he could feel her fingernails dig into his flesh. She leaned against him, full breasts and distended belly meeting the wall of his chest and torso. It was a different experience, he had to admit. Something—*someone*—was quite literally coming between them, and at the same time bringing them closer together. Gavin felt as protective of her unborn child as he did of Lauren.

And then there was this. He enjoyed spending his evenings with Lauren, but he didn't want to spend just his evenings with her and he certainly didn't want things to always end with a chaste peck at her door.

Warning bells sounded. He'd known Lauren mere months, not all that much longer than he'd known Helena when he'd foolishly proposed. Was he doing it again? Was he rushing ahead, letting emotions outpace reason?

He didn't want to think so. The problem was he couldn't think, at least not clearly, while he was kissing Lauren and holding her in his arms. He needed to stop, and then he needed to slow down until he was sure he wasn't repeating past mistakes.

He'd said he would marry again if both the timing and the woman were right. If Lauren was that woman, then once all other obstacles had been removed, their relationship would grow at a more sensible pace. In the meantime they would continue as friends. Just as Gavin reached that conclusion, Lauren pulled away.

"Oh God," she whispered and then covered her mouth with her hand.

The look of horror on her face registered with the same chilling effect as a bucket of ice water dumped over Gavin's head.

"Lauren, I'm sorry. I didn't mean to do that." He laughed gruffly then at his ludicrous explanation. The kiss could hardly be classified as an accident. So he added, "Well, I did *mean* to do that, but I shouldn't have."

Her response to his words shocked him. "I kissed you back."

Indeed she had. "It's okay."

"No."

"Please, don't be so upset about the kiss," he urged.

"I'm... I'm not upset about the kiss, Gavin."

But her face was still pale and her hands were trembling. "Okay. Then why do you still look so miserable?"

"I like you. *A lot*."

"Same goes," he admitted. "*A lot*."

Gavin thought she might smile, but she began shaking her head. "The timing—"

He nodded in understanding since she was essentially echoing his thoughts. "It absolutely stinks. I know that, Lauren. For me, too. But this doesn't have to progress anywhere." He inhaled deeply before going on. "In fact, it would be for the best if it didn't, at least for the time being. We've both got, um, issues to resolve and other things that need to take precedence." His gaze dropped meaningfully to her belly. "Neither one of us is really ready for a serious relationship. We can continue as friends."

That last word left a sour taste in his mouth, but, as solutions went, remaining platonic made the most sense for both of them. To his surprise, Lauren was shaking her head.

"I think I should move out," she announced.

Her words landed like a prizefighter's punch. "Whoa, whoa. Hold on a minute. That's not necessary.

Jeez, it was kiss." A kiss that still had his pulse jumping. "It's not like we slept together or anything."

"Holden's claiming we have."

Gavin staggered back a step, feeling pummeled again. "What?"

"He's alleging that I've been unfaithful during our marriage and citing adultery as the new grounds in our divorce. I think… I think you might be the other man he has in mind."

"That's ridiculous! We haven't done anything. Well, anything like *that*," he added.

"I don't know why he's doing this. I've never been unfaithful to him. He's even requesting a paternity test for our child," she said. "He knows perfectly well what the results will show."

"That son of a—" Gavin bit off the last part as well as the other coarser oaths that came to mind. "I know why he's doing this. He's using the tactic as leverage in the divorce, that's all, Lauren. He's threatening to make things ugly for you because he wants something in return."

She rubbed her arms as if chilled. "I guess so. But he's claiming to have pictures that document my supposed infidelity. I couldn't figure out what kind of pictures he could have, unless they were something he'd had doctored somehow, but now I'm thinking that they might be of you and me."

"Doing what?" Gavin asked, his voice rising along with his temper. "Taking a walk. Sitting on my front porch together talking. We haven't done anything."

"We've kissed before. Maybe not quite like we did just now, but in a photograph…"

He had the sinking feeling she was right. Gavin didn't care for the thought that some hired hack with a telephoto lens had been invading his privacy, any more than he liked the idea his very innocent relationship with Lauren could be turned into something sordid. He'd be having a word with Holden Seville. Right now, though, Lauren needed reassurance. Gavin hated seeing her so distraught. It couldn't be good for the baby, something her soon-to-be-ex clearly didn't care about.

"It's going to be all right." Gavin vowed that he would see to it. "He's just blowing smoke."

"I know. But I still think I should move out," she insisted. "It's not fair to you."

"Let me worry about what's fair."

"But—"

"If Holden wants to drag me into this, let him." Gavin would hire an attorney of his own if need be and sue the jerk for defamation. "I'm not guilty of anything. Nor are you."

He thought that would be the end of it, but Lauren said quietly, "That's not completely true. I am guilty of something. A moment ago, when you kissed me…" Her mouth worked soundlessly and she couldn't quite meet his gaze. Finally, she managed, "I never felt that way with Holden. *Never.*"

Gavin swallowed. How were they supposed to go

back to being just friends when she'd made an admission like that?

"This really complicates things," he said.

"I know."

Whether they intended to or not, whether they wanted to acknowledge it or not, their relationship was heading into uncharted territory.

Lauren was distracted that evening as they ate the roast and vegetables that had simmered in a Crock-Pot for a good portion of the day. More than half of the small serving she'd taken remained on her plate.

"Meat too well done?" he inquired as she pushed it around her plate.

"Wh-what?" She glanced first at Gavin and then down at her plate. "Oh, no. It's fine. Delicious. I just don't have much of an appetite tonight. Sorry."

"Did you call your attorney?" He'd suggested that on their way to her doctor appointment and Lauren had promised she would as soon as she got home.

But she was shaking her head. "No. I didn't get around to it. I'll do it tomorrow."

"You really need to. That's why you're paying the guy, to do the worrying for you." Maybe then she wouldn't be quite so pale.

"I know. Sorry."

"You don't need to apologize." It came out more sharply than he intended. Gavin moderated his tone and continued. "You're always saying you're sorry for things that don't require an apology, at least not from you."

"I'm…" She'd nearly said it again, but let out a sigh instead. "It's a habit, I guess."

"I know it is." He cleared his throat and decided to tell her something that had been on his mind for a while now. "I get the feeling a lot of people in your life have made you feel like you must be perfect and pleasant and agreeable at all times. And when you're not, you need to apologize. Well, for the record I don't expect you to be Mary Sunshine or the soul of accommodation every hour of every day. You're entitled to be distracted, tired, scared, confused, frustrated, irritated or just plain ticked off from time to time. Those are honest emotions that everyone experiences. You're entitled to experience them, too."

She didn't say anything for a long time. Then she admitted quietly, "My parents abhorred drama."

"Life is a drama." He shrugged. "Or it can be a comedy. When you're lucky, it's a little of both."

She smiled as he hoped she would, but then she went on and her words broke his heart. "I wasn't allowed to raise my voice. My parents considered yelling to be proof that I was out of control. My mother is a therapist."

He shook his head, irritated with them, sad for her. "At my house we had regular shoutfests. My folks didn't let them go on for very long, probably out of respect for the neighbors, but they let us blow off steam when it was necessary. Then they would step in, make us sit down and rationally explain what was wrong. We had to work together to figure out a solution." The memories had him smiling.

"Sounds very democratic," Lauren mused.

"Not exactly. Ultimately their word was final, but they took into account what we had to say."

"I wasn't allowed to speak out of turn or to interrupt adult conversations. I wasn't allowed to disagree with my parents either and, believe me, they never took into account what I had to say on a matter."

"So you learned to apologize."

Lauren nodded. "I did."

"What did they do to you when you rebelled or whatever? They didn't smack you around or anything?" His blood ran cold at the thought.

She laughed, but the sound held no humor. "No. They didn't like drama, remember."

"So what did they do?"

"They ignored me. That might not sound like punishment, but it was, especially since they weren't the most demonstrative or involved parents to begin with. Sometimes I almost wished they would hit me. It would have been less painful. We'd sit at the dinner table or our paths would cross in the living room and they wouldn't speak to me or even make eye contact. This went on for days. One time for nearly two weeks. I felt absolutely invisible."

Gavin left his chair and knelt down before hers, taking both of her hands in his. "You weren't invisible, Lauren. They were blind, and so is Holden. But I see you."

She kissed the knuckles he'd scraped leveling the bottom of a door just that morning. "Thank you."

Gavin pulled his hands away and cupped her cheeks. If nothing else, she needed to understand this. His voice was soft but insistent. "I don't want your thanks, Lauren. Do you hear me? I don't want gratitude from you. You don't need to apologize all the time, and you don't need to be so damned grateful just because I treat you the way you should be treated. The way you *deserve* to be treated."

He stroked her cheeks with the pads of his thumbs and because he was thinking about kissing her the way he had in the cottage, he let her go and rocked back on his heels.

He was rising to his feet when she let out a gasp. "Oh!"

Only the fact that she was smiling saved Gavin's heart from stopping. Even so, his stomach seemed to drop into his shoes. "What is it? Are you okay?"

"It's the baby. Here." She grabbed one of his hands and placed it on the left side of her belly. Almost immediately he felt something press against his palm. "Did you feel that?" she asked.

"Yeah." He kept his hand in place and felt it again. Grinning, he glanced up. Lauren was watching him. Her expression mirrored the wonder he felt. "What's she doing in there?" he asked.

"Playing soccer, I think." For the first time all day, she actually laughed. "*He* or she has been pretty active lately."

"You could find out, you know. You could just ask the doctor and end the speculation."

"And end the surprise, you mean," she chided.

"I'm not much on surprises these days."

Although he didn't say it, she knew Gavin's aversion to surprises had come courtesy of his divorce. The crumbling of her marriage had changed Lauren as well, but even more so, the credit went to the baby.

"Until the day I found out I was pregnant, I'd always hated surprises. But that was the best bit of unexpected news I've ever received. I've been a fan ever since."

"Well, boy or girl, either one is a gift."

Where Gavin had touched her with his heartfelt words about what she deserved, this left her staggered. With one simple sentence he'd turned her world on end and made her wish for the one thing that could never be: that he, rather than Holden, had fathered her baby.

"So how did the appointment go today?" he asked as he returned to his chair.

Lauren hadn't been terribly talkative on the drive back from town. In fact, and she wasn't proud of this, she'd actually feigned sleep to get out of having to answer questions such as this one. She couldn't feign sleep now.

"It went okay. Dr. Fairfield said the baby is developing right on schedule."

"So everything is fine?"

"Well, pretty much."

"Pretty much? What exactly does that mean?" he asked.

She fussed with her napkin before admitting, "My blood pressure was a little elevated today when the nurse checked it. It's probably just the stress."

"Is that the doctor's diagnosis or is it yours?" Gavin asked pointedly.

She sighed. "It's mine, but he agreed that stress could be the culprit."

"What does he suggest?"

"Nothing yet." Although she'd spent the afternoon on the Internet and knew that bed rest or an early C-section delivery could be in her future. She didn't mention those possibilities, though. "Just to be on the safe side he wants to see me again in a few days."

"I'll accompany you to that appointment," Gavin announced. Before she could argue, he added, "And I'm not just going to drop you off. I'm coming in. I want to know what the doctor thinks and to hear straight from him what you need to be doing."

Lauren was nervous. She wanted someone there. When she was being honest with herself she could admit she wanted that someone to be Gavin, but she said, "There's really no need for you—"

"Yes, there is. You're not going to do this alone. You don't need to." His voice dropped to just above a whisper. "I want to be there for you, Lauren. Let me be, okay?"

She could have argued, maybe she should have even. But she was so tired of being brave and pretending she wasn't scared. She was a strong woman. She knew that now. But she wanted the luxury of having someone to lean on from time to time.

"Okay," she agreed. "I'd say thank-you, but I've been warned not to."

Gavin smiled. "Who says you're slow?"

He'd expected more of an argument from her. The woman could be incredibly pigheaded at times. He supposed the fact that she'd given in so easily only showed how much she needed someone. Even so, when she left a little while later, she insisted she didn't want him to accompany her to her door.

"I'll be fine," she said when Gavin returned from the hall closet with both of their coats.

"Lauren—"

"No, really. Please. Let's just say good-night here," she pleaded. "Just in case."

Gavin sighed heavily and though he didn't like it, he agreed. He'd let her have her way on this.

He flipped on the back porch light and stood at the door, watching her walk the short distance to the cottage on the walkway he'd recently illuminated with landscaping lights. She moved quickly, despite her ungainly stride, and glanced left and right, no doubt wondering if someone was hiding in the orchard clicking off pictures.

He couldn't blame her. Gavin found himself wondering the same thing.

CHAPTER NINE

GAVIN phoned Holden at his office the next morning to set up a meeting. Lauren hadn't asked him to get involved. In fact, if she knew what he was up to she wouldn't be pleased. But he couldn't sit idly by and allow her and the baby to be subjected to this kind of stress.

"I can't imagine what we have to talk about," Holden said blandly at the beginning of their conversation. "Lauren behind on her rent?"

"I can think of a couple things. I'll come to your office," Gavin suggested. "Ten o'clock. Make sure you're free. I hate to be kept waiting."

"Fine, but I'll meet you someplace where you'll feel more comfortable," Holden replied with an exaggerated sigh.

"Gee, how accommodating of you," Gavin drawled. "There's a coffee shop near Rockefeller Center." He rattled off the address.

"Fine. But don't be late. I can't spare more than half an hour," Holden warned. "My time is at a premium."

"Mine, too."

"Yes, repairs to that house must keep you hopping," Holden said snidely.

"Those and a few other things," he agreed. He wasn't going to get into a mine-is-bigger-than-yours match with the man on the phone. "See you tomorrow."

Without Lauren riding in the passenger seat, Gavin switched the satellite radio from mellow jazz to a bass-thumping rock, turned up the volume to near deafening and shifted the Porsche into high gear, zipping along the highway at a rate of speed that would have earned him several points on his license had a police officer pulled him over. He arrived at the coffee shop in Midtown Manhattan a full twenty minutes before the agreed-upon time, figuring it would take him that long to find a parking spot. He got lucky, though, and secured one on the street in front of the café.

Despite Holden's claims of being busy, he was already there, seated at a table next to the window. When he spied Gavin stepping out of the Porsche, his eyebrows notched up in surprise, but by the time the two men were face-to-face inside the restaurant, the annoying smugness Gavin recalled from their first meeting had returned in spades.

"O'Donnell." Holden extended a hand whose palm was as smooth as a baby's bottom and with his chin motioned to the car parked outside. "You must have gotten one hell of a good trade on the truck."

He ignored the jab. "Hello, Seville."

The other man smiled. "And I didn't realize you had such good taste in clothes. That suit must have set you back a bundle." The smile turned sly. "But maybe you've met someone recently and you're thinking that money is no longer an issue for you."

The implication had Gavin seething, but he managed to say in a perfectly civilized tone, "We're not here to discuss either my clothes or my car."

"So I gather."

A waitress came by to refill Holden's coffee cup and take Gavin's order. He opted for nothing. He was in no mood for refreshments. When she was gone, Gavin got right down to business. "I'm not happy with your treatment of Lauren, and I want it to stop."

"I can't imagine how any of this is your concern…unless you've got a thing for my wife."

With Herculean effort Gavin ignored that taunt, too. "When she went to her obstetrician appointment yesterday, her blood pressure was elevated. Probably because of the stress you're putting her under with your ugly lies."

Holden didn't look overly concerned, even though he said, "I'm sorry to hear she's not feeling well."

"Yeah, I can see how sorry you are."

Holden shrugged. "It's not my fault."

Gavin wanted to shout, but he kept his voice low. "You're accusing her of having an affair. You're claiming that the baby she's carrying might not be yours. You don't think making groundless accusations like that causes a woman in her condition undue stress?"

"The accusations aren't groundless. I have some evidence that suggests the two of you are enjoying something more than a tenant-landlord relationship."

Holden's lips bowed with sharklike cunning, drawing Gavin's gaze to his teeth. Veneers. Had to be. No one had a smile that white and perfect without spending a serious amount of money and time at the dentist's office.

"We are enjoying more than a tenant-landlord relationship. Lauren and I are friends."

"*Just* friends?"

Gavin did his best not to remember the explosive kiss from the day before or the undercurrent of feelings that kept threatening to pull him in much deeper. "*Just* friends. As for your *evidence*, I don't think it will hold up in court since there's nothing going on between us."

"But you'd like there to be." The blinding smile made another appearance.

Gavin's temper flared again, this time accompanied by guilt. The two emotions made for an interesting combination and had his hands wanting to curl into fists. He laid his palms flat on his thighs instead and reminded himself that he was here on Lauren's behalf. Losing his cool wouldn't help matters. Indeed, he would be playing right into Holden's hands.

"What I'd like is for you to stop messing with her mind," he said evenly. "You know she hasn't been unfaithful. You know that baby is yours. I didn't even meet

Lauren until after she'd left you. She was already pregnant at that point."

Holden merely shrugged.

"In her condition she doesn't need any more stress," Gavin insisted a second time.

"I'm not trying to create stress for Lauren."

"It's just a side benefit, huh?"

"She made her own bed."

"Yes, and you were in it at the time," Gavin snapped. He experienced a surprising spurt of jealousy as he made the observation. He wasn't sure he'd felt this jealous when he'd learned Helena was having an affair. Betrayed. Yes, he'd felt that. But jealous?

Now was not the time to analyze his feelings.

"I have to look out for my own well-being," Holden was saying.

Gavin snorted. "And the baby? What about your child's well-being?"

"As you already know, I'm not convinced it's mine," Holden replied blandly.

"God, you're a piece of work." Gavin glared at the man. Didn't Holden know how lucky he'd been? Didn't he realize what he was letting slip away?

Apparently not, he decided, when Holden said, "I want this matter over and done with."

Gavin ached for Lauren. So many people in her life discounted her worth, marginalized her feelings. When she needed them, they let her down. Well, Gavin wasn't going to be one of them. Even if nothing beyond friendship ever developed between the two of them, he would show her the kind of loyalty, respect and trust she deserved. He would show her that she could count on at least one person to look out for her best interests.

He hardened his expression to match his resolve. "So, what's the bottom line?"

"I'm afraid I don't understand what you mean," Holden replied.

"Yes you do. What do you want from Lauren? You want something. That much is clear. That's why you're making this so difficult for her. So, what is it?"

"Are you her messenger boy now…among other things?"

"I'm her friend," Gavin stated succinctly for a second time. Not that long ago, he'd been in her shoes, disillusioned, bewildered and facing the end of his marriage. Oddly enough, his own heartache seemed a lifetime ago. The old bitterness was gone, the disillusionment erased. Had his self-prescribed sabbatical accomplished that or was it Lauren's doing?

"Very well." Holden folded his hands. "You want the bottom line, O'Donnell? Well, here it is. I've worked hard to get where I am. That's a concept you probably don't understand."

"I think I do," he said evenly.

"Then I'm sure you can appreciate that I don't intend to see my standard of living suffer because I have to support a second household."

"You're worried about alimony?" Gavin asked.

"Lauren doesn't want your money. She had a career once and she plans to again. She can support herself."

Holden rolled his eyes. "Not in the style to which she has grown accustomed." He glanced meaningfully at Gavin's suit. "Designer clothing don't come cheaply."

"That's not important to her."

"Wealth is important to everyone, especially those who've never had it." He sneered at Gavin. "And those who are about to lose it."

Gavin ignored the insult directed at him, but the one aimed at Lauren made him seethe. She was anything but superficial. He recalled the previous night, when the baby had moved. She'd been thrilled, awed and radiant with maternal love.

"How is it that you could have been married to her for four years and yet you don't know her at all?" Gavin asked.

"I know her well enough to know she's going to demand child support."

Gavin snorted and shook his head in dismay. "She shouldn't have to demand it. It's your responsibility, your obligation as a parent."

"I didn't want children."

Could the man really be so self-centered? "It's kind of late for that now. You know damned well what a paternity test will show. You can't deny your child's existence."

"Maybe not. But I plan to make sure Lauren doesn't get a penny more than what is necessary. I might wind up having to support the child, but I'm not going to support her." His gaze drifted over Gavin's suit. "Or some down-on-his-luck handyman who thinks he's found his ticket to the good life."

That capped it. Gavin's control snapped. He reached across the table and grabbed Holden by the lapels of his Armani jacket, yanking him half out of his seat. Coffee sloshed. Chair legs creaked. Gavin's lip curled back in a snarl.

"You son of a—"

"Go ahead, hit me," Holden coaxed. "Do it and I'll own that ramshackle house you call home as well as the surrounding acreage."

With an effort, Gavin reined in his temper. Beating the other man to a pulp, no matter how satisfying he would find the experience, wasn't going to help Lauren's situation. He released Holden and stood.

Around them, the other patrons were watching in fascination, their conversations apparently forgotten in the wake of the unexpected drama.

"You're going to regret that," Holden warned between gritted teeth as he smoothed down his lapels. "I might have been willing to let Lauren have some of our joint holdings. Now I'm going to fight her tooth and nail to keep them all. She's going to walk away from our marriage with nothing. Nothing!"

"And yet she'll still walk away," Gavin said. "What does that tell you?"

Lauren and the baby were well rid of him.

"Enjoy the good life while it lasts," Holden sneered.

Gavin meant it when he said, "I plan to."

* * *

He was too keyed up to drive back to Gabriel's Crossing. He needed to talk to someone. He needed advice. He knew where to find it: his brother.

Garrett was two years older than Gavin and half a head taller, but where Gavin was broad and more muscular, Garrett had a lean and rangy build, with longer arms and legs. In a fight—of which there had been plenty while they'd been growing up—they were evenly matched. In temperament, however, they were polar opposites, which is why they made good business partners.

Garrett was analytical, a details man. Where until recently Gavin had tended to move too quickly, Garrett took his time, sometimes too much time, gathering data and weighing facts before reaching a conclusion. Gavin needed his brother's thoughtful input today.

Garrett was in the conference room at Phoenix Brothers going over a set of blueprints with architects when Gavin walked in.

"This is a surprise. Has the prodigal returned?" He was only partly teasing.

"Don't, Garrett. Not today, okay?"

Garrett eyed him speculatively before turning to the other men. "Why don't you work on that revised materials quote and we'll finish this later." Once he and Gavin were alone, he said, "What's on your mind?"

Gavin shoved a hand through his hair and paced to the window. "I need some advice."

"Shoot."

"I just had a meeting with Lauren's husband. The jerk

is making the divorce ugly for her and as a result her blood pressure is up, which is a concern for the baby."

Garrett's brows crinkled. "Lauren? As in your tenant?"

"She's more than that. She and I are…friends, too." God! That word just kept coming up. The more he heard the description, the more he loathed it.

"Gav, look, I know you mean well. She's pregnant, needy and alone. It's only natural that you want to be there for her. But friend or no friend, this woman's divorce isn't any of your business."

"What if I want it to be?" he asked quietly.

Garrett flung his arms wide and swore. "Here we go again! Jeez, and this one isn't even single."

"What in the hell is that supposed to mean?"

"You're doing it again," Garrett accused. "Leaping without looking first. How many cliffs do you have to jump off before you figure out that you can't fly?"

"Lauren's not like Helena," he began.

But Garrett cut him off. "How would you know? You met her, what, a few months ago? She's married *and* pregnant, Gavin. Talk about baggage. At least Helena was just flighty and a flirt. Do yourself a favor—hell, do *me* a favor—and don't get involved."

"What do you mean, do you a favor?" Gavin demanded, his temper rising to match his brother's.

"I've picked up the slack here these past several months while I've waited for you to get your head together out in Connecticut. The name of our company is Phoenix Brothers Development." He slammed his fist down on the conference table for emphasis. "Brothers as in plural. But I've been a one-man show. We had to pass on a couple of good jobs as a result and our competitors were only too happy to land them."

Guilt settled in, taking the place of Gavin's anger. "You should have said something."

"I'm saying something now. I agreed when you said you needed to take a leave, Gav. How could I not? Hell, anybody with eyes could see that you needed one. You were no good to me, to the company, in that condition. But you promised—*promised*—that you'd get your head together and be back at least part-time by this spring. I can't afford for you to jump blindly into another doomed relationship that leaves you a useless husk when it ends."

"That's not what this is."

"Are you sure?" Garrett asked.

"I think so."

"That's not the same as sure." Garrett pinned him with a glare. "You need to be sure, *damned* sure. Because if we have to keep passing on the big jobs, our company could be on the line."

Gavin took his time driving home, and he mulled his brother's words the entire way. They weren't what he'd wanted to hear. Garrett wasn't right about Lauren or their situation. Lauren certainly wasn't a thing like his ex-wife. But he and Garrett had argued similarly when Gavin met Helena, and so his brother's words weighed on him.

* * *

It was nearly dinnertime when Lauren saw Gavin's car zip up the drive. She loved the cottage and the Connecticut countryside, but without someone to share them with their appeal had dimmed. She told herself she wasn't watching for Gavin or anticipating his return. But she was certainly glad when she spotted his car. Besides, she was curious about where he'd been for the better part of the day. He hadn't said anything about being gone, but when she'd gone to the house midmorning to bring him a pastry and talk him into taking a break, no one had been home.

After that, the rest of the day had been quiet and lonely, although Lauren had managed to be productive. She'd finally ordered a crib, changing table and dresser for the baby, as well as a bouncy seat and swing. Lilly had phoned just after she'd placed the order.

"Hey, leave something for your shower guests to purchase," her friend had teased. In the background Lauren could hear a toddler squealing.

Lauren had laughed politely, but said nothing.

"Your mother is throwing you a shower, isn't she?" Lilly had asked.

"She hasn't mentioned anything," Lauren had admitted. "In fact, we've only spoken twice in the past six weeks and both times she called to see if Holden and I had reconciled."

Lauren had accepted her mother's inability to act maternal. She credited Gavin for that. Blind, he'd said, making the deficiency out to be Camille's.

"That's it!" Lauren had just been able to make out

Lilly's muttered curses and hoped no small ears were within hearing distance. "I'm flying out and throwing you a shower."

"I'd love that. Really, Lil. But I know how busy you are with the kids. Besides, I don't really need a shower. I can afford to buy whatever the baby needs."

"I'm not that busy that I can't make time for one of my oldest and dearest friends," Lilly had countered. "And sure you can buy everything you need, but that's not really the point of those things, Lauren. Babies are to be celebrated."

She'd teared up at that. "I know. But who would I invite? My friends from the city would have to drive more than two hours to come. And I don't know that I can count on my mother to show up at all. I'd hate to seem pathetic."

"Leave the guest list to me. Just give me a date."

She had and then her friend said, "Now, tell me about this Gavin O'Donnell."

"Why do you ask about him?"

"Judging from the number of times his name has come up in our recent conversations and e-mails, it sounds like you have some pretty strong feelings for him."

The pause that had followed was as pregnant as Lauren.

"Still there?" Lilly had asked.

"Gavin and I are just friends." She'd rolled her eyes. How often was one or the other of them saying that?

"For now," Lilly had agreed. "But I think eventually the two of you will be much more than that."

Lilly's comment was still on Lauren's mind when

Gavin pulled into the driveway. The little thrill of excitement she felt at seeing him seemed to confirm her friend's assessment. And though she told herself to stay inside and go about her business, not even the threat of being photographed by someone Holden had hired could keep Lauren from bundling up in her coat, wrapping a scarf around her neck and walking out to the garage to greet him.

Leaves crunched underfoot as she approached and Gavin glanced over. He'd been scowling, lost in thought, but when he spied her, his expression brightened and he waved.

"Hello." Noting his business attire, she said, "I didn't realize you had a meeting today. Was it in the city?"

"Um, yeah." The Windsor knot at his collar had been loosened and the top button of his shirt unfastened. He tugged off the tie completely now and wadded it into a ball, which he stuffed into his pocket. He began to scowl again.

"It didn't go well, I take it," she said.

"No. Not like I'd hoped." He expelled a breath and Lauren waited for him to continue, but he didn't.

So, after a moment, she said, "I'm sorry."

"This isn't your fault. So, don't apologize, dammit!"

His near-shout almost had her backing away. The old Lauren probably would have. But meekness no longer suited her, if it ever had. She crossed her arms over her chest and stepped closer until he was within arm's reach. "I'm only being polite."

Gavin closed his eyes and sighed again. "Yes and I'm being insufferably rude."

"I don't know that I'd say 'insufferably,'" she replied.

He opened one eye and squinted at her. "Does that mean you forgive me?"

Lauren smiled. How could she not? He'd stood by her enough times. It felt good to finally be able to return the favor. "Want to talk about whatever it is that has put you in such a foul mood?"

He watched her intently before nodding slowly. "Yeah. I want to talk about it. In fact, we *need* to talk about it. It concerns you, Lauren."

Nerves skittered up her spine. "Me? How? I'm afraid I don't understand."

"I know." He tilted his head in the direction of the house. "Come inside. It's cold out here and you probably shouldn't be on your feet."

"I feel fine." But she followed him up the walk and through the rear door of the house just the same.

Inside the spacious kitchen, she felt instantly at home. She supposed it was because Gavin had allowed her such a free hand in decorating it. He'd picked oak cabinets originally. Those had come down and gone back after she'd mentioned a preference for maple. The light, hand-crafted cabinets contrasted nicely with the dark granite countertops.

Contrasts could be good, she thought. She and Gavin were different, but ultimately they complemented each other much like the room's furnishings.

Gavin took her coat and scarf and motioned for her to sit.

"Can I make you a cup of tea or something?" he asked.

Lauren shook her head. "Nothing for me, thanks."

He glanced at the clock. "I didn't realize it had gotten so late. Maybe I should start dinner."

"It's my turn to cook," she reminded him.

"Not today. You shouldn't be on your feet."

"So you keep saying. I'm not an invalid, Gavin."

"I know that, but I don't want to take any chances with you or the baby."

His concern touched her and helped take away some of the chill she was feeling. "Okay, I'll let you cook, but dinner can wait until after we've had our conversation."

"Right." He tucked his hands into his trouser pockets, scowling again, but said nothing.

"Gavin, you're starting to make me nervous."

"That's not my intention."

"I know. Come and sit," she coaxed, patting the tabletop. "Maybe it would be best if you just said whatever it is you want to say."

He nodded and shuffled over, sliding onto the chair opposite hers. "I went to see Holden today."

She'd told Gavin to blurt it out, but his words were a shock, so much so that she was sure she must have heard him wrong. "You what?"

"My meeting in the city today, it was with Holden."

"My husband asked to see you?"

Gavin cleared his throat. "Um, no. Actually, Lauren, I called him yesterday. I told him I wanted to talk to him."

"You called him," she repeated, her voice rising

slightly. "You called Holden and arranged a meeting with him without telling me?"

He nodded.

Her tone turned shrill when she went on. "You went to see him without asking me if I wanted or would appreciate your interference."

He squinted at her, looking both guilty and contrite. "Yes. I did that."

"Why?" she demanded. "Why on earth would you do something like that?"

"Because he's playing games with you." Gavin stood and paced to the far counter. He shoved a hand through his hair before he turned to face her. "You were so upset after he had you served with those papers. And then you came home from your doctor appointment and your blood pressure was up. What was I supposed to do, Lauren? Just sit back and let him tear you up inside? Don't ask me to do that. I can't."

His words warmed her heart. Still she said, "You might have asked me what *I* wanted, or at the very least you might have mentioned the meeting to me."

"I didn't want to upset you."

"Oh, please!"

Gavin continued, "But your blood pressure—"

"What, you don't think it's up now?"

When he blanched to nearly the same color as his snowy shirt, she almost took her words back, but anger simmered. It was an amazingly exhilarating emotion, Lauren decided, as was the give and take of her conversation with Gavin. She'd rarely experienced anything like it in the past, either with her parents or with her husband, and so she continued. "You went behind my back, Gavin."

"For your own good."

"No!" She slashed a hand through the air as she rose and went to him. "Don't treat me like a child. I'm tired of people telling me what to think, how to act and how to react. I'm sick *to death* of them making decisions for me. I'm quite capable of thinking for myself, you know." She said the words with a conviction she finally felt. Forget exhilarated. Lauren felt liberated, empowered.

"I know that."

"Good. Then start acting like you know that. This is my life, Gavin. It's my business." She tapped her chest with a finger for emphasis.

"You don't want me involved."

"I didn't say that." Her tone softened. "I want to be involved. Okay?"

He pulled her in for a hug. "*I* think I can manage that."

Afterward, as Lauren set the table and he prepared dinner, she asked, "So, what did you and Holden talk about?"

Gavin had gone the easy route: grilled cheese sandwiches and tomato soup. He concentrated on cooking as he relayed the high points of their conversation. He left out the part about grabbing Holden by the lapels.

"By the way, he thinks I'm a down-on-my-luck handyman and you're my sugar mama." He bobbed his eyebrows at her and grinned, hoping to lighten the moment.

Lauren gave an indelicate snort. "He can be such a small-minded snob at times. It's bad enough he's claiming we're having an affair."

Gavin flipped the sandwiches and lowered the heat on the soup. "You know, I've been giving that some thought. He's trying to use it as a bargaining chip in your divorce. Why not let him?"

She frowned. "I'm afraid I'm not following you."

"Under the previous grounds you were going to have to live separately for at least a year before a divorce could be granted under New York law," he reminded her.

"Go on."

"Well, with infidelity as the grounds, the timetable could be shortened."

"So, you think I should just let him make the claim?" she asked.

"I think you should *think* about it. I'm not going to make the mistake of telling you what to do." He held up the stainless steel spatula in surrender, still amazed at what a tigress lurked beneath her seemingly kitten exterior.

"I probably shouldn't admit this, but I enjoyed arguing with you," she said.

"Yeah?"

She glanced away. "Yeah."

Without thinking, he confessed, "It was kind of a turn-on." The words hung in the air between them, as ripe and as tempting as forbidden fruit. He cleared his throat as he felt the heat creep into his cheeks.

"I was going to say liberating," Lauren said.

"Ah." It was the only sound he was capable of making at the moment. God, he felt like an idiot.

"But I like your description, too," she said quietly.

He fiddled with the handle of the spatula, his gaze fixed on it rather than on her when he admitted, "I don't know if I'm supposed to say stuff like that about a pregnant woman."

"I'm a woman first, Gavin. And I won't always be pregnant."

The spatula clattered to the floor, dividing the space between them. He left it there.

Lauren went on. "I won't be married for much longer, either."

He looked up. She was smiling. "Especially, if I take your advice. Holden is claiming I've been unfaithful as a way to ensure he doesn't have to pay me alimony. But I don't want spousal support anyway."

"I told him as much. He seems to think you've grown accustomed to a certain standard of living and won't be able to do without it now."

She rolled her eyes. "Oh, I can do without it."

"I told him that, too."

"You know me far better than he does," she mused.

That was because he paid attention.

"I may wind up getting less than I could in the settlement," Lauren was saying. "But at least the process won't become a prolonged or protracted mess."

"There's that," he agreed.

"Of course, you did once tell me to be careful about giving up everything just to get the divorce over and done with."

"Yeah, I said that. But that was before…" Gavin stared at Lauren, unable to finish the sentence aloud.

Before what?

Before he'd realized what an utter imbecile her husband was?

Before he realized how upsetting the divorce was going to be for Lauren and the stress it would put on her unborn child?

Or was it before he'd realized that he was half in love with her and wanted her to be free as quickly as possible so he could pursue a relationship?

He took a step toward her, kicking the spatula. As it skittered across the floor, Gavin heard his brother's words from earlier in the day: *be damned sure.*

"Gavin, what is it?"

The smell of burning bread rescued him from saying more. He pulled the pan from the burner and waved a hand to disperse the smoke. "It looks like I'll have to start our sandwiches all over."

"You probably should lower the heat," she suggested with a simple smile that made his insides feel as if they were about to incinerate.

"Lower the heat." He repeated her advice with a

vigorous nod. Until he was sure exactly where their relationship was headed and where he wanted it to head, that was the wisest course for all parties involved.

CHAPTER TEN

GAVIN pulled the mail from the box at the road. In addition to the assortment of Christmas cards, a big manila envelope caught his eye. It was for Lauren, the return address the Shaw Advertising Agency in San Diego, California. He frowned.

He was still frowning when he reached her door.

"This came for you," he said, handing her the package after she ushered him inside.

She glanced at the label. "Lilly," she replied on a smile.

"Lilly's in advertising?"

"No. But her husband is friends with one of the top people at this agency. I guess he must have put in a good word for me."

"Are you thinking of applying?"

Gavin waited for her to say no. He wanted her to. California? It was on the other side of the country. Despite the conveniences of modern travel, it might as well have been on the other side of the galaxy.

Her reply was anything but reassuring. "I'm going to

need to get a job at some point after the baby comes. My savings won't last forever."

"But I thought you wanted to start your own agency?"

"I do. Maybe someday I will." She ran a hand over her distended belly. "But that's a pipe dream, Gavin. Pipe dreams don't pay the bills."

"Says who? It doesn't have to be a dream. My brother and I started out with nothing but big plans and egos to match. That's why banks grant people loans, to turn dreams into reality."

"You really believe in me."

It wasn't amazement he heard or gratitude, which he'd already made plain he didn't want. It was something bigger and went far deeper. Something that was binding them together. Strings, he thought. But he didn't try to untangle them.

"Yeah, I believe in you. You're smart, creative, organized." A dozen other adjectives came easily to mind. The woman was amazing. "You could do this."

She nodded. "Someday."

"Why not now?"

"Even assuming I could qualify for a loan, with the baby coming, I have neither the time nor the energy to devote to make it successful. Someday," she said again, sounding less wistful and more resolute.

"I'm going to hold you to that."

Lauren's contractions started just after midnight more than three weeks into the new year and just two days before her due date. The high blood pressure thankfully had proved to be stress induced, and the remainder of her pregnancy had been largely uneventful. Until the first cramping spasm sliced through her abdomen and forced her to curl into a ball beneath her bed's down comforter, she'd felt perfectly prepared to give birth. Indeed, she'd been eager to finally come face-to-face with the little person who had been using her bladder as a punching bag for these past months.

She'd picked out names: Will for a boy and Emily for a girl. She'd washed and sorted the gifts she'd received at the shower her friend Lilly had graciously flown out for and hosted. They'd had it at the farmhouse, in Gavin's much more spacious living room.

Lauren had been touched that several of her old co-workers had come, as well as a couple of neighbors from the apartment she'd shared with Holden. Her mother had not attended, no great surprise there. Camille had called with her regrets a week after the invitations went out. There was a conference in Salt Lake City that she *absolutely* had to attend, so she couldn't make it.

But Gavin's mother had. He'd invited her and she'd come, probably out of curiosity as much as out of courtesy. His sister, Grace, had attended with her. Lauren found both women to be interesting and delightful, even if they had plied her with questions that spelled out rather clearly their concern over Gavin's involvement with her.

As for that involvement it had remained rather

benign given the advanced state of her pregnancy and the slow pace of her divorce. They still ate meals together, talked and took walks when the weather allowed it. But he'd never again kissed her the way he had that day in the cottage.

The baby shower had been small but special. Lilly had seen to that with Gavin's help. The next evening, after Mrs. O'Donnell and Grace had gone home and Lilly had been dropped off at the airport, Gavin and Lauren had spent an hour going through the gifts she'd received. Gavin had oohed and ahhed right along with her when she'd held up tiny outfits, rattles and soft blankets. Then he'd insisted on helping her set up the crib and changing table that had been delivered a month earlier.

At the time, Lauren had felt perfectly calm when it came to impending motherhood. But now, as the hours passed and her contractions intensified, she began having second thoughts.

Major second thoughts.

"Oh, God! I don't think I can do this," she cried as another contraction began. Her panic built right along with the pain.

She tried the breathing technique she'd learned during her Lamaze classes. Gabriel's Crossing didn't have a hospital, so she'd been going to the one in nearby Danbury. A nurse on staff had agreed to act as Lauren's coach. She'd thought about asking Gavin, since he'd insisted he would drive her to the hospital when the time came, but modesty prevented her from doing so. She'd seen the childbirth

video. It was an amazing thing, truly and utterly miracu-
lous, but it was *not* the image she wanted seared into the
brain of the man with whom she hoped to someday pursue
a more-than-friends relationship.

She glanced out the window now. The drive to
Danbury wasn't overly long, but the fact that it had
snowed the night before did nothing to calm her already
frayed nerves. A good three inches of the white stuff
covered the walkway between the cottage and Gavin's
back door, not that she felt up to walking the short distance
at the moment anyway. She picked up the telephone and
dialed his number. Gavin answered on the third ring.

"Hello?"

"Hi. It's Lauren." After saying that she hoisted the
bottom of the receiver up to her forehead so she could
pant without leaving Gavin to wonder if she was attempting to make an obscene phone call.

"Hey, Lauren. Great morning, huh? Have you looked
outside yet?"

"Yes." *Hoo, hoo. Hee, hee.*

"It looks like a Currier & Ives print. The blue sky
really sets it off."

"Hmm," was all she managed. Under other circumstances she would have agreed with him. But at the
moment she didn't want slick roads standing between
her and the epidural she'd been promised.

"I'm thinking of grabbing my camera and walking
into the orchard to take some shots. Feel up for a walk
after breakfast?" he asked.

"Not really." *Hoo-hoo. Hee-hee*.

She realized she'd breathed right into the receiver when he said, "Lauren, everything okay?"

"No. I'm ha-ha-having contractions."

"Now?" He sounded incredulous and almost as panicked as she felt, but he rallied valiantly. "Hang on, sweetheart, I'll be right there."

He was as good as his word. She'd barely replaced the telephone receiver in its cradle before she saw him flying out the back door of the farmhouse. He bolted down the snowy walkway coatless without his shoes.

"How are you doing?" he asked when he managed to catch his breath.

"Okay. Scared," she admitted. "I don't think I can do this."

"Sure you can, sweetheart."

That made twice now that he'd called her that. She'd never been anyone's sweetheart. Other than Borin' Lauren she'd never had a nickname. She rather liked the endearment, especially coming from Gavin.

"Women have babies all the time," he was saying. "There's no reason for you to be scared. None. All right?"

"All right." She let out a deep breath. His words weren't all that comforting, but his presence was. She felt safe with him. Over the past several months he'd showed her one thing: she could count on him.

"Do you have a bag packed?" he asked.

She waved a hand in the direction of the stairs. "It's in the bedroom closet."

"Great. Why don't you call the doctor while I go get it?" he suggested.

"Okay."

Lauren left a message with the doctor's service and then struggled into her coat. Gavin returned in time to help her on with her boots.

Kneeling in front of her, he said, "This probably isn't the best time to mention this, but I've got a serious thing for your ankles."

With her legs straight out, she could just see them over the mound of her belly. "They're swollen."

"I love them anyway." He dropped a light kiss on her left ankle and reached for her boot.

"My feet are swollen, too," she added as he tried to fit one foot into the supple leather. A thought struck her then. Oh, good God! It had been more than a week since she'd last shaved her legs. "I can't go to the hospital!" she hollered.

Gavin glanced up. "Yes, you can. You can do this," he repeated, misinterpreting her panic.

"No. You don't understand. I can't go to the hospital until I shave my legs."

"Lauren," he began in a patient voice.

But she was shaking her head. Suddenly, the most important thing in the world to her was to have perfectly smooth calves when she had to put her feet up in the stirrups and push. And so she announced defiantly, "I'm not going anywhere until I shave my legs."

"Okaaaay," he said on a sigh.

"I know you think I'm being ridiculous, but…" She let her words trail off. She *was* being ridiculous. Even knowing that, however, she wasn't about to change her mind. Everything else was outside her control at the moment. Stubble-free legs were not.

Gavin straightened and held out a hand to help her from the chair. "Just be quick about it so we can go."

Quick about it? It had been a major endeavor to shave them the last time. As she nibbled her lip, Gavin asked, "What are you waiting for?"

"You need to help me."

His mouth dropped open for a moment and he stared at her as if she'd really lost her mind this time. "You want me to shave your legs?"

"Please. It will take me forever." She patted her abdomen and stated the obvious, "I'm not quite as agile as I used to be. It's hard to bend over."

"Right." He nodded. "Do I have to shave your ankles, too?"

"Well, they are part of my legs." She smiled.

"You ask a lot."

"You can handle it," she assured him on a laugh. "My razor is in the shower and so is the shaving gel."

Gavin retrieved the items. When he turned around, Lauren was seated on the closed lid of the toilet seat attempting to roll up her pant legs.

"Let me get those," he offered, kneeling down.

After he put a towel on the floor under her feet, he slathered one leg with the shaving gel and got down to business. After several long, even strokes he'd completed the first one.

"You're pretty good at this," she said.

"Well, I've had a lot of practice."

Her eyebrows shot up at that.

"On my face," he clarified and they both laughed.

He retrieved a clean washcloth from inside the vanity and, after wetting it down, wiped the last of the gel from Lauren's leg. Then he started on the other one. Another time and under vastly different circumstances, performing this intimate chore for her could have been a highly erotic experience, especially as the razor head toured her slim ankles. He filed it away for future reference. He definitely wanted to try it again someday.

After finishing up he dried off her legs, helped her into a pair of socks and rolled down her pants. "Need a haircut before we go? Maybe a perm?" he asked wryly.

"Ha, ha. Very funny." She pulled a face that had him grinning.

Gavin was glad to see some of the fear and panic had ebbed from her expression. The doctor called back then with questions. How long had she been having contractions? How frequent were they? After she hung up, she said, "Well, he says it's a go."

"Okay. What do you say we get your boots and coat and be on our way?"

Lauren nodded, and he could tell by the way she had started to breathe through her mouth that another contraction was beginning to mount. The sooner they were on the road the better, he decided. He grabbed her suitcase and opened the cottage door, but she stopped walking and wouldn't budge. She just stood in the doorway, one arm braced on the jamb, panting as if she'd just run a marathon.

"What is it? Is it the baby?" The image of having to deliver her child himself popped into his head and had the blood draining out of it. He felt a little woozy at the prospect, but he'd do it. He would do whatever was necessary to keep Lauren and her baby safe.

"Not…the…baby," she finally managed. "You."

"Me?"

She motioned toward his feet. "You might… want… to put on some shoes."

"Shoes." Gavin glanced down at his feet. He wore only a pair of navy socks that were soggy from his trek through the snow. He smiled sheepishly. "Yeah. That would probably be a good idea."

"And…a coat."

"Right." He laughed. "Guess I wasn't thinking."

Lauren's contraction was over and from her expression he could tell that some of her apprehension was returning. "Are you nervous, too?" she asked.

Nervous, scared and half a dozen other things. But Gavin pasted a grin on his face, shook his head and reached for her hand.

"Nah. I'm excited. I'm going to meet my second-favorite girl today."

Or maybe not, he realized. At the hospital, Lauren's

labor continued throughout the afternoon. By evening she was exhausted and Gavin was, too. He'd stayed by her side in the labor room, rubbing her back and feeding her ice chips. Early into the process, he'd learned the hard way not to offer her a hand to hold when a contraction came. Lauren had never struck him as a physically strong woman, but when her fingers had curled around his in a crushing, viselike grip, it was all he could do not to whimper and fall to his knees.

After she'd let go he'd half teased, "Was that so you could share a little bit of the pain?"

She'd glanced at him in confusion. "What?"

"Nothing." He'd given his hand a discreet shake, hoping to restore the circulation.

Just before seven o'clock the doctor came in and checked on her progress. Gavin busied himself plumping up her pillows during the exam, feeling conspicuous and a little awkward.

"It will be a while yet. Why don't you take a stroll around the halls," the doctor suggested, nixing plans for an epidural. "I'll be back in an hour, and hopefully things will be progressing by then."

So, they walked the halls in the hopes that would speed up the delivery. But when the doctor checked back around nine, Lauren's cervix had dilated only another half centimeter. It was looking to be a very long night. The baby's vital signs were being monitored carefully and the doctor didn't appear overly concerned. But Gavin was. He pulled one of the nurses aside.

"How much longer is it going to be? Lauren's endured enough. I don't know how much more of this she can take." Or how much more he could handle. It was absolute hell watching her writhe in pain and not be able to do a damned thing to help her.

The woman smiled sympathetically and patted his hand. "It could be another hour or two or even three. It's hard to say. Babies make their own schedules. But don't worry. Your wife is doing fine. Just fine. And your son or daughter will be here before you know it."

Wife.

Son or daughter.

The words made Gavin yearn, so much so that he didn't bother to correct her. He wanted what the nurse assumed he already had. He wanted Lauren as his wife. He wanted her child to be his child, even if not biologically. Eventually, he promised himself, eventuali he would have them. They would be a family.

Half in love with her? Nope. He'd fallen all the way without ever taking her out on a real date. Without ever doing more than hold her hand, stroke her back, kiss her lips. This was different than it had been with Helena, but he was still going to take his time. Lauren needed to settle in to motherhood and there was the not so small matter of her husband still being in the picture. She'd been hurt, emotionally mistreated by both Holden and her parents. She'd come a long way already, but he wanted all of her wounds to heal, just as his had thanks in large part to her.

In the meantime, he had plans to make for their future.

* * *

It was nearly midnight before Lauren's cervix was finally fully dilated and she was ready to begin pushing. Gavin had gone to the waiting room. She'd requested that, but then found herself longing for his presence in those final moments before she gave birth. It wasn't that she relied on him, she realized. She loved him.

I love Gavin.

She'd picked one heck of a time to have such an epiphany. She was moments away from motherhood and months away from being single again. But as she bore down for the final time, she didn't doubt the sentiment's truth. She'd loved him since he'd bought that ridiculous teddy bear, maybe even before. He'd shown her so many small acts of kindness over the months, little things that had kept adding up until her heart simply spilled over.

"It's a girl," the doctor said, holding up a squalling bundle for Lauren to see.

A girl. Just as Gavin had said it would be. Through the haze of her tears she could make out a set of flailing arms and a blotchy, scrunched-up face that already owned her heart. She laughed a little before sobbing hysterically.

"My Emily," she whispered. Here was her daughter. Here, at last, was the miracle she'd been expecting. Could it be that another one was out in the waiting room?

A little later, once Lauren had been moved to a private room with the baby, she turned to the nurse.

"Can you go and find Gavin O'Donnell for me and tell him that he was right? He knew all along that the baby was going to be a girl."

The nurse nodded. "Sure. I'll tell him. Or you could tell him yourself. Would you like me to ask him to come in? I have it on pretty good authority that he's been pacing around the waiting room like a caged tiger since he left your side. He's driving the folks at the nurses' station crazy."

Lauren wanted to see Gavin more than anything, but she raised a hand to her matted hair and grimaced. "How do I look?"

"You look like you just gave birth to a beautiful and healthy baby girl. You're lovely." The nurse smiled then. "All new mothers are lovely."

That probably meant Lauren looked a wreck, but excitement trumped vanity in this instance. "Okay. I'd appreciate it if you'd send him in."

A few minutes later Gavin poked his head around the door before coming fully inside. His face was haggard, shadowed by a day's growth of beard. Worry lines creased his forehead, and his eyes were seriously bloodshot. Her heart somersaulted at the sight of him. Oh, yes, she loved him.

"Hi, Mommy."

"That's me." She grinned.

"The nurse said you had someone you wanted me to meet."

"I do indeed." She held out a hand to him, urging him

closer when it seemed like he would linger in the doorway. "This is Emily."

"Emily, huh?" Gavin's grin spread as he crossed to the bed. "I told you the baby was a girl."

"Yes, you did."

His expression softened as he peered at the tiny face. The baby was wrapped in a striped pastel blanket and wearing a little pink hat. She was sound asleep, a condition the nurse had assured Lauren was not likely to last long.

"God, Lauren, she's beautiful." His tone was low, reverent. "But then I knew she would be. She looks just like you."

"Her eyes are blue when they're open, and she has hair, too." Lauren removed the small cap to reveal a downy, sable-colored thatch that stuck straight up on the top of the baby's head.

"That's some 'do." He chuckled. "She has your chin." He touched it with the tip of his index finger and even though Emily was sleeping one side of her mouth lifted almost as if she knew who he was. "Did you see that? I think she smiled."

His delight was endearing.

"Would you like to hold her?" she asked.

Dimples creased his cheeks as he smiled. "Are you kidding? I can't think of anything I want to do more at the moment."

He scooped the baby up in his hands, taking care to support Emily's neck and head. Lauren had seen the man wield power tools and sledgehammers. He looked equally at home now holding a newborn. As he settled her into the crook of his arm, he lowered himself onto the edge of Lauren's bed.

"What does she weigh? She feels as light as a feather."

"Seven pounds, eleven ounces."

"That's pretty respectable," he said, his gaze never straying from Emily's face. Then he pulled back the blanket and held a pair of tiny pink feet in the palm of his hand. "All her piggies are accounted for, I see."

"Yes."

"You do good work."

All the emotional uncertainty of the past several months, all of the physical pain of the past several hours, none of it mattered any longer. "She's a keeper," Lauren agreed on a sigh.

"Both of you are." He leaned down and pressed a kiss to her forehead. "How are you feeling? It's been a long day and an even longer night."

"I'm exhausted and sore," she admitted. "And wide awake. I should be sleeping. Isn't that the first rule of motherhood? Grab sleep whenever you can? But I don't want to close my eyes. I'm afraid if I do I'll wake up back at the cottage and Emily's birth will have been just a dream."

"She's real, Lauren, and she's here."

"And you?"

"What do you mean?" he asked.

Emotions tumbled. "Are you real, too?" she asked quietly.

He smiled, almost as if he understood the strange question. "Uh-huh. And I'm not going anywhere, either. So, close your eyes and sleep."

She did. With Gavin sitting at her bedside holding her newly born daughter, Lauren closed her eyes and allowed herself to slip into a peaceful slumber.

CHAPTER ELEVEN

IT BECAME a habit, falling asleep while Gavin stood watch over Emily. For the next several weeks, as Lauren tried to get the baby on some sort of schedule, about the only thing she could count on was that right about the time she'd reached her limit—either emotionally or physically—Gavin would be there, ready to lend a hand or take over completely while she took a nap or showered or grabbed a bite to eat. The only time she was on her own was late at night. Even then she knew if she needed him, all she had to do was pick up the phone and call.

The week after Emily's birth, Lauren's parents came out to see their only grandchild. They stayed at a bed-and-breakfast in Gabriel's Crossing and complained mightily about everything during their stay, which thankfully was brief. Three days of their self-absorbed sniping was more than enough for Lauren.

The only bright spot of their visit was that they seemed genuinely thrilled about Emily. They didn't exactly dote over the baby. Camille and Dwight weren't that type. But they did seem interested, which Lauren appreciated. Of course, both of her parents took the opportunity to again lecture her about leaving Holden, but apparently they'd accepted that Lauren wasn't going to change her mind.

When they met Gavin, they were cordial but not overly friendly. Like Holden, they took Gavin at face value, seeing only what he presented, a working-class man who was good with his hands. They would have been impressed had they been privy to the scope of his accomplishments. She saw no reason to enlighten them.

As for Holden, he hadn't seen the baby. Lauren had called him from the hospital to tell him of Emily's birth. She hadn't really wanted to speak to him, but she'd figured, as the baby's father, he had a right to know. He'd asked the pertinent questions—how much did the baby weigh, was she healthy. Beyond that he hadn't seemed overly interested. At least he hadn't mentioned the DNA test. She'd hung up feeling sad for Emily and yet relieved that in the long run Holden wasn't going to be part of the picture. Holden might not want their daughter, but Lauren knew someone who did.

Gavin absolutely adored Emily, and, as winter gave way to spring, the feeling appeared to be mutual. Whenever he peeked over the side of the crib, the baby smiled and waved her small fists in excitement. Like Lauren, she knew she could count on him, too.

In so many ways, Lauren, Gavin and Emily were like a family. Yes, they were *like* a family, and often mistaken for one when they were out, but they were not a family. Just as Lauren and Gavin were like a couple in many regards—sharing evening meals and doting over the baby before Em went down for the night. But they were not a couple.

They were individuals, with separate concerns and objectives, as became clear when Gavin started back to work in Manhattan in late April. He'd made a commitment to his brother. He had an obligation to his company. Lauren understood that. Just as she understood that he'd made no commitment and had no obligation to her.

She assumed they had a future together. At times she felt certain that marriage was what Gavin wanted. *When the time and the woman are right*, he'd said. Of course, the time was far from perfect. But as her divorce inched toward being final, the subject had yet to come up. Now, with her savings dwindling and expenses mounting, Lauren reached a conclusion: she needed to get serious about finding a job.

She mentioned it to Gavin when he came by just after sunup one morning. He'd started stopping in for breakfast before his long commute to Manhattan. Some days, if traffic was heavy or he had to stay late in the city, the morning was the only time she saw him.

She missed their dinners together, their long conversations. She missed him, especially since he spent a good portion of the weekends working in the farmhouse. The renovations were close to being finished and he was no longer doing them alone. He'd hired a three-man crew to scrape and paint the exterior and detached garage, which got a new electric door, and a landscaper had already picked out the perennials and shrubs for the flower beds.

She could all but see the For Sale sign on the front lawn. What then? Lauren opted not to ask the question. Instead, as he fed Emily her bottle, she said, "I've decided to begin my job hunt in earnest."

Gavin glanced up sharply. "So soon?"

"Emily's nearly four months old. I've had a lot more time off than most new mothers." Still, her heart ached. She was hardly sold on the idea of leaving her daughter in someone else's care.

"So, where are you thinking of looking?" He pulled the bottle from the baby's mouth and brought her up to his shoulder to be burped. Lauren watched his big, work-roughened hands pat her daughter's back.

"I've got a few leads." She named off the agencies. She'd already updated her résumé and portfolio. Both were ready to be popped in the mail.

He nodded. "Manhattan, good."

She swallowed. "Of course, Lilly's still pulling for San Diego." Her friend had mentioned it again in their last conversation.

His hand stilled. "Would you consider that?"

"I don't know," she answered truthfully. "Lilly's offered to watch the baby for me while I'm at work."

That was the upside of the arrangement. Emily would be cared for by someone Lauren knew and trusted. The downside was sitting directly across from her. How could she leave the man she loved?

"Don't make any decisions yet."

"At some point I'll have to."

"I know. But not yet." He kissed the baby's head, the gesture as tender as it was second nature. "Promise me you'll wait."

She promised, but it struck her later that Gavin had never said what she was waiting for.

When Gavin couldn't make it to Gabriel's Crossing in time for dinner, he always called. The phone rang just as Lauren put the baby in her carrier seat and prepared to go grocery shopping.

"Hey, Lauren. It's me."

"You won't be home," she guessed on a sigh.

"No. Sorry. Something's come up." Something had been coming up a lot lately. "Hope you didn't take anything out for dinner."

She made a mental note to put the pork chops back in the freezer before they had a chance to completely thaw. "No. Don't worry. I know your schedule can be unpredictable."

"It won't always be." It sounded like a promise. "I'm working on something important at the moment. Something huge."

She smiled at the enthusiasm in his voice, knowing how much he loved what he did. "Want to tell me about it?"

"Yeah, I do. More than you can imagine. But I can't

just yet, Lauren." Curiosity tempered her disappointment when he added, "I want it to be a surprise."

Lauren lay awake in her bed even as Emily slept, snoring softly in her crib. She heard Gavin's car come up the driveway. The light from its high beams illuminated her room for a moment before darkness prevailed. She glanced at the clock on the nightstand. It was after eleven and he was just getting home. She rolled over, thinking that now maybe she would be able to drift off to sleep, but a light tapping sounded at her door.

Pulling on a robe, she went downstairs, flipping on a lamp on her way to answer the knock.

Gavin stood on the opposite side, as she'd known he would. He looked exhausted. His jaw was shadowed, eyes bloodshot. His tailored shirt was wrinkled from the long day and the long drive.

He was a sight for sore eyes. Lauren smiled as she moved in to wrap him in a hug.

"I like coming home to that," he sighed.

"I like having you come home." She felt his arms tighten around her waist, and he whispered something that she swore sounded like "soon."

"I have some pinot grigio in the fridge," she said after a moment, stepping back so he could come inside. "We can sit on the couch, talk. You can tell me about your day."

She started for the kitchen, but as she moved past him, Gavin snagged her hand and pulled her back.

Their bodies bumped. He settled his hands on her hips to keep her there.

"The wine can wait, so can the conversation. Ah, Lauren." He breathed her name into her hair before pushing it aside and nuzzling her neck. She welcomed the intimate contact, reveled in the sensations that showered through her like fireworks.

She found his mouth with hers, eager and greedy for more. It had been a long time. So very long. Need made her bold. She stroked his tongue, nipped his lower lip with her teeth. A moan vibrated from the back of his throat and his hands were no longer anchored to her waist. They'd left their safe moorings to part her robe. He pushed it off her shoulders. Rough palms snagged on the silky fabric of her nightgown, but then Gavin was lifting it, pulling it over her head.

Lauren knew a moment of self-consciousness as she stood before him naked except for a pair of panties. She was almost back to her prebaby weight, but the experience of childbirth had permanently altered parts of her anatomy. Her waist was thicker than it used to be, the skin on her abdomen no longer quite as taut.

Heat suffused her face. "Gavin, I'm—"

Shaking his head, he placed a fingertip against her lips. "You're beautiful, Lauren. Absolutely beautiful."

He made her *feel* beautiful and so her confidence returned, boldness racing neck and neck with desire. She reached for his shirt, unfastening the buttons and letting her lips follow her hands' progress. His shirt joined her clothes on the floor, and Gavin moaned.

She was reaching for his belt when Emily started to cry.

"I forgot we had company there for a minute." He laughed as he said it, but then blew out a deep breath.

Lauren did the same as she scooped up her robe and shrugged into it.

"I'll just be a minute. Ten tops. Help yourself to that wine and pour me a glass while you're at it." She started for the stairs, but then turned. "Don't go anywhere, Gavin, okay?"

He smiled. "I wouldn't dream of it. I'll be here."

And he was. Half an hour later, after Emily finally drifted off again, Lauren found Gavin on the couch. Two glasses of wine were on the low table in front of him. He was shirtless, shoeless and sound asleep.

But he'd kept his promise. He was there.

She wiggled onto the small strip of couch in front of him, resting her head on the corner of the throw pillow he'd commandeered. Though he didn't wake, his arm came around her, protective even in sleep.

"I love you," she whispered as she drifted off.

Gavin woke just before dawn, not completely sure where he was, although he knew perfectly well who was sleeping beside him.

He levered up on one elbow, careful not to disturb her. Lauren mumbled something and burrowed against his bare chest. The heart inside it took a tumble. This was what he wanted, *exactly* what he wanted, for the rest of his life. He'd known it with certainty since Emily's birth, of course, but he'd been biding his time, setting his plans in motion. He'd thought everything out carefully.

The farmhouse was nearly complete and he would be moving back to his apartment, but he had no intention of putting the property up for sale. Nor did he have any intention of living in Manhattan without Lauren and Emily. He'd been working on the guest room there, converting it to a nursery. He had similar plans for one of the rooms in the farmhouse, which they would enjoy as a weekend retreat.

He was going to ask Lauren to marry him. He already had the ring. He was just waiting for her divorce to become final. He leaned down and brushed a kiss over her temple. Last night, if he hadn't fallen asleep, they would have made love. Just thinking of it now had desire stirring. He blew out a breath and reeled in his desire. Maybe it was for the best that they hadn't. They'd waited this long. They could wait till she was legally single again. Till Emily was safely tucked into the care of a trusted sitter. He wanted it to be perfect. Lauren deserved nothing less.

She rolled, shifting to her other side. Her bottom pressed against his front. Gavin closed his eyes on a groan. A moment later, he eased out from behind her, cursing his carefully constructed plans but opting to avoid further temptation.

CHAPTER TWELVE

ON A RAINY Monday in June, Lauren's divorce became final. She went to the courthouse alone except for her lawyer. She hadn't wanted Gavin present and she'd seen no need to bring Emily. Holden hadn't asked to see his daughter.

When the judge made his ruling, Lauren felt no overwhelming emotion, unless one counted relief. It was a surreal moment, staring at the man she'd married, the man who had fathered her child, and realizing their paths weren't likely to cross often in the future, if ever, despite the visitation order that had been worked out.

The proceedings had included few surprises. Holden got to keep the apartment, its furnishings and some of their other real estate holdings, although he'd had to pay her a lump sum for the privilege. It wasn't an overly large amount. In fact, Lauren's lawyer had urged her to seek more. But she'd been afraid doing so would drag out the inevitable and she'd just wanted this done.

Besides, she had plenty to live on. Their joint bank

accounts and investments had been divided equitably, and though Lauren had refused alimony, she would be receiving monthly child support payments for Emily. Holden had also dropped his nonsensical DNA request and agreed to set up a college fund for his daughter.

The daughter whom he had yet to see.

The court granted Lauren sole custody. No surprise there since Holden hadn't wanted to share it and the distance between their current accommodations would have made that difficult anyway. Visitation was set. He was entitled to every third weekend and alternating holidays. Lauren wasn't overly concerned by the arrangement. It had already become abundantly clear that he wouldn't exercise the privilege.

At nearly six months old, Emily had just last week cut her first tooth. She babbled happily, smiled often and had an irresistible laugh. She was beautiful, bright and alert. She was the light of her mother's life. The fact that Holden chose not to share in it was his loss.

Lauren had forgotten her umbrella, and the rain was coming down harder. People dashed past her on the sidewalk, the unlucky ones holding soggy newspapers over their heads. She glanced up at the gray sky with its heavy, hanging clouds and smiled. It was sunny and fair as far as she was concerned.

She pulled out her cell phone and punched in Gavin's number, feeling ready to burst before he finally answered. "Hello?"

"Hi," she said.

"All done?"

"Yes. I just left court and I'm out for a stroll."

"It's pouring rain."

She laughed. "What are you talking about? It's a gorgeous day. I'm a single woman again."

"Single, huh? Well, then I've got a question for you."

Lauren laid a hand over her thumping heart. "Yes?"

"How about a date tonight?"

It wasn't quite the question she'd been hoping he'd ask, but even that didn't dim her happiness. "Sounds wonderful."

Gavin made plans to take Lauren to dinner in Midtown that evening to celebrate. He'd enlisted Garrett and his girlfriend, Amanda to babysit Emily while he and Lauren were out. On a date. Their *first* date, for all practical purposes.

They'd done things a little backward—eating meals and spending quiet evenings together, and of course sharing the birth of a child. But with the exception of a couple of steamy interludes, they hadn't done the things most couples do at the beginning. He planned to rectify that later tonight.

With that in mind, he'd run out to pick up a bottle of champagne. He was putting it on ice for later when Lauren walked into the living room. One look at her and Gavin wished he could fast-forward through the evening he had so carefully planned. He'd never seen her look quite like this, overtly sexy to the point his tongue wanted to loll out of his gaping mouth. He snapped his mouth closed and swallowed a moan.

The dress was a good deal more revealing than any she'd worn in the past, but that wasn't it. She looked confident, determined, as though she knew what she wanted and she knew how to get it. She walked toward him, letting her fingertips trail lightly over the back of the couch.

"I'm ready," she said.

So was he. More than, he thought.

Lauren hadn't worn high heels in months, but she had a pair on now, the strappy black variety that did incredible things for her already shapely calves and delectable ankles.

"You don't play fair," he murmured in appreciation.

"Nope. I play for keeps. While you were gone Cindy came by."

"Cindy?"

"I used to work with her. You met her at the shower. I took the liberty of calling her and asking a favor."

His brain wasn't working. In fact, the closer she came, the harder it was to think. "Favor?" he repeated.

Lauren moved slowly, her gaze locked on his. When she reached him, she settled her palms on his lapels. "I asked her to take Em for a few hours."

"But Garrett and Amanda—"

"I called them, too. Let them know of the change of plans. I had an interesting talk with your brother by the way."

"Hmm?" Her fingers had walked up his chest and were now teasing the hair at the back of his neck.

"He gave me what I consider a compliment, though maybe you can clarify it for me. He said it appeared that your cliff-jumping days were over. He credited me." She kissed his neck, nibbled on his ear before whispering. "Care to explain?"

Gavin pulled her flush against him, eager to return the sweet torture to which she'd just subjected him. "Sure, but not right now. That can wait. This can't."

He kissed her thoroughly and then swung her up in his arms, carrying her past the guest room where her things were stowed, to the master suite. She wouldn't be sleeping down the hall this night.

"I was wondering if we'd ever be alone together like this. It's been hell waiting."

"We didn't need to."

"I felt we did. Timing," he murmured as they helped one another undress. He took his time taking off her sandals, indulging at last in a feast of her ankles.

She moaned softly and then scooted farther back on the bed, until her head rested on the pillows. He followed her.

They made love with the lights on, watching each other's expressions and anticipating each other's needs as passion built and release beckoned.

Gavin waited till the aftershocks had ebbed before he said, "I love you, Lauren."

"I love you, too." She rolled onto her side so she could face him. "You mentioned timing earlier. So the time is right?"

His brow crinkled. "Uh-huh."

"And the woman. Am I right, too?" She was grinning.

He knew where she was heading. Damn, she was stealing his thunder and ruining his surprise.

"You're getting ahead of yourself," he warned.

"No, you've been falling behind. You need to catch up."

"I haven't wanted to rush things," he said.

"I appreciated that…at first. I can admit it made sense given my divorce. But here's the deal, my lease is up soon. I need to find a new place for me and Em to live, and I've got to decide on a job. I've had an offer." She sat up, not bothering to cover herself. "Actually, I've had two."

He sat up as well. "Why didn't you say something?"

"It just happened yesterday and I haven't made any decisions. One agency is in Manhattan."

"And the other one?"

"I think you know where it is. So?" Her lips twitched with the beginnings of a smile.

"Are you playing hardball with me?"

He expected her to deny it, but she grinned. "Yes, I am."

Self-confidence looked so good on her that Gavin couldn't work up to being offended. Still, he wasn't going to let her completely botch all of his meticulously laid plans.

"Well, I've got an offer for you, too." He stood and pulled on his pants. Then he tossed his shirt at her. "Put this on and follow me."

Lauren was baffled. A minute ago she'd been steering him toward matrimony and now she was being led around the apartment in his shirt. What had happened? She'd been sure he'd been about to propose. He loved her. He loved her daughter. Her divorce was final. But now he was giving her a tour of his home, even though she'd already seen most of the rooms before.

"The office is one of my favorite rooms. There's a great view from the window and plenty of cabinet space for files. When you start your business—if that's what you decide you want to do—you could work from here if you'd like. That way you wouldn't have to be away from Emily all day. We could bring a sitter in."

Lauren blinked. "Gavin."

"No, no. Don't say anything now. Just wait." With a hand on her lower back, he steered her to the next room.

The door was closed. Before he turned the knob, he said, "We can redo this if you don't like it, but I couldn't resist."

He shoved the door open and Lauren gasped. The room was painted pink and already furnished with a crib, changing table and dresser. In the corner was a comfy rocker. A tutu-wearing teddy bear similar to the one he'd purchased so long ago was seated on its cushion.

"It was kind of my inspiration, so I bought a second one," he said when he noticed where she was staring. She realized then that the wallpaper border sported a similarly clad stuffed animal. "We can keep the original bear and your furniture in the nursery at the farmhouse. I'll leave that one for you to decorate."

Lauren glanced around the room again, noting all of

the little details, like a night-light and diaper pail, even a wipes warmer on the changing table. "When did you find time to do all this?"

"Those late nights," he said on a shrug. "I wanted everything ready so that when the time was right I could ask you a certain question."

Her eyes filled with tears. "Oh, Gavin."

He'd thought of everything. Planning, plotting, taking his time where he'd once rushed so blindly ahead.

His eyes were bright, too, when he said, "Lauren, I love you. I have for a long time. I love Em, too. In fact, I have since before I saw her because she was part of you."

"We love you, too." She brushed tears from her cheeks.

"I want us to be a family," he said and more tears fell. He blotted them away this time. "Marry me, Lauren. I promise I'll make you happy."

"You already have."

She went into his arms, eager to be there, never wanting to leave them. And when he kissed her, Lauren knew, the future they'd both been busy planning had finally begun.

EPILOGUE

GAVIN grabbed two glasses of champagne from a waiter's tray and started through the crowd in search of Lauren. The artwork on display had earned rave reviews from those in attendance at the gallery opening, but in Lauren and Gavin's case, it wasn't the real draw. They'd needed a night out. They hadn't managed to do anything alone or remotely romantic since the birth of their son, Will, more than four months earlier.

He spied Lauren across the room and felt the familiar kick of attraction. Two years of marriage and it showed no signs of abating. She saw him, smiled, and he knew it was mutual.

She'd gotten her figure back since the baby, though she still complained that certain clothes no longer fit they way they had. He'd told her to buy new clothes. He loved her just the way she was.

And she was lovely. On this night she was wearing a basic black sheath with her blond hair up in a sleek twist accented with diamonds. No one in the room would have guessed that earlier in the day she'd been dressed in khakis, her hair down and one side adorned with little Will's regurgitated formula.

"Here you are." He held out one of the glasses for her and had just taken a sip of his own when he spied her ex. Holden was sneering, and a buxom brunette was hanging on his arm.

"This is a surprise," Holden said. "I was under the impression that this opening was by invitation only."

"Holden." Lauren's tone held a warning.

Not surprisingly, the man ignored her. Turning to Gavin, he said, "I wouldn't think this sort of thing would appeal to someone like you, O'Donnell. But then Lauren knows quite a bit about art. I'm sure she can explain the finer points of the medium to you."

"For your information…" Lauren began.

But Gavin shook his head. "Don't. It's okay. Come on."

They were just stepping away when Holden said in a stage whisper, "That's real champagne, by the way. Apparently one of the artist's patrons doesn't believe in sparing any expense. I hear he made his fortune in real estate."

"Yeah," Lauren agreed. "He's loaded, though you'd never know it from the way he acts. He's not the sort to flaunt it. He's classy." She smiled at Gavin, sipped the bubbling beverage. "Handsome. And incredibly sexy."

Holden frowned. "Wait a minute…" he began.

But Gavin had taken Lauren's arm and was steering

her away. "Sorry, can't," she called over her shoulder. "My husband and I are late for another engagement."

Outside Gavin pulled her into his arms, laughing even as he kissed her. Lifting his head, he said, "That was really bad of you, Mrs. O'Donnell."

"Just setting the record straight." Then Lauren grabbed his tie. Using it to tug him toward their waiting limousine, she added, "Now, if you want to see bad…"

* * * * *

Special Offers
Regency Ballroom Collection

Classic tales of scandal and seduction in the Regency Ballroom

Scandal in the Regency Ballroom
On sale 4th April

Innocent in the Regency Ballroom
On sale 3rd May

Wicked in the Regency Ballroom
On sale 7th June

Cinderella in the Regency Ballroom
On sale 5th July

Rogue in the Regency Ballroom
On sale 2nd August

Debutante in the Regency Ballroom
On sale 6th September

Rumours in the Regency Ballroom
On sale 4th October

Rake in the Regency Ballroom
On sale 1st November

Mistress in the Regency Ballroom
On sale 6th December

Courtship in the Regency Ballroom
On sale 3rd January

Scoundrel in the Regency Ballroom
On sale 7th February

Secrets in the Regency Ballroom
On sale 7th March

A FABULOUS TWELVE-BOOK COLLECTION

 Save 20% on Special Releases Collections

Find the collection at
www.millsandboon.co.uk/specialreleases

Visit us Online

0513/MB416

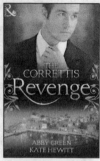